DEATHRISER OF DARKWOOD

FROM THE ASHES

JEN GUBERMAN

UGM Publications

GELIMUND
PROPSHIRE
SUMMERCLOUD GROUNDS
PIPWERRY
BRECHEN
TERETATIAN
DARKWOOD
YULEDARIA
FAUN FARMLAND

SLITHIS
MAGNARIUM
APRENETCH
XLERIA
MOREL
EASTFIELD
TSHI ISLES
LERYNNE

For mom,

Who thought she'd never
like a "book about elves."

CHAPTERS

CHAPTER ONE

A PORTAL IN THE WOODS

"Stupid cat!" Tera grunts, stumbling over a scraggly tabby.

"Rude! What if I called you a stupid elf?" Kiran asks.

"It's different," Tera replies, watching the cat disappear between some trees.

"You're right. Calling *you* stupid would be far worse because you're in school. So, you *should* be smart." Kiran smirks and Tera returns the sass with a heavy punch to his shoulder.

Tera wants to comment on how her best friend is studying to be an animalinguist, but she knows that's one insult that's off-limits. The animalinguist class is almost entirely full of half-elves like Kiran, who only have half the magic strength of full blooded elves like herself.

"We almost there yet?" she asks, changing the subject.

"Just past these trees."

The forest is thick and dark. Trees with leafy branches suffocate the full moon's glow, but the two friends continue to follow the halo of Tera's light orb spell, bobbing like a buoy before them in the heavy summer air.

"I still can't believe you've never been to Summercloud," Kiran says.

"Dad says it's nothing but a scam. 'Too expensive for junk food and cheap prizes.'"

"He's not wrong, but that's not the point."

They step into a clearing in the woods. A shimmering portal floats several inches off the ground. Above it, a splintering sign reads SUMMERCLOUD FAIR in chipping pink paint.

"I feel like this is the kind of portal my mom warned me about when I was little." Tera stops, eyeing the aged wooden sign. "It may as well say, 'Free Toffees, Definitely Not a Trap.'"

"I mean, they *do* have toffees, but they're nowhere near free," Kiran says with a snort. "C'mon."

Tera releases her light orb, watching it evaporate before them. "After you," she says, motioning to the portal.

Kiran walks in front of her, tossing a sly look back before stepping through the portal and disappearing, leaving her in the dark. She huffs, running a hand through her thick copper curls, tucking them behind her long, pointed ears before following her friend.

The forest fades around her, materializing into another dark woodsy space. Instead of the lush nature near her home, this one is full of twisting, leafless trees. Her head spins as she searches for her friend, spotting him already halfway down a steep path just past the return portal.

"Wow, way to wait for me, Kir!" Tera yells indignantly, trotting after him, the compact, hard dirt making soft shuffling sounds beneath her feet.

"We're already running late enough!" he calls back to her. "*Someone* had to flunk her deathrising midterm and get the kingdom's longest lecture from her parents."

"I didn't flunk," she says as she reaches his side and slows to match his pace. "I just didn't do as well on my test as Zeyla did on her lifebringing midterm. I swear the deathrising program is harder."

"Not that I have any experience in either, but that sounds fair. After all, you'd think it'd be easier to heal something that's still alive than bring something *back* to life. Or kill someone, like, permanently. Plus, fewer people actually graduate from the deathrising program anyways."

"Exactly! Thank you! But Mom and Dad treat her like the pride and joy of the family. Maybe if Mom and Dad were deathrisers instead, I'd have an easier time in class. She practically has live-in lifebringing tutors. It's not fair."

"You *picked* it though. They wanted you to be a lifebringer. It could've been easy for you, too. I love you like a sister, Tera, but I'm not hopping into that pity party again."

She starts picking mindlessly at a small scab on her scalp, her mind wandering back to her path selection day. Her older brother, Aston, had picked the lifebringing path five years before her. Their parents were thrilled, but he had acted like it wasn't even a choice. He simply picked the path of least parental resistance. Her little sister, on the other hand, made a huge show out of her decision to follow in their parents' footsteps. Zeyla decorated her room with posters of all the greatest lifebringers in history, bought the overpriced hoodies with "lifebringer" stitched across the chest, and gathered the entire family for her path selection announcement— as if it were a surprise to anyone.

Their parents didn't hide the fact that they were disappointed in Tera's lack of interest in the lifebringing path. They never told her she couldn't pursue something else, in fact, quite the opposite. As much as it pained them to see their middle child go against arboreal elf tradition, they encouraged her to go after whatever she felt most passionate about. Tera waited until the day of her path selection to finally tell her parents she wanted to be a deathriser. She will never forget walking into her family's tiny kitchen later that day to see her mom scraping off the word "lifebringer" in green icing on a congratulatory cake.

"Emmaline and Verity said they'd wait by the fortune teller booth, and Trevitt told me he had to help his dad out fixing one of the rides. He'll join us later if he can." Kiran reaches around, putting his hand flat against Tera's back, urging her to walk faster.

"I'm going, I'm going!" she says, her gaze wandering as she takes in the sight of the towering pink and violet tent walls surrounding Summercloud Fair.

"I don't want to miss out on the whole night. Let's *go.*"

Tera grumbles. "You have longer legs than me. I can't keep up!"

Kiran flashes her a grin, his bright teeth standing out against his rich, indigo skin. "Last one to the ticket booth has to eat an order of fried fish eyes!" He takes off, his silky silver hair fluttering behind him, his thin, pointed ears seeming to bounce with every step.

"That's a *thing?*" Tera sprints after him with a grimace painted on her face.

When she reaches the bottom of the hill, she's greeted by a pair of fauns giggling and juggling flashing balls on either side of the entrance.

"Welcome to Summercloud!" one of them spouts.

"Tickets are to your left!" the other follows.

Tera turns, spotting Kiran handing over a few coins to a man behind the ticket booth. The man holds two paper tickets over the counter. Before Kiran can take them, Tera steps up beside him and snatches them.

"You paid for my ticket?" she asks, holding the two tickets up separately.

"Only because I feel bad for you," he says, feigning a face of pity—scrunching his brow and pushing a frown through an unmistakable smile. "After all, those fried fish eyes are pretty gnarly."

"Stop!" she says with a huff. "You're not *actually* going to make me eat those."

"*Actually,* I am. But don't worry. They might be really gooey in the middle, but the outside is nice and crunchy," he teases, drawing out his words.

"Ugh. Let's just go find Emmaline and Verity."

"Good idea, I'm sure they'd like to watch, too!"

"*Enough!*"

Kiran raises his hands in a defensive surrender.

The two make their way through the crowded fairground, passing booths with intoxicating and warm aromas. Fried foods, fresh doughs, candied meats, and strong brews lace the air, seducing Tera to pause every few steps to suck in a deeper breath.

"Is that Professor Dringely?" Kiran asks, pointing at a towering woman with two small children holding her hands.

Tera spots her and groans.

"I thought you liked her?" Kiran raises an eyebrow at her, slowing in his tracks.

"I do. It's just that stupid test."

Professor Dringely turns, spotting Tera and Kiran. She smiles softly, nodding her head in acknowledgment. One of her little ones tugs at her hand, pulling her attention away only a second later.

After the two friends pass most of the shops and food booths, Tera follows Kiran around a bend and down a stone pathway to a small tent, where Emmaline and Verity stand waiting for them.

"'bout time!" Verity shouts, hands on her hips. Her hot pink bob frames her round, freckled face. In the dim amber lights of the fairgrounds, Tera thinks for a moment that Verity's periwinkle skin almost looks more like the caramel color of her own.

"We were getting worried," Emmaline says, her voice as soft and breathy as always. The faun trots over to Tera and Kiran to hug them, her hooved feet clacking against the stone walkway.

"Hey guys," Tera chokes through Emmaline's tight hug, her strawberry blonde hair tickling Tera's arm.

"Any word from Trevitt?" Kiran asks.

"He left. His dad overdid it again and he had to help him home," Verity answers.

Kiran's face is grave, and he hangs his head. "Poor guy. I swear his dad's been getting worse and worse. He needs to just retire early and take care of himself."

"He can't," Emmaline says. "Too many mouths to feed in that family for the only adult to *not* work."

"I don't know how he's done it as long as he has. Some of those kids are still so little. Ugh. My heart breaks every time I see Trevitt," Verity says. "Sweet gronnet just keeps smiling though."

The friends are quiet. It's been years since Trevitt's mom passed away, leaving him often filling in as a parent for his eleven younger siblings. Even with all the time that's passed, the unfairness of it all never feels right to talk about, so the friends tend to avoid the topic entirely.

"All this to say," Verity starts, "you're stuck with just us tonight."

"Works for me," Tera says, earning a sharp glare from Kiran.

"Be nice," Kiran scolds.

"This *is* me being nice."

"He's nothing but nice to you."

"You don't particularly like hanging out with him either," Tera mutters under her breath, just loud enough for her best friend to hear.

He rolls his eyes and ignores her remark.

"He's just… too much."

"He's never able to hang out much anymore," Verity says, disregarding Tera and Kiran's side conversation. "I mean, I get it, but we'd have a better chance of hanging out with Aeridonis himself than expecting Trevitt to actually show up."

"At least the fair has food," Kiran says with a laugh. "You never know! Trevitt could show up after bringing his dad home. He can't turn down fried food—especially if there's fried fish. Meanwhile, I don't think a wizard like Aeridonis would bother himself with fish pies, funnel cakes, and candied boar belly."

"You never know," Tera jokes. "Maybe Aeridonis has got a soft spot for candied boar belly. I've heard mineral elves are suckers for sweets."

The friends start making their way toward some of the rides when Emmaline breaks the brief silence with a soft giggle. "Can you imagine?" she asks. "The great wizard Aeridonis… stuffing his mouth with sticks of sweets and riding the twirly cups."

Tera and Verity laugh, but Kiran crosses his arms and continues walking in silence.

"What's wrong with *him?*" Verity asks Tera.

"He's a big Aeridonis fan. Has a poster of him next to his bed. I think he tells the poster 'good morning' every d—"

"That's not funny." Kiran's cerulean eyes narrow on Tera.

"Okay, I'm *sorry*. I just mean you have a lot of *respect* for him."

"Because he's one of the greatest wizards the kingdom has ever had, and if it weren't for his help with the Battle of Durnamire, the marrow elves would've continued ruling the kingdom, and my parents never would have gotten together years later. Even if they had, they would've been executed. No breeding 'dirty' half-elves. Aeridonis is a *hero.*"

"I didn't know all that," Emmaline says, her small features crinkling as she looks over at Kiran.

"It's not really a piece of history anyone talks much about. It gets brushed over. But they talk about it a lot in animalinguist classes. I guess because most of us are half-elves that wouldn't exist if the marrow elves were still in control."

The serious conversation lightens as they reach the entrance gate to the twirly cups. They flash their tickets to the ride attendant and shove past each other as they race for the only available cup.

Smooshed in together on the narrow bench, the friends pull down the security lap bar seconds before the cup begins whipping them around in tight circles. Tera hears Kiran moan, and she turns to see his usually dark skin turning pale.

"I don't feel so good," he grumbles. Beside him, Verity squeals with laughter, throwing her hands in the air as the cup continues twirling.

The spinning cups go on just a moment longer and the lap bar releases as soon as they stop. Kiran wastes no time, stumbling from his seat and making his way to the nearest trash can.

"Is he okay?" Emmaline asks, stepping up beside Tera, who was watching Kiran from a respectable distance.

"Too much spinning, I guess." Tera shrugs.

Just as she decides to go closer and check on Kiran, a raven swoops in and perches itself on her shoulder.

Emmaline gasps softly. "Steve!" she coos, hands on her heart.

"Hey, buddy." Tera turns her head to give her pet raven a quick kiss. He holds out the scrap of paper in his beak and she takes it, turning it over and immediately recognizing her brother's handwriting.

> Mom and Dad are home early. I said
> you were at a late-night study session
> with some kid from class because you
> felt bad about failing. Get home soon or
> it's your problem.
> P.S. You still owe me five coins for this.

Tera reads the note a second time while Steve softly pecks at her shoulder, wanting snacks or attention. She groans, rolling her eyes and looking up at her friends. Kiran appears to be feeling somewhat better, and the color is returning to his face.

"Guys, I've got to get home," she says, crumbling the letter and shoving it in her pocket.

"What's up?" Verity asks.

"Mom and Dad are home early, and I'm not supposed to be out. Aston covered for me, but they'll get suspicious if I'm not home soon."

"But you just got here," Kiran whines from his spot at the trash can. "You didn't even get to eat fried fish eyes!"

"Eww." Emmaline shivers. "You wanted to eat *those?* There are so many better options here, Tera."

"Nope. Didn't want to. Wasn't going to. Anyways, I really got to get moving. I'm in enough trouble as-is for the mid-terms. I don't need more."

"You're really leaving already? You can't stick around for just one more ride?" Verity pouts at her.

"You owe me money for your ticket if you leave early!" Kiran says with a weak smile, stepping toward the girls.

Tera brushes him off and turns to Verity. "The last time I was caught sneaking out, my parents put a tracking spell on me for a month. I'm not chancing that again. They questioned everything I did. If I so much as went to the bathroom during class, they'd send Steve with a note asking my professors why I left class."

"Oof, that's a bit extreme," Verity says with a snort. "Your brother can't just cover for you a bit more?"

"He probably *could,* but he *won't.*"

"Fair enough."

"I'll see you guys later. Sorry." Tera waves to her friends and trots off toward the fair entrance.

Near the front of the fair, she passes the juggling fauns who chime, "Thanks for visiting!" as she worms through the bustling crowd toward the ticket booth.

Once outside the fairgrounds, she's overcome by the stillness of the dark forest so unlike the lively one of her home. She slows, taking a moment to look around at the peculiar leafless trees.

Just then, she spots a glimmer deep in the twisting forest. She watches, trying to make out the source. When nothing else happens, she turns to continue up the hill to the portal.

"Quick," a voice hisses from the dark. Tera whips around, amber eyes wildly scanning. Hurried footsteps rustle through

thick and tangling grass. The sound seems to come from all directions, yet she can't see anything but empty woods and the pink portal on the path ahead.

Ignoring her instincts, she takes off into the trees, following the sounds of the footsteps as they rapidly grow fainter. As she sprints deeper into the woods, she can no longer see the path to the portal and can hardly hear the stepping sounds. It's only when she spots the glimmer once more that she realizes where the invisible people must be headed.

Stopping a short distance from the source, she squats behind a tree and peers out, watching. One by one, marrow elves appear in a cluster around a flickering, floating silver orb.

"So, this is him?" One of the marrow elves reaches out a sickly pale gray hand toward the orb, curling his spindly fingers around it.

"Yes," another replies, swatting away the other's hand.

"How did you do it?" asks a shorter one covered in a black cloak.

"Never mind that, it's almost time." He pulls out a pocket watch, staring at it for a while. Suddenly, the shimmering orb bursts, cascading silver from its fixed position in the air. When the glow of the silvery waterfall finally dissipates, Tera makes out the familiar figure.

"Aeridonis," says the elf with the pocket watch, shutting it and placing it back in his pocket. "So nice of you to join us."

Tera clasps her hands over her mouth. She instantly thinks of her best friend and his poster of the great wizard. He would never believe her if she told him about any of this.

Almost as if awakening on command, Aeridonis's gray eyes flick open, locking on the elf with the watch.

His voice—recognizable to everyone in Evalyra—cuts through the stillness of the woods. It feels calm against the low, hissing voices of the marrow elves. "What kind of—"

"Spare us the begging," the pocketwatch elf snips.

Aeridonis's wrinkled and rosy expression remains flat and unchanging as he stares back at the elf. "I wouldn't dare beg. I'll leave that to my granddaughter's dog, Noodle. Actually, I was going to ask what sort of a sad person would kidnap an elderly man while he's napping. Were you raised by boars?"

"Coming from the man who allowed half-breeds back in court. *Disgusting.*" The head elf spits at Aeridonis's feet. "I'm done wasting time," he says, turning his head side to side, and making eye contact with each of his accomplices. "See to it that it's done right this time," he says to one of the hooded elves.

"Me?" the one asks, spinning around to see if perhaps the head elf was referring to someone behind him. Tera can't make out any details of his face, but her few experiences with marrow elves make it easy to imagine. Thin nose, sallow skin, narrow eyes, dagger-like ears. She assumes this one is no different, though his voice lacks that same cold, wet hush of the others.

"Can't we just burn him?" one of the shorter elves asks.

Pocket Watch throws his arm out to the side, blasting the short elf through the air a few yards. He lands on his back with a thump, groaning before he stands and dusts himself off.

"You think he'd be foolish enough to not have protection charms at all times?" Pocket Watch says with a scoff. "No, we need a bigger curse than some childish fire spell. Let's get on with things."

The elf with the warm voice holds up his open hands toward Aeridonis, bowing his head. A few moments later, thick black fog begins trailing like a snake through the damp forest air, slithering toward Aeridonis and slowly coiling itself around his entire body. Tera notices his fingertips twitching, but his arms and legs are still as stones. She wonders why he isn't doing anything until she realizes perhaps he can't.

"Now you." Pocket Watch taps another hooded elf on the shoulder.

The second puts their hands up in a similar fashion, holding firm as a white fog snake seeps through their palms and twists around the wizard.

"Hold." Pocket Watch steps up, stopping inches from Aeridonis's face. "You've ruined everything that once made Evalyra great. But it can still be saved. Can't say the same for you." He steps back, standing between the other two casters and raising his hands but never lowering his head.

Aeridonis, nearly entirely ensnared by the fog snakes, turns his gaze. Tera swears he sees her. Her skin goes cold, and her heart starts racing as she weighs her options, only to realize there are none.

She's always seen photos and paintings of Aeridonis looking strong, proud, and powerful. But at this moment, he looks more human than elf. He stands hunched over, his wrinkled skin loose around his sunken features. His short, pointed ears peek out through his long, wispy hair. Even his thick white beard seems flat and dull.

Tera mouths, "I'm so sorry," and Aeridonis's eyes remain fixed on hers.

"Cinis." Pocket Watch claps his hands together and the two fog snakes burst into a blinding light. Tera and all the other elves involuntarily turn their heads away from the beam.

After the light fades, Tera turns back, only to see that the marrow elves are gone. Aeridonis is also gone, a small pile of ash in the place he stood. Blue smoke pulses in a thin cloud like a heartbeat from the pile for a few seconds before simmering out.

CHAPTER TWO

BUTTER-FLAVORED

Tera gapes at the ash, her eyes welling up, though she isn't sure why. She isn't as educated on Aeridonis's accomplishments as her best friend, and she has no special attachment to him. Even still, she grew up hearing stories about the great, undefeatable wizard. And here he is—a pile of cold ash.

After waiting a moment, listening carefully for sounds of footsteps or voices, she determines the marrow elves have truly left. She scrambles on her hands and knees to the pile.

"Aeridonis? Can you hear me?" She feels crazy even asking, but perhaps an all-powerful wizard could communicate even as a pile of ash. When her question is met with silence, her heart falls into her stomach.

Then, it hits her.

"Oh man," she says with a groan. "Why couldn't someone else have been here for this? Instead, you get stuck with the deathriser who just flunked her midterm. Sorry, dude." She rubs her palms together, warming them before placing them delicately on top of the soft ash. "I'll do my best."

She stays seated, warm palms on the ash, eyes closed. In her mind, she visualizes Aeridonis rising from the ash over and over as she mutters, "Suscito."

The forest is lifeless as she waits. Her eyes shoot open, and she glares at the ash, attempting the entire ritual all over again.

"Suscito."

Silence. Stillness.

"I don't know what to do," she admits, her voice cracking. She stands, pacing back and forth in front of the ash pile. Then, she stops. "Professor Dringely!" Her mind flickers to the image of her deathrising professor with her children at the fair.

"Stay right there!" she commands the pile. Tera turns to leave, stopping to glance back over her shoulder and throw it a quick, "Sorry," before taking off toward the path to Summercloud.

When she eventually reaches the path again, she follows it down to the entrance, racing past the juggling fauns who greet her yet again with a, "Welcome to Summercloud!" Tera stops, trailing back to one of the fauns.

"Have you seen a pyre elf with two little kids? Super tall. Long black hair. Red eyes. Her kids look just like her, but like… little."

The faun smirks and giggles, never breaking her juggling. "Sweetheart, you've just described about a hundred of our guests tonight. Sorry." She shrugs, chirping another, "Welcome to Summercloud!" as a cluster of guests enters the fairgrounds.

"Thanks anyways." Tera groans, leaving the faun and making her way into the crowd.

Shoulders slam into her as she burrows deeper into the mass of people, throwing out the occasional obligatory,

"Sorry." The crowd—far thicker than when she first arrived at the fair—swallows her, making it nearly impossible to see more than the people immediately surrounding her. Dread creeps into her chest, squeezing her lungs. She spins around, desperately hunting for Professor Dringely.

After a few minutes, Tera wiggles her way out of the crowd for a breath of air. Just as she reaches the edge of the horde, the screech of a child's tantrum tears through the jingling sounds of fair games and the chattering of fairgoers. Her eyes instinctively zip toward the source—a small pyre elf sobbing over a jumbo bucket of spilled popcorn in the dirt around him.

"It's okay!" crows the mother, squatting beside him. Tera recognizes her immediately as Professor Dringely. She dashes toward her professor, nearly trampling the second child as she's picking up dirt-covered popcorn with tiny fingers and popping it in her mouth.

"Professor!" Tera cries. "Help!"

Professor Dringely spins to face Tera, eyes wide. "Tera! Are you alright?"

"I need your help. Aeridonis—forest—marrow elves—ash—" she huffs between each word. She pauses to catch her breath and attempt a full sentence. When she realizes she's gripping her professor's robes, she immediately drops them. "Sorry," she says, face flushing deep red.

"Take a breath," Professor Dringely instructs as her little ones pluck ground popcorn like stray chickens. Tera swears one of them even tucks their arms to look like wings.

Tera sucks in a shaky breath, pushing it back out slowly. "Alright, what happened?"

"I was leaving the fair. I saw something and heard someone in the forest outside the fair and I went to check it out. It was a group of marrow elves. Somehow, they had Aeridonis, only I think he was charmed. He wasn't moving—except his fingertips. And he could talk. And then they did some kind of curse together and turned him into a pile of ash. I'm scared his ashes will blow away if we don't do something fast and I didn't know what else to do and I remembered seeing you at the fair and—"

"Are you sure?"

"Am I sure what?"

"Of what you saw."

Tera's face twists and she glares at her professor. "Yes. Positive. You think I made this up?"

Dringely takes a steady deep breath. "No, Tera. I think I was just hoping." She observes her student for a moment as if still trying to decide if her words are true. "This is bad," she says decidedly. Another breath. She places her hands on Tera's shoulders, locking eyes with her. "Okay, here's what we're going to do. Remember what we talked about in class a couple of weeks ago? A deceased person needs a body to resurrect into. You can't bring someone back to life as a pile of ash—it's not something that can function as a living being. It doesn't have to be his original body, but we need to find one no longer in use that we can bring him back into. It could take some time to procure one. In the meantime, I want you t—"

"Mommy!" the little girl screams. Dringely and Tera look down at her as she wails, her brother's teeth chomping down on her hand and a piece of popcorn.

"I've got to report this to security and get my family out of here. If there's someone out there that dangerous, we need to evacuate everyone." Her wide eyes stare back at Tera. "Get home fast– take a friend with you if you can. I'm sure security will want to get the details from you, but we can worry about that later when everyone is out and safe."

"What about his ashes?" Tera asks, her eyes darting between the children and her professor.

"Gather his ashes. Keep them safe and hidden. Bring them to my office first thing tomorrow and we'll figure this out. Just get home safe!"

There's another scream from her daughter. Dringely throws Tera an apologetic frown as she squats down and pries her son's mouth open to release her daughter's hand.

"Gather his ashes in what?" Tera asks, but Dringely is busy scolding her children and telling them it's time to go home. Tera looks around for inspiration, her eyes scanning over the jumbo popcorn bucket on the ground. She swipes it while the kids are distracted by their mother, and she takes off running back to the forest.

It takes Tera a while to find the place in the forest with Aeridonis's ashes again.

"I hope you like butter," Tera says, giving the popcorn bucket a whiff before carefully scooping the ashes into it.

Once she sprinkles the last pinch of him into the collection, she stands, dusting off her hand and carefully clutching the bucket to her chest. "Kiran would never believe me if I told him Aeridonis and I had a sleepover." She smirks, cringing a little at herself. "Sorry."

She takes careful, deliberate steps through the forest, finally reaching the path yet again. This time, she turns to head toward the portal home. Just as she approaches the portal, she nearly trips on something at her feet. Swearing under her breath as she regains her balance and double-checks the contents of the popcorn bucket, she looks around, spotting the same stray cat as before. Tera growls at the cat, turning to leave but stopping just before stepping into the portal.

She looks back at the tabby, who now sits at the edge of the path, licking its paw and wiping it over its ear.

"Dringely said it doesn't have to be *your* body," she says to the popcorn bucket of ash. "This could work. At least for now." She thinks back to a recent lab lecture where Professor Dringely had the students kill toads and resurrect them in the bodies of dead fish. Perhaps she hasn't forgotten as much of the lesson as she thought.

Tera kneels, patting the ground next to her. "Pst, pst, pst. Come here, kitty," she whispers to the tabby, who pretends not to hear her. "I'll make it quick; I promise."

Just then, Tera hears a sputtering sound that catches her off guard. She falls back into the gravel and dirt, scaring the cat away.

She looks around for the source, unable to tell what direction it could have come from. Rubbing at her long ears for a second, she shakes her head and stands to leave after checking that none of the ash had fallen out of the bucket. Then, an unmistakable voice rings out in her head.

You were seriously thinking of putting me inside a cat?

CHAPTER THREE

HEADSPACE

Tera stares down at the popcorn bucket of ash in her hands, willing it to speak.

"Aeridonis?" she asks.

Nothing.

After a few minutes of silence—aside from the chatter of a family passing through the portal—she chalks it up to her imagination. The whole incident in the forest must be messing with her mind. She tries getting the ash to talk one more time, earning her a suspicious look from a couple of parents with their children on their way to the portal.

"I feel crazy." She huffs, shutting her eyes tight and opening them again. When her words are met with silence still, she decides to go home and find somewhere to keep the bucket until morning. As she steps through the portal, her mind refocuses. Time to think of how in the world she'll explain to her parents why she was out so late. And better yet—why she's returning with a popcorn bucket full of wizard.

On the other side of the portal, the familiar lushness of Darkwood's trees greets Tera. On her walk home, she passes Nyana, Darkwood's resident dryad.

"Welcome home, Tera," she says from within her thick tree. "How was the fair?"

"Not great. Long story and I don't have time to tell it—I've got to get home. Sorry, Nyana!" Tera scurries past her with a faint smile, making her way to the grove of tree homes.

Darkwood is home to nearly the entire arboreal elf population of Evalyra, the majority of which are lifebringers like her family. The arboreal elves live in homes built into the sides of monstrous trees that shade the entire forest, staying true to its name of Darkwood.

Tera and her family live in a cozy home about halfway up one of the trees. Rickety stairs zigzag in every direction up the sides of trees, with wooden bridges connecting the staircases at various heights. It's a labyrinth Tera memorized as a child.

She scurries upstairs, tucking the bucket of ashes on the ground behind a clay planter with a bushy flowering plant. Stepping back to make sure it can't be seen when passing by, Tera nods in self-approval. She sucks in a slow, deep breath, summoning big crocodile tears before barging through the front door.

"Esotera!" her mother commands. Tera cringes when she hears her full first name but keeps the tears coming.

"I'm never going to get this stupid class!" she sobs, making sure her mother sees her wiping away a fat tear.

Her mother—a petite woman with copper curls identical to Tera's, equally bronze skin, and a sharp little nose—looks stunned for a moment as she gathers her thoughts.

"Were you out studying?" her mother asks, her face scrunching as she looks her daughter up and down. It sounds as if she doesn't believe the words even as she says them.

"Duh." Tera shoots her an offended look. "I told Aston to let you guys know in case I was going to be out late."

"He—he did," she replies, almost like a question.

Tera gapes at her mom. "Okay? So why are you looking at me like that? Like you're disappointed in me. I already feel bad enough about this freaking test, and I'm never going to graduate and then I'll never get a good job and I'll always just be a failure. They'll have me cleaning seiva just to keep food on the table."

"Language!" Her mother's mouth gapes open.

"If you suck at magic, you could just join the half-elves in the animalinguist classes!" chimes her little sister, Zeyla, who's sitting on top of the dining room table, swinging her feet and grinning back at her. She tilts her head to the side, her copper ponytail swinging.

"That's not funny, Zeyla," their mother warns.

Tera struggles to resist a smirk, but quickly pushes it away and summons more tears.

"I just don't know what to do," she pouts.

"Why don't you get some rest, sweetheart? You've worked hard enough for one day—you need a break. Maybe a good night's sleep will help some of that studying really click."

Tera sighs. "I hope so." She shuffles by her mom, being sure to lean her head pitifully on her mom's shoulder for a moment in passing on her way to her room at the far end of the small house.

When she reaches her room, she throws back a, "Goodnight!" to her family, closing her door and keeping the light off.

That was pretty tricky, says the same familiar voice in her head. She whips around as if expecting the source to come from someone in her room. When she spots no one, she tiptoes toward her bed, flopping back on it and closing her eyes. Was she truly hearing things now?

When she finally opens her eyes again and adjusts to the darkness of the room, she trains them on the paintings on her ceiling. Thick swirls of color fade into black and white across the flat surface. In some places, illustrations of mushrooms and clouds fill gaps in the swirling patterns.

Did you paint that? The voice asks. *It's beautiful.*

A panicked whine erupts from Tera as she launches herself off the bed, checking underneath it for the intruder.

You're not going to see me. Though I must commend you on your eyesight. I forgot what it was like to have young eyes.

"What are you talking about? Where are you?" Tera wildly opens every drawer, cabinet, and closet door searching for the source of the voice. She tears her bedding off the mattress, clothes out of the closet, and trash out of the bin, only to find she's entirely alone. "You sound like Aeridonis," she says, her voice low, "but that's crazy. Am I asleep? If I am, would you be able to tell me if this is a dream?"

I understand it about as much as you do, the voice says, *but it appears I'm stuck in here for now.*

"In where?"

He doesn't have to answer. The voice isn't coming from anywhere in her room. As soon as she asks the question, she realizes Aeridonis is in her head.

"So, you can see what I see?" Tera asks, shutting her eyes tight.

Well, not when you do that.

She opens them again.

Now I can.

"Can't you get out? Why are you here in the first place?"

People always assume just because I'm the "great wizard" that I know stuff. Where do you people get that idea?

"Because you *do* know stuff?"

Eh.

"So… Can you feel what I feel?" she asks, tightly pinching a chunk of flesh on her arm until it turns rosy.

Don't suppose so.

"This is so freaking weird. I've got to ask Professor Dringely about this."

Is that the woman you spoke to at the festival?

Tera nods, then pauses. "Can you tell I nodded? I guess you can see our vision bobbing?"

I don't know how this works either.

Tera sighs dramatically and the wizard grumbles to himself in response.

I suppose she's our best bet for now. And from what I gathered from your conversation with her before you put my ashes in a greasy bucket… He pauses for effect. *She plans to help you in the morning. Listen to your mother and get some rest. We've got a big day ahead of us tomorrow.*

"Okay, you can share my headspace for now, but you can't tell me what to do. That's not how this works."

What else would you suggest we do?

"I'm not suggesting *we* do anything. I'm trying to think of what *I* should do."

Go to sleep. It's been a long day.

"Sleep is the least of my worries right now! I feel like I'm going crazy. You're not in my head. That's not even possible, right?" Tera hurries to her bookshelf, parsing through the old textbooks she never bothered to read for class.

Oh no you don't. You're not trying any spells without your professor. Otherwise, you'll put me in a cat.

"I'm not putting you in a cat."

You almost did.

"Yeah, okay, but I didn't!"

Go to bed, Esotera.

"Don't call me that."

That's what your mother called you. Is that not your name?

"It is, but I hate it. Just call me Tera."

But Esotera sounds more whimsical. I think I'll stick with it.

"Stop, Aeridonis. It's not funny. How would you like it if someone called you Don or something?"

Silence.

"Hit a nerve, did I? Or maybe you like that name! Sounds younger."

Ouch. We're really resorting to age jokes now?

"This has got to be a dream or something. This is so weird." Tera pulls her bedding back onto her bed and climbs into it. She lays on her side, closing her eyes but feeling more awake than ever.

"Hey, Don?" she asks after a few minutes of silence.

Don't call me that.

She lets out a little huff. "I just wanted to know… what path did you take in school? I know you're, like, good at basically all magic. But what did you start with?"

Elemental.

"Oh. Cool," she says, underwhelmed but unsure what answer would've actually surprised her.

The air is cool and silent, and Tera begins wiggling and shifting in bed, rolling over to her other side.

"I'm studying deathrising, in case you wanted to know."

Mhmm.

"I'm not that good at it. My whole family is full of life-bringers, and I just wanted something different from all of them. What paths did your parents take?"

Silence again.

"Don?"

Nothing.

"Sorry, *Aeridonis.*"

Still nothing.

"Did I say something wrong?"

Go. To. Sleep.

"How am I supposed to sleep when I have a literal stranger living in my head? This is everything I can do to not freak out." Her eyes start to sting and a hot tear plummets down her cheek. "I hate this," she says, her voice cracking, "and I don't know what else to do to stay sane besides at least make you feel like less of a stranger. "

She hears him grumble. *Look, kid, I'm tired. I've had a long day. I died. And un-died. I need my beauty sleep.*

"How are you tired? You literally don't have a body."

Do you have a grandfather? A great uncle? Let me teach you something. He pauses to make sure he has her full attention. *Old men like sleep. I don't care if I don't have my own body. I like some peace and quiet. And you're chatty. Cut it out.*

Her chest grows heavy. "Sorry." Her smile fades and she sinks deeper into her pillow, forcing her eyes shut.

Can you hear my thoughts? She tries speaking in her mind. No response. *Don, Don, Don, Don.* When there's still no response, she comes to the conclusion that while he can speak in her head, he cannot hear her thoughts.

She takes a deep breath, allowing herself to settle into sleep.

"Mom might have fallen for that seiva, but I know you were lying." Tera opens her eyes and spots Zeyla peering over her, arms crossed and lips pursed.

"What are you talking about?"

"Last night. The boo-hooing. Where were you?" Zeyla asks.

Tera sits up, combing her fingers through knotted ringlet curls with a wince. "I was studying."

"Whatever. Don't tell me. Wouldn't matter if you studied anyways. No one is going to hire a deathriser from Darkwood. There are already so few jobs for deathrisers that actually pay a good living—they'll never pick you. Leave that seiva to the pyre elves."

Zeyla struts to Tera's bedroom door, pausing in its frame to turn back to her for a moment.

"Oh. Mom said breakfast is ready." She flips her braided hair over her shoulder with a flop, prancing out of Tera's room.

Tera drops a foot out of bed, letting it fall flat on the cold floor. With a moan, she stretches and forces herself up the rest of the way. Eventually, she waddles to the kitchen, where her parents and sister sit around steaming bowls of nutty berry porridge. Her brother, Aston, zips past her, snatching up a bowl and disappearing with it back into his room.

"Morning, Tera," her dad says, a blob of porridge falling from his mouth and into his lap.

"Morning, dad."

"Rough night?" he asks, wiping at his mess with a napkin while he looks up at her. Tera peers down at herself, realizing she never changed into pajamas last night.

"Lots of studying. Brain is fried. Are there any rolls this morning?"

"On the stove," her mom says, pointing to a casserole dish of gravy-drenched biscuits.

Tera slops a couple of the soggy biscuits into a bowl and sits with her family at the table.

That's what you eat for breakfast?

"What's wrong with it?" Tera asks aloud.

"What's wrong with what?" her dad asks, cocking an eyebrow.

"Uh, nothing. Sorry. Just working through school problems in my head."

Both of her parents stop eating to observe her for a moment, only resuming with tentative bites and unblinking stares.

Tera pretends not to notice, popping such a large chunk of biscuit into her mouth that she has no choice but to chew with her mouth open.

Zeyla's nose scrunches and lip curls up as she gawks at her big sister eating. "I'm not hungry anymore." She slides her nutty berry porridge forward and excuses herself from the table.

Nearly finished with her breakfast, Tera scrapes the last bite into her mouth and nearly tosses the bowl into the sink on her way back to her room.

"Tera!" her mother calls.

"Wha-at?" she draws, tossing her head back and rolling her eyes.

"Why are you in such a rush this morning?"

"Professor Dringely promised to help me work through a few of the test questions I missed if I get to school early. I'm trying to go!"

"Okay, okay! You're doing tonight's dinner dishes though, got it?"

"Fine."

Tera scrambles to get ready and hurries out the door, stopping and reaching for the popcorn bucket on the way. A couple of tree beetles found their way into the ash, and she plucks them out, setting their frantically wiggling legs on the banister beside her home.

"Hey, Don?" she asks, trotting down the tree stairs and along the path through the center of Darkwood.

Esotera.

"Do you think this has happened to anyone before? Like, the whole head-sharing thing?"

Do you mean has a student ever decided to resurrect a living being after not paying attention in deathrising classes? Maybe.

"Okay, a bit harsh."

Aeridonis grumbles.

"I'm sorry," she says, quieting her voice as she passes a couple of other arboreal elves on their way the opposite direction. "I didn't know what else to do. I panicked, and you seemed like too important a person to just let sit there as a pile of ash while I went to get help. You could've blown away or something, I don't know."

He sighs. *If it counts for anything, I think you did the right thing. Albeit, not in the right way. For the love of everything holy, I just hope this encourages you to pay attention in class. If it's not keeping your interest, switch paths. It's a pain in the keister, but worth it if you can avoid a lifetime of boredom.*

"I'm not switching paths," she says, nearly in a growl.

What about lifebringing? After all, it comes naturally to arboreal elves like you and your family. I'm sure it would be a breeze to switch paths and catch up to your classmates. You could really thrive.

She picks up her pace, ready to get the wizard out of her head.

CHAPTER FOUR

THE PROTECTION SPELL

The rest of the trip to Pipwerry Academy of Elven Education is quiet. Tera's grateful to catch the portal gronnet right as he sets the school portals for the day. She tosses him a, "Thank you," and steps through, appearing next outside the academy.

Pipwerry has five paths: deathrising, lifebringing, illusionary, elemental, and animalinguism. The school itself has a central hub—a stunning marble castle with a grandiose fountain—and each of the paths has its own floating land mass encircling the Hub. The Hub is home to the path portals, early education classrooms, the cafeteria, and some administrative offices.

Years ago, the floating land masses earned the nickname "islands" from some of the students. Each path's island can be reached by a path portal in the Hub. The deathrising island is home to a tall, black and gray brick tower covered in thorny vines. Outside the tower, deathrising students often hang out in the small courtyard—a graveyard used for practice by the older and more experienced deathrising students.

Tera hurries into the Hub and straight back into the portal room, stepping into the black portal marked by a skull sigil on the wall above it. On the other side, she walks out to the front of the deathrising tower. A few students shoot her a weird look when they see her popcorn bucket of ash, but no one's gaze lingers long. Most students of Pipwerry have seen stranger things within just their first year of schooling.

Professor Dringely's office is several floors up. Once Tera reaches her familiar oak door, she begins pounding on it.

"Professor! Open up, please! It's Tera!"

She keeps hammering her fists against the door up until the second Professor Dringely opens it.

"Goodness, Tera! You scared me. I was just going through the catalog of corpses to see if one seemed suitable enough for someone like Aeridonis."

Tera knows "catalog of corpses" must sound unpleasant to Aeridonis just by the sound he makes in her head. She grins a little, realizing how little the great wizard must know about the deathrising path. The catalog of corpses is simply a binder of information on everyone buried in the island's graveyard. Each one is someone who volunteered to donate their bodies to the school for educating future generations. Some of them are even brought back as themselves, years later. Others—based on whatever markings in the catalog of corpses—choose not to have their consciousness used in their body after death.

"Professor?" Tera asks, eyeing the open door and easing it shut with her foot.

"I spoke with security at the fair," Dringely says with a huff. "They did absolutely nothing. Zero help. I don't see how the fair can hire such absolute imbeciles to protect fairgoers, not with how big the fair is getting."

"Professor?" Tera repeats a little louder.

"I tried to insist they get everyone out. I told them precisely what you told me and they made a joke of it. So now I have to escalate things and get this to the Council bef–"

"Professor!" Tera yells, clasping her hands over her mouth in the immediate, sharp silence.

Dringely focuses on her, interlacing her fingers in wait.

"He's in my head."

Her professor squints, thinking for a moment. "Do you mean you can't get the image of his death out of your mind? I would imagine that was horrific. If you'd be comfortable with it, I can set you up for a visit with the counselor during your lunch period."

"That's sweet, professor, thank you. But that's not what I mean. I mean… literally. He's in my head. Remember when I came to you at the fair? I told you I had tried the spell to bring him back in his own body, but nothing seemed to happen. Only, something *did* happen." Tera sets the popcorn bucket on her teacher's desk. "Aeridonis is literally sharing my headspace. I can hear him. He can see what I see and hear what I hear. He can't feel what I feel, or hear my thoughts, or control my body. It's like he's just an observer, I guess."

Dringely cocks an eyebrow at her.

"What?" Tera asks.

"Now is *not* the time for jokes, Tera. If what you told me last night is true, everyone's in danger and we need to focus on resurrecting Aeridonis so he can tell the Council what happened. If the Council is to believe anyone, it's one of their own members."

"I'm not joking."

"Okay. Explain to me how he's in your head." Professor Dringely crosses her arms and watches Tera with nose upturned.

"If I could explain how, I'd get him out myself. I don't want him here– it's creeping me out, if we're being honest.

I tried resurrecting him myself. Nothing happened. A little after I talked to you, I heard him in my head. Scared the seiva out of me."

Dringely's eyes travel down to the popcorn bucket in Tera's hands.

"Can I see that?" she asks from her seat at her desk.

Tera steps closer and lowers the bucket.

Her professor sighs and starts nibbling on a hangnail.

"Oh my." She reaches her free hand over and taps the top of the ashes as if to test if it's real. "You tried to resurrect him without a body. I didn't realize you actually tried a resurrection spell on him! You just told me he was turned to ash. You know you can't bring someone back without a body! Why did you do that?"

"I–I forgot."

"You *forgot?*"

Tera lets out a half-whimper, half-moan.

"I've never heard of anything like this, but I suppose it's possible."

Glad I'm not a betting man.

"Do you have any idea how we can get him out?" Tera asks, shifting her weight up with her hands on a desk, sitting down on top and swinging her legs.

"I'll have to do some research."

Tera doesn't expect this answer and her swaying legs immediately stop. "Can we not just try the awakening spell again, but with a proper link or something?"

Dringely can't help but perk up, her posture proud. "See? You *do* pay attention in class!"

Tera shrugs. "Not enough, apparently."

"Unfortunately, I don't think that'll work. You're alive. The link is meant to transfer consciousness from one deceased to another. I'd be too nervous to try it on a living person. Besides, it might not move *his* consciousness anyways. It's too risky."

Tera cringes at the thought of her own mind transferring to one of the corpses and Aeridonis living in her own body. "Okay, so if not that, what could we try instead?"

"That's just the thing I don't think you're understanding, Tera. I don't know."

"What about *you?* Any ideas?" Tera asks.

"I'm sorry?" Dringely ceases the chewing and instead stares at her student.

"Not you, sorry."

I hardly dabbled in deathrising. In fact, the Council doesn't even really have deathrising representation at the moment. Is your professor dependable? Do you trust her to find the answers herself, or do I need to direct you to some possible resources?

Tera looks at Dringely. "I trust her, yeah. I think she can do it."

Dringely mouths, "Is he talking to you?" with her eyes wide.

Tera nods.

"Aeridonis?" her professor speaks in an unnaturally stiff voice. "I assure you; I will dedicate every moment possible digging into this until I find a solution. I'll run lab experiments and make sure whatever we end up doing is entirely safe for you *and* Tera. In the meantime, I think I'll hold back on reaching out to the Council. I worry they'll prioritize *you*, Aeridonis, and not keep Tera's safety in mind so much. I'd rather handle this my own way so I can be sure you'll *both* be safe. As soon as you're separated, you can *both* fill the Council in on everything so they can take appropriate action. I'll just need some time if I'm to do this the right way."

Tell her she can take whatever time she needs. I understand the nature of research.

"No!" Tera hops off the table, her heart raging against her chest, threatening to knock the air from her lungs. "It's urgent. This isn't some stupid school project she can take her time with. I need you *out.*"

"I don't need you rushing me," her professor snaps, staring at Tera with bloodshot eyes. It's in that moment she notices Dringely's usually silky black hair is instead frizzy and greasy. "I'm doing everything I can. I came straight here after the fair to work on finding a body for Aeridonis. I had to reach out to several contacts to look for other corpse options. I wrote up a report after security didn't take me seriously. I missed tucking my kids in last night, and I'm sure I'll miss it again tonight. And the next night. And however long this takes. I promise I'm going to work as fast as I can. But I don't want to risk hurting you or him in the process. But that doesn't mean I'm not going to do this as quickly as I can. For your sake and mine. Promise. I just need you to not pester me."

Tera sucks in a slow breath, her eyes hot and stinging as she sinks into the floor. "I thought it was cool at first," she says, "having this all-powerful wizard in my head. I guess it just felt super temporary, like you were going to be able to get him out right away. It's already so overwhelming. When other people are bothering you, you can always escape for a moment by yourself, but until he's out, I won't get that. And it's like that feeling when someone's watching you, except it's someone else watching out of my own eyes. It's freaking me out to even think about it."

Does it help to know that I feel similarly?

"What?" Tera asks, and Dringely picks up that it's directed at Aeridonis.

I mean, think about it. I don't even have a body right now. I'm quite literally a prisoner in yours. At least you can still go wherever you want and do whatever you want. If you want to escape to a café and eat pastries all day, I can't stop you. If you want to visit the coast and sleep in the sand, I can't stop you. But if I want to do any of that, I'd have to ask you to do it instead. And even then, I can't even taste the things you taste, so I wouldn't even taste those croissants. It's a shame. Especially because I'm sure those horrible looking globs of dough you ate for breakfast tasted heavenly.

Tera snickers, wiping a runaway tear from her cheek.

"What'd he say?" Professor Dringely asks. "Are we in agreement?"

"Yeah," Tera says with a semi-reluctant nod.

"Excellent. Don't worry—I'll figure this out. Until then, head on to class. We don't need you sitting around moping until I find a solution."

I'll be quiet. You won't even know I'm here.

Tera gets up, slinging her bag over her shoulder and waving to Professor Dringely as she heads upstairs for her first class of the day: Necromantics.

Professor Leutrix's classroom takes up the entirety of the top floor of the deathrising tower. When Tera finally reaches the top, she tries to stifle her huffing breaths from other students on her way to her seat.

"Sit," Professor Leutrix commands, his voice gravelly and rumbling. "We have a lot to cover today. *Sit.*" His narrow eyes focus on each student as they enter the classroom, willing them to their seats. The second the morning gong rings out across the campus, Leutrix flicks his wrist, the heavy classroom door slamming shut in the face of a latecomer.

Tera pulls her notebook and pencil out, rubbing at her eyes for a moment. Her attention floats up to the tall classroom ceiling, full of hanging pots with lush, vining plants. She sighs, willing every ounce of her attention to focus on her teacher instead.

"The Everdeath spell… What are its effects on the body?" Leutrix paces across the front of the room, snapping in posture each time he changes direction. Tera watches a couple hairs loosen from his usual tight bun of jet black hair every time he turns.

One student raises their hand, straight as a beam in the air. Leutrix continues pacing, ignoring them. The student's arm never waivers or flinches—just waits. Until eventually, the professor finally sighs.

"Since Milling seems to be the only one who knows." Leutrix takes the time to lock eyes with each student before motioning for the one to answer.

"It almost instantly stops the heart. It also leaves a distinct mark on the subject's face as a way of signaling to other deathrisers that the deceased cannot be brought back to life. The death is permanent." Milling quickly stamps out a smile, substituting it for a firm look.

Leutrix waits in silence, and Milling starts to squirm in his seat.

"Why is no one writing this down, since clearly none of you knew this?" Leutrix storms to his chalkboard and begins scribbling out notes for the students.

Every time her eyes wander for even a moment throughout class, Tera feels judged by the wizard in her head, half-expecting him to make some sort of snide comment about how he understands why she's failing her classes. To her surprise, he holds to his promise and stays quiet.

At lunchtime, Tera wanders down to the Hub portal, stepping through and walking to the cafeteria. Across the way, in line at one of the food booths, Kiran waves her down. He stands out in the crowd. Not just because celestial elves are a much smaller population than any other elf, but because of his lack of lumingo—the glowing skin markings distinct to celestial elves. Kiran takes after his elvish father in just about every way except that. Tera remembers his human mother scolding him for complaining about it as a child.

As Tera approaches, she notices his entire posture slumping. His usual beaming smile is absent from his face. Tera raises an eyebrow as she eases her way over.

"What's got you so down?" she asks, joining him in line without looking at the menu.

"Didn't you hear?"

"Hear what?"

"Word got out that Aeridonis missed a Council meeting."

Tera's heart flutters, and she clears her throat. "What's the big deal? Shouldn't he get to skip every now and then?"

"It's not some club meeting, Tera! These meetings are big deals—"

Aeridonis scoffs.

"—and in all his years on the Council, he's never missed one. The other Council members apparently went to check on him and he wasn't even home."

"So, he went out on a bender or something. Wanted to feel young again, I don't know."

Aeridonis chuckles, and Tera smirks.

"I don't know why I bother telling you things sometimes."

They step forward in line.

"I mean, doesn't it concern you even a little bit? One of the biggest names in the kingdom is mysteriously missing. What if something terrible happened to him? If something or someone came for him, the rest of us are screwed. You know that, right? This could be bad. Really bad."

"Kiran," Tera says, grabbing his shoulder and smiling. "Can I tell you something? It might make you feel better."

No.

"If it's sarcastic, I don't want to hear it."

Tera, no. Don't tell him.

"Why?" she asks, and Kiran thinks it's for him. He shoots her a snarled lip and furrowed brow.

"What do you mean *why?*"

Wait until I've got my own body. Then I can tell him myself. Just don't tell him right now.

"You won't ever have *your* body back though," Tera answers.

"What's wrong with you?" Kiran asks, throwing his arms to his sides with a flustered sigh. "You're not making any sense and I'm trying to have a serious conversation."

Trust me. I'll tell you more later. You can't tell him right now. If this takes longer than your professor thinks it will, you're already going to be in enough danger yourself—you don't need to involve your friend right now.

"Danger?" Tera's smile disappears. "What are you talking about? You never told me about any danger to *me!*"

"I can't deal with you right now." Kiran leaves, just as it's about to be his turn to order. He jogs off to the portal room, leaving Tera standing in line.

"Next," the cashier calls.

Tera takes a seat at an empty round table with a plate of garlic potatoes and fish. She sets her silverware down, not even taking a single bite before saying, "Tell me everything."

One step at a time.

"Okay, first of all, why didn't the marrow elves just use the Everdeath spell on you?"

Everdeath? Do you mean the permanent death spell? He chuckles. *The Council has been protected from that spell for years.*

"You can protect against it?" Tera gapes.

I mean, you can't, no. But the Council can.

"Why doesn't the Council protect other people then?"

It's a complicated process, and it only affords resources to protect a handful of people at any given time. It took years to study the properties of the enchantment and I really don't care to get into all that.

"Okay, fine. Then tell me why the marrow elves killed you."

Aside from the fact that they're pretentious turds?

"Aside from that."

They've wanted the kingdom back ever since the Battle of Durnamire. That was the turning point in the war when they knew they messed up. They knew they lost. And frankly, at that point, they stopped truly fighting. They think magic is being made into a joke and that elves should stay within their own cultures. One type of elf shouldn't have babies with another type of elf. You shouldn't marry outside of your culture. They threw around the idea of separate schools, even. Garbage like that. But they never gave up. They've been trying to take down the Council for ages. Specifically, me.

"Why you?"

I know where the draxxi are.

"The what?"

Draxxi.

"Yeah, thanks, Don. I got that." She rolls her eyes. "What is it?"

You're familiar with dragons, right?

"They're *dragons*?"

I didn't say that. Aeridonis sighs. *And you're familiar with cerepents?*

"Yes?"

Draxxi are kind of like dragons in that they're scaley, huge, can fly, and some breathe fire. Most don't. But they're also like cerepents in the way that they understand language and can be immensely vicious. The kingdom has been relying on their protective properties for ages.

"They sound pleasant."

That's one word for them.

"What does it matter that you know where the drackies are?"

Draxxi.

"Whatever."

The marrow elves want them.

"For what?" Tera shoves a forkful of potatoes in her mouth, her cheeks bulging as she chews.

Do they not encourage creativity in school anymore? Problem-solving? Critical thinking? Anything? There are a million reasons you could've at least guessed.

"I don't want to jump to conclusions!" she mumbles through potato.

As I said, the kingdom has been relying on their protective properties for ages. The draxxi provide Evalyra with an absolutely vital protection. The marrow elves cast a nasty curse on the kingdom during the war. Fortunately, we were able to stop the effects, thanks to the draxxi.

"What kind of curse?"

Ehh… Aeridonis mutters for a moment. *It's complicated… And rather dark. Essentially, it'll suck the life out of the kingdom, little by little. Best we keep the draxxi hidden so you never have to find out.*

"I still don't understand what the draxxi have to do with any of this," she says before shoving another bite in her mouth.

They produce an incredibly powerful magical essence needed for widespread protection spells. And those spells need to be cast periodically or they fade. Hence why we need to keep the draxxi hidden.

"Oh." She stops chewing. "That's kind of a big deal."

Understatement.

"What happens if they find the draxxi?"

They'd kill them or steal them for their own purposes. Either way, the safety and well-being of the entire kingdom would be at risk.

"But they killed you, so don't they assume they'll never know the location now? That seems kind of counterproductive."

On the contrary. They've been trying to track me for years, but they've yet to figure out where the draxxi are and how I get to them. But they assume with me out of the picture, someone else will come forward as a secondary caretaker and won't be as careful.

"'Caretaker?'"

The draxxi normally are aggressive, untamed carnivores. These ones have been carefully trained for many, many years. They're also well hidden. Unfortunately, that means they rely on me to take care of them and provide them with food every so often. The valley I've got them in has a little bit of game for them to eat, but it won't keep them full for long.

"So, what does that mean for me?"

Well, first of all, there isn't a second caretaker.

CHAPTER FIVE

A MINERAL ELF FROM MOREL

"Hey, hey, Tera Bear!" Trevitt comes stomping toward her table out of nowhere.

"Oh. Hi, Trevitt."

He drops his plastic food tray on the table with an echoing clatter, splattering some of his stabberfish pasta sauce on her robes. As she lets the chunk of fish on her own plate go untouched, she swears she'll never understand why gronnets are so obsessed with fish.

Tera wipes the sauce away and he doesn't seem to notice.

"What are you doing here, Trev?"

"The school portal master has been griping to the board. He wants to retire, but they don't have another gronnet willing to take the position. Low pay, long hours, ya know? But it's something! And dad could really use the help keeping food on the table. I've got no professional experience, so they're training me!" He laughs, his wet, green skin reflecting the harsh fluorescent lights of the cafeteria. "Can you believe it? *Me!* I didn't think I'd ever get to be a portal gronnet. I figured I'd be stuck following my dad's footsteps in mechanic work."

Tera pokes at her fish, which has gone cold, throwing out a, "That's great, Trev."

Trevitt shoves a plump forkful of noodles in his massive mouth, smacking down with a slurp.

"Anyways, today's my first day training with him. I'm learning how to do lasting portals, source-return portals, view portals– which I didn't know how to do before and they aren't use as often, but they're really neat– and–"

"Uh-huh," Tera urges him to hurry up.

"Oh! Anyways, he got the portals up for me this morning, but I'm supposed to try maintaining them myself when he goes on lunch break. I'm pretty nervous, but I'm excited! If you have any issues with your portal to or from the Hub, I'm sorry in advance!" Another laugh, this time sending a chunk of noodle across the table.

Tera groans, wiping her cheek with a shudder.

"Verity and Emmaline said they were going to take me out for celebratory smoothies later. Wanna come? Kiran can come, too! It'd be great to get everyone together since I missed Summercloud. I re–"

"I have plans," Tera interjects.

"Oh. That's alright! We can hang out another time."

The white noise chatter of the cafeteria isn't enough to fill the awkward silence.

"You gonna eat your fish?" Trevitt finally speaks up, reaching his slimy fingers across the table and swiping a sample of cold fish. Before he can get it to his huge mouth, Tera smacks his hand.

"Don't touch my food."

His wide grin droops. "Sorry. I just wanted to try it, and you didn't seem to want it."

"Who's to say what I want and don't want? I was still eating." Tera picks up her tray, storming off and dumping her food in the trash before leaving for the deathrising island again.

I'm going to need your help if your professor can't find an answer in a timely manner. Aeridonis's tone sounds grave. *Bringing you into that mess isn't ideal, but quite frankly, if we don't feed the creatures, they'll waste away. Not only would that be cruel to the draxxi, but it would cut off the siphoning of that protective essence. It would be putting you* and *the entire kingdom at risk. At least, that's how I'm going to rationalize it.*

Tera keeps walking to her next class, albeit early. "So, you're saying I'm going to be feeding these bloodthirsty things, but they've never met *me* before? They might want to eat me, or they might get territorial, right? It sounds stupid and dangerous. Are you sure this is a good idea?"

As sure as I am that lampflies sleep at night.

"But they don't."

Mmmh.

Tera swallows a lump in her throat. "When do we go?"

Esotera! You've got class, my dear. I can't be living in the head of a dropout.

Tera stops, her face burning.

Kidding. But I don't need you getting in more trouble with your parents. Can't go feeding draxxi if you're not able to leave your room.

"Fine." She continues, passing through Professor Dringely's open door and joining the couple of other classmates who arrived early.

At the end of class, Professor Dringely reaches for Tera, holding her back before she could slip through the door. She stands, holding Tera's arm and waiting for the other students to clear out. Once they are alone, Dringely closes her classroom door and steps over to the stack of books on her desk.

"Did you find something?" Tera asks, nearly hopping toward Dringely's desk, craning her neck to peer at an open book.

"Sort of, but nothing helpful."

"What's that supposed to mean?"

"I found one instance in a book where they reference something similar to your situation. An elderly deathriser tried to bring his wife back after she was ravaged by an animal in the Dreadmires. No idea what she was doing in the Dreadmires in the first place, but that's beside the point. Her body was torn to shreds—completely unsalvageable. He tried bringing her back, and her consciousness joined his. From what I've read, it sounds like what you're experiencing—she was able to see what he saw and hear what he heard, and that's about it."

"How did he get her into a different body?" Tera asks.

Dringely stumbles, trying to latch onto a word to save her. "He… He didn't."

Tera's entire face droops as she feels her lungs tighten.

"They were madly in love, even in their old age. They were more than happy to share a headspace for the rest of the man's natural life. It's actually a really sweet story, however, not helpful to us. But it gives me hope."

"How? How does *that* give you hope?"

"It means you're not the only one this has happened to. And it's unlikely they were the only other ones. So, there's probably something else out there about it. Someone else who has been through it, or at least records of it. And hopefully, a solution is too."

"Now what?" Tera asks, her every muscle tensing up as she awaits the answer.

"Same as before—I keep searching. I'll reach out to some of the other deathrising professors and see if they can point me in the right direction."

"No, no, no! Please don't tell them," Tera begs.

"As confident as I am in my abilities, this situation is far beyond just my expertise. We stand a much better chance of getting this solved with the help of the other professors."

"Please." Her eyes and cheeks start to sting. "They already don't take me seriously as an arboreal elf deathriser. I don't need them knowing I screwed up *this* royally."

Dringely smiles warmly and nods. "I'll present it as more of an academic curiosity. A research project."

"Promise? Don't mention my name."

"I promise. Besides, most everyone is already chattering about Aeridonis's disappearance. While I trust the other professors, I don't think it's safe to go spreading word of your… situation."

Tera nods, rubbing at her eyes and giving her head a quick shake. She takes a deep, steadying breath before speaking. "Okay. I guess there's nothing I can do about it in the meantime, huh?"

"Not really. There's a potion, though."

"A potion? For getting him out of my head?" Her eyes wander to the popcorn bucket of ashes, tucked behind a stack of books on her professor's desk.

"No. It's a silencing potion. It's meant to silence voices in your head. Only lasts for about half a day, but it's cheap and easy to make if you ever need more. It's usually used to help people with other difficulties, but I'd imagine it could silence Aeridonis if he ever got to be… too much." Professor Dringely's shoulders tense up nearly to her ears as she says this. "Sorry, Aeridonis. I'm just trying to look out for the well-being of my student. I hope you understand."

She watches Tera as if Aeridonis could possess her and speak through her.

Tell her I understand.

"He says he understands."

Professor Dringely visibly calms down. "You can get it from the school nurse. I'll write a note suggesting she give you a bottle to keep on hand—just in case." She pulls out a scrap of paper and scribbles a few words and a sloppy signature on it.

After Tera picks up her potion from the nurse, she goes out to sit on the edge of the fountain in front of the Hub. Water spurts up and across to several other spouts in a rhythmic display. A golden butterfly flutters past, and Tera can hear birds singing in the manicured campus trees.

I missed it here.

"I'd imagine it's been a while since you were a student."

Aeridonis lets out a hearty laugh. *You could say that. Though from time to time the Council comes out for visits.*

"Don?"

Silence.

"I'm ready to see where the draxxi are. Just help make sure they don't eat me."

Aeridonis bursts out in uncontrollable laughter while Tera sits, her mouth gaping and confused.

"I—I don't understand what's funny about that."

You should hear yourself, Tera. 'I'm ready.' As if you think I'd show you where they're at right now. Fat chance.

"I don't get it. Why not? You said you need someone to take care of them."

Oh, I do. That's why we're going to go visit my second.

"Your what?"

My second, Fillidren. An elemental mineral elf from Morel.

"I thought you said there wasn't anyone else to take care of them?"

There isn't. He doesn't know where they are, but he knows all about them otherwise.

"It seems pretty stupid that you didn't tell at least one other person where the draxxi are. No offense. I mean, did you assume you were *never* going to die?"

In my defense, Fillidren refused to listen to me whenever I wanted to tell him how to reach the draxxi. He didn't like the idea of knowing because he figured he could be tortured for information, or someone could use a truth serum on him. I never got around to telling him before I died.

"He seems pretty useless as a second. I mean, if it's his job to take care of them when you die but he refuses to hear where they're even kept, how's he supposed to do anything?"

He's a nervous, squirrely little man. What can I say? But heck of an elementalist, I'll give him that. He's done other things to benefit the kingdom over the years.

"So, how do I find him?"

I'll lead the way. Have you ever been to Morel?

Tera shakes her head.

We can probably get that gronnet friend of yours to conjure us a portal to make the trip shorter. Get there and back before your parents even miss you for dinner.

"Who? Trevitt? Absolutely not." She can't help but smirk as if he told a clever joke.

Don't you think you overreacted a bit earlier? So, the kid wanted some fish. Big deal. You weren't going to eat it anyways. Tell him you're sorry and ask him to make a portal to Morel.

Tera begins to pick at an old scab on her head. "I just don't like him. He's annoying and clingy and abrasive… And gross."

No one said you had to kiss the boy—

"Ew!" She pulls up the small scab, inspecting it in her fingers and flicking it into the water.

Esotera—

"Stop calling me that."

You have no room to judge that gronnet for being gross when you're sitting here flicking scabs into the fountain like you're making wishes.

"Stop!" Tera whines, getting up and brushing her robes off. A few passersby give her confused looks, exchanging whispers and stares as they walk by.

I feel like I'm talking to my grandchildren after they steal each other's toys. He makes his voice comically firm. *Tera, go tell that poor gronnet boy you're sorry for hurting his feelings.*

"Fine," she says with an exaggerated huff. She slinks off to the portal room in the Hub, scanning for Trevitt. When she doesn't see him, she rounds the corner to knock on the portal master's office door.

An older, wide-set gronnet in a newsboy cap answers the door. "One of the portals down?" He grunts.

"Um, no," she answers. "I was wondering if Trevitt is in your office. He's a friend of mine and I know he's shadowing you."

"Ye-up. He's in here." He steps aside and Trevitt squishes past him in the tight doorway.

"Oh, hi, Tera."

The portal master closes the door behind Trevitt.

"Sorry about earlier," she blurts out. "That was uncalled for. I've just been stressed out. I didn't mean to take it out on you. Sorry."

Trevitt's wet lips immediately curl into a wide smile. "No problem! I'm glad we could work things out!" He bounces forward a step and crushes her in a hug before she can react.

His arms are hot and moist, and she can feel herself involuntarily recoil at his touch. When he finally lets go of her, she wills herself not to wipe her arms off until he's no longer looking at her.

"I better get back to his office. He's been having me do some paperwork. Nice guy, but not very patient with me. I don't wanna keep him waiting." Trevitt salutes her and turns back to the portal master's office.

"Wait!" Tera calls.

He stops, looking back at her with a raised bushy eyebrow.

"I need you to make me a portal."

Please.

"Please."

"A portal? Why?" he asks.

"I need something for a project," she lies, "and I think I can find it in Morel."

"Morel?" Trevitt's eyes grow wide. "That's awful far to send a student for a project!"

"I mean, she's not sending me there specifically for the project, but I want my project to be the best of the best, especially after I failed the midterm. So, can you help?"

"I should be able to. Anything for a friend!" He steps toward the portal master's office, cracking open the door and telling him he'll be back in a few minutes.

Tera could hear the portal master grunt. Seemingly in approval.

Trevitt starts walking out of the Hub, beckoning for Tera to follow. "This way! Wouldn't want younger students stepping into the portal on accident or something. Gotta look out for other students. Working with portals can be tricky business, and there are a lot of rules to protect people."

He rounds the side of the castle and stops once they're out of view.

"This ought to work!" He interlaces his fingers in a strange symbol, closing his eyes and slowly raising and lowering his hands a few times. A shimmering red and white portal grows in front of him, and once it reaches full size, he stops.

"That's it?" Tera asks, eyeing the portal.

"Sure is!" He beams proudly.

"That's actually pretty cool, Trev," she says with a soft smile, eyeing the portal. "I bet your dad is proud of you for your new job."

Trevitt does a giddy little hopping dance between his two feet. "He really is! And it's not a job yet. As long as training keeps going well, it hopefully will be. The timing couldn't be better. Dad's hoping to retire super soon. He can't really do his job anymore with his health, and someone's gotta pay to feed him, Addie, Merret, Plechet, Dinnie, Ottur, Annet, Prox, Tellie, Dortie, Lokur, and baby Trestie. And me!" He chuckles.

Tera's eyes are wide as she tries to imagine a cottage full of gronnets.

"It's set with a return portal for one hour," he says, drawing her attention back. "If you take longer than that, you'll have to find another gronnet over there to open one back up. But hopefully, that's enough time."

"Is it?" Tera whispers to herself through clenched, faux-smiling teeth.

It'll have to be.

"Thank you, Trevitt."

He grins, putting his fists on his hips. "Happy to help! Hope you find what you're looking for."

Tera nods, her expression flat as she steps through the portal.

On the other side, she's surrounded by towering mushrooms.

"Woah," she says breathily.

Pretty, isn't it? Shame we're not here late at night. Most of the mushrooms here are bioluminescent. They glow at night. Instead of this white and brown everywhere, everything turns vibrant blue and green. Truly magical.

"Where do I go?" Tera's head swivels on her neck, looking up at the gilled texture of the bottoms of the monstrous fungi.

Follow the dirt path down a bit. I'll let you know when to stop and turn.

She starts down the path before her, gravel crunching under her shoes. As she walks past each giant mushroom, she notices doors built into the stalks.

"People live *in* the mushrooms?" Tera stops, gaping at one of the doors.

Not exactly. You'll see.

She picks up the pace, eager to check out Fillidren's mushroom home.

After a few minutes of walking, Aeridonis tells her to stop and turn left. He guides her further and further through Morel, eventually leading her up to a speckled brown mushroom.

"Should I just knock?" she asks.

Are you unfamiliar with the custom?

"What?"

Aeridonis sighs. *Yes, Tera. Knock on the door.*

She reaches her small fist forward, tapping on the door. The sound echoes out in the eerily silent and empty village.

There's a frenzied scrambling of footsteps from within, followed by a clang and crash.

"Should I be worried about this guy?"

Nah. Harmless.

The sounds from within come to a sudden halt, and the door crashes open. A man with frizzy orange hair and a bulbous nose hovers over her, fire erupting from each hand.

"Go away!" he booms, lurching forward and waving his fiery hands in front of her.

Tera stumbles back, tripping on a rock and falling. "I thought you said he was harmless!"

"Who said? Who's been talking about me?" Fillidren says, his words bubbling from his mouth so fast they nearly topple over on one another.

"Aeridonis," she says to him in a loud whisper.

"Where'd you take him? What have you done with him? I've heard the rumors! He's been eaten by a bzeldrine. Don't lie to me!"

A bzeldrine? He really thinks I've been eaten by one of those clumsy beasts?

"A bzeldrine didn't eat him. He's fine!" she shouts, lowering her voice again. "Sort of."

The noise that comes from Fillidren next sounds more animal than elf as he barrels forward.

Tell him his gravy sucks.

"What?" Tera shrieks as Fillidren gains on her.

Do it.

"Your gravy sucks!" Tera screams.

Fillidren stops in his tracks.

"What?" he asks.

Tell him I told you he puts too much roschetta leaf in it. He thinks it makes him a gourmet, but it just tastes like dirty socks.

Tera repeats his exact words, and Fillidren's scrunched shoulders soften.

"It's a long story about how I got here, but if you let me in, I can tell you everything. But Aeridonis is here with me. It's just complicated. I'll explain everything, please."

Fillidren looks her up and down, eventually lowering his hands as the flames putter out.

"Alright. Hurry in, before anyone sees you."

Tera hurries in the open door after Fillidren, who bolts four locks behind her. The space is dark and cramped, but there seems to be no discernible ceiling—it stretches upward through the entirety of the mushroom stalk.

Fillidren guides her down a tight spiral staircase, descending into the dirt. She follows him, her fingers gliding over the cold iron railing.

At the bottom, Tera is greeted by a warm and cozy sitting room. A couple of plush crimson armchairs sit on either side of a lopsided end table topped with a half-drunk tea. Wooden shelves stuffed with worn books line the far wall and a tiny white bird chirps in an ornate metal cage in the corner.

"Sit." Fillidren motions to a chair, snatching up the teacup. He disappears through a doorway and reappears a moment later with two teacups, taking a seat and handing a cup to Tera.

"Thanks."

He nods curtly and jumps right to the point. "Where's Aeridonis?"

She taps the side of her head.

"Excuse me?" he asks.

"Okay, I need you to bear with me on this story," she says before diving into the details of how the marrow elves turned him into a pile of ash, she tried to save him, and now he's sharing her headspace.

"And I'm supposed to believe Aeridonis is in *your* head?" He looks her up and down again, leaning back and crossing his legs. "I get that the kingdom's already in a tizzy. The cheap articles coming out in the papers with wild theories about his disappearance… But this? Absolutely not." His nose crinkles as if he smells something foul.

Tell him I'm threatening to tell you about the thing he did at the Council meeting last spring.

"He says to tell you that he's threatening to tell me about something you did at a spring Council meeting." Tera shrugs. "Not sure what that's supposed to mean."

Or tell him I could tell you about how I'm the only one who knows about what he and sorceress Judy did.

"Okay, now he's talking about something that went down with a sorceress named Judy."

Fillidren slams his teacup down and launches himself forward, getting in Tera's face. "Don't you dare tell her about that!"

Eyes bulging, Tera pulls back in her seat and sloshes tea on the armchair. Immediately, she moves from the seat and tries patting it dry with the hem of her robes.

"I'm so sorry!" she pouts. "I didn't mean to spill the tea."

Fillidren grumbles, holding his hand out and conjuring a flame in his hand.

Tera starts backing up to the staircase, but Fillidren ignores her, setting his hand a few inches over the spill and waiting. The entire time, he never makes eye contact or says a word.

Eventually, he moves his hand and dismisses the flame.

"Should be a bit dryer now." He motions back to the chair.

"Oh. Thank you." Her cheeks burn in embarrassment.

"So, safe to say Aeridonis is in your head. Odd as that sounds. But what does he want from me? I have no idea how to fix your mess."

"He wants you to feed the draxxi."

Fillidren's face puckers and begins turning a ripe red before he sputters out a horrible laugh. His tiny pet bird lets out a screech twice its size, competing to be heard over its master.

"He said you'd know what to do and how, and that we just need to tell you where they are. Since, obviously, he can't do it himself now." She tries speaking over his room-filling laugh.

"Absolutely not," he says, his laughter finally ending.

"Why not?"

"If the marrow elves killed Aeridonis, they'll come for me next. I'm not exposing myself like that. I'm not risking things like that. I'm not risking myself for some nasty, toothy creatures. Not doing it."

Tell him it's his duty as my second. He's already bound to an agreement.

Tera repeats Aeridonis's words, and Fillidren crosses his arms.

"Then I'm breaking the agreement. I'm backing out. I'm done."

He doesn't have a choice.

"He says you don't have a choice."

"I do have a choice. I choose to send you off on your merry way." He stands up, grabbing her arm and lifting her from the seat, directing her to the stairs.

She complies, not wanting to risk a fight she's not qualified for.

He presses her onward, up the stairs and out the door, slamming it shut the second she crosses the threshold.

Well, that was a bust.

"Now what?"

We get you home before the portal closes, and I think of a plan B.

THE FIRESPARK SPELL

When Tera finally makes it back to Pipwerry, Steve swoops over from his perch in a nearby tree, landing on her shoulder.

"Were you waiting for me, buddy?" Tera scratches at his head with a finger before taking the rolled-up piece of paper from his beak.

> Esotera Arlbero, if you don't come home IMMEDIATELY and explain yourself, you're never leaving your room again.

What'd you do this time?

"Heck if I know." Tera grumbles and whines, pocketing the note and hurrying to the portal room.

Back in Darkwood, Tera sprints home with Steve bobbing on her shoulder and occasionally flapping his wings for balance. She climbs the stairs along the tree and bursts into her home, anxious to see what her mother could be going on about this time.

As if she had been posted there since sending the letter, Tera's mother stands a few feet from the door, hands behind her back and deep creases in her forehead.

Steve caws and flies off Tera's shoulder to join her dad at the dinner table, begging for a bite of nuts from his bowl.

Without saying a word, her mother continues staring her down, unmoving.

"Um." Tera shifts her weight between her feet.

Her mom shoots out a hand, a small ticket pinched between two fingers.

"A ticket?" Tera asks, pretending she doesn't realize it's hers from Summercloud.

"You tell me."

Tera steps closer, squinting at the piece of paper. "Yeah, that's from Kiran. He bought me a ticket hoping I would go with him the other day, but I told him I already had plans with some people from class to go over questions we missed on the test."

"Liar, liar!" Zeyla chants from the couch, shooting Tera a snarled look before turning back and pretending to read her trashy romance novel.

Aston appears at the top of the home's narrow staircase to his upstairs bedroom. "Can you guys keep it down?" His shaggy hair is the same copper color as the rest of the family, but pairs with a scruffy face of stubble—something their dad wouldn't be caught dead with.

"Tera's getting what's coming to her—your nap can wait a few minutes," Zeyla hollers to him, almost singsongy, without getting up or looking away from her book.

Aston looks at Tera, whose desperate eyes plead with him.

"Mom thinks I went to the fair the night I was studying after the test. She found the ticket Kiran gave me."

He nods once, scratching at his head. "Mom, I thought I already told you. Kiran came by and dropped that ticket off while Tera was already gone. I put it on her desk. How could she have used a ticket that was *at home?*"

Their mother turns to face her only son, observing his unamused expression for a moment before lowering her hand with the ticket. She walks it to the kitchen trash can, letting it flutter into its open mouth before resuming her dinner preparations as if nothing happened.

Tera mouths a, "Thank you," to her brother, and he mouths back a, "You owe me."

She nods in acknowledgment, walking past the stairs and locking herself in her room at the back of the small house.

She's really got it out for you, doesn't she?

Tera lets out a muffled laugh, not wanting her family to hear.

I don't think you're going to like my plan B.

"Tera!" her mother yells from across the house.

"Hold that thought," Tera whispers before opening her door. At the other end of the house, her mom stands at the front door, Kiran on the other side.

"Hey," he says with an awkward wave and flat smile.

Tera's mom returns to the kitchen, and Kiran steps inside, following Tera back to her room.

"Mom!" Zeyla whines. "Tera's bringing a boy to her room!"

"Do you *ever* mind your own business?" Aston asks.

Tera can't help but grin at the conversation as she closes her bedroom door behind Kiran.

"I wanted to apologize for earlier," Kiran starts, hardly waiting for Tera to sit on the side of her bed.

"Why? I was the one being rude. *I'm* sorry."

Aww. I'm so proud of you.

Tera resists the urge to roll her eyes, not wanting Kiran to think it's directed at him.

"I really do wonder what happened to Aeridonis. I tried asking my parents if they've heard anything, and they told me the Council's been really quiet about it all. The least they could do is dispel some of the rumors going around. Did you hear about the one article? Saying he was secretly dismissed from the Council, and they hired people to assassinate him in his home?" Kiran sits at her desk, running his hands through his silky hair.

Impossible, anyways. No one can see my house. Or any Council member's house, for that matter. Hardcore protection spell renders them entirely invisible. Keeps everyone away—hired assassins, the press, you name it.

"You'd think they'd at least want to tell the public that one's a lie," Kiran says.

"Probably because they don't want to freak everyone out while they try to figure out what to do."

"You're probably right, but that doesn't make me feel any better about what could've happened."

Tera stutters, wanting so badly to tell her friend everything. *Go ahead.*

"Really?" Tera whispers.

"What?" Kiran asks.

If he's trustworthy, yes.

"Kiran," Tera starts, not wasting a minute, "I've got to tell you something."

He raises an eyebrow, urging her to continue.

"Aeridonis is dead."

"That's what I'm worried about, too."

"No, I mean he really is. I witnessed it."

"What?" He shifts in his seat, his eyes locked onto hers.

"After the fair." She begins to explain everything that went down in the woods outside Summercloud, but as soon as she gets to the part about Aeridonis's voice in her head, Kiran's lips can't help but part into a toothy grin.

"While I don't appreciate you disrespecting the great wizard with stupid stories like that, I've gotta say, I appreciate your creativity. I've definitely never heard a story quite like that before."

I take it he's a fan of mine.

Tera groans. "I'm not making it up. Believe me, I *wish* I was. Do you really think I want an old man living in my head?"

Oof. 'Old,' huh?

"Okay, Don, you *are* old, that's just a statement of fact."

Kiran furrows his brow and laughs uncomfortably at her. "It's not a joke, Kiran!"

If he doesn't believe you, we can make him believe you.

"How?" Tera asks.

Ask him if he's familiar with my firespark spell.

"Aeridonis wants me to ask you if you're familiar with his firespark spell."

"Everyone knows about his firespark spell. No one has ever been able to recreate it. It was his own creation that played a huge role in the Battle of Durnamire. Some of the girls in my class even tried to research to figure out how he did it for a history project. In short: Yes, I know about his firespark spell."

Perfect. Get off your bed and make sure you're far away from any cloth or paper.

"Oh boy." Tera sighs, getting up and moving to the far end of her room, motioning for Kiran to get back. "I'm not exactly sure how you expect me to do this."

"I don't," Kiran says.

"Not you."

Kiran scoffs, crossing his arms.

Hold your left hand out in front of you. Fingers together. Palm up.

Tera follows his instruction, her heart thumping faster and faster.

Focus on any warmth you feel right now. Any sense of heat. Focus on it and imagine pulling it into your palm.

She stares at her palm, fixating on it as she notices the warmth of the room.

Say 'Ignus,' or if you can focus enough, you can just say the word in your head. The starting spell for this is one of the easiest spells to do without speaking it.

Quieting every thought in her mind, Tera imagines the word "ignus"—what it would sound like, what it would feel like on her lips, what it would look like, all while focusing on the feeling of warmth throughout her body.

A flame grows before her, floating a mere inch above her open palm. She can feel the heat on her fingers, and she can't help but smile.

Kiran's smirk is replaced by a more serious expression. "Okay, while that's impressive—especially for you—that's not the firespark spell."

"What do you mean 'especially for you'?" She looks into his eyes, glowing from the light of the flame.

"I just mean… I've grown up with you. I know you're not exactly… skilled… at magic. I know you're working hard on it though! You're one of the most dedicated people I know. You just, you know… struggle."

Tera growls.

Good, use that. Keep the flame going, but now focus on the electricity in your room. Not the lights, but the energy. Feel the buzzing in your veins. Imagine pushing it out of your body and through your palm.

She starts to notice a tickling, light zapping feeling across every nerve in her body.

Now, can you feel how hot that electricity is? Keep focusing until you can. Once it starts to burn, say 'ignuscintilla.'

After a moment, the prickling electricity in her body begins to sting like hot needles. She takes a deep, warm breath. "Ignuscintilla."

The flame in her palm begins to flicker, eventually going dark. She almost begins to lower her palm when Aeridonis yells, *Wait!*

She maintains her posture, the stinging heat dissolving. Then, a rush of sputtering orange sparks begins to fly from her hand, fizzling out just before each one can hit the ground.

Close your hand to stop the spell. It gets really big and overwhelming after about five seconds. Close it!

Tera snaps her hand shut, the fiery sparks disappearing, leaving her and Kiran in the darkness of her dim desk lamp.

It was only after a minute of adjusting to the newfound darkness that Tera can make out Kiran's face. His eyes are wide and teary, arms limp at his sides.

"There's no way," he says, his words airy.

"Do you believe me yet?"

"I—I think so."

My plan involves your friend, so I'm glad he's on the same page now.

"Wait, I thought you didn't want him knowing because he could be in danger. And now you want him *involved* in your plans?" Tera spouts.

Plans change.

CHAPTER SEVEN

THE IMPOSSIBLE WALL

"I'm in danger? There are plans? For what?" Kiran asks, his eyes wild.

"Uh—"

If Fillidren isn't going to help me, I'm going to need you instead. But you're not in any shape to deal with that risk just yet. I've got someone I want you to meet. But we need someone to cover for you while you're gone.

"Gone? Gone where?" Tera asks.

I'll explain later. When it's just you. For now, just tell your friend about the draxxi. Tell him I'm training you to be their caretaker until I get a body. And tell him you'll need him to help keep your parents out of the loop.

"Wow, Don. I never expected you to tell me to disobey my parents." Tera chuckles.

"What's he saying?"

"He wants you to cover for me."

"Cover for you? For what?"

Tera explains everything she knows about the draxxi, and Kiran devours her every word, not realizing he's leaning closer and closer, entirely fixated until Tera puts a hand to his chest and gently pushes him back.

"Sorry," he says, scratching his head and breaking eye contact. "The whole thing is just so freaking cool. I mean, ravenous flying beasts hidden away in the kingdom somewhere. And *you* get to feed them?"

"I mean, I guess it's kind of cool." Tera shrugs, not sure what she makes of it all.

"Can I talk to Aeridonis?"

"Um," she says. "Sure."

"Hello, sir," Kiran starts, locking eyes with Tera, who sits there stewing in awkwardness, not unlike that of someone on the receiving end of the happy birthday song. "I'd like to come with. I'll swear any kind of loyalty or secrecy oath I need to. This is the kind of adventure most people could only dream of being part of. I'd be foolish to pass up the opportunity if it's there."

Aeridonis is quiet, and Kiran watches Tera for a reply. After a moment, she shrugs. "I don't know. He hasn't said anything yet."

Is the boy loyal?

"He is," Tera answers and Kiran perks up, grinning ear to ear.

What does he study?

"Animalinguism."

Is he a good student?

"Better than me," Tera says with a lighthearted chuff.

But is he a good student?

"I'd say so, yes."

Tell him he can come with us, but that we need him to cover for you in the meantime. I'm not leading you there until I'm sure you can hold your own. So, depending on how quickly you pick up what you're to learn, he might be waiting a while for this adventure. But an anima-

linguist could prove useful with the draxxi. He'd be a valuable asset to have with you.

Tera nods as she listens, looking to Kiran once Aeridonis is finished.

"Well?" Kiran asks.

"He says yes, but he said you have to wait a while because he has some training he wants me to do. He says you have to cover for me in the meantime."

"Absolutely. Even without Aeridonis, you know I'd do that for you."

The next morning, Tera throws on her school robes after a quick breakfast, rushing off to Pipwerry without saying much to her family. Late last night, Aeridonis told her to get to school early again to talk to Professor Dringely, but he hadn't said exactly why. Just that it's part of the plan.

She takes the deathrising portal in the Hub and races up the tower staircase, barging into Dringely's office without knocking this time.

Dringely snaps to attention at her desk, clearly caught in the middle of a mid-research nap—a stray paper of notes stuck to her cheek, her reading glasses crooked on her nose.

"Oh, Tera," she says, peeling the scrap paper off herself and straightening her glasses. "I'm still working on figuring it out. Nothing new, I'm afraid."

"That's not why I'm here," she says. "Aeridonis told me to get here early in the morning. Said he's got something to ask you. Hasn't told me what it is yet though."

"Explains why you seem so eager to be here," Dringely toys with a smile, rearranging the books and stray pages on her desk into a tidy pile.

I'd like to ask her if you can skip your class after lunch. Ask if she can give you notes or teach you the lecture at a later time. I've got bigger plans for you this afternoon, and if we can do it before the end of the school day, we can get you home before your parents suspect anything.

"Oh, I don't know if she'll go for that," Tera says with a low-hanging head and a soft sigh.

"I won't go for what?" she asks, giving Tera her undivided attention.

"He wants me to ask you to let me skip class after lunch. He has something he wants me to do."

Professor Dringely pauses, nibbling on the inside of her cheek for a minute before saying, "Okay."

Tera shakes her head, doing a double take. "Wait, what?"

"*But—*" She holds up a halting finger, making sure she's got her student's focus. "He has to tell me where he's taking you and when I can expect you back here. I'm not letting a student off campus during class time without at least knowing where you'll be. For safety."

Xleria.

"Where's that?" Tera asks.

"What'd he say?"

"Xleria," Tera answers with a shrug.

Professor Dringely's mouth drops open. "That's *way* too far to be bringing a student without supervision!"

You won't be going without supervision. I may not have a body, but I'm still here. Sheesh. Give me some credit.

Tera giggles. "He thinks you're being unfair not counting him as a chaperone just because he doesn't have a body."

Her mouth stays gaped open as she struggles to dispute the point. When she can't, she closes her mouth and nods. "Alright. Just, please be safe. You've got a raven if you need to send a letter for help, right?"

"Yeah, his name's Steve."

"Good. Use him if you need me."

"Yes, ma'am."

Professor Leutrix's class crawls by, uneventful and slow. Tera's grateful Aeridonis can't hear her thoughts and the fact that she's unable to focus on anything aside from wishful imaginings of what Xleria could be like and what adventure awaits her there.

When lunchtime finally rolls around, she practically sprints to the portal in the courtyard, stepping into the Hub and hurrying to the cafeteria to look for Kiran.

He spots her before she finds him, and he grabs at her arms, steering her around a corner and hiding behind a wall beside the bathrooms.

"What are you doing?" Tera grunts, shaking off his hands and looking at his wild face.

"Sorry," he says, fully removing his hands. "It's Luthais."

Tera grins. Luthais and Kiran have had a friendly rivalry ever since they both chose the animalinguist path.

"Well, technically his brother. I asked a rabbit to deliver a note to Luthais earlier with my midterm grade," he continues, "because I scored three points higher than him. But the rabbit misunderstood and brought it to his brother. I've never seen him turn so red before, and then he threw the letter away and ran. I haven't seen him since this morning, but the two of them were just walking through the cafeteria. It was awful. I don't know if he told Luthais and then figured out it was me. Or if he figured out it was me all on his own."

"That poor guy! You should tell him it was meant for his brother."

"Absolutely not! I'm just going to try to pretend it wasn't me and try to forget this ever happened."

"I can tell him for you."

"No!"

"Fine! I think you're being a baby though. And remember, Aeridonis sees everything I see. So, he sees my adventure buddy cowering in terror at the thought of admitting to a simple mistake. Can't imagine that bodes well for someone that's supposed to help me feed bloodthirsty flying monsters."

Tera makes out the sheer panic and confusion on Kiran's face as he weighs his options.

Suddenly, he straightens his posture and clears his throat. "I'm not afraid. I just would hate to end up so distracted from my studies by something as trivial as a prank gone wrong."

"Yeah," Tera starts, rolling her eyes, "we're both so convinced."

Kiran grimaces.

"Anyways, I was looking for you to tell you something. I can't hang around for lunch. Actually, I won't be in my next class either. Aeridonis is taking me to some place called Xleria for something. He hasn't told me a whole lot of anything, but in case I'm running late getting home and my parents reach out to you, please just come up with something. Got sick at school and I'm stuck in the bathroom, helping give a tour to a new deathrising student, or just staying back in Dringely's office for another tutoring session. Whatever."

"You've got it."

She thanks him, giving him a quick hug before darting out of the cafeteria and into the portal room where Trevitt is resetting the green portal to the lifebringing island, marked by a leaf sigil on the wall above it.

"Hey, Tera!" He immediately bounds over to her, greeting her with a hard pat to the back, nearly knocking the air out of her lungs.

"Hey, Trevitt."

"Portals working alright for ya?"

She nods. "Thank you so much for the portal to Morel the other day. That was such a huge help. I got everything I needed for my project, but now I've got to go to one more place. Do you think you can help?"

Trevitt's wide, plump smile sinks. "'fraid I can't do that."

"Wait, what?"

"Got in trouble for the Morel portal. Not supposed to cast unauthorized portals on campus. They haven't even got me on the payroll yet, and I already almost lost my new position with the portal master. I need this job."

"So, can you just cast the portal off campus?"

"Not that simple, sadly. Portals are an industry, Tera. Now that I'm getting certified, I'm supposed to charge for the service and report all the information for tax purposes. It's a whole ordeal and I could get in a lot of trouble if I do it again. Especially when the portal master's got such a close watch on me. Sorry."

Tera groans. "Okay, thanks anyways."

She walks out to the Hub's fountain, takes a seat on the cement edge, and rests her face in her palms.

What's the big deal? You're telling me you don't have a few coins to order a portal from an actual professional?

"You realize I'm a student, right? And I live with my parents? I don't have a job. Where do you think I get money? I get a little bit for chores and for my birthday. That's about it."

So, use some of that.

"I'm trying to save it up."

For what?

"For—it doesn't matter! It's none of your business what I want to spend my money on."

Look, where you're going, you can most likely get your money back. Consider it an investment.

Tera throws her head back dramatically and whines. "Fine." She stands up, making her way off campus to look for a portal sign in the town surrounding Pipwerry.

Along the edge of the nearby village of Teretatian, she spots the familiar symbol carved into a tall sign. She steps up to the cottage door, tapping gently on its splintering wood finish.

A gronnet peers out the massive peephole on the door. "Where to?"

"Xleria," she answers, holding a satchel of coins from her pocket in view.

The bulbous eye disappears, and she hears a few clicks before the door swings open.

"In."

Tera follows the gronnet inside, past a cluttered kitchen that smells of curry and ale, into a simple room with a coin box on the floor and a wall of different colored lights and numbers.

"One-way, or two-way?" the portal gronnet asks.

"Two, please."

The gronnet picks up the coin box, jingling it in front of him. "Fifteen coins."

"Fifteen? Last time my mom and I took a portal, it was fifteen for *both* of us! I know it's been a long time, but really? Fifteen?"

The gronnet shrugs. "Inflation."

"What?" Tera scoffs, counting out fifteen coins from her satchel, dropping them one by one into the box with a clatter.

"Xleria, you say?"

Tera nods.

He reaches into his apron pocket and fishes out a ticket with the number 46 on it. "Rip the ticket when you're ready to come back here."

"Rip it?"

The gronnet bulges his eyes at her in disbelief, miming a ripping motion.

"Yes, I understand that. But how is that going to get me back here?"

"It's enchanted." He motions to the wall of numbered lights. "Lights up the wall when I need to reopen the portal. Number 46."

Just then, number 15's light illuminates.

"Alright, now you're holding up one of my clients. Let's get you to Xleria."

Tera takes the ticket from him, tucking it carefully into her robe pocket as the gronnet creates a shimmering aqua-colored portal.

"Thanks," she says, stepping through without wasting another minute around the cranky gronnet.

On the other side, she's nearly blinded by the intense light around her. After blinking and squinting for a bit, she can finally make out her surroundings. Before her, a giant landmass full of crystalline structures hovers over a cloud-filled chasm. The crystals glow a radiant blue-white, washing over everything else around the city.

Let's get moving. She should be in the city. It's been a while since I've been out this way, so be patient with my navigation.

"Don, this place is freaking wild."

'Freaking wild'?

"It's so pretty! I didn't even know places like this existed. What kind of people even live somewhere this beautiful?"

Crystal elves, mostly.

"Should've figured," Tera says with a smile, starting toward the city.

She makes out a lengthy staircase bridging the land to the crystal city. Aeridonis instructs her to take it, and she obeys, gawking at the mystery below her. All she sees beneath the bridge is pure white. No indication of how deep or shallow the pit may be.

When she reaches the top, her legs feel as heavy as the crystals themselves. She tries to catch her breath before continuing on Aeridonis's path.

You're too young to be this out of shape.

"Okay, uncalled for, Don. Rude. You don't even have a shape, how about that?"

Is that a 'you don't have a body' joke?

"Sure is," she says, hands on her knees, taking one more deep breath before resuming the journey.

A crystal elf in sunglasses walks past her with a sweet smile and a dainty finger wave.

"Could've told me I'd need sunglasses here, Don. My eyes are killing me."

You'll manage. We're almost there and then we'll be indoors for a little bit.

After a few changed directions, Aeridonis finally leads her up to a doorway chiseled into one of the tall crystals.

"Is this going to be another supposed 'friend' who chases me with fire?"

Friend, yes. Fire, no.

"But they're likely to chase me?"

Not in the slightest.

Tera groans, lifting her balled fist to the door and holding it in the air for a moment before knocking. She steps a few feet back, bracing her feet to run.

Say your name and that you're a friend of mine. Mention that I told you to say I miss painting with her in the elemental courtyard.

Without thinking too hard about it, Tera announces herself and repeats Aeridonis's words.

"What was the point of that?" she asks.

Just then, a giant skull stretches through the door as if the crystal is nothing but elastic. It chomps its jaw open and closed, pressing the crystal until it rips. Tattered bits of the once-solid door now look like sinew on the bones. The skull snaps closer to Tera and she shrieks, bolting down the path.

Go back!

"Nope!"

Aeridonis growls from in her head, but she doesn't notice over the sound of her own panting breaths and thudding heart.

We need her. Go back and tell her I said whipped akaiin cream never tasted so sweet.

"What the seiva is that supposed to mean?" Tera spouts, turning and hiding behind another crystal tower.

We're not going to get into details. Just say it. I'm the only person who would say that to her. And there's especially no way some kid would. Trust me.

"If you get me killed, someone better resurrect me because I want to make sure you never hear the end of it."

If I'm wrong, I'll let you rub it in. Just go.

Tera draws in a shaky inhale, tiptoeing her way back. When she returns, the skull appears to have vanished.

"He says—" Tera's voice fades. She clears her throat and projects her voice with feigned confidence. "He says to tell you, 'Whipped akaiin cream never tasted so sweet.' I don't know what that means and I really hope it's not an insult and that you don't get mad and kill me because I really need your help."

There's a silence and Tera lets her shoulders droop. Just as she's about to turn away, a periwinkle crystal elf with matching hair shimmers into existence mere inches from Tera. Her skin is entirely blemish-free, and thick lashes surround her wide eyes. The crystal elf beams, greeting Tera with a double-handed wave.

Illidara is an illusionist. She's a sucker for concealment spells. Odds were high she would be waiting outside right after you knocked, and that you'd have no idea she was there figuring out who you were.

"He tells me your name is Illidara," Tera says, holding out her hand. "I'm Tera."

Illidara shakes Tera's hand, not letting go as she then pulls, leading her inside the crystalline house, much to Tera's surprise.

"He didn't tell you too much about the whipped akaiin cream, I take it?" Illidara says with a warm giggle.

"Uh, no."

Shutting the door behind her, Illidara ushers her house guest to a living room with tall ceilings and furniture that looks practically new. "Have you heard from my dear friend much?" she asks, releasing Tera's hand and clutching both of her own against her chest.

"Something like that."

Illidara motions to a white leather couch. Tera sits, balancing on the very edge of the couch as if her robes alone would stain it. Once Illidara takes a seat beside her—albeit a bit too close for Tera's comfort—Tera begins to tell her about Summercloud, the ashes, and the wizard living in her head.

"I knew the headlines were wrong." Illidara smiles warmly. "I've been worried sick about him."

I hate that I didn't visit her one more time before...

"He says he's sorry," Tera paraphrases.

"So, he can hear me?" Illidara asks, looking deep into Tera's eyes as if Aeridonis would be visible deep within them.

Tera nods.

"Hello, old friend!" Illidara does a double wave again at Tera.

Tell her I say 'hello, young friend.'

She does, and the woman squeals. "He really *is* in there," she says, tapping her forehead. "Isn't he? This is so strange but very exciting! But I can't imagine he brought you all the way here just to chat with me. Sadly, I don't think I'd be much help getting him out of there, though."

I want her to teach you the impossible wall.

"The what?" Tera asks.

Impossible wall. It's an illusion spell.

"I can't do illusion spells."

Says who?

Illidara simply sits cross-legged, watching Tera's one-sided discussion.

"Ugh." Tera looks at Illidara. "He says he wants you to teach me about an 'impossible wall' or something."

Illidara looks delighted at this request for a moment before her eyes trail off into some empty space in the distance.

"Um," Tera murmurs after a minute, clearing her throat.

"Sorry," she says, shaking her head and making eye contact with Tera again. "Just remembering the first time I used that spell outside of class."

Aeridonis giggles, and Tera tries not to let her imagination run.

"Alright," Illidara says, "when do we start?"

Now, unless you want to pay fifteen coins again to come back here for more lessons.

"Wait, you said I'd get my money back?"

Silence.

Tera grumbles, reaching for the scab on her scalp to scratch at it while Illidara begins rambling about how the impossible wall was one of the first illusions she mastered back in her school days.

"He says he needs me to learn it today."

"Oh! Not much time then. Well, we can certainly give it a go. It's not too difficult of a spell, so with a little practice on your own after this, I have every bit of faith you'll be able to master it."

"Don't get your hopes up too much," Tera mutters.

"Nonsense." She grabs Tera's hands, pulling her to her feet. "Just pose like this." She holds her arms out straight, her palms flat as if pushing against something.

"What does this spell even *do?*" Tera looks at her hands, waiting for an answer before following along.

"Oh! I suppose that would've been good to start with." She smiles softly, letting her hands drop to her sides. "The impossible wall is an illusion that makes those around you see a wall where there is none. Like this. See my kitchen over there?"

Tera looks across the room to a small kitchen and nods.

"Watch." She holds her hands back up, her eyes narrowing on the kitchen.

Tera gasps as a rippling wall of water begins to grow, covering the entire kitchen from end to end. When Illidara lowers her hands slowly, the wall turns to crystal, completely matching the walls of her home. She turns to Tera with a big grin, her hands on her hips.

"Easy peasy!" she says. "Now, it's your turn."

Tera stares at the new wall, stepping toward it, stretching out a hand to touch it. "It feels *real,*" she says.

"That's why it's called the 'impossible' wall. Because you can make people see and feel something that's not even there. And it blends so beautifully with whatever's around it! It's such a fun one. Good choice of spell from Aeridonis." She smiles to herself again, her eyes wandering off as she sighs.

"I'm curious why that's the one he picked," Tera says, trying to prompt an answer.

Unless you're a master mage, it's best to focus on defensive magic rather than offensive. In case the marrow elves figure out I'm in your head, you can protect yourself.

"Fair enough. I see why you picked this one, too. I thought defensive magic was going to be boring spells, but this is so freaking cool!"

"It's definitely cool, but it has its limits," Illidara starts, her smile giving way to a stern look.

"What do you mean 'limits'?"

"Yes, it'll protect you, but there's one catch."

"Of course there is," Tera grumbles, picking at her scab.

"The impossible wall works on just about everyone. Ravens, illusion masters, and consciousless resurrected corpses are the only exceptions."

"Really? The corpses can see through illusion spells? Why?"

"Because they don't have their full mind, illusion masters can't really force their brain to interpret the world the same as we can with living things."

"Oh. I guess that makes sense. Okay, so ravens, mindless corpses, and… who else?" Tera asks.

"Illusion masters. If someone graduated in illusion magic, they're going to be able to see through most illusion spells."

"But not many people graduate from that path, right?"

"Correct. They say about two percent of the elf population ever graduates in illusion magic. It's considered the hardest path to follow, so it's rarely an issue. But I have to put the disclaimer out there. Just in case!"

Tera nods, and Illidara resumes the lesson.

A couple hours pass, and Aeridonis reminds Tera that it's time to go, even though she's yet to have cast the full impossible wall herself.

"Alright, just remember to practice on your own. It takes time, but you're so close! You've got the wall forming, you just have to master that last step that solidifies the texture and color. Don't give up." Illidara hugs her before letting her go on her way home.

When Tera reaches the place where she took the portal to Xleria, she pulls out her ticket, tearing it in half.

"I guess I just wait here?"

I suppose so.

"You've never taken a gronnet portal?"

I have. It's just been a while since I've had to pay. The Council usually covers my transportation.

"Wow. Fancy."

What can I say? Only the best for the best.

Tera snorts.

Before Aeridonis can bite back with a snarky remark, a return portal grows in front of Tera, and she steps through.

She thanks the portal gronnet, who nods and ushers her out the door.

You should let your professor know you're safe before you head back to Darkwood. She seemed worried about you going. I'm sure it's partially because the marrow elves. But mostly because I think she doubts my ability to chaperone without a body.

"Can't say I blame her."

Tera returns to campus from the gronnet's cottage nearby, heading to the Hub. She steps through the portal to the death-rising island and trots upstairs to Professor Dringely's office.

Before she can even finish knocking, the door swings open and Dringely rips her inside, shutting it back behind her.

"Woah." Tera staggers, removing Dringely's grip from her arm.

"Perfect timing." She stares at Tera, nearly vibrating with excitement, "I've got something I want to try."

"Try? For what?"

"To get Aeridonis out of your head."

CHAPTER EIGHT

RAT ASHES

"No way!" Tera starts bouncing.

Wow, okay, I thought we were becoming friends, but that's cool.

"Hey, you can be friends with someone without wanting them to literally live in your head," Tera defends.

That's fair. I wouldn't want you living in my head either.

Tera scoffs and suddenly realizes Professor Dringely has been going on about her findings the entire time.

"And then I wondered about the Clansteden case file, which led me to some research articles about the Lochrodians and how they would sacrifice the elderly to resurrect their consciousnesses into the young warriors of the village so the old wisdoms could be passed down and—"

"Hold on, what?"

Dringely takes a calming breath, her eyes closed for a moment. "Okay. I'm going to try something I found—"

"On me? I thought you said y—"

"On the lab animals, Tera."

"Oh. Okay." She lets out a relieved chuckle.

"I just wanted to tell you about what I found, and I figured maybe you wanted to see the experiment. If it goes well, I'll try it again tomorrow just to be sure. If it doesn't go well, I'll just keep researching until I find something."

Tera agrees, and Dringely asks her to stay put while she fetches some animals from the lab.

Do you think it's going to work?

"Yes."

That's good you have a lot of faith in your professor. That speaks highly of her.

"If nothing else, I've just got to stay positive, right? Manifest good things or whatever."

Mmm.

"What? You don't think it's going to work?"

How often do things work out well the first time?

"Can't we just consider me trying to resurrect you as 'the first time' and say this is the second attempt?"

Say whatever makes you feel better about it.

"You're really not helping."

That seems to be my current state of being anyways. The not-helpful old man who lives in your head.

"Hey, you helped me learn a fire spell the other day. That was pretty cool."

You're not as bad of a student as your family seems to think.

"Okay, woah, uncalled for. Enough of that or I'll take the silencing potion before Dringely even has a chance to separate us."

Aeridonis chuckles, and Professor Dringely walks back in with a dead rabbit, a dead snake, and a live rat.

She sets the animals down on her desk.

"The snake represents Aeridonis, and the bunny is symbolic of the body we would put him in," she says, pointing to the dead snake and limp gray bunny. "The rat is you. Since we can't communicate with the animals—we'd need to involve an animalinguist for that—we're going to test and see if the animals are in the correct bodies based on the behavior after the separation."

Tera gawks at her teacher, nodding like she understands.

"So, we're going to put the consciousness of the dead snake in the living rat. Then, we're going to try to separate it back out and put it in the dead rabbit. If I'm successful, the rabbit won't know how to walk—it grew up as a snake. If the rat's consciousness is the one that gets transferred, the rabbit will be able to walk, as a rat knows what it's like to have legs."

"Makes enough sense, I suppose."

Dringely smiles proudly. "No sense in delaying! Step back a little, please."

Tera obeys, and her teacher holds her hands out, placing one on the living rat and one on the dead snake. Her eyes close, and she casts the resurrection spell.

"How will we know the snake's consciousness is in the rat?" Tera asks.

Dringely pauses, her eyes flicking between each animal. "That's a good question. I've thought of a possible way to test it." She opens a small cup, pulling out a frozen mouse and dangling it in front of the rat. At first, the rat does nothing, but then, it begins squealing and pawing at its tiny ears.

Tera's lip snarls up in disgust. "Is it basically, like, *hearing* the snake? In its head?"

"Probably not hearing it in the sense that we understand, but basically."

"So, the first step worked?"

"I didn't doubt that this step would. After all, it's why you're in my room to begin with."

Dringely then puts her hand on the panicking rat, laying the other on the dead rabbit. She mutters a word Tera can't quite make out, keeping her hands still for a moment before slowly pulling them away.

The two stare at the rabbit, their faces pulling closer and closer to the desk in anticipation.

Tera starts picking at her scab. "How long does it t—"

Just then, the rabbit stirs, giving a few twitches of life before its eyes shoot open. Dringely gasps, and Tera nearly squeals, jumping in place.

"Just wait," Dringely directs, holding up a finger as she watches the rabbit still.

Suddenly, the rabbit goes to move, unable to maneuver its legs, falling once again to its side.

"It worked!" Tera lets out a giddy squeal, dancing around the classroom.

When her celebration isn't met by her professor, she stops, her joy melting from her face as she spots Dringely's serious gaze staring down at the desk.

"What is it?" Tera asks.

Dringely points to the rat, lying lifeless on her desk.

Tera's heart sinks.

Looks like you're stuck with me for a bit longer, kid. Sorry.

"I don't understand," Tera says, poking at the rat. "What went wrong?"

"It could be any number of things." Dringely shrugs. "I'll have to dig back into some findings. But this is precisely why I wanted to test on animals first. It's not ideal, but it's better than testing any of these theories on you and risking this." She picks up the limp rat, putting it in a plastic bag and sealing it up.

Tera sighs, her fingers wiggling through her curls and finding their way back to her scab. "So, back to researching?"

"Back to researching." Dringely looks at her apologetically as she flips one of her books open again.

"Thank you, Professor." Tera smiles weakly at her before disappearing through the door.

Back in Darkwood, Tera makes her way home, passing by Nyana the dryad and giving her nothing more than a quick wave. Not in the mood to talk, Tera keeps her gaze low, watching the wooden steps up to her home gently bend under her feet with a soft creak.

She'll figure it out.

"I know."

Then what's got you so down?

"Just freaked me out, I guess." She pauses, not wanting her family to overhear her from inside as she approaches the door. "The fact that the rat easily could've been me. This is, like, a serious problem. I don't know. It didn't feel as big or scary before. I haven't lost hope yet, but it just kind of freaks me out."

That's entirely rational.

Tera smiles flatly, knowing Aeridonis can't see it.

"So," she starts, a grin growing across her face, "when do I get to feed the draxxi? Soon?"

Eh.

"What do you mean 'eh'?"

Usually that means the person speaking is unsure of something.

"I know what 'eh' means."

Then why'd you ask?

"Because I want to know why you don't trust me yet? You literally live in my head. My life has been a constant trust exercise with you since you moved in up there. Least you can do is start to trust me a little."

And I have.

Tera scoffs.

Let me finish.

"Whatever," she says with a huff.

Aeridonis waits a moment before continuing. *I need you to learn the impossible wall before I'll bring you there. You need to know at least one defensive spell, and it's too tricky to try teaching you from inside your head. Hence why I wanted you to see Illidara. Just in case. I can't let something horrible happen to you. Whether you need it to protect you from the draxxi themselves or from marrow elves or from whatever else.*

"Aww… You care about me!"

Don't get too crazy. If you die, I'm gone forever, too. Plus, no one knows where the draxxi are and no one will take care of them.

"So, I'm a glorified pet sitter?"

'Glorified' if you want to be.

"But hold on, I *do* know a defensive spell!"

Oh?

"The fire one you taught me!" Tera holds out her hand, focusing on all the warmth in the atmosphere, pushing it through to her hand until a flame grows. "See!"

Wow. While I'm thoroughly impressed you're able to replicate a basic flame spell as a deathriser with just one instance of elemental training, that hardly counts as a defensive spell.

"What do you mean? If someone or something attacks me, I'll defend myself with fire!"

Uh huh. And how do you plan on doing that?

"By throwing fire at them?" Tera wiggles the flame in front of her face as if Aeridonis didn't see it.

Go ahead. Show me how that works.

"Well, I don't want to set the entire grove on fire."

Try it. If you set it on fire, I'll teach you how to put it out. But I'm not that concerned.

Tera groans, facing out over the railing of the stairs. She holds out her fiery palm, pulling it back and making a throwing motion. With a sharp yelp, she pulls her hand back toward her, the flame dying out. Cradling her hand to her chest, she notices she's singed her fingertips.

Wow. You sure showed those draxxi and marrow elves, didn't ya?

"Shut up."

No. This is a learning opportunity.

"You couldn't have told me before I tried that it wouldn't work?"

I didn't know exactly what you were going to do. I live in your head; I don't hear your thoughts.

"Fine."

But I could've assumed. And I did. But that's not how you throw fire. You have to imagine surging that heat out and away from your body. It takes immense focus.

"Okay, fine. So, I'll do that if I need to."

The other thing you need to learn is that when I say you need to learn something before you go on a dangerous adventure… you need to learn what I say. I'm not just teaching you things for fun.

"Fine. I'll learn the impossible wall. Then will you bring me to the draxxi?"

Probably.

Tera groans and mutters, "Good enough," before opening the door and walking inside her home, which currently smells of roasting nuts.

Her mother seems too busy with Zeyla in the kitchen to pay her much mind, and she takes the opportunity to hurry past, locking herself in the bathroom to privately treat her burns.

As she's rubbing ointment on, flinching at the stinging burn, her mind begins to wander. "I think we have lab day tomorrow," she whispers to Aeridonis.

Okay?

"I didn't study. I've been too busy with… well, you. Being in my head."

Yeah, that whole thing. What a nuisance.

"What am I going to do?"

About?

"The labs!" She realizes she had raised her voice and immediately resumes a hushed tone.

You expect me to have a magical solution? I didn't study deathrising. That's my least favorite path. No offense. It has its value—it's just not my favorite to study or practice, so I didn't.

"You're supposed to be one of the greatest wizards, like, ever. And you don't know anything about deathrising?"

I have some disjointed deathrising facts in my memory, but nothing substantial enough to help you with your labs. And isn't it enough that I've created many of my own spells? And that I'm a master of the other paths? I don't think you can judge, Miss Master-of-None.

Tera rolls her eyes and groans. "Don't be rude." With a dramatic sigh, she asks, "Can you help me study? You're basically a built-in study buddy."

Do I have to?

"I mean, I'm not letting you sleep. So, what you choose to do with that time tonight is up to you."

Aeridonis grumbles and Tera's mouth pulls into an irrepressible grin. She finishes bandaging up her fingers before stepping out of the bathroom and nearly ramming right into Zeyla.

"Oh." Tera stumbles back a step before trying to squeak past her without any luck. "I thought you were busy in the kitchen with Mom?"

"Who were you talking to?" Her hot breath in Tera's face smells of spices and old coffee.

"Literally no one. Do you often listen in on people in the bathroom? That's kind of weird, Zey. You should probably talk to someone about that."

Her face shrivels up as she scoffs. "As if. I was walking by and I heard you say something."

"What do you *think* you heard?"

"Something about deathrising." Her face returns to neutral and she takes a half-step away from the door.

"Yeah. Wow, what a thought! Maybe because I'm studying deathrising. Maybe because I'm trying to recite things to myself for my lab tomorrow because I want to study. Maybe because the path I picked is harder than yours and actually takes *work.*"

"How *dare* you!" Zeyla shoves Tera backward into the bathroom.

Tera catches herself on the edge of the sink and reacts quickly, holding her hand out and summoning a radiant flame inches from her sister's face.

Zeyla screams, backing up as Tera grins. Her eyes and teeth reflect the vibrant red orange of her flame.

"Mom!" Zeyla runs down the hall and toward the kitchen. Tera immediately dismisses the flame, darting to her bedroom and locking herself inside.

Oooh. You're going to get in trouble, Aeridonis says in a singsongy voice.

"Shut up, Don."

You know your mother is never going to believe her.

"Yeah, right. She'll believe her sooner than she believes me."

Not necessarily. Do you really think she's going to believe that her failing deathriser daughter conjured a flame—something outside her own path—to taunt her sister? Doubtful.

Tera's posture straightens as she processes his words. "You might be right. Perks of being a sucky student, I guess."

Best if we change that, though. How about that studying?

After a late night of working through her deathrising textbooks and sparse notes from class with Aeridonis, Tera wakes up the next morning with few hours of sleep but far more confidence about her labs.

She gets ready for school quickly, not wanting to face her mom or her sister on her way out the door. School robes on, bag packed, and hair hardly combed, Tera takes off in a near-sprint out the door, throwing hardly more than a, "Bye!" to her family.

"Not so fast," Tera's mom asserts, grabbing the back of her daughter's robe just before she can disappear. "We need to have a talk."

Tera's face prickles with a stinging warmth and she tries to steady her voice before asking, "About what?"

"Come inside."

"I'm going to be late for class," Tera whines, trudging a few steps back into the house. Her mom shuts the door behind her and faces her with crossed arms.

There's a burning silence, and Tera tries to brace herself for an interrogation about how she learned fire magic and what would possess her to use it against her own sister. She tries to patch together a believable lie in her head while her mother starts talking.

"Are they talking about Aeridonis in any of your classes?" her mother asks.

Tera's face involuntarily scrunches as she focuses on her mom's eyes. Brows raised, she looks more concerned than angry, which eases her nerves.

"Not really, why?" she replies.

"I'm sure you've at least heard the news? From other students or something?"

"What do you mean?"

"Aeridonis was kidnapped by a group of humans who are holding him hostage with some kind of anti-magic restraints. Apparently, this group has been kidnapping elves for a long time for money. Evil, evil people doing horrible things to these poor elves. And now they've escalated to Aeridonis." She takes a shaky inhale and tucks a stray curl behind her long ear. "All this to say, I need you, Aston, and Zeyla to start walking to school together or with friends. No more walking alone until these monsters are caught. It's not safe."

"Um, mom?" Tera coughs to clear out a laugh caught in her throat. "You don't really believe *humans* could capture Aeridonis, do you?"

Her eyes narrow and she stutters for a moment. "You never know what people are capable of. It's a crazy, dangerous world out there, Tera. Don't argue with me. You're not walking by yourself."

"Fine." Tera crosses her arms and shifts her weight to her other foot. "But I don't want to be late."

"You won't be," Aston says from the stairs as he joins them. "She already gave me 'the talk' and I'm more than ready to get out of here."

"Zeyla's going to make us late. I wasn't worried about *you*."

"Excuse me?" Zeyla snips, poking her head out from her bedroom door. "I've been ready for *ages*. I've been in here reading my book waiting on you two because mom wouldn't let me leave. You don't get to complain."

Tera starts out the door, choosing to not engage with her siblings.

"Have a good day!" their mom shouts as they file out of the house. "Be safe!"

Once at Pipwerry, her brother and sister go their separate ways without another word to each other.

You didn't even eat any of those soggy biscuit things you like. I know you were hoping to get out of the house faster than that, but you don't stand a chance in your labs without some kind of breakfast. How about you grab something to eat from the cafeteria?

"Yeah, I guess. I don't normally eat breakfast here."

Today you should.

"Fine. I guess I'm still a little bit early anyways."

Tera makes her way through the Hub and into the cafeteria, stopping by the menu signage in front of each stand until she finds one that has cinnamon rolls.

Fan of carbs I see?

"You can't judge someone for how many carbs they eat, Don!" She tries to keep her voice down.

Oh, I'm absolutely not. You think I made it to this age without carbs? Please, they're what give me the will to live. Yes, I believe in balance. But I'm not about to shun you for carbs, Esotera.

She grins, trying to contain her laughter as she places her order. As she stands at the pick-up counter waiting for them to call her order number, she picks up a whiff of a smokey burning scent.

"Do you smell that?" she asks, looking around for the source. "One of the cooks must be burning something."

I can't smell in here, sorry.

She looks around some more, stopping when she notices a cluster of young girls chattering wildly nearby. One of the girls frantically flaps her arms at her, and that's when Tera looks down. The hem of her robes has started to burn as a small flame grows at her feet.

When the girl realizes Tera has noticed, she shouts, "Sorry!"

Stunned, Tera starts stamping her feet around, panic growing in her chest and spreading across her body like the fire creeping toward her legs.

"Do something!" Tera yells at the girl.

"I don't know how!" she calls back.

First years.

"They don't teach first year elementalists how to put out fire before they teach you how to create it?"

No, but they probably should. Clearly a firm warning not to practice fire magic in your first year outside of class isn't enough.

"What do I do?" Tera urges.

She catches the sound of a young man snickering at the next closest pick-up counter.

"What's so funny?" she asks him with a snarled lip.

He runs his hand through his shaggy white hair, looking away as if it could hide his smirk.

"If you know how to put it out, do it!"

He chuckles softly, picking up his muffin and juice from the counter, tossing her another amused grin before walking off.

Hands out. Palms down.

Tera immediately obeys, the fire growing faster and warming her legs with burning fabric.

Focus on moisture in the air. Any humidity. Think of any source of water in the room. Even in the cups at the tables. Anything wet you can think of. Imagine pulling it all into your hands.

She focuses, and her hands begin to feel wet as a water droplet falls from her right palm. After another droplet, water begins trickling and eventually pouring from her downturned palms, washing out the fire with a hiss. All the tension in her body relaxes and she lets out a deep sigh. Looking up, she sees the group of girls is no longer there.

"Man. Bunch of jerks."

They're first years. They're probably scared to death they're going to get expelled. Don't be too hard on them.

Tera grunts, looking down at her soaked socks and shoes and her singed robe. From across the cafeteria, she hears someone yell her name.

"Tera!" the voice calls again, growing closer. She looks up and spots Verity shoving her way past a cluster of onlookers.

Her friend stops short, eyeing her wet clothes.

"But you were just… I swear you were just on fire. How did you…"

"It was another student. Some elementalist, I guess. They disappeared," Tera lied, shrugging it off.

Verity furrows her brow for a moment before relaxing and asking, "Are you okay?"

"Yeah, I'm great," she says flatly, staring at Verity. "Really good way to start my day."

"I'm just g–"

"Hey, Verity?" Tera cuts her off. "I kind of need to get a change of clothes before class. Can't hang around and talk." She motions theatrically to her singed and dripping robes.

"Right, right." Verity nods over and over, her pink bob bouncing around her jawline.

"Tell Emmaline I promise to hang out with you both as soon as I'm not grounded anymore!" Tera says before trotting past Verity and out toward the administrative offices for a replacement set of robes.

Who's Emmaline?

"A friend of ours."

Why haven't I seen her yet?

"She's a faun, so she doesn't go to Pipwerry. Why's it matter?"

It doesn't. Just trying to make sure I stay informed. Don't want to fall behind if you start talking to someone and I don't know who or

what you're talking about. Now hurry up and get moving before you're late for class.

Professor Leutrix sits on his desk watching each student as they enter. The desks get arranged differently for lab days, and he waits for the opportunity to belittle a student for taking more than a half-moment finding their place in the new layout. Instead of the normally empty, long tables, today they've got something on each one covered by a black tarp.

Tera hurries into the room, her soggy shoes squelching with each step. Just grateful for the dry robes, she tries to ignore the side eye from Professor Leutrix as she squish-es past him.

When it's almost time for the bell to ring, he leaps off his perch, his cloak swooshing behind him as he soars to the doorway.

"Let's get a move on!" He crows down the hall. "Tick-tock!"

He steps aside as a mousey boy scurries through the door. Before the first chime of the bell even finishes ring-ing out, Professor Leutrix slams the door shut. He flicks his wrist above his head and the classroom lights begin to dim in the tall ceiling.

"Reanimation is a fundamental piece of deathrising as a path and profession. If you have any hope of becoming a master deathriser, you must understand the consequences of improper reanimation. Does anybody remember the number one rule of reanimation?"

Milling's hand shoots into the air, and Leutrix wastes no time calling on him.

"Give the corpse a purpose."

"Give the corpse a purpose," Leutrix repeats louder than Milling. "Do we remember *why?*"

Tera fidgets with her hands in front of her, watching her professor pace.

Go ahead. Raise your hand. You know this one.

Tera lifts her hand a couple of inches from the table, sets it down, and lifts it again.

Higher.

She shoots her hand above her head before she has another chance to second-guess herself, and everyone in the class turns to gawk.

Professor Leutrix halts in place, turning to her and narrowing his eyes. "Miss Tera, is that a raised hand I see? On purpose?"

"Y-yes. Sir."

"Go on."

"If a reanimated corpse isn't given a purpose, it's going to try to fulfill basic survival instincts instead. Feeding, primarily. When you give it a purpose upon animation, it cannot do anything else until that goal is accomplished, after which you can put it to rest again."

Leutrix cocks his head to the side, raising his dark eyebrows. Without a word, he moves on in the lesson.

Atta girl.

Tera can't resist the smile creeping across her face.

After her professor asks a few other questions of his students, he instructs them to remove the black tarps covering their tables. Under each one is a lifeless body. While students from any of the other paths would be mortified by such a sight, the deathrising students are completely unphased. It's just another day in labs for them.

On Tera's table—which she shares with a lab partner—lays a red-headed mineral elf.

"One partner," Leutrix starts, pausing until he has their undivided attention, "is going to reanimate the corpse and provide it with a basic purpose around the classroom. Fetch you a pencil. Touch the door. Something simple. Then release the corpse from the charm as soon as the purpose has been completed. Then, switch roles. Is everyone clear?"

Everyone says, "Yes, professor," in unison.

"Do you want to go first?" asks Tera's partner, a pyre elf with a forgettable face and even more forgettable name.

"Uh, sure." Tera looks over the body, her arms feeling stiff at her sides as she tries to run through the steps in her mind before starting.

Alright, Tera. What's step one?

"One on the heart, one on the head," she whispers, placing her left hand on the body's chest, the other on his forehead.

Good! Next?

"Pull energy from bottom up?"

Go for it.

Tera concentrates, drawing energy from the ground and through her feet, up her legs, her torso, down her arms until it feels like her fingertips are buzzing with life.

"Oriri," she says softly, closing her eyes until she feels the energy leave her.

Open your eyes! I want to see if it worked.

Tera's eyes shoot open just in time to see her corpse testing his jaw and sitting up on her table.

"Oh my gosh," she says breathlessly, watching the redhead.

Don't forget the next step!

"Oh! A purpose."

The reanimated corpse turns and looks at her.

"Get me a piece of chalk from the chalkboard," she says.

The corpse slides its legs over the side of the table, dropping to its feet and standing still for a moment before walking toward the front of the class. It picks up a piece of chalk as Professor Leutrix side-eyes it. When it returns to Tera, it holds out the piece of chalk, dropping it in her outstretched palm. It continues to stare at her.

"Alright. Lay back on the table," she commands.

It obliges, and Tera sets her hands on the corpse's head and chest again.

"Mori," she mutters, and the corpse lets out a sigh before going stiff once more.

"My turn, I suppose," her tablemate says, bouncing on her toes.

Tera steps aside and her partner lays hands on the corpse. *How'd that feel?*

"*So* good!" Tera says, her voice almost entirely washed out by the sounds of her classmates talking to their lab partners and corpses. "It didn't start eating the entire class, so that's a huge win in my book."

Well done, Esotera.

"Thank you." She smiles to herself, wiping it away quickly when Leutrix glances her way.

Tera's tablemate reanimates their corpse and instructs it to knock on the classroom door three times. It gets up and moseys to the door just as Leutrix swoops in beside Tera.

"What a remarkable improvement from the last lab, Tera," he says, his eyes unblinking.

"Thank you, professor," she says, only making brief eye contact. Instead, her eyes wander and watch the corpse knocking on the door.

"I'm glad to see you're finally taking your classes seriously."

"Yes, professor."

He continues staring at her, his focus only breaking when Tera's tablemate speaks up.

"I don't understand," the girl starts, "why won't it come back?"

Their red-headed corpse stands unmoving, facing the door.

"You must be specific, Miss Traella," Leutrix says.

Traella grimaces, looking from the corpse to Tera for help.

"You forgot to tell it to come back when it's done," Tera clarifies for her.

"So did you, but yours came back anyways," Traella whines.

"I told it to bring me something, so that requires it to come back anyways."

"Oh." Traella runs her fingers through her hair with a dramatic huff before trotting over to their corpse, instructing it to return to the table.

When Tera goes to check if Leutrix is still beside her, he's already returned to the front of the classroom to watch over the rest of his students.

Strange fella.

"You can say that again," Tera whispers back.

Later that day, Tera takes her lunch break with Professor Dringely, catching up on what she missed in class the day before. Dringely spends the first few minutes trying to get Tera to open up about what Aeridonis had her doing in Xleria, but he advises her not to divulge too much information just yet.

After repeated attempts to dig for information, Dringely eventually gives up and puts her full attention into helping Tera catch up on missed class material.

"The lab today is pretty easy. It's more of a review of old material than new. In fact, this is one that you should be rather good at after what happened with Aeridonis. That is, if you learned your lesson." She smirks.

Ouch.

"Right?" Tera replies to Aeridonis.

"What'd he say?" Dringely asks.

"Nothing," Tera says, suppressing a smile.

Dringely watches her, expecting details, eventually shaking herself out of it. "The lab is another opportunity for you and your classmates to practice a resurrection spell. I felt it would be useful for everyone to review, especially after what happened with you and Aeridonis. I know the odds are low that it would ever happen to anyone else, but why risk it?"

"So, you're having us bring something back to life?"

"Pretty much. Each student is going to get three dead mice. One of which has been incinerated and will be in a small cup of ashes."

"Okay, wow," Tera says sarcastically, "bit on the nose there. I really inspired this lab, didn't I?"

Dringely shrugs. "Sorry."

"It's whatever."

Apparently it's a good lesson to learn.

"Now you're teaming up against me? If it weren't for me, you and your ashes would've been swept away by the wind! You're welcome."

I didn't say I wasn't grateful, but I'd be remiss if I said you and other students wouldn't benefit from this very specific lesson.

"And you're lucky I didn't remember that lesson from class or you would be in a cat right now."

Aeridonis groans.

Dringely watches curiously, nibbling on her pencil as she waits.

"Okay, so it's safe to say I'm actually prepared for this lab," Tera says to her professor, who replies with a polite smile and nod.

When class lets out for the day, Tera returns home immediately, locking herself in her room to practice the impossible wall.

Feeling inspired by your successful labs today?

"You could say that."

Perhaps you're not as bad of a student as people seem to think. Maybe you just have—

"Don't pull that, 'You haven't applied yourself' seiva. Everyone always tells me that. I *do* apply myself. I just have a hard time remembering things from class."

Maybe it never really felt important or interesting until now. Maybe you never saw practical uses for any of it—except regarding a future career.

Tera shrugs, forgetting he can't see it.

Let's see what you've got then. Go ahead and try the wall. You're on a roll today. I believe in you.

"That's a bit cheesy, but thanks for the confidence," Tera says with a chuckle.

Let's see it.

"Alright, alright." Tera holds out her hands, remembering what Illidara taught her. She focuses, blocking out everything from the day and imagines a wall stretching across half of her bedroom. She pictures the color, texture, and feel of it. A shimmery liquid wall grows in front of her, and she almost loses focus.

Keep going.

Tera continues imagining the wall, her hands up and unmoving. The liquid begins hardening, taking the appearance of her bedroom walls until it looks as if her room has truly been split in half.

She gawks at the fake wall, a sputtering laugh bursting from her gaping mouth. "I can't believe it. No freaking way."

Tera steps up to it, tracing a finger along the cool surface. It feels identical to the real walls of her room.

"So, other people would see this too? But it's not technically there? Their brain just tells them it is and that they can't pass it?"

Yup. Neat spell, isn't it?

"Um, yes!" She giggles again, running her hand along its smooth texture.

Now, get rid of the wall.

"Already?"

Are you just going to keep feeling up the wall? Just get rid of it. You can put up another one later if you want. I want to see you practice taking it down.

Tera sighs in submission, taking a couple steps away and putting her hands up again, palms facing the wall. She imagines the material crumbling in front of her, slowly tracing her palms in a downward sweep. The impossible wall begins to sparkle and fade from top to bottom, disappearing entirely once Tera's hands reach her sides.

"Happy now?"

I'm proud of you! That was excellent. One might even say you're ready to feed some draxxi.

CHAPTER NINE

THE DRAXXI

Tera's jaw drops. "Nuh uh!"

You don't want to now?

"No, I mean, like…" She groans, trying to find words. "I just mean I'm surprised. Excited. I don't know. I didn't expect you to actually ever let me."

A deal's a deal, isn't it? I told you I'd take you to feed them once you learned the spell so I knew you could defend yourself. Especially because they haven't been fed in a while. They could get a bit aggressive, and I want you to be able to shield yourself if they get too excited about dinnertime.

"You basically want me to hide behind a fake wall so they don't confuse me for their food? Why didn't you say that sooner?"

I didn't want to worry you.

"And you think I wouldn't be worried about that all of a sudden?"

It isn't that. I just figure you'd feel better prepared now so it wouldn't be as intimidating.

"Fair enough, I guess. So, when do we leave?"

Tomorrow since you don't have class. Can you contact your friend for help? That half-celestial elf boy?

"His name is Kiran, and yeah. I'll send Steve with a note. What are you thinking?"

Send your raven to your professor first. Ask her to send your parents a note about how well you did in your lab. And that she sees real improvement. It might get your parents to loosen up a bit. We'll take it from there.

Tera opens her window, reaching her head out and whistling. Steve caws from his perch in a nearby branch. He cocks his head at her, and she whistles again.

"Come here, you stubborn bird."

Steve hops a couple steps closer, tilting his head the other way.

"I'm not bribing you. Come here!"

He caws in rebellion, turning his head away.

"Now you're just being rude. You know I feed you! I shouldn't have to give you treats every time I need you to do your job. Come on, buddy."

Steve is silent, ignoring her.

"You know, I could replace you with an owl. Would be a lot easier than putting up with your nonsense."

Steve scratches his head with a taloned foot, giving a little shake of his ruffled feathers.

"You're lucky ravens are better at finding their owners than owls," she says with a sneer. "Plus, the whole seeing-through-illusions thing is pretty cool."

Steve caws in agreement.

"Fine." Tera retreats into her room, pulling a canister of seeds from her desk drawer and giving them a loud rattle. Steve immediately flaps into the room, sliding across the slick surface of her desk as he lands, slipping on some stray papers. His little feet make a happy pattering sound as he dances, waiting for Tera as she reaches into the canister and pulls out a few seeds for him.

"Spoiled." She sprinkles the seeds on her desk and Steve frantically snaps up each one.

As he eats, Tera scribbles a quick note to her professor, rolling it up and holding it out to Steve. It takes him a minute as he finishes the last of his seeds before snatching up the note.

"Bring it to Professor Dringely, please."

Steve hops on the desk before flying back out through the window. Tera closes it behind him and takes a seat on her bed.

"So, what's the plan?"

Well, we have to wait and see if your parents loosen up a bit. If they don't, we'll just have to be a bit more strategic. Whatever our excuse is, I'll guide you and your friend, Kiran, to the draxxi. There's a special path you can take that keeps you out of sight. You'll go there, I'll instruct you on how to feed them, and then you leave immediately.

"Sounds simple enough."

It's not.

"Why's that? Just because they're blood-thirsty killers?"

No. That's the part that worries me the least.

"Oh goody. What's the worst part?"

The marrow elves.

"How come? They think you're dead right? And no one else knows how to get to the draxxi."

They're cruel, but they're not stupid. I wouldn't be surprised if they have guards posted anywhere they suspect is an entrance.

"But if they suspected your hidden entrance was an entrance, wouldn't they have figured a way in by now?"

Aeridonis chuckles proudly. *It's well-hidden. We'll just leave it at that for now. You'll see soon enough. But I just need you to stay vigilant. If you even spot a single marrow elf, I need you to promise you'll leave. Abandon quest. Get out of there. We'll figure out a plan B if we can't get in to feed them tomorrow.*

There's a gentle tap, tap, tap at Tera's window. Steve stands there, pecking at the glass with a note in his beak.

Your bird's fast. He's a keeper.

"Yeah, he's alright when he's not begging."

Tera lets Steve in and reaches for the note. He snaps his head away from her and she grunts in frustration.

"Here." She hands him a seed and he drops the paper. She unfolds it and reads a signed note from Professor Dringely addressed to her parents about how well she did in her lab today and what a drastic improvement she's made since the midterm.

She gives Steve a little scratch on the head before getting up and opening her bedroom door.

"Mom! Dad!" she calls down the hall before skipping to the kitchen. "Look what Professor Dringely just sent!"

She wiggles the note in front of her mom, who's pouring a cup of tea from the kettle on the stove.

"Okay, okay, calm down, Tera," she says, holding up a hand until she finishes pouring her drink. When she's done, she pinches the note from her daughter's hand and unfolds it, her eyebrows rising as she reads it.

"Well?" Tera asks, bouncing and grinning at her mom.

"I'm proud of you!" she says, putting a hand on Tera's shoulder. "You've worked hard to bring up your grades, and this is a great start."

"Am I finally un-grounded?"

Her mom scoffs. "For one week of hard work? Not even remotely. Keep it up and we can talk about it later."

"But Mom—"

"Uh uh," she snips, walking past Tera with her tea and taking a seat on the couch.

"Dad?" Tera asks, turning to her father, who's sitting at the dining room table working on a miniature craft sculpture of a castle.

He looks over the rim of his small-framed glasses, his gaze bouncing between his wife and his daughter. "What your mother said."

Tera lets out a disgusted noise, snatching Dringely's note from the counter and storming off to her room. She slams the door shut and flops back on her bed. "Now what?"

Now we say you're going to be studying with a classmate tomorrow afternoon. We'll have Kiran come by at some point looking for you. It seems like—whether it's a group or just the two of you—you two are always together. When your parents see him looking for you, they'll assume you most definitely are studying. After all, you'd never do anything else without your best friend. Right?

Tera shrugs. "I mean, that seems a bit extra, but okay."

Just trying to erase any doubts your parents might have. Sorry to say, but I don't think your mother trusts you when you say you're just going to study.

"Okay, fair."

After Kiran stops by to look for you, it'll help solidify to your parents that you are, in fact, out studying. We'll be waiting for him at a set meeting place, and once he joins us, I'll lead you to the draxxi.

"Sounds simple enough."

Glad we're on the same page.

Tera gets up from her bed, pulling out another piece of paper and a pen, scribbling a note to Kiran and sending it off with Steve.

"Hey, Don?"

Mmm?

"You're pretty good at this sneaky stuff. Especially for someone so old," she says, laying back down on her bed.

Wow.

Tera smiles, pulling her blanket over herself and getting cozy.

"Here's to an exciting tomorrow, I suppose."

Goodnight, Tera.

The next morning, Tera wakes to Steve staring her down and poking at her nose. She gasps, scrambling to sit up and shoo him away. He flaps over to her desk chair and indignantly preens his wing feathers. Once Tera wipes the sleep from her eyes, she notices a note tied to Steve's foot. She walks over to him and tries to remove it, but instead gets nipped.

"Ouch! Stupid bird!" She lunges at him and he flies across the room. "Give it!"

Tera stumbles over a pile of dirty laundry as she swats at Steve, cornering him and plucking the note from his foot.

"Why are you like this?" She huffs at him, and he squawks in return.

She unrolls the paper. The only word is Kiran's name scrawled in the bottom corner of a sketch of himself giving a thumbs up. Tera smiles to herself, setting the note on her desk before refocusing herself on packing up a day bag.

"What kind of things am I going to need for something like this? What should I wear? Are there any colors that make draxxi mad or anything?"

What kind of question is that? You think they have favorite colors?

"Well, no, I just—"

Wear comfortable shoes, I suppose. Other than that, it really doesn't matter. The younger ones are fond of shiny things, so maybe don't wear jewelry unless you want to risk them gnawing it off.

"See? That's the sort of thing that would be good to know, Don."

Well, now you know. She could hear him snicker.

She finishes packing some snacks, water, and emergency first-aid supplies. After plowing through a quick breakfast, she opts to wear her cozy green pants and a loose-fitting orange top.

Smart choice.

Tera looks her outfit up and down in her bedroom mirror. "What?"

Dressing like a carrot so the carnivores don't want to eat you.

"I don't look like a carrot!"

She looks down at her orange and green outfit.

"Ugh."

It's fine. I'm just joking. You look fine.

Tera slings her bag over her shoulder, making her way to the front door. Stopping in the kitchen, she eyes the knife block on the counter.

Don't.

"What?" Tera asks in a hiss under her breath. Her mother stays unaware, occupying herself with a stubborn sticky spot on the countertop.

You're thinking about grabbing one of the knives, aren't you? One of those isn't going to do anything against a draxxi, so don't bother. You'll just end up hurting yourself if anything. Leave it alone.

Her eyes dart from the door to the knife block until she decides to ignore Aeridonis's advice. She eases toward the knife block, pretending to want a cracker from the bowl beside it. Grabbing a cracker with one hand and pulling out a knife with the other, she carefully slips the knife into her sleeve without her mom noticing.

I'm telling you, it's a bad idea.

Tera sighs and rolls her eyes, turning back toward the door to leave.

"Where are you going? And I hope you're not planning on going by yourself." Her mother calls to her, not looking up from her aggressive scrubbing.

"Study group."

"Again?"

"Well, apparently, I'm still not doing good enough for you, so, yeah. 'Again.'"

"Esotera." Her mother stops scrubbing, her venomous eyes flicking up to her daughter. "I see what you're doing, and it's not working."

Tera stiffens and she forces an eyebrow up. "I don't know wh–"

"I don't feel bad about what I said. I'm proud of you for working hard, but I need to see that you're going to keep your grades up."

Tera feels her muscles release and her posture relax.

"That's why I'm going to study group."

Her mother pauses before saying, "Alright," and resuming her cleaning.

The corner of Tera's lip twitches in a smile, realizing her mother was too distracted by defending her decision to scold her about not having a walking buddy. She drops the knife from her sleeve into her bag in a swift motion.

Without another word, Tera steps out the door into the cool, wet morning air.

"How'd it go?" Tera asks Kiran later that morning as he steps inside the smoothie shop near Pipwerry that the two friends agreed to meet at.

"Fine, I suppose." Kiran shrugs. "Nothing notable. I knocked. Your sister answered. I got an eye roll before I could even say a word. Your mom moved your sister out of the way and told me you were at a study group but that she'd let you know I stopped by."

"So, she doesn't seem suspicious?"

"Not that I noticed, no. Can't say the same for your sister."

Tera scoffs, taking a sip of her aidaberry smoothie. "Nothing new there. Honestly, I'd be more concerned if Zeyla *didn't* seem suspicious."

Kiran laughs, reaching for the second smoothie at their table as he sits down.

"When do we leave?" he asks.

As soon as you two kiddos finish your smoothies.

Tera could feel the impatience in Aeridonis's voice.

"We'll drink the smoothies on the way. Come on."

Aeridonis instructs Tera to take the school's portal to the kingdom capital, Propshire.

As soon as Kiran realizes which portal they're taking, he can no longer contain his excitement. Beaming uncontrollably, he starts babbling about how he can't believe he's traveling to Propshire with Aeridonis himself—albeit in the body of his best friend.

"I mean, I've been there before, but I've never been able to even get near the castle grounds. And like, that's where Aeridonis works. And he's taking us there! You have to tell me everything he can tell you about it. I bet he knows some fascinating things about the castle. Ohmygods Tera! Do you think he can get us into the castle itself?"

Tera's exasperated eyes grow bigger with each sentence out of her friend's mouth as they stand stopped around the Propshire portal.

He's a giddy one, isn't he?

"Something like that."

"What'd he say?" Kiran's head spins so fast Tera swears it almost snaps.

"He's just noting how excited you are. Don't worry about it." Tera grins as her friend begins to panic.

"Oh no, I'm being too much, aren't I?" Kiran's posture droops.

Tell that boy to never apologize for being passionate.

"No, that's cheesy. I'm not saying that."

"What?" Kiran stares at her.

Tera groans before repeating Aeridonis's words.

Kiran's smile creeps back onto his face as he straightens up. "Thank you, sir."

"Okay, let's get a move on," Tera says, stepping through the Propshire portal.

Propshire itself is small, housing hardly more than the Council's castle. The land around it is lush and vibrant with colorful life—small flowers dotting the soft grass on either side of the cobblestone path encircling the castle.

Keep going like you're headed to the castle itself, but then take a left when you get to a dirt path.

Tera follows his guidance with Kiran keeping pace beside her. When they reach the dirt path, she turns left, walking until Aeridonis tells her to make another turn, cutting through the grass until they reach a small gate in the wall around the castle. She reaches for the handle, giving it a rattle to no avail.

"Shocker, it's locked," she says, waiting for instructions.

Aurum clavis.

"What?"

Say it. Keep your voice down. Put your mouth practically to the lock itself.

Tera's brow scrunches before she squats down, her lips an inch from the lock as she whispers, "Aurum clavis."

The lock clicks and Tera stands, pulling on the gate. It's heavy, but it swings open slowly. Her and Kiran pass through, closing it behind them. She paws around at the back of the gate, trying to figure out how to lock it again.

It locks on its own, so don't worry about it. There's going to be a door into a special corridor of the castle. Head around the left until the ground begins to dip down. Then stop.

The friends continue in silence, both of their heads swiveling around at every little noise.

"Where is everyone?" Kiran asks softly.

Almost no one is allowed on the grounds except the Council and groundskeepers. And they don't typically work this late in the morning on a weekend.

Tera repeats Aeridonis's words, and Kiran nods, his shoulders softening from their stiff hunch.

Once the ground starts to go downhill, they stop.

"Now what?" Tera asks.

You see that rune on the ground? A couple steps ahead of you?

Tera's eyes scan the grass for a stone rune with a strange symbol carved into it. "Uh-huh."

Stand over it. Hold your friend's hand.

She steps forward and puts out her hand for Kiran, who stares at her with a raised eyebrow.

"Just take my hand. Aeridonis's orders."

Kiran joins her, grabbing her open hand

Close your eyes. Kiran too. And then count back from ten.

Hesitantly, Tera closes her eyes and instructs Kiran to do the same. When she tries to peek one eye open, Aeridonis hollers at her to shut it again and start the countdown over.

"Ten, nine, eight," she begins quietly.

She resists the urge to look again when she feels a cold rush of air across her arms.

"Seven, six, five…"

Alright, open them.

"I didn't get to zero," Tera protests.

It's alright. You counted kind of slow anyways.

"What d—" her eyes shoot open, and she stops talking. Instead of the castle grounds, she now stares down a darkly lit stone hallway.

"Woah," Kiran says, releasing Tera's hand.

Follow this hallway for a bit. I'll tell you when to stop.

"What even was that? How did we—"

It's a telerune. Not common anymore, but I still have a couple from back in the day. This part of the castle isn't accessible any other way. There's still one more lock, for extra security. But we're almost there.

"I have so many questions," Tera says, her words echoing in the claustrophobic hall.

"Me too." Kiran keeps looking over his shoulder at the even darker space behind them.

Save them. We don't have time for a Q and A.

A few moments later, Aeridonis tells her to stop.

"But there's no door," Tera observes, looking all around them.

There is.

"What's he saying?" Kiran asks, stepping closer to her as if he'd be able to hear Aeridonis himself.

See that stone that doesn't match the rest?

"What?" Tera turns, scanning the walls on either side of her until her eyes lock onto a stone in the rough walls that looks cleaner and smoother than the rest.

Precisely.

She steps up to it, reaching out and feeling the smooth, cold rock.

Aperio ostende.

Tera repeats his words into the stone, which gets sucked into the wall as if the entire thing is liquid. She gasps, jumping back as the wall drains like water into a drainage hole in the floor.

"What did you do? What was that? Is it supposed to do that?" Kiran rushes to the now-empty space, stretching his arm out and waving it through the darkness before him.

Walk through the new opening.

"But I can't even see a foot in front of me that way," Tera says. It was as if the new path resisted any trace of light from the rest of the hallway.

Trust me.

She lets out a half-whimper, half-groan as she shuffles into the pure darkness, her hands outstretched. Kiran follows without question, taking hold of a bunch of fabric at the back of her orange shirt as they blindly go, allowing the darkness to swallow them whole.

A few minutes in, she begins to panic. With nothing to tell which way she's going or which way she came from, the darkness suffocates them. It presses in on her senses until the only thing she's sure of is Aeridonis's voice in her head.

Keep going.

"Am I even going the right way?"

You need to trust me.

Tera closes her eyes, trying to convince herself the darkness is her own doing—that she has control over it. She feels Kiran behind her, still gripping her shirt tight. After a few more steps, things suddenly glow red beneath her eyelids and her eyes shoot open to blinding light.

She blinks back the bright sunlight, eventually making out the shapes of the valley. Tall trees covered in speckled mushrooms and viny overgrowth form a barrier to the outside world. Behind her, it appears as if they had entered through the mouth of a cave.

Aeridonis starts babbling in her head about some protective spell over the valley that keeps the draxxi contained and prevents outsiders from seeing anything but an empty valley, but all Tera can focus on is the growing number of long, scaley faces poking out from behind the trees to watch her.

Kiran still clings to Tera's shirt as he points a shaky finger at a bush just several yards away.

A smaller draxxi peers around the leaves, its slender face black and covered in metallic-looking scales. Aside from its bright and unblinking eyes, it has no other discernible features. Tera can't make out its ears, nose, or even mouth.

"Don," Tera starts softly, "what do we do now?"

More and more draxxi begin peeking out at them until the valley feels full of giant black scaled faces and gleaming eyes that seem to devour every move the friends make.

Everything in the valley is still for a moment. The baby draxxi from behind the bush rears up on its hind legs, towering over Tera and Kiran. Its face elongates until suddenly, it reveals a wide set of needle-like, brilliantly white teeth.

"Don!" Tera's voice shakes. She takes a step back, and the other larger draxxi all crawl out from their positions, rearing up on their hind legs and flaunting their teeth. Several stretch out their leathery wings, sending a gust of wind her way as they thrash.

"Wait," Kiran says, his voice firm as he locks eyes with the baby draxxi. He stretches his arm out in front of Tera before taking a few steps forward.

"What are you doing?" Tera panics.

Kiran hushes her, easing closer to the draxxi, stopping a few feet away from it. He drops to one knee and shows his open palms to the creature, who responds with a wet snarl.

"Kiran!" Tera wails, and several other draxxi hiss and flash their teeth.

He doesn't break his posture or eye contact with the scaled beast, and after a moment, it closes its mouth over its teeth and lowers itself onto all fours. It tiptoes closer to Kiran, who reaches out a hand and places it on the space between the draxxi's eyes.

Such a beautiful scene.

"What? Why didn't you say something earlier! They could've killed us. Still could!"

I wanted to give your friend a chance to use his strengths and communicate with the draxxi. They're insanely intelligent creatures and they're an absolute joy to interact with.

"Wait, he's *talking* to them?"

Well, at least that one, yes.

"I've never actually seen him do the stuff he learns in class. This is kind of really cool."

Animalinguism is an underappreciated path, but honestly, it's far more unique than any of the others. The others all work similarly, but animalinguism is a whole other animal. Joke intended.

"Kir," Tera calls out, her voice gentle. "What's it saying?"

The draxxi flares back on two legs again, glaring at her and hissing. After Kiran draws its attention once more, it calms down.

"They don't trust you," he tells her.

"What? Why? What'd I do wrong?"

"Your bag."

"My bag?" She stops, remembering the kitchen knife. Slowly, she lowers her bag from her shoulder and gently tosses it out of her reach. "Is that better?"

A pause. All the draxxi seem to visibly relax, lowering themselves onto four legs and concealing their teeth.

"Did they… did they say what about the bag bothered them?" Tera asks, wondering if it was just a lucky guess that she has a weapon.

Kiran waits before replying, "Knife."

Tera's jaw drops. "How?"

Her friend shrugs before standing up and turning back to her. His newfound draxxi friend butts its head against his shoulder until he reaches back over to pet it.

"I take it they're ready for some food?" Tera asks.

Kiran chuckles.

"What's so funny?"

"Nothing." He smirks, patting the draxxi.

Tera looks between the two and starts picking at the scab on her head. "Whatever." She rolls her eyes. "Let's just feed them. Don?"

It's easy. There's already a set of powerful spells that keep a constantly growing supply of food, but it's important that it's controlled. The draxxi tend to get a little… overkill… about their food.

"Where even *is* the food?"

You see that patch of dirt to the side over there?

Tera turns and spots it. "Yeah."

It's right there.

"What?"

You mean you can't see it? Hmm. Maybe this won't work after all.

"What do you mean?" Tera's heart begins to race, and she hurries over to the dirt patch, looking all over as if expecting the food to reveal itself.

I'm joking, Esotera. Powerful illusion spell. Keeps it concealed.

"Oh." Tera runs her hands through her curls, her face growing warm but grateful that Aeridonis can't see it. "How am I supposed to take down the spell? Or put it back up?"

Technically, you won't. You'll just be temporarily lowering it. It comes back on its own extremely quickly. You'll have time to grab food for one draxxi before it reappears. Prevents them from stealing from the stash before it can properly replenish. You'll lower the spell once per draxxi.

"Sounds easy enough."

Step one would be counting the draxxi. Might be a better job for your friend.

"You don't know how many there are?"

Some are born, some die. The numbers fluctuate. Should be about a dozen, but it's important to know exactly.

"Kiran," Tera calls, "Aeridonis says we need to count the draxxi. He said you'd be better for that."

"Sixteen," Kiran says without pause.

"You didn't even co—"

"So?" He looks to the draxxi beside him, nodding. "Sixteen," he repeats.

"Alright," she says with an amused scoff.

You might need his help for this part too. They can be a bit heavy.

"*What* can be a bit heavy?"

You'll see. Get him over here and then I want you to hold your hands out over the dirt and say, "Ostendo." Then be ready to heave the meat out and over to the draxxi.

Tera nods and summons Kiran, who has a hard time convincing the smaller draxxi to leave him be for a moment.

She fills him in on the details, and the two brace themselves as Tera lowers the illusion spell. Before them, a sort of tunnel opens, exposing a pile of deer carcasses. She shudders, collecting herself quickly so she and Kiran can lift one from the tunnel's opening, taking it and setting it in the middle of the valley.

Two of the larger draxxi thunder over to the first deer, their needle-like teeth sinking into opposite ends. They snarl and snap in an ugly game of tug of war until the deer splits in two, showering the grass with innards.

Tera's eyes bulge, and she whips her head away from the gory scene.

Impatient buggers. Best you don't watch them eat. Just keep focused on feeding. You're doing well.

Tera and Kiran work together to feed all sixteen draxxi. As the creatures eat, Tera keeps her back turned, opting to focus on a brightly colored mushroom on a tree. Kiran, instead, watches the feasting with fascination.

"Are they almost done yet?" Tera calls back to him, refusing to turn around.

"That squeamish, huh?" He laughs. "And no, not yet. A couple of them are still eating."

She groans, feeling her stomach do a flip as she visualizes the deer ripping apart again and again in her mind.

Quiet.

"What?"

Be quiet. Now. You and Kiran.

Tera stays silent, trying to figure out what Aeridonis is listening for when she hears it.

"I wonder how Aeridonis even tamed these things in the f—"

Tera turns, grabbing Kiran's wrist and throwing a finger to her lips, her eyes wild. He stops talking, tilting his head and letting his eyes roam. When he hears it, he throws a hand over his mouth.

They found us.

CHAPTER TEN

THE ELEMENTALIST

"Get back," Tera whispers to Kiran, pulling him behind her as she holds her hands out, trying to remember every step of the spell from Illidara, unsure of where to place the impossible wall.

"I still don't understand how you figured out this girl has any connection to Aeridonis," says an approaching voice.

Block them in the cave.

Tera turns to face the mouth of the cave they had come through, focusing her mind on the look and feel of the stone walls.

"I can't see anything," another voice says.

"Keep going," says a third.

Tera's heart begins jumping around in her body, as if fighting against her stomach and lungs for space.

Focus.

"I'm trying!" she whines under her breath to Aeridonis.

Not hard enough. This could be life or death. Focus on the wall.

She squints, arms outstretched as she imagines feeling the cave wall where there is none. Her eyes burn hot as she stares at the mouth until a liquid wall shimmers into place at the entrance. It solidifies into believable stone and Tera can feel her shoulders soften around her neck.

Atta girl.

The voices grow louder still, and Kiran panics, concealing himself behind a tree as the draxxi disappear into the valley. Tera freezes, watching her wall illusion as if simply blinking would cause it to crumble before her.

"You know what happens if you're lying to me about this, Garridan," one of the voices warns.

"Yes, sir. I assure you; she went this way."

"And you're certain this girl knows where the draxxi are?"

"Positive."

Tera's mouth gapes and her entire body begins to feel hot. "I don't understand," she says under her breath. "We were so careful. How would anyone have even known where we were going?"

I'm not sure, but don't beat yourself up over past weaknesses. Use them to make stronger moves in the future.

"Do you really think they're just going to turn around and leave just because of my wall? If they don't, there won't *be* a future."

We'll have to see.

"What?" Tera fumbles for words, still not breaking her stare. "What happens if they don't?"

I'm feeling optimistic.

"Oh," Tera says with a scoff. "I'm glad you're feeling sunshine and crystal elves about it, but we need a plan B, Don!"

He shushes her, and she gnaws on her lower lip in wait as the voices grow closer.

"And she's no threat?" one of the voices asks.

"Hardly." Tera figures that response comes from the one called Garridan. "I accessed her grades and have been watching her since shortly after we took out Aeridonis. When I visited his second, he pointed me in her direction, but his word is hardly trustworthy. All I really gathered is that she came to him on Aeridonis's behalf. I'm honestly not sure why she even has any connection to him, but I know she does."

Probably best I never told Fillidren how to find the draxxi.

Tera throws a look over her shoulder, hoping to meet Kiran's gaze and ask if he's hearing all of this, but he's nowhere to be seen. She turns back and focuses again on her illusion in front of the cave mouth.

"It's a dead end."

"What are you talking about?"

Tera can hear their dry hands run against the rough stone of her wall, growing ever so slightly quieter as they continue tracing their fingers along the length of the inside of the cave.

"I knew we shouldn't have listened to him. He's nothing but a sympathizer."

"Garridan knows what happens if he misleads us," a voice repeats, wet and hissing. "Don't you, boy?"

Garridan doesn't acknowledge the others, and they move on to whining about the darkness.

"Can't you use an illumination spell?" one moans.

"You think I haven't tried that? It isn't working in here."

The voices continue to bicker, growing quieter. Tera begins to feel a smile creep across her face, but it instantly melts when she spots one of the marrow elves stepping through her wall.

Locked in place, she watches him. First his foot, then his leg, torso, and head until he's entirely inside the valley.

Hide.

Tera ignores Aeridonis, her eyes narrowing on the intruder.

Now, before he sees you!

She focuses on heat. Anger. Letting it course through her until it begins to burn her palms.

Esotera, no. Bad idea. Stop, stop, stop!

The intruder's head turns, spotting Tera in the empty valley.

Tera lets out a near-animalistic growl, her hands igniting in hateful flames.

The intruder barrels toward her and in her shock, she nearly loses focus, her flames flickering out for a moment before growing again. When she looks down to check on the fire spell in her hands, she loses sight of the intruder. Suddenly, she's knocked backward, stumbling on her feet and losing her flames entirely. He appears out of nowhere, shoving her against a tree.

He trains his strong hand against her neck, keeping her pinned to the bark with his body. She whines, the sound weak as it escapes her throat. As soon as her eyes meet his, she's hit with instant recognition, and by his widening gray eyes, he knows it.

With his other hand, he places a shushing finger to his lips. He releases her, and before she can catch her breath to speak, he disappears.

"Looks like Garridan was wrong," one of the voices says from inside the cave.

"His loss."

"An honest mistake, sir," Garridan says. "Perhaps I should have observed her a while longer before acting."

"You won't make the same mistake again."

The voices grow quieter until they're indistinguishable.

Tera thinks back on the young man's familiar shaggy white hair. His skin is richer than the corpse-like flesh of a full-blooded marrow elf, but his angled features are unlike that of any other type of elf. "He was the one who laughed at me when that first-year set my robes on fire," she says as the memory fully surfaces.

He was one of the elves that killed me.

"He was there?" Tera thinks back, trying to recall any faces she caught a glimpse of from her hiding place in the woods outside Summercloud, unable to remember his.

Wasn't just there. He was one of the ones that participated.

"What was he doing at my school?"

You heard the same things I did. Following you, apparently.

Tera's skin crawls at the thought of being watched.

After a moment of silence, she notices the eerie emptiness of the valley. "Where's Kiran?"

"Up here!" Kiran shouts from the back of the same small draxxi as before. Beside a couple of the adults in the sky, the baby looks only a quarter of the size of the rest. It soars and lands gracefully in front of Tera.

"You're kidding, right?" Tera asks, staring at her friend as he dismounts the creature. "There's no way that thing let you ride it."

"I mean, I don't know what to tell you. You know what you saw." Kiran beams from ear to ear, patting the draxxi's head.

"Does it have a name?"

"It's a he, and yes, he does. Obviously not in our language, so we had to work something out."

"'Obviously.'"

"His name is Elo. He's the youngest one of their pack."

Tera nods to Elo, who turns to look at Kiran.

"I already told him you're friendly. And I explained the whole Aeridonis thing to him. He's just a bit skeptical. You can understand."

"Sure, sure." Tera's mouth flattens, and she nods animatedly.

"So, your wall worked, huh?"

"Did you not see—" Tera stops, gaping at him. "You didn't see any of the stuff with the guy who attacked me, did you?"

"Someone attacked you?" Kiran's goofy grin gives way to horror.

Tera tells him about everything he missed from his safe spot above the trees. She mentions that both her and Aeridonis recognized the boy.

"I think his name is Garridan," she says. "I don't even know how he was able to get through the wall when none of the others could," Tera says.

Illusion master.

"What?"

Remember the drawback to illusion spells. Illusion masters are rare, but you just so happened to meet one today. And he saw right through your spell.

"Okay, so he's an illusion master and can see through illusion spells," Tera repeats out loud so Kiran can catch up. "But that's not even the weirdest part. He disappeared and lied to the marrow elves about me being here. He could've told them about my spell. They could've figured out a way in or waited me out. Something. But he lied to them, and they left."

Aeridonis is silent, and Kiran simply shrugs.

"Why'd he let me go?"

Your guess is as good as mine.

Frustrated at the lack of clarity, Tera goes to grab her bag from where she discarded it earlier. She does so slowly, watching the draxxi as they peer at her from around the trees again.

"Tell them I'm not going to hurt them, Kir. Plus, we fed them. We can go home now, right?"

For now, but you need to be better prepared next time. I'll take the blame for that. I shouldn't have sent you here without taking more precautions. At least now we know you're being watched. We can use that.

"Use that? How?"

I didn't say I have a fully fledged plan right this second. Your generation is so impatient.

Tera scoffs. "'My generation.' Sure. Okay."

It's all about instant gratification. Just let an old man think for a bit without having to have everything in place right away. The young people today need to learn some lessons in patience.

"If you don't stop talking seiva about 'my generation,' I'm going to use that potion from the nurse. Shut you up for a bit. Maybe someone ought to teach the older generation that not everyone wants their unsolicited advice on things like patience."

Kiran's eyes bug out of his head as he watches his best friend arguing with the voice in her head. Elo creeps over to her, as if wanting to hear Aeridonis's side of the debate. He gets mere inches behind Tera's shoulder.

"And maybe if you wouldn't have distracted me, I could've taken on that guy when he f—AH!"

Tera screams, throwing herself away from the hardened face of the young draxxi over her shoulder. Elo rears back, startled by the noise. The entire valley of draxxi begins hissing and snarling, baring their teeth from their positions in the woods.

"Tell them to stop!" Tera cries at Kiran.

A moment later, the valley quiets down. Kiran walks over to Tera, putting an arm around her and giving her a squeeze.

"You're okay," he says with a light chuckle.

"They freak me out."

"*You* freak *them* out."

"If I've got to keep feeding these things until we get Aeridonis a body, you're coming with me again."

"Gladly. I'd love to see them again. They're absolutely in-credible." Kiran's eyes light up as he watches Elo, who flaps his leathery wings as he trots over to a larger draxxi.

Tera and Kiran leave through the cave entrance, following Aeridonis's directions back through the castle and grounds until they reach the portal back to Pipwerry.

"Hey guys!" calls Trevitt's wet and gravelly voice on the other side of the portal. "What were you doing in Propshire?"

"Nothing," they answer together.

Trevitt's smile fades. "Oh. I get it." His head sags. "I'll leave you guys to it. I've got work to do anyways."

He starts to walk away, and Tera and Kiran ex-change silent sighs.

"Wait, Trev," Tera calls.

You're not telling him about the draxxi, Esotera.

"Do you want to come with us to get smoothies?"

Trevitt's lips curl up in a wide smile.

"We already had smoothies today," Kiran says, immediate-ly snapping his mouth shut as he realizes how his words sound.

Trevitt's short-lived smile fades. He scrunches his brow and glowers at the friends. "No, thank you. I'll see you guys later." He turns again, leaving them behind in the portal room.

"Way to go," Tera says, punching Kiran's shoulder.

He yelps. "Okay, rude!"

"Yes, you were. We both were."

Wow. Is this growth I'm seeing?

Tera rolls her eyes and lowers her voice. "Stop. I just feel bad for him sometimes."

Kiran and Tera go their separate ways, agreeing to work together later to figure out a plan to protect themselves and the draxxi next time. Tera hopes there is no next time, and that Professor Dringely gets Aeridonis out of her head before then, but she can see the thrill in her friend's eyes at the thought of another draxxi visit.

At home, Tera's stopped by Zeyla at the door.

"How was *studying?*" She smirks, her arms spread between the open door and the doorframe, blocking Tera outside.

"It was fine. Let me in."

"Who'd you study with?" Her head tilts to the side, her eyes unblinking.

"Some classmates. Since when have you cared about my academics? Get out of the way, Zey."

"Which classmates? Some of my friends are friends with deathrisers. Maybe I know of them!"

Tera scoffs. "Stop lying."

"I'm not lying! They really are friends with some people in your class."

"No, I meant about having friends."

Zeyla's smug grin falls off her face, replaced by hatred burning in her eyes. She slams the door shut in Tera's face with a huff.

Tera rolls her eyes, opening the door and stepping inside. "Was that really necessary?"

Her sister is already in her own room, and Tera instead walks in on her mother scolding Aston for never sitting with the family for dinner.

"I'll make it up to you, Ma. Swear. I'm just a little busy right now." Aston hurries up the stairs to his bedroom, gripping a plate of paraletti bird pie.

"I have an idea," Tera whispers almost imperceptibly.

She rushes up the stairs after her brother, her mother questioning it with hardly more than a curious glance over her shoulder. When she reaches the top of the stairs, she beats on the door a couple times before letting herself in, shutting and locking it behind her.

"Woah," Aston says from his desk, mouth already full of food. "Can I help you?"

"As a matter of fact, you can."

After filling him in on everything since Summercloud, Tera watches him while rocking back and forth from her seat on his floor.

"And I need a favor," she says.

At this point Aston still hasn't said anything. He sits, thick brows raised high as he observes his sister.

"The next time I go to feed the draxxi, can you please come with? None of my friends are lifebringers, and I'm sure as hell not asking Zeyla, Mom, or Dad." Her eyes start to sting, her cheeks rosy as she stares off in space. "Aston, I'm scared." Her eyes flick to him. "I want someone who can heal. In case things go bad. And maybe healing won't be enough, but at least it's something. If nothing else, I think I'd feel safer."

Aston's cheeks puff out as he lets out a slow, dramatic exhale with his eyes wide. He runs his fingers through his messy copper hair and then leans forward in his chair.

"I don't know how else to tell you this, Tera, but I can't help you."

Tera's heart falls into her stomach. "What do you mean? *Can't* or *wont?*"

"Can't. I'm not a lifebringer."

Tera's left brow cocks up and she narrows her eyes at her brother. "Huh?"

"I switched paths. Years ago."

"Do Mom and Dad even know?"

Aston shrugs. "They'll find out when they see me in a yellow cloak at graduation."

"Yellow? Elemental?"

He holds out his hands, conjuring a small flame in one and a swirling ball of snow in another.

"Woah."

"Good at it, too. Not to sound full of myself or anything." The corner of his mouth twitches in a subtle smirk, and he dismisses the spells. "But that means I wouldn't be much good as a healer. I hardly made it through any lifebringing classes to begin with. I can do the very beginner healing spells and that's about it."

Tera sighs, folding her arms over her bent knees and hanging her head. "I don't know what to do."

"If you're telling the truth about Aeridonis, why isn't he helping you?"

I'm still thinking.

Tera shrugs. "He hasn't come up with anything yet I guess. And I'm surprised you even believe me at all. Honestly, I was expecting you to laugh at me and kick me out of your room."

"Honestly, what you said isn't any more or less believable than the seiva everyone else is spouting about his disappearance," he says. "And why'd you even bother telling me any of this if you felt that way?"

"I had to try. I didn't know what else to do or where else to go."

"For the record, I believe you because I've never seen you stressed out like this before. I know you get a bit upset about grades and stuff, but not like this. You're hardly recognizable right now. It's a bit weird."

Tera looks up and smiles weakly.

"Wow. Convincing," Aston jokes.

The two sit in the quiet warmth of the room for a moment before Aston clears his throat.

"I could, uh," He adjusts himself in his seat, sitting up straighter. "I could still help you, if you wanted."

"How?"

Aston flicks his wrist in a rapid snap, and suddenly his trash can across the room bursts into flames. Tera jumps to her feet, the bright flames mirrored in her nervous eyes.

No. Absolutely not.

"Can you teach me?" Tera asks, a smile teasing at her face.

Esotera, no.

Aston shrugs. "Don't see why not. My little sister should be able to protect herself if she wants." He waves a hand in front of his face, a small cloud forming over the garbage, sprinkling water onto it with a soft sizzle until the fire dies out.

Tera can't help it, and she throws herself at Aston, hugging him tight.

"You tell Mom and Dad though and I'm telling them everything," he threatens.

"Our little secret." She pulls away and offers him a hand.

He accepts, shaking it. "And I'm still coming with to see the draxxi."

CHAPTER ELEVEN

SUMMONING STONES

O ver the next week, Aston spends his evenings teaching Tera basic elemental spells in one of the empty extracurricular meeting rooms in the Hub after classes. Each time, they're careful to shut the door and keep their voices low in case the marrow elves are following.

"So, you said that one marrow elf boy got through your spell, but he didn't hurt you?" Aston asks, sitting on top of a desk and swinging his feet slowly.

Tera nods, picking at the scab on her head while allowing her eyes to wander the room.

"Sounds like he thought you were cute or someth—"

"What? No! Stop that." Tera immediately stops picking and instead stares at her brother, her nose crinkled up at him.

Aston shrugs. "If he comes again, I'll just set fire to the deadskin myself."

Deadskin?

"Rude term for marrow elves," Tera answers. Aston looks at her with a raised brow, but she brushes him off. "To be fair, *I* don't use that word. I used to think it was because they're pale and look like walking corpses, but Kiran taught me it's because of some psycho marrow elf dude during the war who skinned other elves and sold it as some kind of nasty leather to other marrow elves."

I know what it means, I just haven't heard it in a long time. I'm impressed your friend knows that story.

"Are you talking to him right now?" Aston asks, sneering.

Tera rolls her eyes and resumes picking at her scab.

"What are they even teaching you in your deathrising classes right now?" he asks, changing the subject. "Anything at all useful for any of this?"

She shakes her head and sighs. "I mean, not really. Leutrix is teaching us how to resurrect corpses from a distance, and Dringely's class has just been talking about what kinds of plants we shouldn't pull from for spells. Basically, just talking about protected plant species so we don't kill them."

Aston laughs and shakes his head. "How does any of that kill plants?"

"Do you not know how deathrising works?"

"I mean, you're kind of an outlier in the grove, you know that right? Kind of weird for anyone in Darkwood to study deathrising."

She shrugs. "Deathrising kills plants because you can't just bring someone back to life without pulling life *from* something. That's why the deathrising professors have so many potted plants in class. And they're always replacing them. Because the students kill them to bring back the corpses."

"Huh." Aston raises his eyebrows and tilts his head. "Learn something new every day."

"Speaking of learning new things, I think I've got it down." She stands, focusing her gaze on a standing target on the other side of the room.

"Now remember, be careful when you aim. Anything you cast fire onto is going to catch fire. Once something's on fire though, it's going to act like a normal fire. Hence why you can put out a magical fire with something like normal water. If you cast a fire on something surrounded by dead trees, they'll probably catch fire too. If you do it on something surrounded by, like, wet laundry, the stuff around your target probably won't catch on fire. Unless your aim sucks and you actually hit the wet laundry."

"'Wet laundry'?"

Aston shrugs. "Best example I could come up with. Alright, responsible disclaimers aside, let's see what you've got."

Her body grows hot, and she forces the energy through to her hands. As if throwing a ball, she tosses aggressively toward the target, snapping her fingers together as she does. There's a loud whoosh as the target bursts into flames.

Tera lets out an airy laugh. She puts her hands on her knees, looking down at the floor and then back up at the fiery target. "That's so freaking cool. Almost cool enough to switch to elemental. I can see why you picked it over life-bringing for sure though."

Aston smiles softly and nods to himself. "Lifebringing just wasn't me. But setting stuff on fire? Yup. That's it."

Tera bounces on the tips of her toes, full of energy. "I don't know how you don't go around setting stuff on fire all the time."

"Ha! I mean, it's tempting. Apparently, we both have a knack for fire magic. Wouldn't Mom be proud?" He scoffs.

"Boy, you got jokes." Tera says with a sniff, crossing her arms as she watches her fire die out. "But glad I'm not going to be the only disappointment in the family."

"Geez, thanks."

"I didn't mean it like that."

"I know."

The two are quiet for a minute as they watch the last bit of the fire fade, leaving behind a pile of ash in place of the target.

"For the record," Aston says, "she doesn't think you're a disappointment."

Tera rolls her eyes. "She would never say it to my face, but I can tell."

"I think she's more concerned than she is disappointed."

"Concerned? About what? Her reputation?" Tera groans, kicking a stray pencil across the floor.

"Tera, you're literally the only deathriser in Darkwood. It's completely contrary to arboreal elf culture. She's worried you won't find a good job, that you'll be stuck working in the factories or something instead of in the Healer Tree or one of the care centers, that you won't be taken seriously, that you'll regret your choice." He shrugs. "You know. Stuff like that."

"Wow." Tera sighs. "That doesn't necessarily make me feel better." She lets out a nervous laugh.

"I mean, she has a point, but just because things are probably going to be hard for you doesn't mean they're impossible. Just means you might have more work ahead of you than Zeyla."

Tera groans and rolls her eyes. "I hate that."

"I know you do." He chuckles. "But enough whining and pity parties. I want to teach you how to set fire to multiple things at once."

Tera's posture straightens and she bites back an excited smirk.

I have a plan.

It's been another week of lessons with her brother, and Tera lies in bed staring at the ceiling in her dark room. She imagines Garridan surprising her in the valley, and this time, she'll be prepared.

Didn't you hear me, Esotera? I have a plan.

The image of her confidently setting fire to Garridan and the marrow elves dissipates from her mind, and she groans. "What kind of plan?"

A plan that takes care of the draxxi and keeps you, your friend, and your brother safe from the marrow elves.

"I'm listening."

Your friend, the gronnet. He's the key.

"Absolutely not." Tera closes her eyes and rolls over.

Young lady, you will listen to my plan! Enough of the attitude.

"Old man, I will not."

He's silent for a moment. *Just listen to me. If you don't like the plan, we'll have a discussion. How about that?*

"A discussion?" She scoffs. "Fine."

We'll purchase a summoning stone set and give one to Kiran and one to your gronnet friend—

"'*We*'?"

Okay, you will purchase a summoning stone set.

"What even *is* a summoning stone?"

They're used for portals to very precise locations. If you have a summoning stone and rub it, the portal gronnet with the partner stone can use that to create a portal directly to the other's location.

"Huh. That's kind of cool." She rolls onto her back and lets her eyes trace over her artwork on the ceiling. "But why do we need them?"

If you'd let me talk, I'd get to my point.

Tera grumbles, biting her tongue.

We don't want to involve a stranger in this. I trust your gronnet friend to keep things confidential more than a public portal one. Of course, we spare him as much detail as possible anyways. Odds are, he will have some of these stones on hand—most portal gronnets do. Once Kiran is with the draxxi, Kiran can rub the stone and the gronnet boy can create a portal to him. You and your brother can take that.

"That sounds a bit excessive."

We can send your brother with Kiran, to play it safe. I don't feel like the marrow elves are watching either of them, but it doesn't hurt for them to have each other's backs. But the marrow elves are most definitely onto you. They're likely watching and following you from a distance. If you take a portal, they won't know where you're going, so they can't follow you. It keeps the location secret.

"I see what you're getting at, and while that plan sounds all sunshine and crystal elves, it won't work."

Oh?

"Trevitt hates me now. He's never going to agree to this plan."

I highly doubt that's true.

"Don, dude, seriously? You're in my head. You were there. He's fed up with me."

That's why you're going to beg for forgiveness.

Tera's laugh squeaks out of her, and she sits up, picking at her head scab. "Good joke, Don, but we need something serious. What's your next idea?"

Nope. That's… uh… That's it.

Tera sucks in a dramatic breath, huffing it out and flopping back again in her bed. "I mean, I *do* feel bad about how I treat him. He's just so overkill, you know? He's too loud, too messy, too clingy, and too energetic. He's too much."

An apology doesn't mean you're asking him on a date or asking him to be your best friend. I've been around for a few years and—

Tera snickers.

Ha. Funny. Yes, I'm old. What a fun joke. I'm being serious, Esotera. All I'm trying to say is I've learned some important lessons over the years, and one of them is how to keep healthy boundaries while still making sure people around you feel loved and cared for.

"Okay, fine. So, let's say I beg for his forgiveness. What if he still says no?"

That's his decision to make. We're just going to have to hope he says yes.

"That's it? You're just *hoping* he agrees to put his career at risk to help me with something he knows nothing about?"

Do you have a better idea?

"We c—"

One that doesn't involve massacring all the marrow elves because you think you're some kind of badass now just because you know some basic fire spells.

Tera grumbles and rolls her eyes. "I guess not."

First thing tomorrow. Get to school before classes start. He should be there if he's been working closely with the portal master—start of the day is busiest for classes, so they'd need to be there in case of portal issues. Head straight to him. We can focus on the rest of the plan if and when we get a positive answer from the gronnet.

"Fine. Can I go to sleep now?"

Wouldn't you rather stay up thinking about how awkward you were when you presented your essay in class this morning? I think I counted about thirty 'um's.

"Why would you say that?" Her face scrunches and her eyes shoot wide open. "I practiced! You know I did! Oh gods, is that why Cathalda and Markut were laughing in the back of class? They were laughing at *me!*"

Woah, Tera, my dear, I was joking. You did marvelous. Your classmates were laughing at that tall fellow sitting in the back of the room.

He took a drink of his tea and spilled it in his lap. You were too focused on your presentation to see it. Stop worrying yourself sick.

"You want *me* to stop? You're the one who put that thought in my head. Leave me alone and let me sleep or I'm using that potion from the school nurse to at least give me a night of peace. *Enough.*"

Silence.

"Better."

The next morning, Tera gets to school early as planned. She makes her way to the portal room but doesn't see Trevitt. The portal master steps out of his office just as she reaches out to knock on the door.

"What?" The portal master glowers at her, Tera's small fist still up as if about to knock.

"Have you seen Trevitt?" she asks, lowering her hand.

"Check the cafeteria. Move."

She steps awkwardly aside and watches as he waddles through the portal room and out the front door.

With a slow and shaky breath, she collects herself and calms her nerves before walking down the hall to the cafeteria. She steps slowly through the room, scanning the seats and food stalls for the familiar gronnet until her eyes land on him. In the far corner of the cafeteria, he sits at a lopsided table by himself, a meat roll in either hand as he alternates which he bites from.

"Hey, Trev," Tera calls softly, tossing him a smile and a half-hearted finger wave.

He looks up at her, grease and crumbs from his breakfast smeared across his face. Without a word, he slides his second tray of food over, as if clearing the spot next to him.

"Thanks," she says, sitting down beside him.

"Where's your breakfast?" Trevitt asks her, hardly making eye contact as he chomps down on the meat roll in his left hand.

"Oh, um, I haven't gotten any. Not that hungry."

He grabs a plate of eggs and fish sausage off one of his trays, setting it in front of her.

"You don't have to give me your food, Trev. I appreciate it, though."

"It's no problem. Please eat."

The two sit in aching silence, only broken by the occasional crunch of Tera's fork and knife through sausage casing.

"Why were you looking for me?" he finally asks.

"What?"

"You never want to sit by me. Why'd you come over here?"

"I wanted to talk to you," Tera answers.

He turns to look at her.

"What do you want?" he asks.

"Forgiveness."

"Please don't lie to me, Tera. You might not like me, but at least respect me enough not to lie to me."

"I—"

"You just want me to make you another portal, don't you?"

She gapes back at him.

Trevitt sighs and drops his breakfast on his tray. Little chunks of meat tumble from the half-eaten rolls.

"I can explain," Tera says.

"I really don't need you to give me excuses and stories. I'll do it. But please stop pretending you're my friend. Either you are or you aren't. Stop using me."

"I really can explain everything!" Tera's face burns hot as she stammers through every word.

"No thanks. Not really interested in hearing it. Just tell me where you want the portal to. I'll do it after I finish my breakfast. Just a reminder though, we've got to go off campus, and I've got to charge you. Dad had to quit his job even sooner than he planned, so I'm the only one providing at home anymore."

Tera's hand shoots over her mouth. "Oh, Trev. I had no idea. Have they started paying you here yet? How are you getting along?"

"They're paying me half-rate. I explained my situation and they had sympathy, so until I go full-time, I'm at least making something. But it's not enough. I'm doing private portal work on the side now. But since I have nowhere to actually set up a shop, I'm just getting the clientele the public portal gronnets turn away. These people get involved in some shady stuff, but I try to keep my nose out of it and just make the portals."

Tera gnaws on the inside of her cheek, a prickling of guilt in her stomach.

"So, as long as you're willing to pay, I'll do it. And it's gotta be off campus. I got in trouble last time, remember?"

Tera sighs. "I'm so sorry."

"Doesn't matter to me if you mean that or not. Just hope for your sake that you're doing all this portal jumping for a good reason."

"Thank you."

"Okay."

He picks his breakfast back up and continues eating.

"Trev?"

He stops mid-bite, pausing and staring off into the cafeteria, waiting for her to speak.

"Can we do the portal later tonight, actually? It's a bit of a complicated situation."

"Okay," he repeats.

"And do you have any summoning stones I could buy?"

"What do you need a summoning stone for?" he asks, looking her in the eyes this time.

"I thought you didn't want the details?"

"Well, consider my curiosity piqued."

CHAPTER TWELVE

THE UNEXPECTED LETTER

That afternoon, Tera buys a summoning stone from Trevitt and passes it along to Kiran during lunch, filling him in on the plan. With Aeridonis's help, she reminds him of the steps to get to the draxxi and he repeats them back to her several times to make sure it's cemented into his memory. Next to them, Aston kicks his feet up on the table. Kiran scowls, scooting his lunch tray further from his best friend's brother's feet.

"I still don't see why I can't just come with you," Aston says to Tera.

"I already said this," she says with a groan. "I'll be portaling from a safe spot. As far as we know, they're watching *me*, not you guys. But they almost found the draxxi before. In case they come back, Kiran needs protection on the way there."

"How do we get back safe after we're done though? If they're already suspicious of the area, won't they have someone nearby watching? They'll see you leave, and it'll blow the whole thing," Kiran questions.

"We'll use the summoning stones, the same way we'll use them to get me *to* the valley. Trevitt will have the partner stone to the one I gave you. You rub your stone, and Trevitt will get the message that it's time to put up a portal for me to get to you, and then again to bring us back. They'll never know where we went."

Kiran nods, his expression flat.

"So, when do we leave?" Aston asks.

"Immediately after the last class period lets out. You two will head straight there. Kiran knows the way. Once you're there safely, rub the stone in your hand to let Trevitt know it's time to send me over."

"Sounds simple enough," Kiran replies.

After the last class that day, Tera slowly makes her way down to the portal room to meet Trevitt. When she enters, he's there, recasting the green lifebringing portal while a couple of first years watch him.

"Thank you!" the smaller of the two squeaks at him, her wide smile beaming. "I was worried the portal was closed for the day and I left my textbook in class. My dad would kill me if I missed another homework assignment. You're the best!"

Trevitt smiles warmly, waving the two first years toward the portal. "Don't mention it! The portals are supposed to always stay open, so I'm glad you let me know it was fading. If anything, *you're* the best!"

The two high five him on their way through the portal, and Tera waits until they're both gone before she approaches Trevitt. When she does, his smile immediately melts from his face and is replaced by indifference.

"Kiran hasn't signaled me yet. You're early," he says flatly, waddling over to a nearby bench and taking a seat. He stares at the wall directly ahead of him.

"I know. I wanted to tell you how important what you're doing is, and how much I appreciate it."

"Uh-huh."

"You have no idea how much you're really helping. Th—"

"You're right. I don't."

Tera shifts awkwardly from where she stands, her fingers trailing up to her scab. "Trev?"

He grunts.

"If I tell you what we're doing, do you promise not to tell anyone?"

Don't.

Trevitt perks up and immediately catches himself, pretending instead to be indifferent. He shrugs.

"It's really important that you don't tell anyone. I can't tell you if I don't have your word that it'll stay a secret."

Esotera, stop. You don't know how much danger you're putting him in by telling him. And the draxxi. And you. And the entire kingdom. The more people that know, the higher the risk there is even going to feed them.

Trevitt crosses his arms and locks eyes with her.

Tera pauses, taking a breath and looking around the portal room to make sure they're alone. "I'm saving the kingdom. From the marrow elves."

His brow furrows.

"Do you think I'm stupid?" he asks in a deep growl.

"What?" The question catches her off guard. "No! I just felt you should at least know why it seems like I'm using you. This is really important, and you're literally a hero."

"Save it. I'd rather you not say anything at all than spew ridiculous lies at me like that. Like I'm some kind of kid… or an idiot. You're lucky I'm even making this portal at all! After this, I'm *done*. I'm not making any more portals for you—I don't even want you talking to me after this. I could use the money, but I respect myself too much to talk to jerks like you. I'm not the pushover you and Kiran and everyone else seems to think I am."

"We know you're not a pushover! You—"

"Stop."

"I—"

"Stop."

Tera sighs and hangs her head in defeat.

I told you not to tell him a single thing.

"Shut up," Tera grumbles under her breath.

Trevitt shoots her a side eye. "What did you say?"

"I was telling myself I need to shut up now."

Trevitt scoffs.

Just then, he perks up and reaches into his pocket, pulling out a smooth gray stone, the center of it glowing a hot red. "Looks like they're ready for you."

Tera nods and follows him out of the castle and down the short road to Teretatian. They round the corner of a couple small cottages and stop in an alley. Trevitt holds his hand out expectantly, and Tera reaches into her pocket, feeling for her coin bag. It's empty, and she fondles it frantically, as if coins would magically appear. She nibbles on the corner of her mouth, drawing her empty hand out of her pocket.

"Can I bring you money before class?"

With nothing more than a pause and a sigh, he holds his hands up and conjures an opaline portal. His face scrunches as he looks at his creation.

"Is something wrong?" Tera asks, eyeing it.

"No, I've just never made a portal this color before. It's pretty, but weird."

"Is the color a bad thing?"

"Not necessarily."

"What does the color mean?" she asks.

"It's complicated."

She stares at the portal, inching closer as if it's likely to explode.

"It's fine. The portal itself is safe. Can't say anything for wherever you're going, but the portal is fine. What are you waiting for? I've got to get back."

She makes a hesitant noise, checking Trevitt's face one more time for reassurance but not finding any. With a deep breath, she steps through.

The light of the valley blinds her for a moment, as she blinks back the sun and spots Aston and Kiran petting Elo, the young draxxi. Aston greets her with a wider smile than she's ever seen on her brother's face—even bigger than the time their parents got him a miniature snapping drake for Leaf Fall Day.

As soon as the draxxi notices Tera, he tenses up, snarling his needlelike teeth at her.

"Seriously? Even after I fed you last time, you're still going to act like that around me?" She crosses her arms and stares at Elo. "Ungrateful."

Elo snaps his jaw at her, and she holds firm, not letting Elo see her flinch this time.

"He's doing it to get a rise out of you," Kiran says with a chuckle, patting Elo's head as he conceals his teeth and settles in again for more pets.

"This is the coolest thing ever!" Aston buzzes with energy, his eyes floating around the valley, taking in the sights of the draxxi perched on rocks and flying high above the trees. "How come no one sees them up there?"

"Powerful illusion," Tera answers, tossing a glance over her shoulder toward the cave opening.

"But wouldn't illusion masters still see them?"

Remember how I told you the draxxi provide the essence for a powerful protection charm over the kingdom? When that same essence is used with a spell I developed, it also works to conceal their location. It's not a standard illusion spell, either, so it's undetectable from the outside, even to illusion masters. I thought this all through carefully, don't worry.

Tera regurgitates everything Aeridonis explained, and Aston and Kiran devour her every word.

"*This* is why Aeridonis is considered the master of master wizards! Who else could have created a powerful spell like that?" Kiran looks on at Tera with starry eyes.

"Enough fan-girling, Kir. Let's go ahead and feed them." She looks over at the cave mouth again. There's a faint flapping noise, and Tera freezes in place.

"You good?" Aston asks, walking up beside her.

She flails her hands, whacking his shoulder and shushing him. He leans in, eyebrow cocked, and long ear tilted to the cave mouth.

The flapping grows louder, and Tera yanks Aston's wrist, guiding him behind a tree. Kiran follows their lead, hopping on Elo's back and shooting into the sky.

Tera silences her breathing, watching her chest rapidly rise and fall from her position pressed against a scratchy tree trunk. Every muscle in her body begins to tense as the sound grows near.

There's a sudden pinch on her shoulder and she lets out a scream, conjuring a fire spell.

Aston bursts out laughing, pointing at her shoulder. Tera turns and Steve nibbles at the tip of her nose in greeting. Her face starts to grow as hot as the fire magic in her hands. She dismisses the spell and lets out a shaky exhale.

"You scared me half to death, Steve!" She scolds her raven with a reluctant smirk, giving him a little scratch on the head. Her muscles relax before she notices the letter tied to his ankle. Plucking it from his foot, she unravels it and tries to make out the sloppy writing.

"Who's it from?" Aston asks, reaching for it. She hands it over with a shrug.

"I can't even read it."

Aston squints, checking the back of the letter and finding nothing. "It's practically scribbles."

"I don't like this," Tera says, eyeing the cave mouth again as she shoves the note into her pocket unceremoniously.

"It's just someone trying to mess with your head, I'm sure."

"I already have an old man living in my head, I don't need help messing my head up *more.*"

"Let's just feed the draxxi and we can get a portal out of here," Aston says, a hand on Tera's shoulder to usher her along.

She nods, taking a step forward when *BANG.*

The draxxi take off, disappearing almost instantly into the tops of the trees and into the sky. Tera and Aston drop into a crouch behind the nearest greenery-covered boulder just as Garridan steps through the cave mouth. Behind him, marrow elves begin pouring into the valley. Tera peers out from the side of the boulder, her heart thumping deep in her stomach and threatening to burst out. She hides completely behind the boulder again, throwing her brother a panicked look.

"Why weren't you able to find the entrance the last time we were here?" asks a familiar voice. Tera peeks, recognizing the speaker from Aeridonis's murder—*Pocketwatch.*

"Powerful illusion spell. I must not have noticed it last time. Whoever cast it concealed it well. That's why I wanted to use her bird."

"Good thinking, my boy."

Garridan nods stiffly, standing in place as the marrow elves keep filing in.

"So, the girl's here somewhere," Pocketwatch says, scanning the valley. "Do something about it."

"I hardly think she's a true threat." Garridan raises his voice. "If she's watching, let her learn from this that it's not worth resisting us."

Pocketwatch smiles, patting Garridan on the back. The two silently watch their people getting into place for a while before he speaks again.

"You know the plan!" Pocketwatch calls out, his serpent voice crawling down Tera's neck and sending chills rippling across her body. "Get them to the tower."

"Where's the animalinguist girl?" another marrow elf asks, his head spinning.

Just then, a petite mineral elf with nearly human-like little ears steps through the mouth of the cave in a long lilac cloak. She flips her waist-length blonde waves behind her shoulders. Hands together as if in prayer, she looks up at the sky.

Pocketwatch leans over and whispers something into her ear, but she seems to ignore him. One by one, the draxxi draw out from their hiding places, soaring through the valley and landing in the clearing.

"What are they doing?" Tera hisses under her breath.

It's the girl. She's enchanting them.

"Enchanting? They can do that? Kiran can't do that!"

It's advanced magic. And frowned upon by most animalinguists. They believe in free will, not in using their abilities to force animals to obey. Even if Kiran could do that, he likely wouldn't ever choose to.

"Oh my god, Kiran!" Tera gasps, cupping her hand over her mouth. Last she saw, he disappeared into the sky on Elo's back.

"Looks like that's all of them," Garridan says after a few moments, when the flapping of leathery wings finally quiets.

"What about that one?" Pocketwatch points to somewhere in the sky. "The small one. Looks like it's got a friend on its back, too." He turns to the blonde girl. "Get that one down."

She slowly lowers her gaze, turning to look at him with sharp eyes. "I'm trying."

"Your sweet-talking isn't working. Enchant the beast and get it down here or we'll make sure you're their first meal tonight."

"I'm not doing that." She turns her head back up to the sky. "Have patience."

Pocketwatch groans, leaving her side to talk to some of the other marrow elves, who all straighten their posture as he approaches.

"Enchant it now, or we'll just kill it instead," Garridan warns the girl. She shoots him a fierce glare, but then her shoulders slump as she turns back to Elo. Lifting her hands, she stares at Elo, her jaw moving as if talking with her lips shut. When she finally stops, nothing happens.

"I don't understand," she says breathily.

"I'll handle this." Garridan shoves past the girl. He cups his hands together, staring into them as a wispy orb of green and black swirls and grows. Lifting the orb, he lines it up with Elo and Kiran, flicking his wrists outward and sending the orb hurtling their way.

Elo dashes to the side, but the orb chases him. Just as he tries soaring higher, the orb crashes into Kiran's back. He drops his grip and screams, sliding and only stopping his fall by catching hold of Elo's foot. Elo screeches, flapping desperately to compensate for the displaced weight.

The animalinguist girl locks eyes with Elo and smiles softly, motioning to an empty space on the ground below. Elo obliges, lowering himself and Kiran gently to the ground. Kiran's arms drop from Elo's foot, and he begins writhing in the grass. He lets out an unnatural wail, which all the marrow elves seem to ignore.

Aston grips Tera's arm tight, his eyes begging her to stay put.

If you do anything, they're going to kill your friend. Don't move.

"Then I'll bring him back," she whispers in return.

How'd that work the first time? With me? Besides, you won't be bringing anyone back if you rush out there and they kill all of you. Think about this. Wait until they leave, then tend to your friend. We'll figure something out about the draxxi, but there's nothing you can do right now to fix this.

Aeridonis's words echo in her head as she stares wildly at her pleading brother for a moment before sinking back against the boulder. She resorts to pulling at the rough edges of her scab as she tries to tune out the pained sounds of her best friend.

"Get them out to the portal before it closes," Pocketwatch says. "We don't have time to waste."

Garridan steps before Pocketwatch, facing the draxxi and crossing his arms above his head. He holds his pose for a second before ripping his arms away from each other and bringing them back to his sides. A thunderous crash echoes through the valley, turning almost instantly to persistent metallic rattles.

Tera peers around again, eyes wide as she makes out the shapes of over a dozen draxxi bound by chains. The creatures erupt in indignant screeches and growls, thrashing against their magical bindings.

"This wasn't part of the plan!" the blonde girl yells, storming up to Garridan and only stopping when her face is an inch from his.

He looks down at her, a smirk twitching on his lips. "Neither was this." He repeats the motion before the girl can react. The chains begin warping their way across her body as she screams and smacks at Garridan in vain.

Pocketwatch claps Garridan on the shoulder before leading the way out of the valley. Several other marrow elves stay back with the draxxi. They raise their hands together, and the chained creatures all begin to rise about a foot off the ground. With a swish of their hands, the marrow elves send the floating and bound draxxi off toward the mouth of the cave. Elo shoots Tera a look, his normally fierce face soft and helpless before he disappears into the dark cave. The remaining marrow elves follow after. Kiran's screams of pain ring out louder than ever in the silence of the now-empty valley.

Tera dashes out from her hiding place, hardly waiting a second to be certain the marrow elves have left the cave. She skids across the slick grass, her face scrunched as she kneels beside her friend. Kiran twists, his limbs knotted, and his skin so swollen it begs to burst.

Aston squats beside her and pokes Kiran's purpling arm, to which Kiran wails and curses.

"What are you doing?" Tera slaps her brother's shoulder. "Fix him!"

"Fix him? How am I supposed to fix him? Put him out of his misery with a fire spell?"

"You took some lifebringing classes. Heal him!"

"I think you fail to realize just how quickly I switched paths, Tera. I don't know how to do any of that. I can basically just heal cuts and scrapes. That's it."

"What are we supposed to do?"

Aston shrugs, his brow furrowing as he looks down at Kiran. "Maybe he'll die soon and you can just resurrect him?"

It won't kill him.

"What?"

Aston looks at her. "I mean, I—"

"Not you," Tera cuts.

The curse won't kill him. It'll just make him wish he were dead.

"What is it?"

Well, we know Garridan is an illusion master. Odds are, it's a nasty illusion curse meant to trick the body into having some sort of reaction. I've seen similar ones before. They're not pretty. Only way to fix it—aside from the spellcaster calling it off—is to have a lifebringer cleanse it.

"Aston," Tera says, her wild eyes shooting open, "do you have any lifebringer friends?"

He scoffs, but his smile awkwardly fades when he realizes she's serious. "Um. No."

"I don't want to have to do this, but we might need Mom and Dad."

Aston cringes.

"I know, but what else am I supposed to do? He's suffering!"

With a sigh he says, "I'll call the portal. Let's get him home quickly." He reaches into Kiran's pocket, muttering a quiet, "Sorry," as he pulls out the summoning stone, giving it a rub.

The next few minutes drag on, as Kiran's body keeps shifting colors and swelling. Finally, an opaline portal grows a few feet away.

"Help me get him up," Tera says, lifting Kiran under his shoulders as he screams, his voice wet and his face puffing beyond the point of recognition.

Aston grabs Kiran's ankles and the two shuffle to the portal, lifting him carefully as they step through.

On the other side, Trevitt stands in wait, his arms crossed and expression flat. As soon as he spots Kiran's contorted and bloated body, his huge mouth drops open and shapeless words begin tumbling out.

"Wha—di—izzy d—oh!" he babbles, hovering over the friends as they step out of the portal and into the small alley-way of Teretatian.

"Trevitt," Tera starts, "I know I promised I wouldn't ask you to make more portals, but I really, really need you to make a portal to Darkwood. We don't have time to get to the portal room back at Pipwerry—I need to get Kiran to my parents *now*. I'll pay you later. Just, please!"

Trevitt nods frantically, immediately holding his hands up. The opaline portal fades away and is replaced by a swirling dark green. He steps out of the way, gesturing to the portal with his mouth still gaping.

"Thank you." Tera guides the top half of Kiran through the portal with Aston following.

The two step in unison through the forest until they reach the stairs up to their house. Tera climbs faster than Aston, and he drops Kiran's feet with a thunk. Kiran howls through inflated lips. Flustered, Aston scrambles to pick his feet back up.

"You're going too fast!" he yells.

"Then go faster! Keep up."

"No. I'm going to drop him again and then we might really kill him. And nature knows just how much you suck at resurrection spells. Go slower. Step when I say so"

Tera grumbles but nods once.

Aston takes a deep breath. "Step."

The two take on one stair.

"Step."

Another.

"Step."

When they finally approach the door, they set Kiran down. Tera reaches for the knob, but the door swings open.

Zeyla stares back at them. "Holy seiva. What did you do?"

CHAPTER THIRTEEN

THE BURDEN

"Zey, please, he needs help. Where are Mom and Dad?" Tera asks.

"Gone. They're at the neighbors for some potluck thing." She watches Kiran with eerie calmness. "What happened to him?"

"Long story. Illusion curse. He's in a lot of pain and we don't know what to do. We need someone to cleanse it."

"Why can't Aston do it?" She flicks a hand in her brother's direction.

"Uh," he hesitates. "I switched to elemental."

Zeyla's mouth splits into a wide grin. "No freaking way. Mom and Dad are gonna flip!"

"Okay, focus," Tera dismisses her. "Can you help him or not? Please, Zey."

Zeyla steps closer to Kiran, her eyes scanning him and stopping on his face, his eyelids swollen entirely shut now. She nods. "Bring him to my room."

"Thank you," Tera says softly, picking up her best friend with the help of her brother.

They carry him into their sister's room, nearly setting him on her bed when she crows at them.

"Ew! No. He's all puffy and gross. Set him on the ground."

Tera looks at her sister in disgust and disbelief before rolling her eyes and gently lowering Kiran to the ground.

"Move." Zeyla shoos her older siblings away as she sits beside Kiran. She places her hands carefully on his chest, closing her eyes. After a pause, she takes a deep, soft breath.

With a slow and steady exhale through her pursed lips, she lifts her open palms to the sky. Her hands swim through the air in a strange dance before her as she breathes in again. Slowly, she lowers her hands to Kiran's chest again, this time pressing her weight into his chest with a grunt.

The swelling starts to fade in his face first. In moments, his eyes are visible again, his thick neck slims out, and his limbs loosen and fall limp into Zeyla's green shag rug. Tera can feel her own body relax as her friend heals before her.

Only once all the swelling disappears does Zeyla remove her hands from his chest. She sits back on her feet and watches Kiran for a minute as he eases himself up, checking over his body.

He turns to look at his best friend's sister, her face serious as she seems to stare off at absolutely nothing. "Thank you," he says, and her eyes snap to look at him.

She nods, rising to her feet and stretching. "I'm going to make a snack and some tea, and I want you all out of my room when I get back."

When she goes to leave, she stops in the doorway, clutching her stomach before taking off down the hall. Tera hears the bathroom door slam.

"Zey?" Tera hurries after her. "Are you okay?" She stands outside the bathroom door, waiting for a reply.

"Go away!" Zeyla grumbles.

She's got the burden.

"What?" Tera asks under her breath.

She cleansed a pretty gnarly curse. She's going to be feeling it for a bit.

"I've never seen my parents get sick after working at the Healer Tree though."

They probably aren't healing massive curses every day. And even still, your sister is just a student. It's going to affect her more regardless.

"Zeyla," Tera calls through the door, "thank you again. Do you need water or anything?"

"Tea."

"You got it. Be right back."

Tera heads into the kitchen, passing Kiran and Aston in the hallway. They follow close behind her, trying to get her attention as she puts a kettle on the stove for her sister's tea.

"What are we going to do about the draxxi?" Kiran asks, keeping his voice low.

"What do you mean?" Tera asks coolly, measuring out some tea leaves from a bag labeled "Zeyla's: Do NOT Touch!"

He scrunches his eyebrows and cocks his head. "What? The marrow elves! Taking the draxxi! How are we going to get them back?"

"They mentioned some kind of tower, right? I say we go to the tower and *take* them back."

Aeridonis laughs in her head.

"Something funny, Don?" she asks.

What kind of response was that? Are you trying to sound tough or something? "We take them back." He laughs again. You sound ridiculous. Three students taking on a bunch of marrow elves to rescue the draxxi. Yeah, okay. I'm sure that'll turn out totally fine. The draxxi have higher odds of just freeing themselves.

"Well, what do *you* propose?" she asks, feeling her face burn hot.

We need to talk to your professor again. If she's nowhere closer to a solution, we need to involve the Council before the marrow elves' curse starts taking effect. The protection spell should hold for a while, but there's no time to waste. It'll be hard to even get the opportunity to speak to the Council with me stuck in here, but this is beyond you now.

"They're going to look at me like I'm crazy."

"It's alright," Aston says, "we already think you're crazy."

Tera rolls her eyes. "Not you guys."

Aston looks at Kiran, and Kiran shrugs back at him.

They have ways they can verify that I'm in your head. I'm not worried about that. I'm worried about getting them to see you in the first place.

"What do you mean? What if we just go to one of their houses or something like we did with Fillidren and Illidara and explain the situation? If they can check that you're in my head or whatever, I don't see what the problem is."

The Councilmembers' houses are well-protected. You won't even be able to see them without them allowing it. The only option is to do this the official way.

Tera groans, and the kettle on the stovetop begins to scream.

It's best we get on their appointment wait list sooner rather than I—

"Stop talking, Don," she says, pouring the water over the leaves.

Excuse me?

"Sorry. *Please* stop talking."

There's silence before he mutters, *You have some nerve, Esotera.*

She runs her fingers through her hair with a dramatic huff before snatching up the teacup and walking it to the bathroom just as Zeyla opens the door.

Her sister takes the tea without a word and disappears into her bedroom, shutting and locking the door behind her.

"She almost seems more pleasant than usual," Aston says, observing them down the hall from the edge of the kitchen.

Tera scoffs and flops down on one of the couches in the living room. Kiran comes and sits next to her, while Aston sits on the arm of the couch and fidgets with a wooden figurine on the side table.

"You doing okay now?" Tera asks Kiran.

He instinctively pats over his face and arms, giving a nod. "Yeah. I think I'm all good. I know you've had some issues with your sister over the years, but I really appreciate what she did for me today."

"Ten coins says she tattles to Mom and Dad before they even step all the way in the house later." Tera lowers her head into her palms for a moment before sitting all the way back on the couch. "I'm going to be grounded for literally the rest of my life, which is just going to make all this stuff with the draxxi ten times harder."

Aston laughs. "They might go easy on you if she also tells them I'm not studying lifebringing."

"Yeah, you might even have me beat. Their pride and joy firstborn… an elementalist." Tera smirks.

Aston thwacks her shoulder with the back of his hand and lets out a sarcastic "ha-ha."

"Serious question," Kiran interjects, the lighthearted mood instantly dying out. "What are the marrow elves going to do next? Now that they have the draxxi?"

Tera shrugs, half-expecting Aeridonis to speak up, but he doesn't say a word.

"We need to take out their leader," Aston says, accidentally snapping a piece off the wooden figure he was playing with. He awkwardly sets the figurine and the broken piece on the table and turns to the other two. "Cut off the head of the snake, ya know?"

Bad idea.

"You expect us to just go up to him and kill him?" Kiran asks, and Tera cuts him short, holding up a shushing finger.

"Don, what do you know about their leader? The dude with the pocket watch."

His name is Fedrae. If I can be candid for a second, the man is a complete ass.

Tera grins. "I mean, we gathered that much. Do you know a lot about him? What's his motivation here? I know he wants to take over the kingdom, but do you know anything specific?"

Of course I do.

Tera's smile falls flat as she realizes he's waiting for prompting. "Can you *tell* me?" she whines at him.

Aeridonis clears his throat and Tera rolls her eyes, knowing he has no physical throat to clear.

"Magical and genetic muddying," he calls it.

"What?"

That's what he calls it. "Magical and genetic muddying." Fedrae, and quite frankly the marrow elves as a whole, believe you should marry and have children with your own kind. Marrow elves with marrow elves, arboreal elves with arboreal elves, humans with humans, you get the gist.

"Why do they even care that much? What difference does it make?"

They believe it taints the purity of magic and diminishes the potency. Basically, they think a pure-blooded marrow elf would be more powerful and valuable to society than someone who is a mixed elf.

"That's stupid. They don't have any proof of that anyways."

Precisely why the Council and I fought so hard to protect that right. Though I will say, I didn't expect it to extend to humans and elves to-gether. Once I noticed that trend, I tried to pass a ruling that celebrated those marriages but discouraged them from having children. While I absolutely believe any elf should be able to marry any other kind of elf, or marry a human, years of research shows that half-elf, half-human children bear weaker magical abilities. Over time, a great portion of the magical population will die off.

"Wait… You supported that ruling?" Tera could feel her hands ball into tight fists as she grits her teeth.

Of course. I believe in freedom and equality, but I also don't want magic to die off. It's a truly tricky balance that I'm proud to say I found an appropriate answer for. Unfortunately, the ruling fell through during Council voting, so the public never heard of the threat to magical lineage. I have nothing against children of elf-human couples. In fact, it was my idea to include them in court and Council.

Kiran and Aston both stare at her, leaning in little by little as if they'd be able to hear Aeridonis speak.

"What's he saying?" Kiran finally asks.

"Uh," Tera hesitates. "Just some raellie-brained political stuff."

"Okay, first of all… Hate that phrase," Kiran says. "Raellies are smart little creatures, actually, and no one gives them enough credit. Second, is what he's saying something that can help us with the marrow elves though?"

Tera scoffs. "No."

"I feel like you're hiding something." Kiran narrows his eyes at her, crossing his arms and leaning back in his seat.

"If it was important, I'd tell you."

"I think your friend's a bit mad his idol lives in your head and not his," Aston says with a smirk, getting up from his seat and wandering to the kitchen.

"I'm not jealous. I'm not a child." Kiran's indigo skin turns a deep purple. A vein on his forehead begins to pulse, and he erupts from his seat. Pacing the room for a moment, he stops in front of Tera. "I just wish you wouldn't keep secrets when anything could be important right now. The marrow elves basically tortured me, and who knows what they're doing to Elo and the other draxxi. It's not time for stupid inside jokes with your best friend, Don."

Tera's face twists in disgust, rising from her seat and glaring up at him. "For your information, I just found out Aeridonis supported a ruling that prohibited elves and humans from having children together. Is that what you wanted to know?"

"Woah," Aston says from the kitchen, rummaging through the cupboard for a snack.

The color fades from Kiran's face and every muscle in his face seems to sink with the gravity of her words. He takes a step back, lowering himself to the ground.

"He really said that?" Kiran asks, his voice soft.

Tera doesn't answer, instead, she takes off down the hall and into her room, slamming the door shut behind her with a crash.

"What's wrong with you?" Tera snarls at Aeridonis under her breath. "You're nearly as bad at Fedrae and the marrow elves. What were you thinking?"

What was I thinking? I was thinking of the future of magic in the kingdom. I didn't want to forbid elves and humans from marrying and having happy futures together. I just wanted to make sure they didn't breed out all the magic over the generations. I know it sounds bad, but it comes from a good place.

"You can't just tell people who is and isn't allowed to have families!"

Clearly. The ruling didn't pass anyways. The Council had other ideas they wanted to look into to preserve magical genes.

"All this and we still don't know how to save the draxxi and stop the marrow elves, and you're still stuck in my head, and now Kiran hates me, an—"

He doesn't hate you, Esotera. And I already told you… I don't want you trying to stop the marrow elves. Leave that to the Council. We just need to get you an appointment with them.

"I'm not doing that."

Yes, you are. That's the only logical thing.

"Unfortunately for you, you don't really get a say in this."

You're making a mistake. You're putting yourself, your friends, your family, and the entire kingdom in danger if you make so much as one move in the wrong direction with them.

"Then I won't move in the wrong direction."

When Tera comes back out of her room later that day, Kiran is already gone, and her parents are back home.

Before bed, she checks in on her sister. Zeyla hardly says more than a word, simply shooing Tera out of her room so she can keep reading her romance book in peace from her cocoon of blankets on the bed.

Tera leaves, returning to her own room and carefully shutting the door behind her. She flips on her desk lamp and sits down, pulling her knees to her chest—the way she feels most comfortable in her chair.

There's a fluttering of wings followed by a little, "I'm here!" caw from Steve on her windowsill.

She turns around and smiles softly at her bird as he wiggles his foot, a loosely tied piece of parchment hanging from his leg.

Tera gets up and trades Steve a seed for the letter. Turning it over in her hand, she sees Emmaline's name in a curly font with a little heart dotting her "i."

"You've been to her family's farm for treats again, haven't you?" Tera asks her bird. "They're spoiling you. You're going to get too fat to fly." She pokes Steve's belly and he squawks, nipping at her finger.

With a sigh, she sets the letter down on her dresser, vowing to get to it later. It doesn't feel possible to think about things as normal as plans or gossip with friends right now.

Steve flaps back out the window and Tera returns to her desk, crawling back into her strange position in the chair.

Abandoned sketches and watercolor paintings lay scattered across her desk. She slides these aside with her arm, pulling out fresh paper and a dull pencil. Absent-mindedly, she doodles a sketch of a draxxi soaring through the clouds.

Just as she's adding the details to the wings, there's a loud crack outside her window.

She jolts upright, tilting her long ears to listen for more. Something in her stomach feels uneasy. She forces herself to creep toward her window to take a look.

Garridan gives her a little wave from his perch in a branch.

Tera's outstretched hand bursts into flames as she leans out her open window. "I should kill you!" she shouts, but before the flames can leave her hand, Garridan disappears with the snap of his fingers.

Close the window, shut the curtains, and just ignore him! Don't egg him on.

The flames die out as she scans the forest, ignoring Aeridonis and looking for Garridan's shaggy white hair against the green. Just as she's about to lean back into her room, he appears inches from her face.

"What fun would that be?" he asks with a smirk.

Tera gasps, falling back onto her floor. She collects herself, standing and quickly slamming her window shut, crushing Garridan's fingers. He yelps, pulling them back.

From her side of the window, she sticks her tongue out and then smiles, proud of herself. Garridan presses a bloody middle finger to her window, leaving a red smudge before disappearing again. She locks her window and pulls the curtains tight with a disgusted grunt.

I told you so.

That night, she keeps waking and checking the lock on her window.

CHAPTER FOURTEEN

STOLEN FISH PIE

Tera makes a point to get up extra early the next morning, giving up on the notion of sleep and deciding instead to pay Professor Dringely a visit before class. When she reaches her teacher's classroom door, she knocks, waits a few minutes, and lets herself in.

She doesn't see Dringely behind her desk or at her bookshelf. Tera scans the room, spotting a tall ladder. Her eyes follow the ladder upward until she sees Dringely at the very top, pulling potted hanging plants from a large bin on the side of the ladder and hanging them up on the ceiling.

"Professor?" she calls politely from the ground.

Dringely finishes hanging a dewvine plant before acknowledging her with a, "Yes?"

"Have you…" Tera pauses, turning and shutting the classroom door. "Have you made any progress? To get him out of my head?" She looks up at her professor hopefully, tapping her fingertips together as she watches Dringely climb down the ladder.

"Not yet."

Tera's face melts and she can feel her eyes burn. "You still haven't found anything at all helpful?"

"Well," she hesitates, "I haven't expanded my research all too much."

"You've given up?" A hot tear dives down Tera's cheek. "N—"

"You can't give up! What am I supposed to do? I can't live like this forever! You don't understand. Aeridonis needs a body and I need him ou—"

"I haven't given up, Tera."

"You just said you stopped researching! You gave up!"

"I've been taking a different approach," Dringely says, her voice calm. She crosses her arms, watching Tera.

"What do you mean?"

"I've involved Professor Leutrix."

"You *what?*" Tera bellows.

"He's the most experienced deathriser on the entire staff board. I figured he'd be a better asset than my collection of books."

Tera groans, sinking into the nearest chair and letting her forehead hit the tabletop with a thud.

"It was either that or nothing," Dringely admits. "I kept hitting dead end after dead end. Professor Leutrix hasn't found a solution just yet, but he's experimenting with some things that hadn't even occurred to me and hadn't been mentioned in my books. I'm really optimistic, Tera. I am."

Tera lets out a theatrical moan. "This sucks."

"I know it does." Tera can hear Dringely's sharp heels click against the floor as she approaches her, setting a cold hand on her shoulder. She pulls out the seat beside Tera, sitting down. "I know you're tired of this, but every day we get closer and closer to a solution. We haven't given up. You just have to be patient a bit longer. I'm so sorry."

Tera sucks in a breath, lifting her head and revealing her tear-stained cheeks and bloodshot eyes. "It's fine. I guess. What's another day? Or week? Or…" She sighs. "I've got to get to Leutrix's class."

Without exchanging another word, Tera hurries out of Dringely's classroom, leaving the door open behind her as several students walk in past her, clutching their books.

As usual, Leutrix watches over each student as they enter his classroom and take their seats. This time, however, when Tera enters, he swoops over and stands hovering over her as she sits.

"If I even suspect that you're receiving help in class from your… *new friend,*" he says in a hushed hiss, "you'll be sent straight to the nurse's office for a silencing potion. And I'll make sure she *watches* you take it before you can return. Is that clear?"

"Yes, professor," Tera says, focusing all her energy on not rolling her eyes until her professor has redirected his attention to Tera's lab partner, Traella, as she enters the room with tattered robes.

"Couldn't be bothered to put on a decent pair of robes for my class today, Miss Traella?"

Traella sniffles, running her fingers along the black shreds. "Someone resurrected a corpse and left it in the hall." She whimpers. "It kept lurching at students walking by. It tried to eat me."

Leutrix's lips pucker before he turns and storms out into the hall. When he returns, he slams his classroom door shut behind him and marches to the front of the room.

"Perhaps I overestimated you, Miss Traella. If you can't rest a corpse, I don't know what you're doing in this class."

"I'm sorry, Professor. I didn't—I wasn't—I think I just panicked. I know how to rest a corpse, I swear!"

Leutrix watches her with narrowed eyes, turning to the metal drawers at the back of the classroom. He swiftly pulls one open, revealing the body of a deceased gronnet. He places one hand on the body's head, one on its heart, and within a moment, the gronnet is up and moving. It stares lifelessly into Traella's eyes as it rages toward her, giant mouth hanging open.

Traella screams, scurrying away from the reanimated gronnet, her tattered robes fluttering with every step.

Help her.

"Absolutely not," Tera whispers back. "I'm already on his bad side right now. She'll be fine. He won't let anything happen to her."

The gronnet corners Traella, snapping his wet mouth at her hungrily. She drops to the floor, and just before she can throw her arms up in self-defense, the gronnet corpse sticks her entire head in its mouth with a sickening suction sound.

The energy in the classroom shifts, as students begin panicking and telling one another to do something. Leutrix's robes are a blur as he races to the scene, putting his hands up and muttering. The gronnet is pulled slowly from Traella's head, trailing a thick strand of mucus. Leutrix mutters to the gronnet, who calmly walks back to its drawer. It climbs in, and Leutrix puts it to rest again.

Everyone's eyes are on Traella, who sits in a shivering ball, her hair and face completely encapsulated in slime. She checks her cheeks with her hands, stretching out a web of goop as she pulls them back out.

Without even turning to face her, Leutrix calls from his place by the drawers, "Someone help escort Miss Traella from my classroom. Take her to the guidance counselor and let them know she's to be placed in the introductory deathrising classes immediately."

The students watch Traella in horror, nobody rising to help her. Leutrix closes the drawer and steps deliberately to the front of the class, his hawk eyes looking over each student, waiting for anyone's uncomfortable twitch to single out his target.

"Miss Tera." His voice slices the silence. "Since you and Miss Traella are lab partners, it makes sense for you to be her escort, does it not?" His veil of faux concern for his student is thin, but Tera stands, approaching her lab partner and reluctantly offering a hand.

Traella's petrified eyes flutter up to meet Tera's before she slides her sticky fingers into Tera's palm. She rises, following Tera's lead out of the classroom. Leutrix slams the door shut behind them and Traella nearly jumps out of her skin at the sound.

"Are you okay?" Tera finally asks, offering her an arm for support as she notices just how shaky her lab partner is walking.

Traella stops, glaring at Tera. "What do *you* think, Tera?"

"I—"

"I've been humiliated in front of the entire class. For no reason. And now I have to take remedial classes? For what?" Her voice grows squeakier with every word. "That dead gronnet was running right at me! What was I supposed to do?"

"I—I think he wanted you to put it to rest."

Traella groans. "I'm not here to learn how to make dead things dead again. I don't even get why we'd need to do that."

"Probably in case something like today happened." Tera motions to the girl's tattered robes and then her goopy face. "Or, you know, if we end up working in the production plants."

"Whatever. Let's just get this over with before anyone sees me."

Just as the two reach the bottom of the stairs, there's a whistle from above.

Tera looks up to see Garridan just a flight above them, sitting on the railing and swinging a leg as he wiggles his fingers at her.

"Hi, *Tera,*" he says, his voice sharp on her name.

"Stop stalking me!" Tera says with a growl, igniting her hands and racing up the stairs.

Snap.

Garridan disappears again.

"Stop doing that, freak," Tera calls, her head spinning.

"Maybe you should stop threatening me," he whispers in her ear.

She screams, jumping away from him.

"Tera!" Traella calls. "Stop flirting and let's *go.*"

"Flirting?" Garridan smirks. "Is that what we're doing?" He drapes an arm over her shoulder.

"No." Tera slumps, letting his arm fall off her as she trots down the stairs back to Traella.

"Oh, come on now," he teases. "Where're you going?"

"Apparently, I don't have to tell you. You'll just follow me anyways."

"Clever girl."

Tera snatches Traella's arm by the crook, guiding her out of the deathrising tower and toward the portal.

"I didn't know you had a boyfriend," Traella says as they step through to the portal room in the Hub.

"I don't."

"Good. He seems like an ass."

Tera can hear Aeridonis chuckle in her head.

"He is." She continues to pull Traella toward the front offices, turning to a door marked for the guidance counselor.

Tera lets herself and her now-former lab partner inside. She all but shoves Traella into a seat.

The guidance counselor adjusts her glasses, staring in shock at the slimy student in her office.

"Leutrix said to put her in the intro death classes," Tera says before exiting and shutting the door promptly behind her.

With her hand still on the knob, she stares at the door.

"Aeridonis?" she calls under her breath.

Mmm?

"What am I supposed to do about Garridan? He's following me. Do I kill him? How do I kill him? He won't stop disappearing. Just catch him off-guard?"

Woah. Calm down, killer.

"He's part of the reason you died and are now stuck in my head. He's the reason the marrow elves have the draxxi."

I know. Just act like a normal student. He knows you and I are connected somehow, but I don't believe he knows how. As much as I enjoy our conversations, maybe keep them to a minimum until either you meet with the Council, or your professors separate us. Got it?

Tera sighs. "Fine."

"What happened to your slimy friend?" Garridan calls over, leaning against a wall on the other side of the hall.

"Get lost." Tera's mind buzzes, wondering if Garridan heard her conversation with Aeridonis. She was certain no one would have heard what she was saying.

"Hard to do around here. I know the school like the back of my hand."

"Congratulations. Have a gold star."

Garridan raises his eyebrows as he lets out a huffy chuckle. "You're spicier than you let on."

"Spicy? I'm not a meal."

"That's not what I mean by spicy, and you know it." His eyes roam down and back up. "Besides, you're not a *meal,* you're a snack."

A snack? What's that supposed to mean? Ask him what that means, Esotera.

Tera lets out a frustrated whine and rolls her eyes. "You're insufferable." Though she's speaking to Garridan, she hopes Aeridonis knows her comment is for him as well.

He steps into her path but she blows past him, slamming her shoulder into his as she walks back to the portal room.

"I liked it better when I didn't know you were stalking me," she calls to him before stepping through the black skull-marked portal.

She returns to Leutrix's class, copying the notes she missed from one of her classmates upon her return. Her mind fixated on Garridan and the marrow elves and the hurt faces of the draxxi in their chains, Tera struggles to focus in class. She repeatedly pinches the skin on the back of her arm, forcing herself to be present. When Leutrix finally dismisses his students, she looks down at her arm, noticing the angry red patch and rubbing it as if to erase it.

Next block is Tera's free period. She doesn't feel hungry, so she decides to skip lunch and attempt to study in the graveyard outside the tower. Realistically, she knows studying in her current mental state is pointless, but at least it might keep Aeridonis quiet, satisfied that she's acting like a normal student.

She lowers herself onto the grass, leaning against a tombstone and pulling her knees close to her chest. The air feels cool and wet as she takes a deep breath, closing her eyes.

All of a sudden, a hand shoots up from the dirt, gripping Tera's foot tight. The wrinkled skin clings to thin bones, and gnarled fingernails crack and chip as the hand pulls. She screams, kicking and flailing to get away. Almost as quickly as it appeared, the hand releases her. She scrambles backward, and the fingers ball into a fist. The middle finger pops up with a crack.

"What th—"

Her eyes scan the graveyard, spotting Garridan sitting in a tree. He grins, waving his hand through the air as if clearing smoke. The hand fades away, leaving the ground beneath it completely untouched.

Tera gets up and storms back into the tower, not stopping until she's inside Dringely's room. She slams the classroom door shut immediately behind her, locking it and stomping over to Professor Dringely, who sits behind her desk, snacking on a jollyberry cake and a cup of tea.

Dringely looks up at Tera, eyebrow cocked as she wipes crumbs from around her lips. "Is everything okay, Tera?"

"No. I need your help with something."

What are you doing?

"What's going on?" Dringely sets down the half-eaten cake and clears her throat.

"As a deathriser, what's the best way to stand up for myself against other paths?"

"What do you mean? Is another student bullying you?" She begins to pull out her harassment report forms from her desk.

"Not exactly. Let's just say this is all theoretical, okay?"

Dringely hums and lets her hand hover over the paperwork.

Tera leans across her professor's desk, her eyes wild and unblinking, and her words fast. "If someone were to be abusing their abilities as an illusion master by tormenting a deathriser... how could—how might—like... how can the deathriser show that they shouldn't mess with me? I mean *them!* The deathriser."

"Tera, if someone is bullying you, I'm obligated to report it to the administration. It'll stay anonymous."

"It's not a student."

"Oh?"

"Can you just give me the advice?" Tera asks, clenching and unclenching her fists. "Please?"

Professor Dringely takes a deep breath and sighs slowly. "Okay, how about this…" She leaves the report papers in the drawer and closes it. "I won't file a report. I won't tell administration—unless your life is in danger—but you tell me what's going on. That way I can help you better."

Tera crosses her arms, challenging her teacher. When Dringely doesn't flinch or speak, Tera eventually drops her arms. "Fine."

She pulls a chair over to her professor's desk and takes a seat with her elbows on its surface.

"It's one of the guys who killed Aeridonis. He knows Aeridonis and I are connected somehow, but I don't think he knows how or why. And he's been following me and watching me everywhere I go. But to make things even worse, he's been driving me nuts. He's an illusion master, and he keeps disappearing and appearing out of nowhere." She proceeds to tell Dringely about Garridan sitting outside her bedroom window, appearing in the deathrising tower after the incident with Traella, and what happened with the hand illusion in the graveyard.

"Tera!" Dringely's face is stern. "This man is dangerous. You can't just play pranks on him. I know he's bothering you and following you, but it's best if you just go about your life as normal as you can while Professor Leutrix and I work on separating you two."

I told you so.

Tera's face flushes red and she shoots up from the chair. "Forget I asked." She leaves, slamming the door again and pacing back and forth in front of it in the stairwell, her fingers snaking up to her hair and tangling themselves in her curls.

It's only when she spots Traella trudging out of another classroom door that the idea hits her. The corner of her lips twitch as she suppresses a smile, trying to stay casual as she heads upstairs to Professor Leutrix's classroom.

She knocks gently on the door, pushing it open enough to peek inside. Leutrix swoops to the doorway, seemingly out of nowhere.

"Miss Tera. Class doesn't start for an hour. What are you doing up here?" He peers through the crack.

"I just have a question."

Silence.

"I know we've been learning how to resurrect from a distance, but what if the corpse is underground?" Tera asks.

Stop it, Esotera. Leave that boy alone. You're going to cause more trouble.

"With or without consciousness?"

"Without."

Leutrix disappears from view and the door swings open. Tera steps inside, and her professor stands at his chalkboard, scribbling words in a messy font. She closes the door behind her, quietly locking it in hopes of keeping Garridan out.

"Sit," Leutrix commands, setting the chalk down and turning to face her. He motions to the seat closest to the board.

"Uh, okay." She joins him, sitting in the quiet before he finally speaks.

"Oriri obex."

"Wh—"

"Repeat it."

Tera scrunches her face at him.

He mimics her face. "If you're not interested in learning, you can leave my classroom now."

"I *am* interested, I'm sorry. I just—you caught me off-guard. Okay…" She fixes her posture. "Oriri obex."

"Good. As with any spell, with practice, you won't need to use the words. But until then—why aren't you writing this down?"

Tera's eyes bulge and she hurriedly pulls out her notebook and pen, scribbling the words down.

"This spell raises the dead in a state without conscious thought. It works through barriers and obstacles such as dirt, water, and brick. Similar to the spell we've been discussing in class recently, start with a hand on your head and one on your heart."

He displays the motions, and Tera mirrors him.

"Feel the energy charge from within. Pull the life essence from the plant life around you. More corpses require *more* energy and focus. For the sake of demonstration, I'm going to focus on teaching you how to raise one corpse through a barrier for now."

Tera nods.

"Focus your gaze on the direction of your corpse. If you need, you can close your eyes while you're pulling energy. Once you feel the energy peak, say the spell and flick your palms out." His hands swish in the silence of the classroom as he flips them around.

She repeats his move, and he nods, seemingly satisfied.

"Are you ready to practice?" he asks.

"Wh—right now?"

He looks at her expectantly.

"Uh… sure?" she replies.

Leutrix steps around his chalkboard and toward the morgue drawers against the wall. "This one here." He points to one of the drawers. "I want you to resurrect this one."

Tera can feel her heart thumping all the way in her stomach as she focuses on the one drawer, her hands on her head and her chest as she pulls energy from the plants hanging above. Energy pulses like electric waves through her feet, legs, stomach, until it reaches her fingertips with a stinging warmth.

"Oriri obex." She flicks her wrists out toward the drawer, feeling the energy tug at her fingertips and disappear suddenly.

Nothing happens.

She looks at Leutrix, who stands stiff, watching the drawer with his hands joined behind him.

"Did I d—"

Clang.

Tera stops, her eyes shooting toward the drawer just as it lets out another deep, metallic clang.

Just then, the drawer pulls open clumsily, bit by bit until its resident finds their way out into open air.

The deceased pyre elf from the drawer throws his legs over the side of his metal bed, dropping to the floor with a quiet *plat* of his bare feet on the stone floor.

"Can I put him to rest from a distance too?" Tera asks, carefully watching the pyre elf from the corner of her eye as she faces her professor.

"Very good, Miss Tera. Same as the standard resting spell but pull the energy and sweep inward."

Tera nods, half out of confidence and half out of need for self-assurance. She observes the pyre elf as he gathers his bearings, exploring the room around him for a moment. He reaches Leutrix's chalkboard, fingering a piece of chalk, picking it up and biting into it with a dusty crunch.

With a slow breath, Tera holds her palms out, her hands hovering in front of her forehead and chest as she pulls energy back from the corpse.

"Mori."

She flips her hands back to face her, and the pyre elf crumples like a doll on the floor with a thud.

Good gods, Esotera. If only more people pissed you off, you might actually be a half-decent student. Is that all you needed this whole time?

Tera groans, but when Leutrix glances at her, she turns it into a cough and a throat clear. "Excuse me," she says, patting her chest.

"Excellent work today," her professor says, lifting the pyre elf and setting him back in the drawer. "I think that's enough for one day. Make sure you get something to eat during your free period—there will be no snacking in my classroom because you neglected basic self-care."

"Yes, sir," Tera says. "Thank you."

She leaves, making her way to the Hub portal to grab a quick lunch with the remainder of her free time.

You might be able to answer this for me. As you know, deathrising is the only path I didn't truly bother studying, so you'll have to excuse my ignorance. That resting spell. "Mori." It means "die," doesn't it? Is it technically a killing curse?

"Technically, yes. Takes a *lot* more energy and focus to use it to actually kill someone. Doesn't take as much to put down an unconscious corpse because they don't have as much of a life essence." Tera pauses. "And before you ask, yes, I paid attention in class when Leutrix taught that. It was one of my first ever deathrising lessons, and one of my first ever experiences with Leutrix. Honestly, I think I just remember it because I was scared of what he'd do if I didn't." Tera chuckles, stepping through the portal and into the lobby of the Hub.

Makes sense. Thanks for the quick lesson. Enough talking to me for now. No way to tell if Garridan is listening.

Tera grunts and takes off toward the cafeteria.

Inside, she makes her rounds of the room, scanning the day's menus at each of the kiosks and stands. When she spots Kiran in line at the pastry bake shop, she hops in the queue behind him.

"Hey, Kir!" she says with a chirp.

He turns, eyebrow cocked and face flat. "Who died and took over Tera's body?" He looks her up and down. "What's got you so pleasant today?"

Her smile fades and her hands find their way to her hips. "What's that supposed to mean?"

"Nothing, I just didn't figure you'd be in such a good mood, all things considered."

She shrugs. "That's fair. I guess I'm just excited."

"About?"

"I can't really talk about it just yet, but I'll tell you when it's done."

"Wow, neat," Kiran says, his words laced with sarcasm.

Tera huffs. "It's not a big deal. I just… someone has been watching me. I can't talk too much."

"Watching you?" Kiran spins around completely to face her now, his eyes wide. "Are you talking ab–"

"Don't worry about it, I've got it under control."

Aeridonis scoffs, and Tera rolls her eyes.

"Why'd you r—" Kiran cuts himself off. "Oh. *He* said something, didn't he?"

Tera nods subtly, and her friend flips his silvery hair over his shoulder as he turns his back to her.

"What are you mad at *me* for?"

"I'm not mad at *you.*" He steps forward in line, ordering his food.

"Okay, so don't turn your back on *me!*"

He turns to her. "What am I supposed to do?"

"Same as always," Tera calls to him as he walks over to the pickup window. "As if he's not even there."

"But he—"

Tera throws her finger to her lips to shush him.

He purses his lips and sighs before giving a nod of acknowledgment.

"Thank you," Tera mouths, stepping up and placing her order at the counter.

Once she gets her food, Tera says a quick goodbye to Kiran and hurries off to the deathrising graveyard again. Just as she turns the corner to step out into the garden of tombstones, she trips over something invisible. Her thrasherfish hand pie flies from her grip, nearly falling to the grass, only to freeze in mid-air.

Garridan fades into view as if thick fog cleared out of the air around him. In his hand, he holds Tera's lunch, albeit a bit smooshed.

"Watch your step, Tera. Could've hurt yourself," he warns with narrowed eyes, holding out a hand.

She glares up at his hand, smacking it away as she stands on her own and brushes dirt and grass blades from her robes. "Enjoy the fish pie, asshole," she says, adjusting her curls before flouncing past him with her nose upturned.

"Oh, come on now," Garridan urges, holding out the mashed hand pie to Tera, who ignores him and strolls leisurely up and down the rows of tombstones. "Don't you want to eat something for lunch?"

"I would, but I gave it away to the needy."

Garridan chuffs, taking a greedy bite of fish pie, flaky crumbs fluttering to his feet. He walks over to the tall tree that looms over the far end of the graveyard, leaning against it while he eats.

Tera continues scanning the etchings on the headstones, occasionally throwing a glance Garridan's way.

"So, I overheard you in the valley," Tera calls to him. He looks up from his food, his sharp ruby eyes nearly black in the shadows of the tree.

"So what?" he says through full cheeks.

"You don't think I'm a threat," Tera states, "because you saw my grades."

"My guess is the free rent at your parents' house is the only reason you're not a drop-out."

The comment stings, slicing at Tera's chest like a razor. "You gather all that about me just because I'm not good at school?"

You are *good at school, Esotera. You just don't apply yourself.*
She scoffs.

"I've seen elves like you a million times," Garridan says. "Ones who pick a path they think sounds cool, but then go to that first class and realize it's actually a lot of work. They do just well enough to not get kicked out of the program and either drop-out eventually *or* graduate by some miracle of the gods and end up never finding a job because who would want a worker that doesn't truly know the basics of their path?"

Tera's silent, moving onto another row of graves, squatting at one labeled *gronnet*.

"Which will you be, Tera?"

His focus returns to his half-eaten hand pie just as students begin filing through the graveyard on their way to classes after the free period.

Tera takes advantage of the distracting crowd. She places one hand on her head and one on her chest, pulling energy from the thick grass tickling her legs.

"If it makes you feel better"–he pauses to swallow a bite–"I'm sure a lot of these other kids are the same as you. So at least you're not the only one."

She flips her palms out and mutters, "Oriri obex," under her breath.

What are you doing? Don't do this!

The grass around her starts to wither and die.

"I noticed you have siblings, Tera. Are they as big of disappointments as you?" He sucks the grease and crumbs from a finger, rubbing the now-wet finger on the hem of his robes.

Tera sighs, keeping a straight face as she stands and walks over to him. He doesn't even look up at her, instead, he picks at a stray cuticle.

"I think you underestimate me," she says plainly, cutting him a look.

"Hah. Maybe I underestimated your inability to get a hint. Arboreal elves aren't meant to be deathrisers. You're kidding yourself if you think otherwise. I'm not sure what value Aeridonis sees in you or why he's working with you."

The ground at the base of the gronnet's headstone begins shifting. Tera's eyes dart toward it and she forces herself to refocus on Garridan, raising her voice.

"If I'm not a threat, you'll have no problem telling me where you took the draxxi."

"Is that your play here?" He laughs. "You're acting weird—but I'm sure that's normal for you. Didn't figure you'd try a blatant attempt at getting intel. You're even dumber than you let on."

"Me? Dumb? *You're* the one who doesn't think I'm a threat."

"Cute," he says, his tongue leeching sarcasm.

Tera shrugs with a smirk.

Just then, the ground beneath the tombstone parts as the gronnet corpse digs its way through. It hoists itself onto its two legs. Nostrils flared, it holds its head high, wetly sniffing the air.

Students walking by to access the tower side door shoot the gronnet a glance over their shoulders, not giving it much thought. Resurrected corpses in the graveyard are hardly anything unusual for a deathrising student.

At this point, the gronnet has Garridan's attention. He looks over at it nonchalantly. Once it's latched onto Garridan's fish pie breath, it turns to face him. Its huge mouth drops open, revealing a green, wet cavern. The gronnet's fat lip quivers, a thick strand of saliva oozing to the ground, which it promptly steps in as it marches toward Garridan.

He lets out an airy chuffle, looking at the pastry crumbs left on his hands. "Fish. Clever." Beckoning to the gronnet with a finger, calls out to it.

Tera takes a few steps back, observing.

Once the mindless gronnet corpse is hardly more than a few feet away, Garridan snaps his fingers and disappears. Tera can feel herself tensing up as she watches, hoping and praying her idea works.

The gronnet continues its pursuit, reaching out with slimy fingertips. It grabs onto something—Garridan—who yelps before the gronnet slurps his head right into its mouth in one swift motion. The illusion spell fades, and all the passing students stop to watch as the gronnet noisily sucks on Garridan's head.

A couple of girls stop in the doorway, pointing and giggling at the scene. Tera beams, watching with her arms crossed. She allows it to continue for a moment, watching

Garridan's legs kick blindly as the spit begins soaking through the fabric on his shoulders and chest.

She finally decides to release him, not wanting to be late to class and not wanting to leave a mindless corpse at large in the graveyard. The gronnet goes limp, flopping to the floor and tugging Garridan down with it.

Tera steps over to his side, nudging him with the toe of her shoes. "Can you hear me?"

There's a muffled gurgle and a thrash of splayed legs.

"Good. I just want to know, Garridan… Boy who underestimated me and learns to leave well enough alone… or corpse-brain who needs to be taught another lesson: Which will *you* be?"

She turns her back to him, leaving him to struggle with the weight of the gronnet. The campus crypt keeper will rebury the corpse tonight and lay fresh sod, and Tera doesn't care if it takes Garridan all day to break free.

CHAPTER FIFTEEN

DEADSKIN IN THE LIBRARY

"You need to tell me what's going on, right now." Zeyla snatches Tera's arm just as she walks through the front door, whisking her off to her bedroom and shutting the door behind them both.

"I can't," Tera says.

"That's a load of seiva."

"I *can't*. I'm not making it up this time to tease you or anything. It's really for your own good that I don't tell you."

"It's clearly something bad. Kiran's curse was no joke. I've never felt so sick in my life. But you trust Aston and not *me?* You can tell me!"

Tera shakes her head, her expression grave.

Good job, Esotera. I know it's hard keeping this secret, but it's for your family's safety.

A heavy pit grows in Tera's stomach when she sees the genuine hurt on her sister's face.

"Fine. I'll figure it out myself then. Always do. Get out." Zeyla opens her door and shoves her sister out—her strength surprising for someone with such a tiny frame.

"I'm sorry," Tera says as Zeyla slams the door shut. She sighs, moseying down the hall to her own room.

To her surprise, Aston is already inside, sitting at her desk. She turns, spotting Kiran cross-legged on her bed. She glances back and forth between them, but they just look at her with confused and scrunched faces.

"Why are you guys looking at me like *I'm* the one who shouldn't be in here?" she asks, closing the door behind her and standing between them, hands on her hips.

"We've got to do something about the marrow elves and the draxxi," Kiran says without a second's pause.

"Yeah, duh. I know that."

"So, what are you doing about it?" he asks.

Her lip curls up and she stutters, searching for words. "I'm working on it!"

"Are you though?" Aston chimes.

Tera's face begins to burn, and she cuts him a harsh look.

"I'm just wondering," he says, holding his hands up in surrender. "We haven't heard anything yet and I don't feel like this is the kind of thing we can just sit on and wait."

Tell them you'll be making an appointment with the Council. You kids don't need to be taking this on.

"Enough!" Tera shrieks, and the boys jump in their seats at the sound. "I don't know what to do, okay? I just want things to go back to normal. It's too much and I'm not cut out for a rescue mission. It was one thing when he wanted me to go feed his pets, but this is something totally different. I can bring mindless corpses back from the dead and I can set stuff on fire. And I can make a pretend wall. That's literally all I know how to do. So, if you've got some great idea, s—"

Her bedroom door opens and her mother peers in, her brow furrowed. "Is everything okay in here?"

"School drama," Kiran bursts back.

She looks between her son and daughter, who just stare at her expectantly.

"Alright. Don't stay up too late—you've got school in the morning," she says, easing the door closed again.

"I *know!*" Tera whines back, loud enough for her mother to hear through the walls.

You don't have to be cut out for any of this Tera. Let the Council handle it. Please.

"I don't even want to have to deal with the Council, okay?" she spouts, staring at the ground as she speaks. "I want you out of my head so you can deal with this mess! I'm done."

"You want *who* out of your head?" asks a fourth voice.

The friends all turn to the source. Garridan leans against Tera's window from inside her room, smiling as though he belongs.

Tera stands speechless, shutting and opening her eyes several times, fully convinced he's nothing more than a hallucination from too much stress.

He finger waves at Tera. "Hey, Tree Girl."

I told you to be careful.

"You jus—I don—this isn't fair! Get out of my room!" Paralyzed by the situation, she freezes in place, looking at the ceiling and blinking rapidly to will the bubbling tears back into her eyes before they can tumble.

She takes a slow, shaky breath before looking Garridan in the eyes.

"What do you want from me? What will it take for you to leave me alone?"

"Tell me where Aeridonis is and what it is he wants with *you.*"

"I assure you, he wants *nothing* to do with me."

Garridan sneers. "Stop toying. You want people to see you as some sort of badass who's different from everyone else, but you act like literally every other teenage girl I've ever met." He begins stepping closer and closer to Tera as he speaks. "Get a backbone and start making some big girl moves, or tell me what I need to know so you can go back to scraping by in classes, gossiping about boys, and getting smoothies with your besties."

At this point, he's inches from her face, looking down on her. She can't help but to stare back at him, completely disarmed. As soon as she breaks away from his gaze, she realizes they aren't in her room anymore. Instead, they're in an empty library with towering oak shelves covered in worn leather books. The edges of the shelves seem to disappear in endless darkness, and only the space around the two of them is warmed by the amber light of lanterns strung from the ceiling.

"Where—what happened?" she asks, stumbling backward.

"Don't worry about it. Your friends are safe. This is just a bit of privacy so we can talk."

"Talk?" Tera scoffs, running her fingers through her curls and latching her hands on top of her head as she scans the room for an exit. "I don't *want* to talk to you. What aren't you getting about that?"

He pops into view directly in front of her again, grabbing her face between his cold hands. He takes one hand and taps her forehead with a long, slender finger.

"How'd he get in here?" he asks softly.

Tera feels a boulder in her stomach as the room begins to spin.

"What's happening?" she asks, her vision turning to static and her ears beginning to ring.

"Oh, probably just the blood loss."

"Blo—" She looks down, squinting through her fuzzy vision. Her left arm dangles there without a hand, the flesh marred and tattered like old rags. Blood pours from her bare wrist, landing in a thick puddle on the library floor with heavy drips.

Tera's body begins to feel like it's hardening, turning into a statue as she freezes, panicked and disoriented.

Garridan reaches out his arms to catch her just as her legs give out.

"What's hap—" Her words fade and her eyelids flutter.

"What's happening is I'm inside your mind. None of this is real. You're still back in your room with your friends. But I can make this go on for what feels like eternity. Or I can make it all stop now. Your choice."

Tera's vision begins to clear, and the warmth travels down to her fingers and toes again. She holds her arms up, wiggling the fingers on both hands. The floor shows no trace of blood.

Garridan disappears from behind her, no longer offering her support. She stumbles, and he appears again in front of her.

"So, what's it gonna be, Tree Girl?"

Tera struggles for words before she breaks down sobbing, curling up on the floor and putting her head between her knees.

Garridan lets out a mixture of a sigh and a groan, taking a moment before sitting beside her. "Was that a bit too extreme?"

Tera's body heaves with every cry, and Garridan tentatively places a hand on her back.

"It's okay. Maybe I shouldn't have done that. I'm truly sorry. Here, let me see your hands. Are they okay?"

Her sobs begin to slow to shakes and sniffles, and she peers over her knees at him. He's holding his palms out and open, giving her a nod and a soft smile. Her stomach flutters, and she slowly extends her arms out, placing her hands in his.

"Ahh," he says, his entire expression softening. "See? To-tally fine!"

He holds up her hands, her fingers gnarled at the joints, bent in every sort of direction like a beast had gnawed on them.

She screams, ducking her head down between her knees and shaking.

"Ohh," he coos. "Do you want it to stop?"

"Please!" she says through whimpers.

He sniffs, smirking as he drops her hands and stands to his feet, looking down on her. "You *know* how to make it stop."

"Why does it matter how he got in my head?" she asks, never looking up.

"You don't have the leverage here to ask your own questions, Tera. Just tell me and I can let you go."

"But you won't though."

"Yes, I will."

"Not really. Once the marrow elves know everything, things are only going to get worse."

Garridan sighs, squatting in front of her and reaching out a hand. He tilts her gaze up with a finger under her chin. When her eyes reluctantly meet his, he smiles.

"They have no qualms with you. Only him. Tell me what I need to know and I can assure you, they'll separate the two of you. Your mind will be your own again."

Tera scoffs, rolling her eyes and wiping her nose with the back of her hand. "It doesn't work like that. No one has been able to separate us. It could kill me. Or wipe my conscious-ness and give Aeridonis my body."

"What?" He snorts. "What kind of incompetent elf do you have working on this? Of course we can separate you two! And *you'll* be perfectly safe."

"What about Aeridonis?"

Garridan shrugs.

"No," Tera says. "I can't tell you."

Garridan's gentle expression mutates. His brow buckles at the center, eyes searing through Tera, and a vein rages at his temple. He stands again, walking a few steps away from her before turning back again.

"I tried to be nice." He flicks his hand out and Tera wails as one of her ribs makes an audible snap.

"Enough!" booms a voice, echoing through the dark halls of the library.

Garridan freezes, his head spinning on his shoulders as he searches for the source.

"Where are you, wizard?" he calls out, backing into a shelf.

Aeridonis steps from the darkness, the lantern glow illuminating his weathered face.

Tera stares back at him, her mouth gaping open. She tries to speak, to ask questions, but all that comes out is sputtered and broken syllables.

Aeridonis shoots her a brief look of amusement through his crinkled eyes before he turns his focus back to Garridan.

"Had your fill of bullying yet?" he asks, slow-stepping closer to the boy.

Garridan holds his position, straightening his shoulders and keeping his head high.

"You think they value you, boy?" Aeridonis asks.

"Of course they do. That's a stupid question. Why do you think they picked me to finish you off, old man?" Garridan takes his time with his words, savoring each one. He looks Aeridonis up and down, devouring him whole from top to bottom like a snake with its prey.

"Need I remind you, you didn't quite succeed." Aeridonis chuckles warmly. "It seems Miss Esotera might even be a better student than you ever were."

Tera's face stings at the dig, but she sits quietly, easing herself into a standing position while the men bicker.

Garridan scoffs, his eyes flicking toward her as he snaps his fingers. Both of her legs buckle beneath her weight, and she crumples like a ragdoll to the ground.

"Enough!" Aeridonis claps his hands together with a boom. The shelves rattle and Tera's vision goes completely white. When she reopens her eyes, she's lying in her bed, with Kiran and Aston hovering over her.

"Oh, thank gods." Kiran heaves a sigh of relief and puts his hands over his eyes, running his fingers back through his long hair.

"W-uh?" Tera murmurs, propping herself up with an elbow. She squints, blinking rapidly to clear the fuzzies from her vision.

"I thought you died or something," Kiran says. "The guy disappeared and then you were like totally catatonic. Eyes rolled back in your head and just kinda keeled over."

"He was in my head," Tera mumbles, rubbing the side of her face and sitting up.

"What do you mean, 'in your head'?" Aston asks.

"One minute I was in the room, the next minute, I wasn't." She begins to explain to them about the library, the torture, and Aeridonis saving her.

"Woah," Kiran says. "That's freaking wild. Like, you could physically see Aeridonis this time? In his old body?"

"Yeah, I guess."

"That's so wild," Aston mutters, staring at Tera's forehead.

"Can we stop talking about Aeridonis for once and focus on the real issues at hand?" Kiran asks, his expression stern, arms crossed tight over his chest.

Tera and Aston exchange surprised looks.

"What?" Kiran snaps.

Tera starts, "It's just, you're–"

"Not anymore," he finishes.

Wow. Bit of a sensitive one, isn't he?

"Regardless of your personal feelings," Aston says, "we need his help with this."

You're still not going to confront the marrow elves. You're going to talk to the Council and let them handle it.

"Are you for real, Don?" Tera spouts, sitting up further in her bed. Aston and Kiran jump at her sudden outburst.

"What's he saying?" Aston asks.

"Who cares?" Kiran replies.

"Shut up!"

"Guys." Tera cuts them a harsh look. "Stop."

"What's he saying?" Aston asks again.

Tera holds up a finger to shush him so she can speak to Aeridonis.

"You can't seriously just tell me to sit back and let this keep happening until the Council thinks it's convenient to meet with me. They're not going to believe me in the first place." Tera's eyes begin to well up with hot tears. "I can't go through this again. Garridan's never going to leave me alone."

That's why you're going to visit Illidara again. See if she can teach you something to keep an illusion master from breaking into your headspace again.

Tera goes silent for a moment, thinking about his idea. She nods slowly to herself, sniffling. "Okay. That'd be a good starting place, at least. Then we'll discuss talking to the Council. Maybe. But I'll do anything to keep him from doing that to me again."

Aeridonis sighs. *I'll take it. For now.*

CHAPTER SIXTEEN

PERIPETEIA

The next day, Tera skips her first class. Sending Steve with a letter would be too risky, so she sends Kiran to let Professor Dringely know she'd be absent. She forces down breakfast, puts on her school robes, and waves goodbye to her mom as she would any normal morning before school.

After taking the portal to Pipwerry, she leaves the Hub quickly, hurrying along the path to Teretatian.

"How did you get him out of my head?" Tera asks in a hushed voice, keeping pace and checking over her shoulders.

A lucky guess.

"What?"

I've never been in that situation before. To be fair, I've also never lived in someone's head before. I was down the hall and heard voices for the first time. I went to check it out and saw what he was doing to you. I had to make a logical guess on a spell to knock his focus and get him out of your head. I cast an illusion interrupt spell to break his focus. Luckily, that's all it took. But I can't keep him from coming back in—not when I'm stuck in here. He should leave you alone for a bit though. I used a pretty heavy-duty stunning spell. He'll probably be a bit dazed for a day or two with migraines.

"Huh. Well, thank you." She pauses for a minute. "Wait a minute. You said, 'down the hall.' What does that mean?"

I was in the study.

"My brain has a study?" Tera scoffs with a wide grin.

I mean, it's kind of just a room with an empty desk, papers, pens, and a lamp. So, I assume it's a study.

"Maybe it's a drawing room."

Aeridonis mutters. *You know, that's probably what it is. Anyways, yes. There are just a few rooms. I tend to hang out in the study... err... drawing room. There's an armchair in there that's good for napping. That's also where I watch through your eyes. Just sort of appears on the wall. Pretty hard to miss. Anyways, the library is just down the hall.*

"That's kind of cool." Tera smiles to herself, her joy fading quickly when she spots the letter nailed to the village portal gronnet's cottage.

Out for personal matters.

Please visit Yuledaria for the next

nearest portal gronnet.

Thank you.

"What am I supposed to do now?" Tera asks, stepping closer to reread the note. "I can't walk all the way to Yuledaria! I'll miss half the school day. Leutrix won't be nearly as forgiving as Dringely. Bet ten coins he'd immediately send my parents a note. They'd never let me walk to school alone again."

You might have to try your luck with your gronnet friend.

Tera tosses her head back and moans. "Please, no."

It's either that or another date night in your head with Garridan.

Her head shoots straight again. She takes a deep breath and nods. "Fine. I'll try."

She begins the trek back to Pipwerry, her fingers slithering up her scalp and searching for the rough edges of her scab.

When she rounds the corner of the portal room, a sharp voice bites through the white noise of student chatter. Tera nearly launches out of her skin, fire spell at the ready in her hand.

"Tera!" Verity calls. "Where have you been?"

"Uh," she stammers.

"Emmaline has been asking about you, and I haven't had any kind of answers for her because for all I knew, your parents murdered you for sneaking out and going to Summercloud. She said she sent you a letter a while back and you never replied."

"Oh," Tera says with a whine. "I'm so sorry. I didn't mean to ignore you guys. It's just been a rough month. I've had my hands full trying to pick up my grades. I swear I'll plan some kind of girl's night or something soon, okay?"

Verity's stunned face says it's not, in fact, okay.

"I promise," Tera begs. "I've just got a lot going on right now. Nothing fun. Nothing nearly as good as hanging out with you and the group. I miss it so much. Which is why it'll be the first thing I do when my parents loosen up a bit. But at this rate, I'll be grounded for life. I really need to go get some pieces together for this project. But I promise!"

Tera's eyes are wild, and Verity analyzes her for a moment before giving a half-hearted nod.

"Alright. Just take care of yourself. We're getting worried about you. Plus, you're lookin' rough." She smirks, giving Tera a quick hug and bounding down the hall to the cafeteria.

Once Verity disappears, Tera turns her attention to the portal master's door. She grits her teeth and wills herself to knock.

The door opens and there's an immediate, "How can we h—" before Trevitt stops, his cheery smile falling. "Tera."

"Hey." She raises a limp hand in an awkward greeting.

He steps out of the office, gently shutting the door behind him and turning to face Tera, his arms crossed. "How's Kiran?"

"Much better. Zeyla was able to heal him. Thanks for asking."

The silence is only broken when a couple of younger students walk into the portal room, chatting and giggling on their way into the lifebringing portal. Tera's eyes glance out of her peripheral, waiting for them to step through the portal. When they're gone, she clears her throat and takes a deep breath.

"You already know what I'm here about," she admits, "and I wish I wasn't doing this again."

Trevitt's entire face contorts and twists like green putty until every feature seems to be pursed. "I'll do it, but only because I need the money. That is, if you remember to pay me."

Tera nods, her gaze and head low.

He opens the portal master's door, exchanging a few words with the gronnet behind the desk before heading out of the Hub. Tera hurries to catch up, surprised at his speed for such short legs and a wide body.

"Where to this time?" he asks when she catches up, following his lead along the path back to Teretatian.

"Xleria," she whispers.

"No doubt for some kind of" –he mimes with finger air quotes and rolls his eyes– "class project."

"Something like that," Tera mutters almost to herself as they near the village.

A few minutes of awkward silence pass before she speaks up again.

"How's your dad doing?"

The corner of Trevitt's mouth twitches into a frown, but he quickly steadies his emotions. "This is just business. You don't have to act like you care anymore. You're just a client now."

Tera's mouth hangs open a little and she racks her brain for something to say to show she cares, but it comes back blank.

When they pass by a couple quiet storefronts and trail down some narrow alleyways, Tera grabs the front of Trevitt's shirt and tugs him after her.

"This way," she urges, picking up the pace and checking over her shoulders. When they reach a restroom shed outside the village market, she pulls him inside with her, shutting the door and locking them in the dark room with its eggy stink.

"What's your problem?" He growls at her, crushing her hand and throwing it off of himself.

"I can't keep asking you to help me like this—"

He scoffs.

"I'm serious." She takes a shaky breath, running her hands through her hair and feeling the rough bump of her scab tempt her fingertips. "I didn't want to tell any more people than I absolutely had to, but I feel like I have to tell you why I need your help."

What are you doing? You're putting that boy in danger if you tell him. Esotera, stop! You've told too many people already. You don't understand wh—

Trevitt sits down on the loose toilet seat, and it creaks under his weight. "It doesn't matter what you say."

"I know it doesn't. Nothing will fix the damage I did to the friend group or to you. I know you've been feeling used, and I don't blame you for that. But I hope you'll at least understand why I did it if you just let me explain."

He's silent, thinking for a moment.

"Just let me make you this portal and move on with my day. I have to get back to work."

"No. Listen…" Tera covers the moon-shaped cut-out on the wooden door, hoping to stifle as much sound as possible. She begins filling him in on the details about the draxxi and Aeridonis living in her head. She skips as many random details as possible, like *how* Aeridonis wound up in her head.

"Oh my gods, Tera, you'll do anything for attention won't you?" he says with a snarl. "The man's missing and you're using that for pity? That's disgusting."

"If you don't believe me, you can ask my professors," she adds.

Trevitt shakes his head. "You shouldn't be telling me this."

"I know. I didn't want to involve you in this, but I wanted you to know I haven't been doing this for some stupid selfish reason. I'm trying to do what Aeridonis needs me to do to keep things from getting worse while we try to figure out how to get him out of my head."

"Stop," Trevitt commands, standing up and shoving her aside. He bursts through the restroom door and back out into the searing daylight. "I don't want to hear all this."

"I'm sorry, I just—"

"Stop," he repeats, turning a corner and walking down another alley. "Let me make this portal and then leave me alone."

Tera's jaw cocks to the side and she rolls her eyes. "Fine."

He raises his hands, drawing up a shimmering aqua portal.

Just as she raises a foot to step through, Trevitt shoots his arm across her path. She gives him a scrunched look, which fades to relief when she spots the summoning stone in his hand.

"Oh." She giggles nervously. "I can't believe I almost forgot one. Thank you."

"Consider it a rental."

She smiles flatly, giving a singular nod of her head before closing her fingers around the stone and stepping through the portal.

The harsh brilliance of Xleria stings Tera's eyes, and she instinctively ducks her head, shielding her face with her arm. She grunts, her eyelids fluttering rapidly until her vision adjusts enough to squint and take in her surroundings.

Xleria sparkles in front of her, with its towering crystal structures hovering over the clouds below.

"Gods," Tera says with a deep sigh. "I don't think anything in Evalyra could beat this place."

What do you mean?

"It's like walking in a painting. I thought it'd feel less beautiful the second visit, but I think I like it even more this time. Well, what I can see, at least." She rubs her eyes, vibrant colors melding against the insides of her eyelids as she does.

Focus, kid.

"Yeah, yeah, old man. I'm working on it. If you were actually here, we'd still be waiting on you to catch up to us in the village anyways, so don't whine to me about hurrying up."

Is that another old person joke?

She snorts, grinning to herself as she approaches the long staircase above the cloudy chasm.

I know you think I'm old, Aeridonis says, *but your old people jokes might have me beat.*

"Whatever you say," she dismisses him, taking two steps at a time until her legs begin to grow heavy.

When she reaches the top, she stops to stretch and catch her breath. Looking around, she realizes she doesn't remember where to go beyond this.

"Hey, Don?"

Silence.

"Don?"

More silence.

"Aeridonis?"

I'm giving you the silent treatment.

She snuffs, smiling. "You're not supposed to tell some-one when you're giving them the silent treatment."

Well, you weren't getting the message.

Tera groans, running her fingers through her curls. "You know, when people tell you to stay young and all that, they don't mean do childish stuff like giving someone the silent treatment. This is serious."

Wow. So, you are *able to tell when matters are serious? Could've fooled me.*

"Stop joking around." Her smile fades and she crosses her arms. When a couple of crystal elves wander past her, deep in conversation, she bites her tongue and pretends she's still stretching.

Once they pass, she speaks again, her voice lower this time.

"I forgot how to get to Illidara's house."

Your generation is the worst about that, you know that? You don't pay attention to your surroundings, so you never remember how to get places. You'd be lost without me, admit it.

"Well, at this rate, I'm lost *with* you, Don."

He grumbles something indistinguishable and tells her to take the path to her right.

Aeridonis continues to guide her through the crystal city, having to redirect her attention at one point when she pauses, admiring her reflection in the side of one of the iridescent crystal buildings. She picks at her coiled curls, watching them spring back into place as she tilts her head and watches the way the warm colors of her skin look against the cool crystals.

If you're done making yourself look pretty, can we move on?

"Aww, Don! You think I'm pretty?" Tera coos and giggles.

He doesn't have to say anything for Tera to feel his disdain. She looks at herself grinning in the glassy surface for a sec-ond longer before turning on her heel and continuing along the way. Every time she passes another crystal elf, she throws them a nonchalant head nod or wave and keeps moving.

Recognize it yet?

"Yeah, I think so. It's the one that looks like a big crystal," Tera says flatly, her eyes scanning over the front doors of a half dozen crystal homes.

Don't sass me. I was asking a question. The second one. To your left.

"Thank you."

Tera reaches a fist up to knock on the door, but before she can, it begins melting, sliding down the wall and globbing together in a sticky-looking puddle at the base of the building.

She eyes the blob of door by her feet, nudging it with her toe. It sticks to the tip of her shoe as she pulls her foot back, stretching it into a strand of shimmering slime.

"Eughhh."

I wish I could tell Illidara this is no time for her games.

"Illidara," Tara calls out, shaking her foot free from the goop, "I really need your help. Please. I don't know where else to go."

The door almost instantly appears back on the wall. Tara glances down at the floor and the glob is gone. When she looks back up, Illidara stands there, hands on her hips.

"Why didn't you say something sooner?" she asks, ushering Tera in. "Come!"

Tera obliges, and Illidara closes them both inside the house.

"What's troubling you, love?" Illidara asks. She sits on her couch, patting the seat for her house guest.

"It's this illusion master marrow elf. He knows Aeridonis is in my head. He, like, went inside my head and took me with. I don't really know how or what exactly it was he did, but it was like a library or something. And he did all this stuff to me in there. Made it feel like my arms were ripped off and stuff like that. Aeridonis stunned him, and the marrow elf and I both got knocked out of there but I'm so scared he's going to do it again an—"

"Oh, dear," Illidara coos as Tera begins to blubber.

Illidara gets up, disappearing into another room and returning a moment later with a teacup, rattling against its matching saucer as she hurries back to her guest.

"Thank you," Tera manages, taking the tea from Illidara's outstretched hands. She tries to bring herself to take a polite sip, but pauses, her lip quivering. "Can you help?"

"Absolutely!" She nods over and over, her hand placed gently on Tera's knee. "Ugh, you poor thing."

"It's fine. I really don't need you feeling bad for me." She sniffles, running the back of her wrist against her nose and quickly sweeping away the tears on her cheeks with her thumbs. "I just want to keep him from doing that again. It's bad enough I feel like he's constantly there watching me, but it's another when he's literally in my head, too."

"Well, he's most definitely not in my house. I'd be able to see him." Illidara smiles and sits up straighter. "It's just me and you. And Aeridonis." Her eyes flick to Tera's forehead as if addressing the wizard's physical presence.

Tera visibly relaxes into her seat, allowing herself to sip at her tea.

"So, you know how you said you were in a library in your head?" Illidara asks.

Tera nods, taking another drink of hot, bitter tea.

"That's basically your memory bank. It's in the heart of your mind. And there's a door that leads into it from the outside. Keeping intruders out is actually a lot easier than you might think." When she sees Tera's look of pleased re-lief, Illidara beams at her and continues. "Basically, you just lock the door!"

"What? How?"

"Here…" Illidara takes the teacup and sets it on a short table. "Do this." She clasps her hands as if in prayer in front of her chest and then closes her eyes.

Tera follows her lead. When nothing happens, she peeks through one eye at her instructor.

"You need to clear your thoughts. Don't focus on anything. Not sounds, sights, smells, feelings, ideas. Easier said than done, I know."

"Okay?"

"Fortunately, this is a lot easier to do if you've been in your own headspace before. Which, you have! Once everything else is clear from your mind, paint the picture of that library in your mind. Make the thought so strong it takes over your senses until it's as if you can feel the books with your fingertips."

There's silence for a moment.

"Then," Illidara continues, "find the door. Lock it."

Tera's eyes shoot open. "What?"

"Lock the door," Illidara repeats, cocking an eyebrow.

"There's no way that does anything."

Illidara's smile fades and she glares at Tera, snapping her fingers. Suddenly, the high crystal ceiling and cozy couch of the living room are no more. Once again, Tera finds herself inside her mind's library, curled up on the cool wooden floor.

This time, Illidara hovers over her with crossed arms. "Get up."

Tera obeys, and the second she's on her two feet, Illidara snatches her by the wrist and pulls her down several rows of old books. She stops when they reach a heavy wooden door in a dark corner of the room.

"See that?" she asks Tera.

She nods and reaches for the thick metal lock, turning it with a thunk.

"Okay, while that's good in theory, I'm already in here." She unlocks the door. "Lock it when there isn't someone hanging out in your mind."

"What about me?" Aeridonis asks, peering out from around one of the bookshelves.

Illidara gasps, her face illuminating as she bounds toward Aeridonis, wrapping him in a bear hug. "How are you, dear friend?"

"I mean"–he looks down at his body, arms out–"it would be nice to have my body back, but I suppose it's gone for good."

"Once we get you outta here, I'll cast the best body illusion spell you've ever seen. We'll get you looking just like you should." She slaps him on the back a bit too aggressively and he lurches forward.

He smiles half-hearted. "As I should? Somehow I doubt you mean you'll make me look like the hunk I once was."

Tera tries not to laugh, biting her lip and distracting herself with a frayed cuticle.

"I see you laughing, Esotera," Aeridonis calls over to her.

Tera steels herself before turning to face him. "What? Oh, no. Sorry, I was just thinking about something from earlier."

"He really used to be quite the looker back in the day," Illidara defended.

Tera stares at her, her brow scrunched. "You don't look like someone who shares the same 'back in the day' as Don."

"Beauty illusion." Illidara winks.

"Nuh uh." Tera shakes her head, refusing to believe it.

The young and bright crystal elf before her begins to meld into a pale pink old woman with wrinkles spiderwebbing from the corners of her hollow eyes— one of which is shrouded by the veil of a cataract.

"Absolutely stunning." Aeridonis beams at her, his hands clasped in front of him.

"Stop it, you!" Illidara says, her laugh warm and deep.

"I hate to kill the reunion," Tera interjects, "but I've really got to get going. Can we just practice the thing? Sorry." Her cheeks sting as the two elder elves lock eyes with her.

"Yes, of course," Illidara says, her beauty spell erasing her age once again.

After exiting Tera's mind space, Illidara runs her through the exercise a few times until she is able to successfully keep her instructor from invading her head by locking the door.

"So, because I locked it, is it locked for good? Until I unlock it?"

Illidara shakes her head. "Sadly, no. Its natural state is to be unlocked, so the brain will keep fighting the lock. Just check up on it every now and again, especially when that pesky marrow elf is around."

"And why can't Aeridonis lock it?"

"He's not technically of your mind, so he can't manipulate anything meaningful in there. He's just a presence. Almost like a ghost." Her voice begins to chill, sounding distant and icy. "Just floating around." Illidara looks down at her hands and sighs.

A shiver ripples across Tera's skin and she can't help but feel a tug deep in her chest.

"I really appreciate your help," she tells the crystal elf.

"Always happy to share what I know." Illidara takes Tera's hand in both of hers. "You're always welcome back. And next time, I won't even melt the door!"

Illidara escorts Tera out with a hug goodbye. Just before she closes the door, Tera turns around to speak.

"We're going to get him a body of his own," Tera says in a whisper, "I promise."

"When you do, you send him my way." Illidara winks. "And don't forget about me. When I said you're always welcome, that's not just limited to when he's in there." She taps on her temple.

Tera nods, thanking her again before making the walk back toward the edges of the floating city.

"Don't think I didn't pick up what was getting put down back there," Tera says with a smirk, beginning the descent down the long flight of crystalline stairs over the cloudy void.

What are you talking about?

"The flirting! You have a thing for her, don't you?"

Out of nowhere, Garridan pops into being, blocking Tera's path down the stairs.

"I tried to play nice," his slithering voice cuts.

She turns to run, but in one swift movement, he launches her over the side of the railing and down to the clouds below.

CHAPTER SEVENTEEN

WHAT LIES BEYOND THE CLOUDS

Tera rips through the clouds, plunging toward white nothingness. She screams, but her voice seems to disappear into the light around her. The staircase above shrinks until it disappears entirely. She's enveloped in nothing but blinding white.

With no way to tell which direction is up and which is down, her stomach starts doing flips.

Esotera! Hands out. 'Non cado.' Say it!

She wails, clawing at air.

Hands out.

More screams, drowning out Aeridonis's voice.

Now! ·

Tera shoots her arms out in front of her.

Non cado.

"Non cado!" she screams through the clouds.

Her body lurches, stopping mid-fall. She floats there, hovering in white, with copper curls flowing around her as if underwater.

She coughs, her lungs desperately grabbing for air. When she finally catches her breath, she lets her arms fall to her sides.

"Don? How do I get down? Or… up?"

Swim.

"What?"

Oh, don't tell me you don't know how to swim.

"I can! But in… like… air?"

Um… like… yes?

"No need to be snarky," she says, gradually beginning to kick her legs and scoop her hands in front of her. She can't help but smile as her body rotates.

Kick your legs more. You're just going to keep spinning.

Tera moves her legs, feeling weightless. There's no resistance as she paddles her feet.

Are you going the right way?

"I don't know," she says with an airy laugh.

After a few minutes, her joy begins to melt away and the sickening chill of panic leeches in. The white of the abyss below Xleria seems to never end. No color or shapes show themselves in the clouds—only more white. The air begins to feel suffocating.

It's only during Tera's next hesitant move that she spots it. A smudge of rich green tears into the blinding white expanse, growing larger and larger with each stroke. She swims toward it with renewed drive.

The closer she gets, the clearer the shapes become. Lush trees bloom from the green, reaching out to her in the clouds. She stretches a hand out when she nears them, but the weightlessness of the sky gives way to gravity.

Tera crashes down toward the tree with a scream. She throws her hands out, clawing for a grip on the branches. Limbs scrape her face and arms as she tumbles through thick leaves, coming to a sudden halt when her arms finally find a branch to wrap around.

Eyes wide and heart racing, she hangs from the tree. Legs dangling above wispy dew-covered grass, Tera takes a breath, bracing herself and dropping. Her feet hit the ground, but her balance fails and her legs crumble. Faceplanting into the wet grass with a thud, she groans.

I don't know if you can hear, but I'm clapping. What a fun dive!

She roars in a pathetic moan, leaving her face buried in the grass for a moment before working up the motivation to stand and assess herself for any injuries.

Her ankle stings from the poor landing, several shallow scrapes decorate her cheeks and arms in bright red blood, and her robes suffered some tearing, but all in all, she considers herself in good shape.

"Why didn't you tell me the spell would stop working?" she asks.

Seems like there was a point where the sky beneath Xleria transitioned into the sky above wherever we are now. Interrupted the spell or something, perhaps. Or, more likely, you just lost focus. He chuckles.

She groans, rolling her eyes.

Now able to focus on her surroundings, Tera looks over this new land. Almost immediately, her entire face scrunches.

"What the..." she trails off, taking careful steps toward the familiar structures of homes built into trees. "Darkwood? Something doesn't feel right."

I don't think it's your home.

"I don't think so either," Tera says, her eyes locking on a singed and moss-covered skeleton at the base of a nearby tree.

She wills herself forward, closer to the homes. Up above, the white sky she had fallen through melted out into an unending, starless dark sky. The circle of white sky appears to be the main source of light in the darkened forest, its light tracing the leaves in white. The air is still, but silhouettes of branches dance across the grass before Tera as she moves underneath the trees.

"Where is everyone?" Tera asks quietly, taking soft steps up the side of one of the oversized trees.

I—

Aeridonis never replies.

She reaches the front door of the first home on the first level of the tree and gives it a gentle knock.

A minute passes with no answer. She knocks again with a little more force.

"Hello?" she calls, but no one replies.

Tera moves onto the next door, her veins going cold when she sees it's hanging off the hinges. The edges of the wood are blackened and splintering. Against her better judgment, she peeks her head into the home.

Wooden children's toys litter the floor, and the smell of must and smoke choke the air. She steps further inside, recognizing the layout of the home as similar to her own. Tera walks deeper into the home, picking up a piece of a wooden train and turning it over in her hands.

"Hello?" she tries, with no response.

She turns to leave, stopping dead in her tracks when she spots another skeleton. Protected from the elements, this one is free from growth and greenery, instead covered in dust. Bones lay scattered against the floor and the seat of the couch. Tera wonders how the bones even got into that strange position, but she doesn't plan to stick around long enough to find out.

A newfound urgency to her steps, she nearly sprints back to the front door, only pausing when she sees a name scribbled on the inside of the doorframe. Beside ticked lines at varied heights, sloppy child's handwriting spells the name *Garridan*.

Tera scoffs at the coincidence, but she can't shake off an uneasy feeling churning in her stomach.

Is Garridan a common name?

"Heck if I know. I just want to get out of here." She hurries the rest of the way out of the home and opts to go back downstairs.

She speed walks through the eerily familiar forest, never pausing to catch her breath. The air is completely still and silent, yet she feels a haunting presence lurking somewhere in the darkness. The hair on her neck pricks up at random, and she picks up the pace. It's only when she reaches the edge of the forest that she stops.

"Woah."

The forest's edge gives way to endless white sky at her feet.

"The sky needs to stay *above* me. This is too much." Tera motions to the clouds. "I just want to get out of here."

What if you go through again?

"Do I have to? Can't I just use the summoning stone?" She feels for the cool stone in her pocket.

Aren't you curious what's on the other side?

"Would *you* do it?"

Since when have you ever wanted to do what I would do?

"Since now."

I'd go for it.

Tera grumbles. "I was kind of hoping you'd say something else."

Like what?

She shrugs, knowing he can't see it.

With a deep breath, she steps off the land's ledge and into the clouds. Plummeting down once again, she thrusts her hands out before her and screams, "Non cado!"

Her fall stops and she begins floating, but it feels for a moment as if her stomach wants to *keep* falling.

"Ugh," she says, clutching her gut.

Everything alright?

"I just don't feel well. I kind of wish I just went to class and had a normal day."

You know it wouldn't have been normal though. That boy would have tormented you any chance he'd get. You needed the lesson from Illidara. The getting shoved over the stairs part, on the other hand...

"Let's just keep moving," she says, beginning to kick and stroke her way through the clouds again. "Poor Trevitt is stuck waiting around for me to summon him."

He's probably not just waiting around. I'm sure he went back to work.

"True. He's been pretty serious about that job. It's weird to see him so serious about anything."

Sounds like he doesn't really have a choice.

Tera frowns. "I know. I wish there was something I could do. I know we're not actually close, and I'm not saying I want him to start hanging around us again–I don't–but he's a good guy and doesn't deserve what's happening with his dad."

I can't really help you with this one, Esotera. Just do what you feel is right.

As she swims, she starts to notice a pinkish purple smear growing larger in the white sky.

"Looks like we're about to find out where we're headed next."

Stay focused this time. Be ready to recast the spell if you feel yourself falling. Don't want a repeat of the trees.

Tera nods to herself, readying her arms as she kicks a few more times.

The white gives way to the sharp tops of pastel-colored crystals. As she takes in her new surroundings, the spell breaks again, and she starts rapidly falling.

Hands in front of her, Tera calls out, "Non cado!" Her fall stops and she floats there, face-down and looking at the top of Xleria.

"There's no way," she says through a disbelieving chuckle.

Magic's a beautiful thing, isn't it?

"This hurts my head to even try to make sense of it."

Who said you need to make sense of it?

"Um. Don't you want to?" Tera begins swimming down toward the city, aiming for an open space between some of the crystalline buildings. "You can't honestly tell me you don't care to find out *how* we just fell through the sky beneath a city, landed in a place way too much like my home, fell through more sky, then landed on top of the city we fell from under. It hardly makes sense to even say that. Don, I'm so confused!"

Xleria hasn't always had the sky beneath it. I only know it opened up after we took control from the marrow elves. Xleria used to float over a forest on flat ground. I suppose I just assumed it was gone forever. Obliterated and left as an empty crater. I never would have guessed it fell beneath the crystal city. Truthfully, the Council never searched for it. I guess that's our fault for making assumptions.

Tera sighs. "There's no way I'm going to be able to pay attention in class today. The odds were already low when I started my day, but it's not happening now."

You'll have to at least show up for as much as you can. We can't have your parents buckling down on you too much. We've still got to get you to a meeting with the Council. After that, you're allowed to get as grounded as you'd like.

"Wow, gee, can I?"

Yes, you can.

Tera's expression goes flat, and she rolls her eyes.

As she nears the ground, she reorients herself to land feet-first. Gently, she eases herself down until the soles of her shoes make impact. She feels the spell lift as gravity drops her hair back into place around her shoulders with a springy bounce.

"Let's get out of here," she says softly, trotting toward the staircase once again. This time, she clings tight to the railing the entire way down.

At the edge of Xleria, she stops, reaching for her summoning stone and giving it a hurried rub. Minutes pass, and a portal eventually grows before her. Her chest drops as she heaves a huge sigh of relief. The second the portal fully forms, she throws herself into it.

On the other side, Trevitt stands with his arms crossed.

"Took you long enough," he says with a grunt. "Had to miss lunch. Didn't want to get caught in the middle of a meal and have to leave for a portal call."

"It's after lunch time?" Tera's heart flutters and a surge of energy bursts through her. "I've gotta go. Thank you!"

She reaches into her coin purse, pulling out some money and dropping it into Trevitt's outstretched hand before taking off in a sprint down the sidewalks of Teretatian.

Tera reaches Leutrix's classroom, the door already—unsurprisingly—closed. She picks at her scab for a moment before shaking her arms at her sides to let out the nervous energy. With a deep breath, she slowly turns the doorknob and pushes the door open just enough to squeak through the gap.

Everyone in class turns to stare, but she tries her best to ignore them, taking long strides to her desk and taking a seat.

"Kind of you to bless us with your presence, Miss Tera," Leutrix mutters, never turning to face her as he scribbles notes on the chalkboard.

"I'm sorry, professor," Tera says, her chair screeching against the hard floor as she sits.

He replies with a disgusted grunt but doesn't pause his frenzied scribbling.

The entire time in class, Tera's mind keeps fluttering back to the eerie village beneath Xleria. She wonders how many people even know about it, and what exactly happened to the people who once lived there.

There's a loud clap, shocking her out of her daydream.

"First, you have the audacity to show up late to my class, but then you refuse to answer questions when asked. Miss Tera, you're truly trying my patience today." Leutrix's stare burns through her and she sits upright.

"I'm so sorry professor, I'm just not feeling like myself today. May I go to the office?"

"Go."

Tera rises, tripping on the leg of her chair and knocking it to the ground. The sound echoes in the tall classroom. When she looks up, face stinging, she spots Garridan in the far back corner of class. He's biting his lip and trying to cover his mouth as he holds back a laugh. Once he has Tera's eyes, he snaps his fingers without making a sound, disappearing once again.

"Leave me alone!" Tera screams at him. "Stop following me!"

"Miss Tera, I need you to leave my classroom," Leutrix says, his eyes wide and brow furrowed.

"I—" She glances back at her professor and then at her classmates, who all look on in horror. Without another word, she dashes for the door, slamming it shut behind her.

She races down the stairs and only stops when she reaches the graveyard.

Trampling through the fresh sod, she stomps over to the maintenance shed at the far end of the graveyard. She hides behind it, praying to the gods that no one finds her.

Almost as soon as her back hits the wooden wall of the shed, she breaks down sobbing. Her entire body convulses with wet gasps, and she lowers herself to the ground, resting her face in her arms, bent over her knees. She takes a few deep, shaky breaths, focusing on her mindspace until she can see the door, locking it.

"I didn't figure you'd survive that fall." Garridan's voice rings out in the quiet graveyard.

Every nerve in Tera's body shocks to life and she scurries to her feet.

"I mean, it was rather impulsive. I'm not technically supposed to kill you or your brain buddy. I saw an opportunity and went for it. Bit reckless of me." He struts over to her and leans against a tree just across from her.

Tera watches him, her eyes searing with rage and sweat beads threatening to fall from her forehead.

He pushes away from the tree, stepping slowly toward her as he speaks.

"If I can be honest, I was a bit relieved to see you falling back down on Xleria. I wasn't sure what was under there–if anything at all. What'd you find?"

Tera snarls her lip at him. "Why're you asking me? It was your name I found down there."

"My… what?" Garridan's sneer fades and he narrows his eyes at her.

"Your name. Written on a door frame with little height markers or something."

"There was a house down there?"

"Bunch of them. Looked a lot like Darkwood, actually, but dead and empty. Come to think of it, it seems like some kind of illusion spell you'd pull just to screw with me." She furrows her brow even deeper.

Garridan's jaw slacks to the side and his eyes scan her face. "Huh," he says, pulling away from her while he thinks.

Tera crosses her arms and stares at him, but he doesn't say a word. Instead, he just stands there, rubbing at the bridge of his nose. His eyes look bloodshot and wet as he looks off into space.

When she's sure he's too invested in his own thoughts to follow her, she turns on her heel and tries to tiptoe away. Garridan's attention snaps back and he grabs her shoulder. Spinning her around to face him, he leans in close.

"You're lucky Mister Big Wizard's grown to care for you. I'm not so sure you would've survived the fall without his help." At this point, he's inches from Tera's face, and her hands grow hot. "Or maybe he's just trying to keep you alive until he figures out how to get out of there." He taps her forehead with a cool fingertip.

Tera roars in rage, swinging her fiery hand up to hit his head, but he snatches her wrist instantly. His grip is tight, and her fingertips go numb as her fire spell flickers out. He leans in even closer, his red eyes fixating on her. She can feel his warm breath on her cheek as he speaks.

"Woah there, Tree Girl. It's not safe playing with fire."

"Let go of me!" she wails, sending her foot crashing through his legs.

He releases her wrist and doubles over, clutching himself. She takes the opportunity to sprint for the portal, leaping through and stumbling to the cold stone floor of the Hub. She scrambles to her feet, ignoring the confused stares of several elemental students in the room.

Not sure where to go, but sure she doesn't want to stay in Pipwerry, she keeps running. Just as she steps outside the Hub, Garridan pops in view in front of her again.

"Where do you think you're going?" he asks, his smirk sending a cold shiver across her entire body.

"What will it take for you to leave me alone?"

"They're not going to get off my back until I come back with information. I need to know how he got in your head. That's all." Garridan saunters over to her, and she takes a step back. "I'm really not asking for much."

"But what are they going to do once they know?" Tera asks, tiptoeing backward for every step forward he takes. "They're going to kill me, aren't they?"

Garridan smiles and shakes his head. "Their fight isn't with you. You're just some student who got in the way. They want to separate you two so we can deal with Aeridonis. Since killing him didn't work the first time, they've thought of some additional… uses."

Tera shakes her head. "I can't let you do that."

He huffs. "You're not a hero. And you don't need to be. Let us separate you and you can go back to your underwhelming life."

"There isn't a safe way for you to remove him from my mind and you know it."

"You don't know that."

"I'm pretty damn sure."

Tera's next step bumps her into a wall. Garridan continues walking toward her, leaning his arm against the stone wall, blocking her in.

"Don't make me pay your mind another visit. I'm better prepared to see your friend up there this time."

"Tera!" Zeyla shouts from the castle fountain with her friends. "You finally bribed a boy to date you?"

"N—"

"She sure did!" Garridan calls back, his voice sweet and his smile softening. He leans closer and plants a kiss on her forehead. She shudders at the warmth spreading through her body, grimacing at him.

"He's not my b—"

"Do Mom and Dad know?" Zeyla asks, cocking her head to the side.

"He's n—"

All of a sudden, one of Zeyla's friends drops her smoothie, spattering the fountain and Zeyla's robes. She hops up, reprimanding her friend as she shakes frozen berry chunks from the cloth with a twisted look on her face. Tera takes the opportunity to slip out from under Garridan's arm, running back into the castle.

She realizes he isn't going to stop following her, and she knows she can't go home this early in the day. Instead, she makes her way to the nurse's office, stepping in quickly and shutting the door behind her.

The nurse, in her turquoise gown and cap, turns from her ingredient shelf and greets Tera.

"How can I help you, dear?" She walks over to a table with a small glass vial, turning its contents into a mortar.

"I'm having a bit of a day. I just need like… a mental health break. Can I rest in here for a bit?" Tera asks, motioning to a bed.

The nurse nods, turning her attention back to her table as she begins grinding an herb with a pestle.

Tera lays back, watching her chest rise and fall as she tries to slow her breath. Every so often, her eyes shoot up to look at the door, expecting Garridan to barge in at any point. After a little while passes with no intruder, she rolls onto her side and allows herself to sink into sleep.

Tera stays in the nurse's office the rest of the class day. Grateful the nurse respected her request and didn't question her, she thanks her and takes her leave. She braces herself for the walk home, knowing Garridan is probably following her.

She's surprised when she makes it home with no unwelcomed visits from her stalker.

Once she enters her home, she makes her way to her room. Zeyla rounds the corner, following just a couple steps behind her, shutting the door behind both of them once they're in Tera's room.

"I need you to tell me what kind of curse that was I cleared from Kiran," she demands, voice hushed and arms crossed tight.

"I can't," Tera says, sitting in her desk chair and leaning back.

"You *can,* but you *won't.*" She hops up on Tera's desk, taking a seat. "Look, I already know it's a marrow elf spell."

It's as if a boulder crashes into Tera's chest, knocking the air from it. "What?"

"I've never had the burden so bad in my life. Whatever that curse was… it was nasty. I did my research. I know it's specifically a marrow elf illusion spell, and I want to know what you were doing screwing around with marrow elves."

"Zey, I can't tell you. It's not safe."

Zeyla's bloodshot eyes lock onto Tera's and her copper hair frizzes around her face. She lowers her voice even further. "If you don't tell me, I'm telling Mom and Dad you've been running around with marrow elves. Better yet, I'll just ask your marrow elf boyfriend."

Tera smacks her hand over her sister's mouth. Zeyla glowers at her with wild eyes, ripping her hand from her mouth.

"Don't *ever* do that again!"

"Sorry." Tera grimaced, knowing it was too far. "I just… Please keep your voice down."

Zeyla climbs down from Tera's desk, putting a couple steps between the two of them. She crosses her arms again, watching her sister expectantly and shifting her weight on her feet.

"I *can't,*" Tera says in a hushed whine.

"Fine, I'm asking the marrow elf." She spins on her feet and prances toward Tera's door.

In a panic, Tera conjures an impossible wall, concealing her door.

"What the hell?" Zeyla turns to Tera. "I don't know what stupid spell your teachers taught you, but this isn't okay. Let me out!"

"Not until you promise me you won't go anywhere near him."

"Who? The marrow elf? Why? Afraid I'll embarrass you or something? I promise, you're doing a great job of that yourself."

Tera sighs, running her hands over her face as she thinks. *Don't you dare.*

"I can't let her near him, Don. He's dangerous," Tera whispers almost indecipherably.

"Oh my gods, are you talking to yourself now?" Zeyla smirks.

"If I tell you everything, you have to promise not to tell anyone."

Zeyla uncrosses her arms and steps closer to her sister. "I'm listening."

"I'm serious."

"I know." She whines, tossing her head back. "I won't tell anyone! I haven't told anyone about dealing with the burden, so I wouldn't tell them about *why* I've had it. I promise."

Zeyla sits back on Tera's desk again as Tera tells her everything that's happened since the night at Summercloud. She battles several dramatic eyerolls from Zeyla, threatening to stop the story. Each time, Zeyla throws out a half-hearted apology and adjusts her posture into one she feels displays respect and attention.

"Let me get this straight…" Zeyla chuckles lightly, her big eyes locked on the ceiling as she speaks. "You didn't pay attention in class–no surprise there–and you screwed up like… a *signature* deathrising spell. Aeridonis… *the* Aeridonis, is in your head . Just, like, hanging out? Because he didn't have a body to go into. And you can't get him out?"

"Yeah, basically."

"I've heard the rumors and stories going around about him. If it weren't for that nasty curse, I'd figure you're lying. You're lucky Kiran got cursed, huh?" She smirks.

Tera stares back flatly.

Zeyla laughs but then suddenly freezes, locking eyes with Tera. "Wait, can he like… see everything? All the time?"

"I mean, yeah, he sees what I see."

"Eww." She cringes. "You mean he can watch you shower?"

"Gods, Zeyla! Stop!" She smacks her sister's shoulder.

"It's a serious question!"

"No! I shower with my eyes closed now. Don't be gross."

If it counts for anything, I'd respect your privacy regardless. I'd go take a nap or something.

The corner of Tera's mouth twitches in a subtle amused smile that Zeyla misses in her dramatic display.

"So, that curse was from the boy you've been hanging out with?" Zeyla asks, nibbling on her nail.

"What? No. I mean, yes, the curse was from him, but I'm not 'hanging out' with him. He's a horrible person. If one of the draxxi were to kill him, they'd be doing the kingdom a favor."

"So, *not* your boyfriend?"

"No!"

"Just checking." She puts her hands up in defense.

The two sit there in awkward silence for a minute before Zeyla speaks up again.

"I guess that's all I wanted to know. Can I go now?"

"Fine." She releases the impossible wall spell, revealing her door.

Zeyla opens the door and strides out. She pauses in the doorframe, freezing for a moment before turning to look back at Tera.

"Thanks," she says before leaving.

That night, Garridan doesn't visit.

A few times during the night, she tries talking to Aeridonis about the Council. Each time, he hushes her and says he'll explain tomorrow after a full night of sleep. One Tera doesn't get. Instead, she tosses and turns until the sun comes up.

In the morning, she reluctantly joins her family for breakfast. Their mom persistently tries to engage her kids in conversation, but each of them keeps their heads down as they pick at their food and lazily eat.

"What's going on?" she eventually asks, setting the tray of jollyberry scones on the stovetop and putting her hands on her hips. "You're all acting weird."

"Nothing, Mom," Aston is the first to reply. "Just been a crazy time at school for everyone. Lots of rumors of students cheating on tests, so they've been buckling down. I think we're all just feeling the pressure from it." He looks at his sisters expectantly.

They reply with delayed but enthusiastic nods.

"Totally!" Zeyla says with a dramatic frown.

Tera shoves a bite of scone in her mouth, washing it down with tea. "I'm going to head to school," she says, abandoning the rest of her breakfast.

"Me too," Zeyla says, setting her scone down just before she's about to take another bite.

"I guess I better get going too." Aston groans, stretching backward in his chair before getting up and grabbing his bag from the counter.

The three leave home in succession, their mother watching with raised eyebrows. She throws her husband a look as if begging him to question the whole thing, but he never peers up from his papers. Tera closes the door on the scene before they can ask any further questions.

The walk to the Pipwerry portal is quiet, and it's only when the three siblings step into the portal room that Aston finally breaks the silence.

"You told her, didn't you?" he asks Tera.

"That obvious?" she asks.

He grunts and Zeyla beams at them both.

Tera's eyes flicker over to Trevitt, who stands nearby, resetting the animalinguist portal.

"Well, some of us have classes to get to," Zeyla says, stepping toward the green portal. "Have fun with the voice in your head, crazy!" She wiggles her fingers at Tera and steps through.

Trevitt looks from the green portal to Tera, their eyes meeting for a moment before he quickly refocuses on the animalinguist students waiting on their portal.

"Any clue yet where the marrow elves took the draxxi?" Aston whispers in Tera's ear.

She shakes her head. "No idea, but I think I'm just going to follow Aeridonis's advice and talk to the Council. I've had enough and I'm ready for someone else to take over."

He sighs. "It would've been cool to see it through ourselves, but I don't blame you. Let me know if you need someone to go to the Council with you."

She smiles warmly back and thanks him. "Aeridonis promised to help me put in a request for a meeting during my free period. Just hoping the waitlist isn't too long. He told me this morning about some kind of code word to put on the request. Secret 'code red' sort of thing. We're hoping it gets me an appointment sooner."

"Wow. That works, I guess."

"Hope so."

The two say goodbye and part ways, taking their respective portals.

Tera walks into the deathrising tower, making her way to Professor Dringely's classroom a bit early. Dringely stands with her back to the door, digging through her bookshelf. At her desk, Professor Leutrix hovers over a stack of open books.

"Professors?" Tera calls, announcing her presence.

The teachers continue, unphased.

"Here, look at this," Leutrix calls to Dringely.

Dringely pulls a book from the shelf and joins him, looking over his shoulder.

"I'm just going to sit down, I guess," Tera narrates, looking at her professors for a response. Getting none, she walks over to her usual spot and sets her books down, taking a seat. Across the classroom, she can see the popcorn bucket of ashes stored away in a glass case along with preserved clippings of strange plants and a taxidermy of a hackthorn.

"Do you think it would work? What about…" Dringely asks, pointing at a passage in the book.

"We'd have to substitute that part. It would take longer, for sure. But there's a chance."

"And if it doesn't?"

"If what doesn't work?" Tera calls, louder this time.

Dringely and Leutrix look up at once.

"Tera, when did you get here?" Dringely asks.

"Uh—"

"We're trying to find a solution to your problem. We'll share details with you when you need to know details," Leutrix snaps.

"I—sorry."

Leutrix slams the book shut, snatching it from the desk and soaring out of the room.

Tera looks at Dringely, who just shrugs at her.

"He's right though. No sense troubling you with some of the details until we sort through them," she tells her student.

Tera groans, sliding down in her seat and accepting defeat.

CHAPTER EIGHTEEN

ORIRI OBEX OMNES

Tera's morning classes with Dringely and Leutrix both consist of pop quizzes and essay work about their planned careers.

Dringely makes sure to remind the students–consisting mostly of pyre elves–that their essay is due before the upcoming Hearth Holiday. The announcement about shortened classes and no homework the next week elicits excited chattering and huge smiles from her classmates. As the only arboreal elf in her classes, Tera is the only one who doesn't celebrate Hearth Holiday. But she's silently grateful for the break from homework.

When her free period arrives, she races out of class, knowing she's working with limited time before she has to be back.

She takes the Propshire portal in the Hub as Aeridonis fills her in on some of the procedures for requesting an appointment with the Council.

Pick up the pace, Esotera.

"I'm going, I'm going!" Her calves sear as she speeds toward the Council's castle.

If Garridan is following or has any idea what you're doing, he's not going to let you put in a request with the Coucil, you know that, right?

"I'm well aware, thanks," she says with a groan, pushing past the pain and taking off in a run for the castle.

The small building to the right. Just outside the castle gates.

Tera turns as she reaches the front of the castle gates, making her way toward a squat structure butted up against a cluster of manicured trees. A well-maintained wooden sign swings on a post outside, labeled REQUESTS.

As she's focused on reading the sign, she rams into the back of a portly human in a sweat-stained shirt and fraying overalls.

"I'm so sorry!" she says, stumbling back a step, holding her hands out in apology.

"That might be the fastest anything's moved in Propshire ever," the man jokes with a deep chuckle. "Get comfy. Line ain't moved in a while."

"Line?" Tera's eyes travel before the man, scanning over a single-file row of people wrapped around the request building.

I was worried about that.

"What was the point of rushing?" Tera whispers to herself after the man turns forward again.

Hoped we'd beat the lunchtime rush.

Tera sighs, shooting a look over her shoulder, crossing her arms tight across her chest.

Every so often, the line moves forward a couple steps. Her fingers, with a mind of their own, work their way up to her scalp and begin picking at the rough edges of her scab. She feels a sting as it comes loose. When she pulls her hand away, there's a little blood on the tip of a finger. With a grimace, she wipes it on the side of her robes and hopes no one notices.

With nothing more to hold her attention, she starts looking over her shoulder again, much to the annoyance of the mineral elf now in line behind her. She tries shooting the woman a casual smile, but it's met with a scowl.

It's finally almost Tera's turn. The man in front of her turns to her with a friendly smile. His thumbs tucked in his pockets he leans against the stone siding of the request building. "What brings you here today?"

"Uh—" She scans her brain for a plausible answer.

"Sorry, not try'na pry." His smile disappears and he rubs his stubbly head, looking down at his feet. "Just makin' conversation. S'pose I should've started with something like, 'How 'bout this weather?'"

"That's alright." She smiles weakly. "What brings *you* here?"

His smile returns almost as quickly as it left. "Some friends and I have been comin' by once a week to request a change to employment requirements for humans. Used to be humans had just as much a chance as elves at management positions in some industries. I understand being limited to certain fields—tech, agriculture, shipping, merchandising, crafting 'n such. It doesn't require magic. But we should have an equal chance to lead. No offense–I have no problems working for y'all. It's just some of us have been workin' years for these jobs and every time we're looked over for some hot shot young elf. Feels like you're cheatin' the system if you can use magic to get the job done. Used to be magic wasn't allowed during interviews and all that. Nothin' can substitute ole' fashioned hard work, ya know what I'm sayin'?"

Tera's eyes wide, she waits to make sure the man's done speaking. "Wow, I had no idea that was an issue. That makes sense. I can see why that'd upset you–it sounds totally unfair. I hope they're able to do something to help."

He takes his hands out of his pockets and pats her on the shoulder. "You seem like a good kid. I hope they can help you with whatever you're here for, too."

She flattens her lips into an unenthusiastic smile. "Me too."

When the man turns back around, the gronnet in line in front of him exits the building, holding the door open for him.

"Welp," he says, waving to Tera. "Looks like it's my turn."

He disappears into the building, the heavy door slamming shut behind him.

Seems like a well-intentioned man. Shame the Council likely isn't reading his requests.

"What?" Tera asks. "Why not?"

Some of the Council members are a bit more money hungry than myself. Not to say they're bad people, but if they don't see a financial gain in changing that policy back to the way it used to be, they probably won't touch it.

"That's so messed up."

I never said it was right.

The man opens the door on his way out, holding it open and standing aside for Tera. She nods to him as she enters, and he gently releases the door behind her.

Somehow, the building feels even tinier from the inside. A square table sits in the center of the room with a stack of parchment and a pen. In the middle of the table is a narrow slit.

Explain—briefly—the situation. Put the word "gogneau" at the top of the page. It's just a random code word the Council developed a long time ago for emergencies. Hopefully, it'll help escalate things.

Tera follows Aeridonis's instructions, scribbling out as legibly as she can what happened at Summercloud, what happened with the draxxi, and even a brief mention of Garridan. She signs it, folding it in thirds.

"I'm assuming?" She holds the letter over the slit in the table.

You'd be assuming correctly.

She releases the parchment. It drops into the slit and disappears.

"Oh." She stares at the table. "I'm not sure what I expected, I guess."

That's all. Let's get you back to school. Don't need you to be late to another class.

Tera nearly sprints back to the Pipwerry portal, tripping on her way through and landing on her face in the Hub.

"First time using a portal?" Garridan asks, standing on the other side of the portal room with a tuftplant stem bouncing from his lip as he chews on it.

She chooses to ignore him, resisting the urge to roll her eyes. Standing and patting the dust from her robes, she makes her way over to the black deathrising portal.

"Wait, are you giving me the silent treatment?" He scoffs, smiling so wide the stem drops from his mouth. He steps on it walking over to her.

Just as she's about to walk through the portal, a strong hand grips her shoulder and yanks her back.

"Where do you think you're going, Tree Girl?" he asks, leaning his head around her.

"To class."

I'm not sure if I'm impressed or worried by your newfound restraint. If I know you, and I'd like to think at this point I've got a fair understanding, it's killing you not to make a snide comment right now. Careful, I might just be proud of you.

"What's the point of class?" he asks.

She turns to face him, narrowing her eyes.

"Serious question. You've got uh—" He looks around the room with mock paranoia, a smirk creeping across his face. "Someone." He taps his temple.

"And?"

"You don't need to learn anything. You're just going to act out anything he tells you. Otherwise, you'd be dead by now. Trust me, I've watched you enough to know nothing substantial about you is your own doing."

"What's that supposed to mean?"

Esotera, no! Don't engage. He's just taunting you.

"I just mean you're not really…" He pauses, humming to himself. *"Memorable.* Special. Or altogether talented."

Her face sears and she begins to feel the heat burning her hands. Resisting the fire spell, she swallows her anger down like an oversized pill.

"That's funny," she says, her eyes flicking up to lock onto his, "coming from a puppet. You think *you're* special? Fedrae is using you. Is this what he does for people that mean something to him? Assign them to stalk students? Wow. Seems important." She laughs. "He's just trying to keep you busy so you stay out of his way."

"You have no idea what you're talking about." A thick vein begins to appear on his forehead as he glowers at her. "At all."

"Sure, sure." Tera smiles and nods. "If you don't mind, I'd like to get to class. Some of us aspire to be more than worker corpses."

His lip snarls at her, but he doesn't stop her from taking the deathrising portal. She half expects him to follow her through, tormenting her the whole way to Leutrix's class. If he is following her, he doesn't make himself known this time. Tera feels her shoulders relax and fall, rather than staying scrunched by her ears in stress.

Leutrix's door is wide open, and her classmates all scurry through to their seats like terrified mice under the watchful eyes of a hungry hawk. When Tera enters, her eyes can't help but gawk at the ceiling and the shelves along the walls. Plants are nothing unusual in a deathrising classroom, but she's never seen quite this many. The hanging plants at the ceiling push out at all kinds of strange angles because every inch of spare space is occupied. Many of these plants have longer, fuller vines snaking down toward the anxious students beneath. Even Leutrix's bookshelves have been cleared of their usual ancient textbooks to make room for more potted plants.

At first, Tera doesn't even notice the row of resting corpses laying at the far end of the room in front of the mortuary drawers. One by one, her classmates' eyes travel from the collection of plants to the row of bodies.

I've got to give you deathrisers some credit. The other paths don't have classes quite this wild.

Tera lets out a light and breathy chuckle to herself, earning her a side eye from one of the other students.

Leutrix shuts the door behind him, his usually quick steps slow and deliberate. He takes his time walking over to the bodies, looking over each student on his way. Tera can feel his glare over her, but she chooses not to acknowledge him. Instead, she pretends to write in her notebook.

"Whether you like it or not," Leutrix starts, stopping at the row of corpses with his back to the students, "most of you won't even pass for graduation. Those of you who *do* graduate, the bulk of you will end up in the production plants. It's not a glamorous job. No one will ever see you as a hero. But if it weren't for the corpse keepers in those important positions, we wouldn't have many of the things we take for granted in life. It's arguably one of the most important jobs in Evalyra."

He turns to face them, looking over each of them again, his face less harsh than usual.

"Can anyone tell me how the production plants obtain and use worker corpses?" he asks.

Milling's hand pierces the air.

Leutrix sighs, waiting a moment before inevitably calling on him.

"Anyone is eligible to become a worker corpse in death." Milling sits up straighter, tucking a loose strand of hair behind his ear. "You can register with the Council's Provision Program. When you pass away, your family is given time to mourn and perform any funeral rites for your culture. Afterward, a corpse keeper is sent to collect your body and transport it to the production plants to raise and rest you daily for whatever job your corpse is placed in."

Leutrix nods. "And can anyone tell me what the families get out of this deal?"

Milling's hand waves through the air.

"Someone that isn't Milling again."

Milling puts his hand down, his smile fading.

Tera raises her hand halfway, nibbling on the inside of her lip.

Leutrix's eyes shoot her way. "Go on."

"Most worker corpses are only used for a one- or two-year contract. The family has no say—if in life the person signed the registration contract, it's binding. But the family gets paid. If they signed a one-year contract, the family gets payments for two years. If the person signed a two-year contract, the family gets paid for five years. It's a win-win. The deceased gets to continue providing for their family, the family gets additional support, the kingdom gets the labor it needs, and living citizens don't have to risk themselves doing dirty or dangerous jobs that could kill or hurt them. And in the end, the corpse is still given a proper burial after their contract expires."

Wow. I didn't realize you knew so much about how all that works.

Tera scribbles in her notebook for Aeridonis to see.

*Believe it or not, I did my research before
I picked my path.*

Leutrix turns to his chalkboard and begins scribbling something. The students all crane their necks to read it, but as soon as he turns back to face them, they all snap back straight in their seats.

"In today's activity, you'll be performing solo. No lab partners."

The students begin nervously chattering amongst themselves.

"Enough," Leutrix says in an exasperated moan. "If you have any hope of actually pursuing deathrising as a career, you're not going to be able to rely on a lab partner. Line up. Single file."

Everyone begins standing and he swipes his arm through the air, sliding all the desks and chairs against the wall at once.

Tera gets in line behind a few of her classmates after several nervous ones shove anyone they can before them in line.

Leutrix steps beside the row of corpses, standing motionless in wait.

The students find their places in line and the talk dies down under the crushing pressure of Leutrix's stare.

"Mister Daellyn," Leutrix greets an unusually short pyre elf with shoulder length coal-colored hair. "You're going to attempt to raise all seven corpses at once. Give them a purpose. Put them to rest. Move to the back of the line. We're going to continue until everyone has had a turn. If one of your classmates fails to properly complete any of the steps, you are not to interfere."

Silence.

"Does everyone understand me?" Leutrix asks with a growl.

"Yes, sir," a bunch of students nervously whisper out of sync.

"Now, Mister Daellyn," Leutrix puts a hand on his student's back, guiding him forward a few steps, "You remember how to raise one corpse from a distance, I presume? Not just by muscle memory, which at this point I expect from all of you, but the steps and the feelings behind it. You remember those?"

Daellyn's head nods so fast it seems to bobble on his neck.

"How about you kindly remind your classmates how it's done?" Leutrix sweeps his arm out to gesture to the students in line behind Daellyn.

"S-sure." Daellyn turns to the rest of the line. "Put a hand on your head and on your heart. Feel the life energy from the plants. Pu-pull it to you. The energy, I mean. Not the plant." He chuckles nervously, his eyes full of panic. "Say, 'oriri.' Then, like…" He flicks his wrists out. "Do that. And—and push the energy with it."

Daellyn looks over to Leutrix, the silence agonizing. When Leutrix nods, a smile pops onto Daellyn's face and he visibly relaxes.

"Multiple resurrections at once works much the same," Leutrix says, his eyes flicking over to the row of corpses. "The only difference is the spell and the energy needed. Instead of just oriri, the spell is oriri *omnes*. And you need to draw *more* energy. Enough for each corpse you want to resurrect. It can take practice to pull the exact amount. In order to pass today's activity, you must raise at least three of the seven corpses."

A couple students nod. The one in front of Tera starts rocking forward and back on her feet as she waits.

"Professor Dringely has given me inspiration for this activity today," Leutrix continues, "in that there will be a… twist."

Nervous chatter amongst the students again, and Leutrix extinguishes it with nothing more than a harsh stare.

"If any students manage to successfully raise all seven corpses—and follow the rules of the assignment, *naturally*—I will award five points extra credit toward your final grade."

Tera can't control her mouth, which gapes open at her professor. She covers it and tries to play cool, but her classmates around her share her excitement.

"This could save my grade from the midterm," Tera whispers almost imperceptibly to Aeridonis.

Then make sure you blow him away. You can do this, Esotera. I believe in you.

"That makes one of us."

I know Garridan has gotten in your head about things. But I wasn't the one who set a resurrected gronnet on my enemy. And while I still hold to it that it was reckless, it was nonetheless impressive and clever.

Tera nods to herself, pulling her attention away from her anxieties just in time to see Daellyn raise four of the corpses and instruct them to high-five each other before laying back to rest. Clearly surprised by himself, he whips around and tries to high-five Milling behind him, catching him off-guard and accidentally slapping another student in the face.

Daellyn apologizes profusely, and the slapped student just glowers at him as Leutrix directs Daellyn to the back of the line.

Milling steps forward, rolling his wrists with a crack before placing them on head and heart. Everyone watches in quiet anticipation—the tension in the room like a frayed rope waiting to snap. After a moment of energy-pulling, Milling whips out his wrists with a quiet, "Oriri omnes."

Six of the corpses begin stretching their limbs, easing themselves back onto their feet. Before they can stand, Milling—with obvious disappointment—tells them to run a lap around the room and rest again. The corpses obey, and the entire time, he watches the seventh corpse with dying hope.

As the six corpses lay back to rest, Milling's shoulders slump. He makes his way to the back of the line without making eye contact with anyone.

Two more students take their turns. Tera looks up at the lush greenery hanging above as vines shrivel and brown, the life leaving them with each successful cast.

When it's Tera's turn, she realizes how aggressively her heart thumps inside her chest, seeming to collide into her ribs with each beat. She takes a couple steps forward and places her hands on her head and heart.

Do it like Garridan's watching. For all we know, he might be. And now's your chance to show him you're not to be messed with.

The nervous flutters turn to searing rage and Tera begins to siphon life energy from the plants in the room. Electricity seems to rattle inside her every cell until she feels her entire being vibrating. In the corner of her eyes, she sees plants wilting on the shelves beside her.

Students begin whispering in the background, but she pushes aside their voices. When it feels as if her skin is about to burst with power, she flicks her wrists around and commands, "Oriri obex!"

She quickly throws out an "omnes" after realizing her mistake.

Nothing happens for a moment, and she's fully convinced she botched the spell with her mistake. The whispers behind her grow louder.

There's a sudden metallic rumbling that washes over the murmurs. All seven corpses begin stretching and standing, and the handles of nearly all the metal body drawers at the back of the room begin shaking. Several students scream and back up.

A command, Esotera! Give them a purpose.

Tera's eyes wide and hands shaking, she raises her voice to the seven corpses. "Help them," she says, pointing to the drawers.

The corpses begin pulling open the metal drawers one by one, and more reanimated corpses begin sitting up, stretching their limbs and dropping to their feet.

She chews on the corner of her cheek, her brain scrambling for a purpose for all the corpses before her. "Dance," she tells them, her voice cracking. She clears her throat. "Dance," she says again, louder and with confidence.

The group of corpses begins dancing and wiggling in place, awkward and disjointed. The sounds of grunts and shuffling fabric of their tattered clothing take the place of music.

She directs them to rest again, and the seven original corpses take their places on the ground. The corpses from the drawers join the others on the floor. Her face burns with embarrassment when she realizes they needed specific instructions to go back into their drawers.

Tera turns to walk to the back of the line, and every other student's eyes burn as they watch her in stunned silence.

After a minute, Leutrix clears his throat. "Excellent work, Miss Tera. The cap is five extra credit points, so don't expect more for the others." He motions to the pile of corpses resting at the back of the room.

That's all he has to say about that? That man's about as strange as a natwelly fly in the desert.

Tera doesn't question what a natwelly fly is or why they don't belong in a desert. Instead, she tries to focus on ignoring the continued stares of her classmates.

Leutrix calls the attention of his students again, instructing the next one to take their turn.

While in the back of the line, Tera's eyes travel around the room, realizing just how many plants died during her turn alone. As she scans the crispy brown potted plants along the far wall, her eyes lock onto Garridan, who sits perched on one of the desks along the wall. He gives her a single nod, clapping slowly and silently before disappearing again.

I was kind of just using him as motivation to get you to try even harder. I didn't actually expect him to show himself in your class. Bit ballsy.

Tera can't help but stare at the place Garridan disappeared from, wondering if he's still there. She wonders why he bothered coming into her class, especially when the odds are slim of anything pertinent to his mission coming up in a classroom setting.

By the time all the students take their turns, only two other students manage to raise all seven corpses. One unfortunate student only raises two, and Leutrix instructs him to return for further practice at the end of the day.

He dismisses the class, and everyone begins filing out. Just as Tera's about to pass through the doorway, she's yanked back into the class by her arm.

Leutrix looks down at her, not saying anything until the very last student leaves the room.

"I need you to tell me if your little… associate"—his eyes flick up to her forehead–"helped you in any way today."

"No, Professor."

His brow furrows and he waits expectantly.

"I promise," she insists. "He's actually not experienced in deathrising."

Tell him he can check my old class records with the front office. They have kept every student's record since Pipwerry's inception. No doubt he can find everything he needs about my experience and training from there.

"He says to tell you to check the student records at the front office if you don't believe me."

Leutrix sniffs, tipping his nose up at her. "Alright. I suspect our recent lesson had a bit too much staying power in your mind, perhaps."

Tera can feel her cheeks sting at his words, but she bites her tongue. "Sir?"

He clearly calculates his every word before speaking again. "You've never cast a mass resurrection spell before. I can't imagine you knew the spell before today."

"No, sir. I got nervous and blurted out the first similar spell to come to mind. I tried to correct it and I guess it worked."

"In a way. You didn't precisely do as asked—I wanted you to cast oriri omnes, not oriri obex omnes."

"It was a mistake, professor."

"Made for a good show. Oriri obex omnes is the spell for mass resurrection *through an obstacle.*"

Tera's eyes grow wide as she pieces it all together. "Oh woah. I had no idea. I swear."

"I'd be more upset if I felt you hadn't paid attention. However, you displayed better focus than I've seen from you yet in all your classes with me." His eyes narrow. "How'd you draw in so much energy this time?"

"I suppose I got mad, sir."

"Mad?"

She nods.

He smirks. "If that's what works for you, I suppose keep at it."

"Thank you."

He waves her off and she hurries down the stairs without looking back.

I'm proud of you, Esotera.

She tries to resist smiling, but it pushes through. "Thanks, Don. And thanks for the… encouragement."

He chuckles, and she smiles at herself the rest of the way to the Darkwood portal. For the first time in a while, she doesn't worry about what'll happen if Garridan shows up.

CHAPTER NINETEEN

LINES THAT CAN'T BE CROSSED

That evening, Tera enjoys the break from homework for Hearth Holiday. She even allows herself to paint for the first time in what feels like ages. Dragging a chair across her room and positioning it below an unpainted space on her ceiling, she grabs her cracked paint pallet and favorite brush. She steps up on the chair, her arms out for balance as it settles into the ground. Without thinking too hard, she dips her brush in a vibrant orange paint and begins making quick streaks and swirls, covering her makeshift canvas in painted flames.

When her mother calls her out to dinner, she drops her brush in a cup of foggy paint water and bounds down the hall.

"You seem chipper," her dad observes.

She smiles without meaning to. "Just having a good day, I guess."

"Wow! Don't think I've heard you say that in a long time. Something happen at school?" her mom asks.

She tells them a little about Leutrix's class, leaving out some of the details. While her parents try their best to be supportive of her path, she knows deathrising makes them uncomfortable. As her dad tried to explain to her when she first picked her path, their job as lifebringers should *prevent* death, and deathrisers are a reminder of the times they've failed. And on top of that, deathrisers are typically the only elves able to kill someone permanently. Once a deathriser casts the Everdeath spell, their target can never be brought back. Tera's parents don't believe anyone should have that kind of power.

"I'm proud of you, Tera!" Her mother beams at her as she scoops some cabbage and bark-roast beast on her plate.

Anxiety tugs at Tera for a split second, reminding her of the draxxi, held captive who-knows-where. And then her mind wanders to the curse over the kingdom, wondering just when the protective spell will wear off. She reminds herself the Council should be able to handle it better than she ever could. It's just a matter of time before they read her letter and see Aeridonis's code word to take action fast.

Aston saunters downstairs and drops into his seat at the table, grabbing his fork and immediately shoveling food in his mouth.

"Where's your sister?" their mother asks, eyeing Zeyla's empty spot. "I don't remember the last time you both beat her to the table." She chuckles to herself, going to set the pan back on the stovetop.

"I haven't seen her since this morning at school," Tera says. "I figured she'd be walking home with her friends."

Their mother looks over at Aston expectantly. He shrugs, his cheeks bulging with food.

She grumbles and goes back to dishing up food.

The family eats together—without Zeyla—talking about the beautiful decorations up around Evalyra for Hearth Holiday. Tera has hardly noticed the annual appearance of enchanted candles and lanterns posted up along every walkway in the kingdom. She almost envies the pyre elves. Every year, Hearth Holiday is a chance for pyre elves across the kingdom to gather around the grand hearth of Magnarium—the hometown of most pyre elves in Evalyra. They celebrate with decadent cheeses and mead to honor their ancestors who didn't survive the eruption that destroyed their original homeland. It always feels far more meaningful to Tera than the biggest annual celebration in Darkwood: The Hallowing.

"If you see your sister, tell her I put her plate in the fridge," their mother says, rinsing off a dish and handing it to their father to dry.

"You'll see her before we do," Tera says, fully planning on painting the rest of the night.

"Your dad and I have a work function. Training some new members of the night shift tonight. We'll be back late."

Just then, an owl barrels through the open kitchen window, its feet sliding across the slick table in its landing.

Tera's father swears in surprise, bumping into his wife and dropping a plate. The dish shatters on the ground, and both of them immediately bend down to pick up the pieces.

That's the Council's parchment. Grab it!

Tera unties the ribbon and snatches the small scroll from the owl's leg, shoving it down her shirt. The owl sits on the table, watching her. She waves at it with her hand, trying to shoo it away. When her parents pop up from the ground, they toss plate shards in the trash and turn to look at the owl.

Tera's mother looks at the owl's legs, clearly figuring it's a messenger owl. She looks from the owl to her daughter.

"No message?" she asks. "What's this owl doing in our kitchen then?"

Tera tries to be nonchalant, shrugging and putting her hands on her hips. "I'm as confused as you are."

Her mother's gaze lingers on her another moment before she reaches her arm to the owl. The bird steps up, wobbling on her arm as she lifts it and leads it back to the window. "Go home," she tells it, and it takes off with a powerful flap of its wings.

Tera promises to tell her sister about the plate of food saved for her, and then she scurries off to her room before they can ask any further questions.

You're arguably getting worse at lying. You know that, right?

"Shut up," Tera hisses at him.

She closes her door and locks it before sitting on the edge of her bed, digging the small scroll out from her shirt. She unrolls it, looking over the words in their fancy and elegant font.

> Miss Esotera Arlboro,
>
> Thank you for taking the time to leave the Council a letter. Your request has been received. Your presence is requested at a Council hearing on the 23rd at precisely sunrise.
>
> We look forward to speaking with you.

Tera skims over the letter a few more times, unsure of her own eyes.

"The 23rd?" she asks with a huff. "Are they joking? That's not for over two weeks! What about the code word? Doesn't that mean anything to them?"

Perhaps they don't believe you. I'm not sure where they presume you got the code from, but my guess is they don't believe you. After all, with all these ridiculous stories about me going around, I'm sure they're getting plenty of letters from people claiming they know where I am. I'm grateful they at least accepted your request. We're just going to have to be p—

"Don't you dare say we just have to be patient. You saw how the marrow elves treated the draxxi! And it's my fault they were captured in the first place. I can't just leave them like that, Don. We've got to do something."

There's nothing we can do for now. Perhaps we can go tomorrow and leave them another letter explaining once again the urgency. I'll come up with something else you could perhaps tell them to speed things up. Don't panic though. We'll get this taken care of and everything will turn out fine.

"You're way too calm about all of this."

What good does it do to worry you about this? It isn't your place to interfere.

"Arguing with your brain buddy?" Garridan's voice rings out from her bedroom window.

She rolls her eyes, trying to focus on locking her mind's door before sighing and looking over at him.

"What do you want from me? Come to harass me about how he's in my head again? I already told you, I'm n—"

"It isn't that."

She squints at him, crossing her arms in wait.

"It's your sister," he says, his usual smirk absent.

A cool rush floods her veins, but she maintains her steady tone. "What about her?"

"When was the last time you saw her?"

"This morning." She watches him as he climbs in through her window, stepping toward her.

She stands, steadying herself in a wide stance.

"Relax, I'm not going to hurt you." He puts up his hands and stops walking. "I'm here to help."

Tera full-belly laughs at him.

"Alright, that's fair," he says with a deep sigh.

He watches her as she stares at him in wild amusement, and it isn't until she stops laughing that he speaks again.

"Fedrae has her."

CHAPTER TWENTY

TAKE A LOOK

"That's not funny." Tera can feel her pulse in every inch of her body, and she has to fight the fire spell flickering at her fingertips.

"I know. And that's why it's not something I'd joke about," Garridan says.

"Why do I have any reason to believe you?" she asks.

"You don't."

"So, I shouldn't."

"Depends on if you want to save your sister."

Tera sniffs, arms still crossed. She cocks her head at him, looking him up and down. "Why would you *ever* say anything *remotely* helpful?"

I don't trust him. But when we go write another letter to the Council, we'll mention this and it could get you in sooner. They won't let anything happen to her.

Garridan frowns, looking down at his feet. A stray lock of nearly-white hair slips from behind his ear, swinging in front of his pale face. He tucks it, his eyes looking up at her. "I don't think it's a fair move."

"Meaning?"

"Using someone's family."

Tera scoffs. "Wow. It has moral boundaries?"

"'It'?"

"You've been nothing but awful to me since we met."

"To be fair, it wasn't like I volunteered for this." He stands upright, his lip snarling at her.

"You enjoy harassing me too much to have *not* volunteered."

"I swear. I wanted to be in charge of watching over the draxxi. Way more badass than stalking a mediocre-at-best student. Trust me, I didn't ask for this."

"Even if you didn't, you act like this job comes with overtime pay."

"I think at this point, you'd feel lonely if I wasn't around." A grin teases at his lips, his eyes darting down again.

"Absolutely not." Tera stands firm. Unblinking.

"Whatever." His smile transforms into pursed lips, his forehead scrunched. "Save your sister, don't save your sister. I did my part and told you—my conscience is clean."

Tera waits, watching him. He's wringing his hands, shifting his weight from foot to foot, throwing her occasional glances. "So," she says with a stiffness to her voice, "if you happen to be telling the truth, where would you say Fedrae is keeping my sister?"

He stops fidgeting, locking into place. His gaze travels to her again.

"Lailerynne." His voice cuts the silence of the messy bedroom.

"What?"

"Lailerynne," he repeats. "It's a coastal town. Normally, it's a quiet fishing village. Handful of fauns lived there and not much else until we took over."

"What do you mean *lived* there?"

He shrugs nonchalantly. Tera tries to shove down her impatience, distracting herself with the scab on her head.

"Why do you do that?" he asks, watching her.

"Do what?"

He mimics her picking at her scalp, and anxious heat instantly surges through her face and chest. She drops her hand, and can't help but think of the half-lifted crusty scab, begging to be plucked.

"I'm not judging. Just wondering if you were even aware of it."

"Don't change the subject," she said with a hiss.

"What more do you want me to say? Fedrae has your sister. She's in Lailerynne. Not much else to the conversation."

Tera throws her arms up with a bewildered half-snarl, half-groan. "Oh yeah, no big deal. Just a casual conversation. You're telling me he kidnapped my little sister! I'm going to need a little more to work off of."

"There's a tower. She's in there. You can't just waltz into the tower though. Fedrae has basically turned that place into a home base. It's surrounded by enchanted draxxi and pissed-off marrow elves."

"So, help me get in."

Tera can hear Aeridonis make some sort of snide comment, but she can't make it out over Garridan's laughter.

"You might not be that bright, but at least you've got good jokes," Garridan says, leaning casually against the wall.

We can check if he's telling the truth. If he is, we'll tell the Council. We'll do everything we can to escalate things and get her home safe.

"How do we see if he's telling the truth?" Tera asks under her breath.

"I can hear you, Tree Girl," he says in a singsong voice.

"I don't care," she sings back, rolling her eyes.

A view portal.

"A what?" Tera asks, her eyes zoning out on the ground as she focuses on his voice.

Garridan narrows his eyes, leaning in as if he'd be able to hear Aeridonis.

Portal gronnets can cast them. They're a lesser version of a normal portal. It basically just lets you view a location, rather than actually travel there.

"So, we'd be able to look in the tower?"

Theoretically. Might need to cast several view portals to get a good look unless you can get him to tell us where exactly in the tower Fedrae may be keeping your sister.

"Garridan?" Tera asks, looking up from her fixation point on the floor. "Do you know where Fedrae is keeping Zeyla?"

He grimaces for a second, scratching his head. "I mean, *could* be the first floor."

Tera nods frantically, taking mental note.

"Or the second."

She nods again.

"Or the third. Maybe the fourth or fifth. Y'know… could be the sixth." The smirk starts creeping onto his face, but when he sees Tera's eyes growing wet with anger, he stops. "Sorry. I'm not sure. If I had to guess, I'd say either the storage room in the basement or, if he was feeling generous, somewhere in the living quarters on the fourth floor. I can't promise either of those are right though. He didn't tell me, and I didn't stick around to watch."

"'Watch'? You saw them bring her in though?"

His lips flatten. He sighs impatiently. "Yes. But I left shortly after."

"Did he take Zeyla just to get to me? He wants me to turn myself over to him?"

"Enough questions. I've already told you way too much. Don't make me regret it." His eyes feel threatening for the first time that night, and a chill ripples down Tera's neck and spine.

"But wh—"

Before she can finish her question, Garridan disappears.

"I need to talk to Trevitt," Tera says to Aeridonis. "Mom and Dad are gone for the night—it'll be easy. But I need to know if he's telling the truth."

You won't catch any arguments from me there.

"Even if I did, you should know by now I won't listen." Tera smirks, pulling the vial of silencing potion from the school nurse, wiggling it in front of her own face. The amber liquid sloshes like tiny tidal waves in its glass home.

I wish you could see me roll my eyes just now. I think I'm spending too much time around you.

"Get used to it… apparently."

She opens the door to leave, nearly walking right into Aston, his ear pressed to her door.

"Dude!" Tera stumbles back, hands up and lip curled at her brother. "What the hell are you doing outside my door?"

"I just thought I heard something. Wanted to make sure you were okay."

Tera scoffs, crossing her arms. She refuses to break eye contact or silence, knowing her brother will break. He copies her, crossing his own arms and staring back at her with a cracking frown.

A moment later, he says, "Fine," and slumps his shoulders. "I thought I heard another voice. Figured maybe it was Kiran. Thought maybe you didn't want to include me on the plans anymore or something. I don't know."

"Nothing really changed," she says, feeling her own tension relaxing. "Just an added step."

"Tera," Aston says with a grumbly sigh. "I heard the conversation. I don't know everything you guys said, but I know something is wrong and Zeyla might need help."

Oh. He really did *hear everything.*

"I wouldn't believe that guy if I were you," Tera says. "Or me. *I* don't believe him. But I've got to do my due diligence and all that. Just in case he *is* telling the truth for once, I need to be sure."

"I'm coming with you," he says. "Just in case."

"Fine, but I'm leaving now. Before Mom and Dad get home."

"Don't let me slow you down." Aston steps out of the way, motioning for her to lead.

The two hurry to the Pipwerry portal. The evening air is crisp, and the off-and-on winds slice against their bare arms. Overhead, the moon stipples light through thick leaves to the lush grass underfoot. In the tree homes around them, honey-colored lights turn on and off as other arboreal elves move from room to room. As they pass Nyana the dryad, they both throw her quick waves, dismissing her attempts at a friendly conversation as they continue their trek to the portal just past her.

Aston trots to keep up with his sister as she takes long steps through the forest.

"Hold up," he calls after her, huffing and puffing. "What exactly is the plan, anyways?"

"I thought you were listening in on the conversation," she replies, never breaking stride.

"Well, yeah, but I can't hear what *he's* saying to you."

Tera summarizes the plan to cast a view portal and look for Zeyla, and upon finishing, Aston stops in his tracks.

"Is Trevitt even going to be there this late?" he asks.

"We can use the calling panel, if nothing else," Tera says, only slowing her pace a little.

Aston finally catches up, still keeping a fast pace to stay beside her. "But won't that call the portal master instead of him?"

"Doubt it. I haven't actually seen the portal master do any work since Trevitt started. I think he just kind of has Trevitt do *everything* nowadays."

Aston gives a "fair enough" tip of his head.

They reach the portal to Pipwerry and Tera steps through first, with Aston only a second behind.

Once in the portal room, Tera immediately beelines for the portal maintenance door. Without hesitation, she raps on it, the heavy thwacking echoing through the emptiness of the Hub.

Silence swallows her knock. She clears her throat, waiting just a second before trying again.

"Try the calling panel, I guess," Aston reminds her.

She looks over to the stone protrusion at the end of the portal wall. The calling panel is nothing more than an enchanted stone carving of a gronnet face in the wall. Her fingers lay across the rough, cool stone as she presses down with her whole palm. The border of the panel glows a soft golden color and she steps back.

"He's not here," Tera says, pacing back and forth in the portal room.

"Be patient. You *just* pressed it."

She tosses her head back in a gurgling groan, throwing her arms across her chest and continuing her back and forth soldier march around the room.

"Tera?" Kiran's voice bounces. "What are you doing here?"

She turns around to see Kiran standing in front of the purple animalinguist portal—marked by a paw print sigil above it— with his hands cupped together in front of him.

"I could ask you the same thing," she replies, eyeing his hands. "Zeyla hasn't come home. I'm looking for the portal master. Or Trevitt."

"Trevitt's not here, but the portal master should be back in a minute. He was on the animal island swapping out some old hinges on the front door when I left."

"They've got him doing castle maintenance now?" Aston asks.

Kiran opens his mouth to answer, but Tera cuts him off.

"What's that?" She motions with a nod of her head to his clasped hands.

A smile erupts on his face and he trots a couple steps toward his best friend. "It's a tirabet chick!" He opens his hands just enough for Tera to see the downy green puffball look up at her with tiny, beady black eyes.

"A what?"

"They're not that common anymore, sadly. But they're one of my favorite animals. Did you know tirabets actually build their nests underneath awnings to stay out of the rain? They're fascinating little birds! Unfortunately, I haven't seen one since I was little. At least, not until recently. A pair built their nest right above my bedroom window. I happened to be walking home at the right time, too. Heard this little one practically screaming for help when it fell from the nest and got snatched up by a fox."

Kiran tucks a finger into the space between his hands, wiggling it against the baby bird's fuzzy back. It chitters a squeaky chirp at him and he beams even wider. Tera swears if he smiles any bigger, his mouth will rip open.

"And why'd you bring it here? In the evening?" she asks.

"Um, it was hurt? Duh?"

Tera's brow teeter totters in confusion, waiting for an explanation. When it doesn't come, she asks, "Why bring it to Pipwerry though?"

"Oh!" He chuckles warmly. "Professor Aeckmage is fantastic at helping hurt creatures. I sent her a message that I needed help and she agreed to meet me at school. I wanted her to take a look at it to help me decide what to do. Especially with it being so endangered. And they are delicate, let me tell you! You've really gotta take care of them."

"Uh huh." Tera catches herself glancing over her friend's shoulder, hoping to see the portal master sooner rather than later.

"Want to see it?" Kiran gestures out to Aston with his enclosed hands.

"Uh. Sure."

Kiran goes over to show Aston his finding, and Tera stands staring at the portal, tapping her finger on her crossed arm.

"So you said Zeyla hasn't come home?" Kiran asks, returning to Tera.

"Yeah. You know how Garridan has been following and harassing me?"

He nods, his eyes full of sympathy.

"He said something earlier, and I just want to look into it. I'm a bit worried about Zeyla, but I also don't trust him. Aeridonis—"

Kiran's caring expression melts away and he groans.

"I know you're mad at him, but can you please just listen?" Tera whines.

"Fine."

"Anyways," she says with a huff, waiting and watching Kiran for a moment before continuing, "Aeridonis suggested

I use a view portal to check for Zeyla. I doubt we'll see her. I'm betting she's out with her friends and forgot to tell Mom and Dad, and Garridan's probably just screwing with me. But I've got to check."

"Well shoot, I wish you would've said something sooner! Let me see if I can get the portal master to put the hinges down for a bit and help out. And I want to come with, but I've got to leave this sweet widdle fuzzball with Professor Aeckmage." He peers between his fingers again, cooing and baby-talking the bird. "Be right back!"

He steps through the purple portal and disappears, leaving Tera and Aston in the portal room alone. The calling panel still glows on the wall, and Tera lets out another impatient grumble as she picks up her march again.

The two siblings don't exchange a word in the waiting. It's only when Kiran returns with the portal master that the silence finally cracks open with the gruff voice of the old gronnet.

"I heard you want a view portal," he says.

"Yes, sir," Tera replies.

"You know I can't do that on campus, right?"

"Yes, sir," she repeats, this time with a wobbly-headed nod.

"Yer mom and dad ever teach you about portal fees?"

"No, but I'm familiar with how it works."

"Good. Let's get moving." He brushes past her, his oversized wet feet slapping the ground with each step.

She exchanges a look with Aston as the three follow the portal master to Teretatian.

The portal master doesn't say much on the walk. He doesn't ask why she wants a view portal—only *where* she wants it to.

"Lailerynne, huh?" he asks.

"Yes. Fourth floor of the tower. I wan—"

"I don't need to know. 'slong as you have the gold. And ya can't take too long. I've got to get back to campus. You've got a few minutes."

"I need a few view portals in the same building. Is that possible."

"Ye-aap."

Tera sighs in relief, picking up the pace to keep up with him as they near the village.

They turn down a few streets until the portal master decides they've gone far enough from campus.

"This'll do," he says, looking around at the clearing in a small garden of purple flowers with a memorial bench against the edge. "Ready?"

Tera replies with a "yes" and drops a few gold coins into his open and eager hand.

He pockets the gold and shoos her away to make room. He begins swirling his hand around as if mixing something in a bowl, only his fingers are pointed upward. A cloudy miniature blue portal opens at about face-height.

The portal master steps back, motioning to his creation without a word.

"That's it?" Tera asks. "How do I—"

"You put your face in it. Stand in place. Keep your feet steady— don't want to get dizzy and fall. 'less either of you boys is a lifebringer and can fix her up?"

Kiran and Aston shake their heads.

"Didn't figure." He turns back to Tera. "Wide stance. Face in the portal."

Tera eases herself toward the little blue portal as if it could grow and swallow her whole. She looks down at her feet, scooting them out and steadying herself.

Every muscle in her shoulders and neck are tight, ready to pull back into the safety of Teretatian as she eases her head through the portal.

CHAPTER TWENTY-ONE

THE RESCUE MISSION

The walls and floor look as if they could splinter off and shatter into a million pieces. Tera isn't sure what she expected the oceanside tower to look like, but this wasn't it. Crooked and dingey windows decorate each wall of the room. Heavy-looking scarlet curtains full of small burn marks hang on either side of the largest window. Looking from side to side, all she sees is an empty bed with no linens, a wardrobe with chipping yellow flowers painted along the side, and a shattered mirror. It doesn't look like anyone has lived in this room in a long time.

With a relieved sigh, Tera pulls her head out of the portal and looks over to Aston and Kiran. She shakes her head and sees the boys visibly relax.

"It doesn't even look like anyone has been in that room in like a hundred years," she tells them.

"Is that it, then?" the portal master asks. He watches her, using a jagged nail to dig a piece of mushy food out from between his teeth. After inspecting it, he pops it back in his mouth and swallows.

"No," she replies. "There was one more spot I wanted to check. Same place, but the storage room. In the basement."

He raises an eyebrow at her. "Not that it's any of my business," he says with a chuff, "but is everything alright? Ain't you lookin' for yer sister?"

"Yeah, it's just somewhere she might be." She didn't feel like coming up with any detailed excuses. She can tell he doesn't really care anyways.

He grunts and dismisses the blue portal, swirling his fingers in the air again. An identical little blue portal appears once again at face-height.

"There ya go," he says, backing away and gesturing out to it.

She nods in appreciation, stepping closer again and carefully moving her face into the view portal.

On the other side, the near-total darkness swallows her. She blinks, her eyelashes fluttering like insect wings as her eyes desperately try to capture any light they can find. When they draw in the slight illumination of a fat candle on the far end of the storage room, she's able to make out rough edges of shapes in the room.

A few barrels sit pressed against a wall—or at least she assumes that's where the wall is. She can't see beyond it. All she makes out is a pile of hay, a glass bottle perhaps, and a sleeping figure in the pile of hay. Her heart seems to pause, her eyes locking and unable to shut as they use every drop of light to paint the details. The copper curls. The little upturned nose. The leaf-shaped patch on the shoulder of the school robes.

"Zeyla!" Tera shouts at the figure.

She doesn't flinch. Tera squints, watching carefully for the steady rise and fall of her sister's chest. Yes, she's breathing. Tera sighs when she spots it.

"Zey!" she calls again. "Zeyla, can you hear me?"

Just then, Tera feels a strong tug. The dark storage room instantly turns to a moonlight-coated garden. Tera's back in Teretatian with Aston, whose hand still grips the fabric behind her neck tight.

"What the hell, dude?" Tera swats his hand away and he releases.

"You saw her?" he asks, jumping straight to the point.

"I think so."

"You *think* so? You need to *know* so."

"Maybe I could've if you wouldn't have pulled me out!"

"Tera." He spins his sister around and grips her shoulders tight. His eyes are wild and his curls seem to frizz with electricity. "Do they have our sister?"

Tera feels her bottom lip quiver, but she sucks it in and gnaws on it before nodding.

Aston releases her shoulders and straightens up. "I guess we've got to go get her."

What? Is he out of his damn mind?

"Maybe," Tera replies to Aeridonis, "maybe not."

You're not doing this.

"If they have my sister, I absolutely *am* doing this."

They clearly think they can use her if they have her. They aren't going to do anything to her if they need her. We'll go to the Council and get them to act fast this time. They'll listen to this.

"Uh uh. I'm not waiting."

Esotera, please.

"I'm. Not. Waiting."

You don't know what you're getting yourself into. This isn't just a bad idea, this is a death sentence. And if you die, no one there is going to bring you back.

"I don't really have a choice."

But you do!

"Stop!" Tera screams, her voice pulsating through the silence of the village.

She turns, looking to the portal master and Kiran. Kiran appears hardly phased by his best friend seemingly arguing with herself, but the portal master looks on at the scene with a wrinkled and scrunched face.

"Look," he starts, putting his hands up. "I don't really care what you kids are doing. I don't. I'm retiring soon. I don't give two flyin' faun farts if you kids are doing something shady. I just want your word that you keep my name out of your mouths if you get caught. Got it?"

Tera nods once, her eyes locked on him.

"So, where do we go?" Kiran calls over to her as he walks her way.

"All I know is she's in the storage room in a tower in Lailerynne. But I've got an idea," Tera says. She steps away from the makeshift huddle the boys begin forming with her. She feels a lump in her throat at the thought but swallows it away and clears her voice. "Garridan!" she calls out to the darkness of the village around them, her voice hardly above a speaking volume. "I know you're here, creep. You're literally always here. I believe you now. Happy?"

Garridan hums from behind her. "Sorry, what was that? Can you say it again?"

She groans, rolling her eyes and throwing her head back dramatically before turning to face him. "You were right. They have her. In the storage room. How do I get her back?"

He laughs. "Oh ho no! I didn't say anything about helping you and your little raiding party go on a heroic quest to save the girl. I did my part."

"Actually, no you didn't." Tera's hands find their way to her hips, and she tips her nose up to him. "What good is it for me to know they have her if I don't know what to do about it? After all, you said it yourself that I'm pretty incapable."

Garridan grits his teeth, running his hands through his hair. "I can't."

"Fine." Tera turns to Kiran and Aston again. "He's a lost cause. We'll do this ourselves."

"You're as good as dead," Garridan says.

"Then *help* us."

He lets out a mix between a groan and a growl, disappearing without another word as if he was never there.

Tera pauses, racking her brain for ideas. The last thing she wants is to just barge into the tower to save her sister without a plan. But Garridan—her inside knowledge—won't give any further information, and Aeridonis—her living encyclopedia—won't stop telling her what *not* to do. She just wants someone to tell her what *to* do.

Aston grabs Tera and Kiran by the crooks of their arms and pulls them aside, his voice hushed.

"What if we just went nearby and scoped it out for a bit?" Aston proposes. "From a distance. Just watch. See if anything sparks a genius plan."

Kiran looks between the two siblings, waiting for Tera to say something.

"I mean, it's as good an idea as any, I guess," Tera says with a shrug. "We've just got to be careful. Find a hiding spot fast and stick to it."

"So, let's focus on just observing," he says. He clears his throat, returning to the portal master, who stands there still preoccupied with the food in his teeth. "Can you take us to Lailerynne? As far on the outskirts as possible."

The portal master holds out his empty palm, his wide eyes flicking between each of the three elves.

Tera looks at her brother expectantly.

"What?" he asks, his voice full of surprise.

"He's asking for payment," Tera clarifies.

"Yeah?"

"Can you… you know?"

"Don't you have any?" Aston asks, crossing his arms.

"I'm almost out. This whole ordeal hasn't been cheap."

Maybe it's a sign you shouldn't go.

"Guys, enough, I've got it." Kiran's already placing the gold coins in the portal master's hand. The gronnet closes his sticky fingers around the metal discs, burying them within his pocket.

"Outskirts of Lailerynne?" he asks to clarify.

The three nod and back out of his way. He puts his hands up, tracing them through air as if stroking an invisible painting. A glowing blue portal grows in the space before him. Once it's full-sized, he steps back, standing like a soldier beside it.

"After you." Kiran motions to Aston.

"Me?" He grunts. "Alright." Without hesitation, he walks through the portal, keeping his head low.

Kiran takes a deep breath as if about to plunge underwater. "Are you nervous? I'm nervous. Or excited. I can't t—" He steps through the portal as he babbles.

Tera exchanges a look with the portal master, giving him a wordless nod before stepping into the blue portal before her.

The salty air stings her eyes and fills her nose, instantly wiping out the floral cloud of the garden. Black, porous boulders decorate the land before her. Over the tops of them, she spots the tower itself. Hateful waves relentlessly beat against the cliffside near the tower. Opposite the cliff, she makes out the speckles of village homes and shops along the tower's base. The wet sand of the shore along the village perimeter sprouts all kinds of seagrass and seaside plant life Tera doesn't recognize, especially from afar.

She snaps out of her daze, searching for cover to hide behind. Settling on one of the boulders, she scurries over the rough and uneven terrain until she's behind a large enough rock to conceal her and the others.

"Get over here!" Tera hisses to the boys, who stand a short way away, looking across to the tower.

They scan the area for the source of her voice, spotting her and hurrying over.

"Is that where they've got her?" Kiran asks, motioning with his gaze to the rickety and narrow tower that seems to sway with every crash of the waves.

Tera takes a second to fill him in on exactly what she saw in the view portal.

"Well…" He lets out a huffy chuckle. "At least we don't have to go up a bunch of stairs to get to her."

Tera returns his attempt at a joke with a blank stare.

"Sorry. Not funny," he admits.

The three peer over the side of the boulder, watching the ocean and the swaying tower. After a moment, Tera speaks up.

"We're not going to be able to get in." She points to the door of the tower, where two figures stand posted at either side. "Look."

You didn't expect to just waltz in there, did you? I told you not to come here.

"Shut up, Don."

Excuse me? You don't have to be rude. I'm j—

"Enough. Please. The Council doesn't care about me or my sister. They'd take their sweet time and tell me I can meet with them in a few weeks to discuss my 'concerns.' I'm not waiting, and that's final."

"Ew," Aston says with a smirk. "You sound like Mom."

Tera rolls her eyes and can't help but to grin.

"Anyways," Aston says, "I have an idea."

Tera raises an eyebrow, turning her body fully toward him. "A storm."

She watches him, expecting more.

He just stares at her.

"Okay, you don't have to be all dramatic about the presentation, dude, just tell me your plan. Actual workable details."

He sighs and drops from a squat to a full seat behind the boulder. "What if I create a storm over the tower? A really wild one. Drive the guards inside while we look for a way to sneak inside?"

"You can do that?" Kiran asks.

"Um, yeah." Aston holds out his arms, palms up. A few tiny raindrops sprinkle down on the three, stopping immediately when Tera whacks her brother in the chest with the back of her hand.

"Are you trying to point a big flashing arrow right above us? Knock it off!" she says.

"Sorry." He grimaces. "But yes, I can, to an extent, control the weather. Learned storms in one of my most recent classes. I'm not as good at it as fire magic, but it's not that hard. Practiced enough on the elemental island. Actually, caused some flooding in the downstairs classes." He sits up tall, his chest puffing out like a bird.

"Alright," Tera says, looking back over at the guards by the tower door. "So, you create a bad storm. The guards go inside. We look for a way in. What if that front door is the only way in, and the guards are right inside waiting out the storm?"

"I can't imagine it'd be the *only* way in," Kiran says. "Check it out."

Tera and Aston look at him, following his outstretched arm and pointed finger, making out a winged figure soaring in circles high above the tower.

Tera gasps. "Is that really—"

"Draxxi." Kiran beams at her. "This must be where they're keeping them, and if we can get close enough, I can communicate with them. They can get us up to a window or something at least."

Tera mulls the details over in her mind, imagining all the ways it could go horribly wrong. While she isn't completely sold on the plan, it's the best they've got.

"Once we have Zeyla, how do we get home?" Aston asks. "Just take a draxxi back out?"

"I don't think that's a good idea," Kiran says. "Unless we keep the storm going so the guards can't see us and curse us out of the sky."

"Can they fly in a bad storm though?" Tera asks.

Kiran hums to himself in thought. "That's a good point. Probably not well. Maybe short bursts enough to get us up to a window, but not enough to fly through it and out of the village safely." He groans. "I didn't even think about the storm."

"We'll have to figure a different way out of there then," Aston says. "If we stop the storm too soon, the guards will definitely come back out and we'll be screwed."

"Wait!" Tera throws her hands out in front of her, eyes wild. "I think I know what we can do!"

Aston and Kiran watch in wait.

"Okay, now who's being dramatic?" Aston grumbles.

"No, I'm thinking it through first, sorry. I think it'll work. We can just jump out a window. Don taught me a spell to fall safely. As long as we're careful and quiet, we can get Zeyla upstairs to the living quarters. When I used the view portal, it looked like no one had been in that room for a long time. If we can sneak in there, we can jump out the window and use the spell to get to the ground safely. We'll get Aston and the four of us can bolt."

"And then how do we get home?" Aston asks.

"Easy. We ju—" Tera freezes, the excitement on her face peeling away as panic and realization burrow deep. "I—I forgot to ask the portal master for a summoning stone."

"What?" Kiran asks.

"We have no way to portal home," she admits.

Aston's face scrunches as he glowers at her. "How did you forget t—"

"You didn't say anything, so clearly you didn't think about it either!" she defends.

She pats her pockets, desperately hoping her memory serves her wrong. Perhaps she simply forgot an entire conversation with the portal master. When her hand meets a round, hard lump in her pocket, a relieved huff of air escapes her mouth and she smiles. She fishes her hand in the pocket for the stone, pulling it out and frowning.

"Wait a minute," she says, looking it over. "This is Trevitt's summoning stone. I never gave it back."

"Will it work? Could we just use him to bring us home?" Kiran asks.

"I mean, maybe? I'm really not sure, but it might be the best… only… hope we have." She tucks the stone back into its home in her pocket.

"Can we get going on this?" Aston says, his leg bouncing. "I'm worried the longer we sit here, the bigger the odds are of us getting caught before we even get to the tower."

"I mean, you're literally step one of the plan. I think if you're ready, we're ready," Tera says.

Aston rubs his hands together with a wicked grin. "Forecast is calling for rain, my friends."

"Cheesy." Tera rolls her eyes and her brother ignores her, his hands out at his sides with his palms up. He stares at the tower.

A small cloud begins to form over it, growing darker and larger, pulsating like some sort of living being until it's nearly black. There's a feeling of static electricity buzzing in the air until suddenly there's a crack. The steady swelling ocean sounds seem to turn to static, washed out by the rumbling thunder. In a split second, fat raindrops start somersaulting from the black cloud, spattering against the sandy ground around the tower.

Tera can see one of the guards motion something to the other, and the two quickly retreat into the tower. Just in time, too. The rainfall is so thick that she starts to struggle making out shapes through the sheet of gray.

"You going to be alright here?" Tera asks her brother, his arms still outstretched and his smile wide. He looks up at the storm as it creeps across more and more of the sky.

Thick rain begins spilling from the sky above them as Aston's storm stretches the span of Lailerynne. His eyes crinkle at the corners as he watches his creation obeying his command.

"I think he's good," Kiran says, tugging Tera's sleeve and leading her toward the castle.

The two trot and hop carefully across the rocky slope down toward the village. As they near the tower, even the storm isn't enough to dull the angry protests of the ocean, punching against the cliffside.

Tera tries to ignore the cold squelching in her soaked shoes, squishing water between her toes with every quick step.

Kiran speeds ahead, rounding the side of the tower and pressing his back to its rickety wooden wall. He beckons Tera over with a frantic hand, and she flicks away a clump of wet hair clinging in front of her eye before picking up her pace.

She joins him, then follows his stare up to the dark sky above. Unable to keep her eyes open through the downpour, she throws her gaze down to her feet, blowing away rain droplets that seconds ago clung to her lip.

"Do you see them?" she asks.

"No, but I hear them," he says with a warmth. He grabs her shoulder—a bit too firm—and lets out an excited squeak. "They hear me too!"

She looks over to him just in time to see his smile fall.

"What?" she asks, straightening up and trying to follow his eyes to the sky again.

"Th—It's—Something's wrong."

"What is it?" Tera repeats, her heart thundering in her chest. "They won't help?"

"I—"

His mouth gapes open and he squints up at the sky.

Just then, one of the draxxi swoops down, knocking Tera and Kiran both to the wet ground with one beat of its wings. Tera scrambles away in a crab walk. Kiran sits there frozen. The draxxi rears back on its hind legs, bearing its razor teeth at him in a hateful hiss.

"Kiran, move!"

Tera jumps to her feet and plows into her friend, shoving him to the side just before the draxxi strikes, its jaw snapping at the air where Kiran sat a second ago.

"No, no, no!" Kiran whines, holding his hands up in mercy. "We want to help!"

"Kiran, let's *go!*" Tera abandons the plan, grabbing Kiran's hand and trying to pull him along with her back up to Aston, but he digs his heels into the wet sand. The two slide as she pulls desperately, and it's only when the draxxi rears its head again that she lets go, preparing to jump out of the way.

"Why won't it listen to me?" Kiran wails, his feet planted in place, staring the draxxi dead in the eyes.

Didn't Garridan say the draxxi are enchanted? What are the odds he was telling the truth?

"How do we un-enchant them?" Tera asks, the muscles in her legs tensed and ready as she watches the staring match between Kiran and the draxxi.

Unfortunately, you *don't.*

"Kiran!" Tera calls. "Do you know how to break an en-chantment?"

Kiran stutters, not giving her a clear answer as his nerves break. The draxxi senses it, lurching forward and snapping again, narrowly missing him.

"Kiran, let's *go!*" she tries again.

"I can't just leave them like this," he says, looking at her with a sunken face. "We've got to save them."

"We can't do anything for them when they're like this. Now let's get out of here and regroup." She tries once again to urge him back up the hill, but he refuses.

"Wait," he says, almost indecipherable under the crashing thunder and pattering raindrops on the dense sand. He holds up a finger, tilting a long ear up to the sky. His smile stretches back across his face and he nearly bounces. "It's Elo!"

Tera's eyes wide, she gawks at her friend. "So what? An-other draxxi coming down to eat us? Enough, Kir! Let's go get Aston and figure out what else we can do."

"No, he's okay."

Tera shoots the enchanted draxxi a look over her friend's shoulder just before it propels itself back into the sky.

Elo lands in its place. Far smaller than their previous attacker, Elo stands there, tilting his head at Kiran.

Kiran smiles and pets the creature on the jet-black head. Rain pings off the slick scales, and his bright eyes shine through the dark weather.

"Is he willing to help?" Tera asks, trying to look up at the sky for the other draxxi, her body still tense and ready to run.

There's a pause. Kiran looks at Tera and nods confidently. She lets out a shaky sigh, unsure if it's relief or new anxiety.

Kiran squats down, cupping his hands together as Elo lowers himself to the sand. Tera's groan is drowned out by the sounds of the storm. She eases herself over, taking tentative steps.

Elo rears his head up, flashing his bright, needle teeth like a wicked grin. Tera throws herself back with a gasp.

"Not funny!" Kiran scolds Elo, who eases himself back down. He looks back at Tera, exchanging his disappointment for sympathy. "He's just teasing. Don't be dramatic. Come on."

"Hah," Tera says in a huffy scoff. "No. I'll find another way up."

"He says you won't."

"I will. I don't trust him."

"No, he means you physically won't be able to get up any other way. The only way in is the front door or the windows. And the first floor doesn't have any windows."

Tera's eyes shoot to the side, looking up and down the side of the tower.

"You're wasting time," Kiran reminds her, "and your sister's in trouble."

Tera steadies herself with a deep breath and a nod. "Fine." She lifts her head with faux confidence, walking up to Elo and stepping into Kiran's cupped hand so he can lift her onto the small draxxi's back.

"Why isn't he enchanted?" Tera asks no one in particular.

Enchanting him didn't seem to work in the valley either, remember?

"I'm not sure," Kiran answers. "Maybe he's too young?" He stands, pulling himself onto Elo's back right behind Tera. "Or maybe he's just special."

He smiles endearingly and pats Elo's side.

The young draxxi stretches his leathery black wings, thrusting them and lifting into the stormy sky. Tera bites her tongue to hold back a surprised yelp. She throws her chest down on Elo's back. His smooth scales offer no grip or resistance, and she feels herself slide. Kiran giggles in her ear behind her as he grabs her waist and holds her still.

"You're fine," he reassures her. "He won't let anything happen to us."

"I'm glad *you* trust him at least," she says, immediately regretting the snark in her voice.

"Fourth floor, right?" he asks, and Tera can't believe they've already reached the fourth-floor window.

She looks over the side of the draxxi at her foot dangling in the open air, spotting their small footprints in the sand below.

"Woah," she murmurs, feeling lightheaded.

"Any chance the window is just… like… unlocked?" Kiran asks with a chuckle, reaching out to try it. Before his hands can make contact, Elo turns to face the tower. He pulls his head back and rams it into the window, which shatters into sparkling pieces of glass before them.

"Oh gods," Tera says. "There's no way they didn't hear that."

"In case you forgot," Kiran stops, pointing to the sky, which thunders in agreement.

Tera breathes, trying to slow her heart and regain her now-swimming vision. While she focuses on her breathing,

Kiran wraps his sleeve over his fist before knocking over a few remaining sharp shards of glass in the frame.

"I'll go first and then I'll help you in," he offers.

"If you get off first, he's gonna drop me."

"No, he won't. You've got to trust him. And me. I literally have never let you down before!"

Before she can protest, he's already pulling himself through the empty window frame, falling into the vacant room on the other side. He pops back into view a second later, throwing her an overexaggerated thumbs-up.

"Please don't let me fall," she says, looking at the back of Elo's head. "I don't even know if you understand me, but I thought I'd try asking nicely."

"He doesn't understand you, but he gets the vibe. C'mon." Kiran holds out his hands to help pull Tera through the window. When she's through, she falls into him with a wet smack.

The two let out an "oof," and Kiran pushes Tera off of him.

"Geez, thanks," she says, pushing herself up into a sit.

"Sorry, you're heavy."

She gapes at him, and his eyes grow wide when he realizes what he said.

"Sorry, you know I didn't mean it like that!"

She smirks, rolling her eyes and standing to her feet. She checks herself for cuts from the window frame, only spotting one along her left arm. Dabbing away some of the trickling blood with the bottom of her shirt, she winces a little and then shakes it off. She looks back up at Kiran, who stares at her in disgust.

"Did you seriously just wipe blood on your shirt?" he asks.

"Uh… yeah? I don't exactly have a bandage with me."

"That was a nice shirt." He crossed his arms, pouting.

"Thanks."

"I said *was.*"

"Whatever." She glances at the cut again. The bleeding is slow, and she isn't too worried about leaving a trail in the dilapidated tower. "Let's just figure out how to get to the storage room."

He nods in agreement, shooting a glance to the window frame. Elo is gone, and all they can see from the empty frame is the gray wall of rain outside. It rages against the tower walls, far louder than Tera expects. She feels herself relax a little knowing there's no way the guards downstairs could've heard them break in.

She turns her attention from the window, looking at the room around her. It's exactly as she saw in the view portal.

"What next?" Kiran asks, as if they were simply moving through a vacation itinerary.

Tera's face scrunches and she begins pacing, keeping her steps light on her toes. "What if we…"

She trails off, muttering something to herself. Kiran leans in expectantly.

"Yeah, I got nothing," she admits, stopping.

"I'm going to go look at the stairwell," Kiran says, walking toward the only door in the room.

Tera resists the urge to hide while he peeks. After all, what if someone spots him? Instead, she focuses on any warmth she can find—which turns out to be hard in the cold, damp tower—building it up into a flame in her right hand. Just in case.

The door lets out a quiet creak and Kiran peers his head around the side of the doorframe. He lingers, and Tera's fingers twitch. If it weren't for the fire spell in her palm, she knows she'd be picking at her scab. It's as if she can feel it growing on her head, just begging to be peeled.

Kiran tucks back into the room, softly closing the door again. He looks over at Tera, his eyes traveling to her hand and back to her face. "I didn't see anyone. Should we just… like… go for it?"

An airy scoff pops out of her mouth before she can stop it. "'Just got for it?' I mean…"

Don't tell me you're actually thinking about it.

"I don't really see a better way down there," she finishes. "But I have an idea."

Kiran's long ears perk up. Tera steps closer to him and lets go of her fire spell.

"The Impossible Wall," she says. "If we even *think* we hear someone coming, just, like, flatten yourself against the wall next to me. I'll cast it, and it should just look like part of the tower wall. They won't see us. Unless any of them are illusion masters. But we just kind of have to eat those odds, I guess."

Kiran shrugs and lets out a deep sigh. "Works for me."

She nods, leading the way to the door. After throwing a "ready?" glance over her shoulder at Kiran, she peels the door open.

The staircase matches the forgotten and decaying look of the fourth floor. Wooden stairs sit full of splintering shards and stains from years of dirty shoes treading up and down it. The staircase's safety looks questionable, but Tera's sure it's the least of their concerns in a tower full of marrow elves.

She opens the door further, sliding her way through the gap into the stairwell and taking the first uneasy step onto the aged wood. It lets out a soft, pained groan with the weight of her foot. She pauses, tilting her head to listen carefully for anyone who may have heard her.

When no voices or steps respond to the cry of help from the old stairs, she continues tiptoeing carefully down, with Kiran only a step behind her.

Suddenly, Tera hears a step creak from above them. Her entire body goes rigid and her hand shoots out behind her to stop Kiran. He freezes, too, listening. When there's a second step in the stillness, she presses her back to the wall, with Kiran following suit. The staircase is narrow, and anything jutting out too far would seem suspicious. With her hands hardly more than an inch in front of her, she focuses, conjuring a rickety looking wall before her and her best friend.

She silently sucks in a long, slow breath, feeling her chest press against her conjured wall. It doesn't move, but it feels like it's closing in on them, pushing her into the rough walls of the tower. Tera wants nothing more than to look at Kiran for reassurance, but the wall sits so tight on them that she can't move her head without scraping her nose. Instead, she just stands there, focusing on her breathing and the loudening steps descending closer.

When the steps sound like they're right in front of her, the wall seems to shimmer, allowing Tera to see through it like a thick screen. Garridan appears in view for only a moment—long enough to grin and wave at Tera before disappearing and descending further down the stairs.

Tera's mouth gapes open, looking where he stood only a second ago. The shimmering seems to fade away, leaving a solid wall in its place once more. She listens, realizing his steps were the only ones she heard. Without another second's wait, she dismisses the impossible wall, her chest expanding with a full breath of relief.

She turns to Kiran, who looks more confused than relieved. Before turning and continuing their walk down the stairs, she throws him a quick shrug and blank look. Unsatisfied, he squints at her, but follows.

They reach the third floor, second, and then first, pausing occasionally to listen for foreign steps or voices. Any voices they hear along the way never draw closer, seeming to stop at the second floor as their destination.

The staircase ends at the entrance to the first floor, but beside that entrance stands a thick, slatted wood door. Tera looks down at the bulky padlock connecting a chain from the wall to a chain on the door.

You didn't really expect to just walk into the room with their prisoner, right? I don't like to say, 'I told you so,' but…

Tera bites her tongue, rolling her eyes at the old man in her head once more.

She looks between the door, the lock, and the wall, desperately trying to think of a solution.

Just then, there's a voice on the other side of the first-floor door beside them. Tera's eyes wide, she throws her back against the far wall, getting her hands ready to cast the Impossible Wall spell. She looks to her side and Kiran hasn't seemed to notice the voices. Instead, he's fidgeting with the padlock.

Tera hisses under her breath, trying to get his attention. As the noise registers, he looks up and over at her just as the door begins to open. In a moment of panic, she throws up an Impossible Wall, mouthing a "sorry," knowing he won't hear or see it. She disappears behind the illusion just in time to spot the look of hurt on Kiran's face.

CHAPTER TWENTY-TWO

THE PILE

"Who are you?" a slithering voice asks, muffled by Tera's Impossible Wall.

"I-I—" Kiran's voice cracks.

"He's trying to rescue our prisoner, no doubt," another voice adds. "Thinks he can be a little hero. Cute." Tera can almost feel the spittle in their words.

"Take the half-elf to Fedrae," the first voice says.

The other mutters something Tera can't make out. Kiran's yell pierces through her wall, rattling her bones and sending a ripple of goosebumps across her body. Her bottom lip quivers and her eyes burn hot, but she blinks back the tears, willing herself to keep it together.

"Shut up!" the other voice snarls, and there's an electric crackling, followed by another yell.

One of the scorching tears plummets from Tera's eye and down her nose, hanging on at the tip. She squeezes her eyes shut tight, and another tear finds its way out.

"On second thought," the first voice says, "I'm coming with. I've got something to discuss with him anyways. Namely, how this sneaky bastard managed to creep his way inside."

She doesn't hear Kiran anymore as the voices and foot-steps seem to make their way upstairs. One of the footsteps sounds clumsy, dragging and thunking reluctantly with the others.

When the steps and voices are completely gone, Tera releases the wall and folds forward, catching herself on her knees. A cry sits high in her throat, begging to be let out. She swallows it, taking a deep and shaky breath before standing upright.

No going back now.

She nods. He's got that much right.

The keyhole on the padlock watches her and she frowns at it.

In a whisper, she asks, "Are there any spells for locks?"

Unfortunately, no. I mean, I'm sure someone has created something that works at least some of the time, but there's no universal spell for locks, no.

She runs her finger across the lock, moving it up along the thick iron chains until it meets the wall. She pauses, trac-ing her finger on the ragged wood wall. A smile starts to creep onto her face, and she drops her hand to her side.

Warmth begins to creep through her body, surging down her arm and tingling in her fingertips. With a soft snap, a flame floats in her palm. She steadies it over the iron loop holding the chain to the wall. The flame just barely licks the wooden wall.

That flame isn't going to melt iron. You'll be here a while w—

Just then, the aged wood around the loop begins to crack-le and char, peeling and crumbling away until the loop falls from the wall with a metallic clatter. She dismisses the flame, instead focusing on any moisture in the tower, which isn't hard. Everything around her feels damp. She conjures the only water spell she knows—from when Aeridonis helped her put out the fire on her robes in school—to put out the small fire growing on the wall.

With the entire chain and its lock now on the floor at her feet, she pulls the door open. It's heavier than she expects, and she feels a stinging in the cut on her left arm. A fresh droplet of blood beads up and dances down to her hand. She dabs the whole thing off on her shirt again before slipping through the opening in the storage room doorway and easing it shut behind her.

"Leave me alone, you deadskin *creeps!*" Zeyla spits in a fit, exchanging her snarl for a squint when she realizes her visitor doesn't look like her marrow elf captors.

"Shut up or they'll come looking," Tera hushes her, waving frantically.

"Tera?" she asks, her thick eyelashes batting back the sliver of light from the doorway, trying to make out the shape of her sister.

Tera carefully walks down the storage room steps with nothing but candlelight to guide her feet. As she does, she feels for the summoning stone in her pocket, rubbing its smooth surface with her thumb. Even if she has to stay behind to get Aston and save Kiran, she wants to make sure Zeyla is home safe first.

"Rumor has it my needy little sister got herself in trouble," Tera jokes in a whisper when she reaches the last step.

"Real funny, considering *you're* the reason they took me."

"Right." Tera grimaced. "Sorry."

"At least you came to get me out of *your* mess."

Tera sighs, swallowing the words that want to find their way up and out.

"What happened to your arm?" Zeyla asks.

"How did you even see that?" Tera asks, holding up her arm and furrowing her brow as she tries to get a look at her cut.

"I've adjusted to the awful lighting in here, I guess." She pauses. "Well, come on! Give it."

Tera hesitates for a second before stretching her arm over in front of her sister. Zeyla puts her open palms out over it, her hands dancing through the air as she closes her eyes and hums softly. The cut begins to stitch itself together, the gap filling in with fresh skin. When Zeyla lowers her hands, the only trace of the wound is the blood smeared on Tera's arm and shirt.

"Sick," Tera says under her breath, twisting her arm around in the low lighting. "Thanks."

"Mmm."

Tera keeps rubbing the summoning stone, anxiety prickling at her chest as she wonders if Trevitt can even see her calling.

"So, what's the plan?" Zeyla asks, crossing her arms and shifting her weight side to side.

"Uhh…" she mumbles, rubbing the stone even harder and faster, as if it could make a difference. She whispers down toward her chest, "Please, Trevitt."

The door crashes open, blinding light surging into the dark storage room.

Hide, now! Put a wall up!

Only listening, not thinking, Tera throws her palms up and builds an Impossible Wall where she stands, enclosing herself in a corner of the room.

"What's going on?" Zeyla asks with a whimper—her voice different than Tera has ever heard it.

"We're moving you. Let's go." It's one of the voices from earlier—the marrow elves that took Kiran.

Don't, Aeridonis says, reading Tera's silent panic.

Stuck in complete shock, Tera's palms smack the conjured wall in front of her. Her face contorts as she swallows a scream, her heart rioting inside her ribcage. She can't just stand here and let them take her sister again.

She releases the wall, and it fades away in front of her, revealing an empty storage room. Frantic, she runs up the crooked stairs and peers out the door, but she just finds an empty stairwell. Her eyes travel down to the chain and padlock on the floor.

They must've thought Kiran was the one who did that. You're lucky they don't know you're here.

Tera steps back into the storage room to think. As she paces, she realizes she's still been rubbing the summoning stone. She blames it on her nerves and takes her thumb off of it, realizing it was too late to send her sister through a portal home anyways.

"It's your fault," Tera says softly, pacing the room. "I shouldn't have listened to you."

What would you have done to stop them, Esotera? Truly?

"I don't know, but I would've at least tried! I did *nothing*. I hid."

Suddenly, a glowing golden portal begins growing in the darkness of the storage room. Tera stops in her tracks, monitoring the portal with narrowed eyes.

She watches it from a distance, not ready to leave the tower and abandon her best friend and siblings. In her mind, she apologizes to Trevitt for the false alarm. As she does, Trevitt himself steps through, his feet making a wet *plat-plat* as he does.

"Give me the stupid stone back," he says, not wasting any time. He holds out his hand, folding and unfolding his fingers as if to speed things up.

"What?" Tera asks, stunned.

"You're driving me insane. You've been rubbing the stone and I'm trying to cook dinner for my family. Knock it off."

"Trev, I needed your help. I'm sorry to interrupt your dinner." She recognizes the spice in her voice and cringes, reminding herself to reel it in if she's to expect his help later.

"I'm not doing this anymore. Give me the stone."

"No, please," she begs, "it's—"

"Important?" he scoffs. "Yeah. I gather."

"I know, I know, but this time is more important than ever. They have Zeyla. The marrow elves took her."

"Give me the stone."

"Didn't you hear me?"

Trevitt sighs, lowering his arm and rubbing the bridge of his nose. "Tera, just give me the summoning stone so we can be done with this."

"You don't believe me, do you?" she says in a shaky sigh. "I promise you, the marrow elves took my little sister—"

"I know they did."

"—and I— Wait… What?" Tera stops, watching him.

When he doesn't answer, she prods, "What do you mean you know they did?"

He takes a deep breath and lets it out in a hot, wet sigh.

"Trevitt?" Tera straightens up, taking a step backward.

"I've tried telling you. My dad's not well, and it's nearly impossible to feed the whole family with just my income."

The nerves in Tera's entire body begin rattling. Her hands shaking, she runs them through her curls, looking around the room for an explanation.

"They offered me all the money I could need to take care of my family, Tera," Trevitt says, his tone flat, as if reading a grocery list or reporting the day's weather.

"You didn't," Tera says, shaking her head over and over, feeling tears stinging her eyes.

"It was either your sibling or all of mine," he says, his voice cracking, taking a step closer to her, "and I will *always* choose mine."

He reaches into his pocket and pulls out the partner stone to her own. "I'll just get a new set of stones." Unceremoniously, he holds out his hand and opens his fingers, letting the stone fall to the floor with a small clatter.

Tera's eyes follow the stone to the floor, and when she looks back up, Trevitt and his portal are gone, and the storage room is once again empty and dark.

She sucks her lips into her mouth, biting down on them and clearing her throat.

Tera—

"No. I don't want to talk about it."

Are you—

"I said I don't want to talk about it," she repeats, her voice gravelly.

I just w—

"Shut. Up." She growls, her hand finding its way to her other pocket. "I've had enough of you telling me what to do. Your way doesn't work. I shouldn't have ever tried to bring you back."

Her fingers wrap themselves around the cool glass bottle of amber silencing potion. From within her pocket, she flicks the cork off so Aeridonis can't see.

Esotera, I'm—

"Stop calling me that." She pulls out the open bottle, the smooth mouth of it meeting her lips. Before he can protest, she throws her head back and chugs the bitter potion.

Her rage is met with nothing but silence.

She looks down at the empty bottle. A droplet clings to the lip of the bottle, trickling down the side of the glass as Tera holds it up to the candlelight, processing what she just did.

"Don?" she asks, her voice quiet.

No response.

She swears under her breath, chucking the bottle into the hay pile that recently served as Zeyla's bed.

The realization begins to sink in that she has no idea where the marrow elves took her sister or Kiran. Her mouth begins to feel dry and her fingertips begin to tingle. She takes a deep, shaky breath and tries to collect her thoughts.

With a groan and an eyeroll, she pauses and then softly calls out, "Garridan!"

Nothing.

"I'm not asking for a sidekick, I just want to know where they're taking them," she clarifies.

There's a scoff from the far corner of the room. She stares at the darkness, her eyes trying to create the familiar shape of her stalker. After a moment, he allows her to see him. He's leaning against a wall, one ankle crossed over another.

"If anyone's going to be a sidekick, it isn't me," he says, pushing himself from the wall and striding toward her.

"Well, you're certainly not going to be the hero." She crosses her arms.

"That's not how you convince someone to help you.".

"I'm disgusted with myself enough for asking in the first place. Don't make this worse."

"Oh, no, I absolutely *have* to make this worse." He smirks, now standing only a foot from her. "You know that."

Her stomach battles her heart for room in her chest as she stands her ground, straightening her posture to look taller.

"Tell me where they took my sister and my friend," she says with feigned respect.

He simply raises an eyebrow at her and waits.

With a dramatic eye roll, she throws in an almost indecipherable, "Please."

His grin grows even wider, and he takes a step back. "That wasn't so bad, was it?"

Her jaw cocks to the side as she stares at him with arms crossed tight. "Stop wasting time."

"Wow, right to it," he says, holding his hands up in playful surrender. "Alright. Odds are pretty high Fedrae's got them up at the top of the tower with him and a handful of guards until he figures out what to do next."

"The very top?" Tera's stomach and heart both sink to the floor.

He nods. "You'd have better luck getting them to come out of the tower than you'd have getting up to the top. Not to mention getting out of there alive."

Tera sighs. Before she can say anything else, Garridan disappears and the storage room door creaks open slowly.

She decides it's best to get out of the tower and regroup with Aston rather than try to take on all the guards in the tower herself. Maybe together they can think of another way to get Kiran and Zeyla out of there.

Without wasting another minute, she hurries up the rickety stairs and into the stairwell, pausing to listen.

"I'm going to try the front door," she says under her breath, pausing for a second. When Aeridonis doesn't answer, it hits her that she's truly alone in this. Regret burns at her throat and chest, but she pushes it aside and makes her way to the first-floor door.

She presses a long ear to it, trying to take in even the most minute sounds. When her ears are met with nothing, she wraps her fingers around the knob and turns little by little, pushing the door open.

The first floor is practically empty. With no windows, no furniture, and no elves in sight, it feels forgotten except for the brilliant crimson portal shimmering and glowing in the dead center of the room. Her eyes lock onto it, wondering where it leads.

She hugs the wall, quick-stepping around the far edges of the room as if the portal could suck her into oblivion if she gets too close. When she reaches the front door on the other side of the room, she pauses.

There's no thunder. No rain. No guards waiting out a storm from inside.

Frozen, she tries to quickly process. She assumes Aston must be at the top of the tower with the others, but now the guards will be outside the front door again.

She could try to make a run for it, but they'd stop her.

She could try to save them all from the top of the tower, but Garridan didn't seem to know for sure if that's where they're being kept. Did she want to risk capture if it turns out he's wrong?

She could try to take the fourth-floor window, but then what's she supposed to do?

The options overwhelm her—none of them seeming promising.

The fourth-floor window feels like the best option to her, so she skirts the perimeter of the room back to the stairwell. She makes her way back up, pausing occasionally to listen for marrow elves—or even her friend and siblings.

When she reaches the fourth floor, she lets herself into the room and shuts the door quickly behind her. She leans over, hands on her knees while she tries to catch her breath after holding it for what felt like the entire staircase.

Once her heart rate and breath feel somewhat steady again, she walks over to the busted out window, sticking her head out to look around. The storm has definitely cleared, and more draxxi are out circling the tower than when they arrived. With nothing more than one calming breath, she crawls through the window frame. She pauses, teetering at its edge for a second before pushing herself out of the tower.

"Non cado!" she says softly to the wind ripping through her hair.

Her fall stops, and she begins to float in place. With a sigh of relief, she starts to swim down toward the wet, dense sand below.

When her feet meet the ground, she releases the spell and feels gravity return. Her curls bob around her head as they sink back into place.

Knowing the guards are at the other side of the tower, Tera decides to continue forward to look for a safe place to rest and think.

She makes her way around to the village, hiding behind the worn shacks every so often to listen for others. The sounds of crashing waves heaves, filling the village with wet breath. The salty wind worms its way through the old wooden shacks with a soft whistle.

A chill scurries up Tera's spine and she shutters. Across the way, she spots an empty shack, its door swinging back and forth like the waves on the shore just beside the village.

She takes cautious steps closer to it. When she hears the voices of a few marrow elf guards, she darts inside, pinning herself to the wall behind the swaying door.

"They're starting to stink," one of the marrow elves says as they grow closer.

"Yeah, that happens when they rot, stupid." Another marrow elf groans. "Though to be fair, you'd think all the salt in the air around here would preserve them, huh?" She laughs, but the other doesn't seem to find her dark joke amusing.

"Should we let Fedrae know?" the first asks.

"What? No, that's stupid. You trying to join the pile? He said only to get him if there's an emergency. Doesn't sound like an emergency to me, so it sure as hell won't sound like an emergency to *him.*"

"What're we supposed to do with them, then? The stink's gonna get in the tower sooner or later."

"The fauns here've been throwing their dead to sea for years." The words come from a third, louder voice. Tera leans in toward the door, recognizing the voice as Garridan's. "Just toss them out there. That's what I told the siege to do when we first took the place. What's one more pile out there?"

The other two voices are quiet for a moment.

"Maybe that's why Fedrae keeps you around, kid," the second voice jeers.

The first scoffs. "We know that's not why. Smartass over here could do just about anything he wants, and daddy'll look the other way."

"'Daddy'?" Tera asks herself under her breath.

A fourth voice joins them, and Tera can hear this one panting for breath. "Dremir caught some elves trying to free the girl. He's got them in his office, and he moved the girl to another floor. One of them was caught outside and we're not sure if he had anyone else helping."

Tera's chest tightens as their words confirm her suspicion. Aston has to be the outside one they're talking about. She imagines him trying to fight back as the marrow elves sneak up on him, and her face begins to burn. It takes every bit of self-control in her to refocus on the marrow elves for anything that might be helpful to save the others.

"Fedrae wants all village guards to interrogate the villagers. See if anyone is hiding elves." The fourth marrow elf seems to run off, the sounds of scraping feet in wet sand growing faint.

She strains to listen even closer, but the three wander too far on their patrol for her to hear.

After waiting, Tera peers out of the shack and hurries through more of the small village. All of a sudden, she stops in her tracks, staring ahead at the pile of rotting fauns heaped up in the town center.

Dead bodies are nothing new to Tera, but something about seeing them outside a classroom setting sets her heart on a strange beat. She feels every thump of her pulse through her body—deep in her throat and down through her arms. She swallows a lump and forces herself to look away. As soon as the initial shock fades, the smell creeps into her nose. She lurches, clutching her mouth and focusing on the salty smell of her own sweat on her finger below her nose instead.

All of a sudden, a shrill scream rips through the air. It seems to put the crashing waves on hold as the entire atmosphere waits for the next cry. Every hair on Tera's neck pricks up. She bolts behind the nearest weathered shack, pressing her back to the splintering wood. After a moment's hesitation, she throws up the Impossible Wall and stands in wait.

"Please, stop!" a woman pleads. Her voice seems to come from the village center. "We haven't seen anyone!"

One of the marrow elves from before—the one who didn't want to tell Fedrae about the rotting bodies—warns the woman to stop struggling and go where she tells her.

"She said she hasn't seen anyone," the first marrow elf says, his voice tired, like this is all nothing more than an inconvenience keeping him from getting home in time for dinner.

"I don't care if she has or not," the second says. "There were footprints on the west side of the tower headed toward the village."

"Okay?"

"*Foot*prints, stupid. Not hoofprints. So, it wasn't a villager, and it wasn't one of us."

The first marrow elf says nothing else, and the second raises her voice. "Whoever else is trying to break into the tower has got ten seconds to make themselves known or I'm making faun burgers for dinner tonight."

"Euughh," the first elf says with a moan.

"Too far?" asks the second.

"Mm hmm."

 It's silent for a moment before she speaks up again.

"I stand by what I said. Come out or I roast the faun alive."

Just then, Tera hears the familiar crackling of a fire spell.

"What do I do?" she asks under her breath.

When Aeridonis' voice is still missing, she remembers the potion and feels an ache in her stomach.

"I don't know if you can hear me," she whispers, "but I can't do this without you. I should've known better. I've never been able to do any of this on my own. I don't know what I was thinking. I can't show myself though. They have a pile of bodies already, and that was before I ever got here. Me revealing myself isn't truly going to save her. If anything, it'll just kill Zey and Aston and Kiran, and I just can't."

"Six…five…" the marrow elf counts down over the whimpers of the hostage faun.

"I can't do it. Gods forgive me," Tera pleads breathily, "but I can't."

"Four…"

Tera sucks in a cool breath and turns in her makeshift room behind the shack until she faces the direction of the village center. With one hand on her head and one on her heart, she searches for the essence of life around her.

"Three…"

Slowly, she pulls enough from the sparse plant life of the village square. Feeling the life tingling at her fingertips, she flips her palms outward, mouthing, "Oriri obex omnes." And a moment later, palms still out, she mutters, "Attack the marrow elves."

"Two… One."

Just then, there's a snapping like stepped-on glass, and the air fills with a different scream—one of the marrow elves.

Tera's hand finds its way to her scalp as she mindlessly picks at the healing scab in wait, focusing all her energy on listening through the conjured shack wall.

"What're you doing?" the female marrow elf shrieks. "Don't just stand there! Kill them!"

"They're already dead!" the other whines. "Or, at least, they're supposed to be!"

Tera clears the Impossible Wall, tiptoeing to the side of the shack to peer around at the chaos. Right before she can look around the corner, a faun bursts past her without looking back and without stopping. Startled, Tera puts her Impossible Wall back up.

"I'm getting Fedrae!" the one marrow elf calls out.

"No! This isn't an emergency. If you can't handle this, I'll do it myself."

Tera hears a squelch and a thud. Followed by another, and another.

"See?" the female marrow elf says through exhausted breaths. "Handled."

"Whatever. The bodies didn't just come back to life on their own. Someone's around and messing with us. I think that's worth telling Fedrae."

"We'll tell him when we find them."

Despite the increased threat, Tera can't help but smile to herself. "I hope you can still see and hear," she whispers. "I did it. *And* I have an idea how to get them out of the tower."

CHAPTER TWENTY-THREE

EVERDEATH

The two marrow elf guards move on through the village searching for her. Every so often, she can hear a crashing door and some yelling. The sounds grow further and further away, and once she's sure they've moved on to the other parts of the village, she lowers her Impossible Wall. She takes advantage of their flustered hunt and goes for the one place she knows they won't look for her—out in the open in the village square.

Several half-rotted fauns litter the square, necks severed and bodies splayed in unnatural positions on the wet sand. The pile of bodies still stares her down, hardly smaller than before. Her nostrils flare out and her face scrunches as she gets a whiff of sea spray and decay.

She stops a few feet from the pile, looking over at the tower. It seems to tilt and sway in the wind even more aggressively from this angle. She half expects it to crack and split at any moment.

In her head, she maps out the shortest path to the tower before redirecting her attention to the lack of plant life in the village square. She roams around the area, throwing an occasional glance over her shoulder when there's another crash and yell deeper within the village. A hint of dull gray-green catches her eye, and she trots over to it.

She doesn't recognize the tall, thin plant, but assumes it's some sort of coastal grass. Standing over the patch, she places her hands on her head and heart again, pulling every ounce of life from the grass at her feet, feeling it crisp and drying around her legs. With a deep breath, she mutters, "Oriri obex omnes," waiting only a moment before adding, "Follow me to the tower."

One by one, fauns pull themselves up from the pile of colorless, stinking bodies. Nearly a dozen of them gather around Tera, waiting for her to lead them. She looks into the eyes of one of them, feeling a pull in her chest. The faun's features sink into his face, and his eyes look back at Tera without a thought behind them.

She looks over at the pile, wishing she could raise even just a few more, but the dead plant life around her feet forbids it.

When it seems the last resurrected faun lifts itself from the never-shrinking pile, she takes off running toward the tower, only stopping once to make sure they all follow suit. In a sort of clumsy line trailing behind her, the corpses tag along, some of them stumbling over their own feet as they slow to meet Tera.

"When we reach the tower, attack the guards," she instructs, like the coach of a makeshift team of misfits.

They stare back at her with dead eyes.

"Alright. Go team."

She turns back to the tower, her neck popping as she tips her head up to take in the height of the building. With another deep breath, she continues the short journey back to the tower entrance.

As Tera and her modest undead army near the front door, the guards spot them. One of them calls over to the other, who lifts his hands and summons a purple fog over the ground just before the entrance. He smirks at the corpses, tilting his head to the side.

"Nice try, deathriser," he calls out to Tera. "They're not getting in the tower." The purple fog grows thicker and thicker until suddenly, it clears. The front door disappears with it.

The ground below begins to rumble and creak like an ancient floor until it splits open before her.

The other front door guard traces a finger through the air, drawing out the crack in the ground.

Before Tera thinks to command them to stop, her corpses begin running toward the guards, falling one by one into the split in the earth. Without waiting for the last ones to fall, she takes off running for the village again. She hopes the front guards have been commanded not to leave the door as she tucks off into the cluster of splintering shacks. It's only a matter of time before they report her to the other guards, but she knows everyone in Lailerynne is already hunting her down.

Once she's reached the far edge of the village, she darts behind a house and walls herself in with the Impossible Wall once more. She takes tabs on all the guards she's come across so far. Clearly, one of the front door guards is an illusion master. The other—who ruptured the ground—must be an elementalist. So is one of the patrol guards in the village. The second one—the male marrow elf from the village patrol— is a mystery.

"There's no way I'm getting into the tower again," Tera realizes out loud. Talking to Aeridonis makes her feel safer, calmer, even though she isn't sure he can hear her. "I can't talk to the draxxi, and for all I know, Elo might be the only one who won't eat me. And even that's questionable. The front door isn't an option either. I can't even get close with those guards around."

Her chest begins to ache, and her stomach pulls tight as she pictures her loved ones all locked in a tower full of marrow elves who want nothing more than to kill her and the wizard in her head. She's just grateful marrow elves rarely pursue deathrising—the odds of any knowing the Everdeath spell are slim to none.

The longer she thinks about Kiran, Aston, and Zeyla with the marrow elves, the tighter the muscles in her core twist. Her chest feels heavy, as if she's trapped in the narrow space between the staircase wall and her Impossible Wall again, unable to take a full breath. Pins and needles prick her fingers and toes, and she starts furiously rubbing her hands together to make it stop. When she looks back up, her fishbowled vision makes her surroundings spin. Breathing feels near impossible, yet she can't stop doing it faster and faster.

"No, no, no." She moans, shutting her eyes tight and rubbing them with her palms. "I don't have time for this. They need me."

She hugs her arms in tight, keeping her eyes shut and focusing on her breathing.

In. Slow. Out. Slow.

The tingling in her hands and feet begins to fade, and the weight on her chest slowly lifts.

"You're okay," she reminds herself. "We're going to get them out of the tower, go home, and figure out how to get Don out of my head so he can deal with all this. And everything will be fine." She lets out one last long, shaky breath before opening her eyes.

"I can't get in the tower," she repeats slowly, as if mulling over each word in her head.

But then she remembers Garridan's words.

She huffs and smiles to herself. "So, I'll just have to get them *out.*"

Tera waits for her nerves to fully settle down but they never do.

"You don't even have to say anything. I can feel you rolling your eyes right now. Sorry, Don, but I'm doing this."

She lowers her Impossible Wall and listens to the rolling waves for a second, making sure the patrol isn't nearby before she takes off for the beach.

Before reaching the shore, Tera passes through a thick barrier of more seagrass, lining the entire length of the beach. She sighs in relief as it tickles her arms and legs while she steps through.

The haunting air of the village hangs overhead like a sorrowful presence watching her as she pulls further from it and nearer the ocean.

On the other side of the grass, she's greeted by lazy waves lapping at gray sand. She takes careful steps toward the water, as if her presence alone would anger it.

With her feet at the growing and shrinking edge of the ocean, she pauses, looking behind her at the tower looming above.

"No going back."

Tera presses her lips shut, taking a slow breath in and out through her nose. The salty smell of seaweed and iodine fills her as she closes her eyes, one hand on her head and the other on her heart.

She feels the life from the seagrass slither through her veins, warming her every nerve.

He said they bury their dead at sea.

Life begins to vibrate through her cells, green and white flashes of light dazzling behind her closed eyelids.

If she can't get into the tower, she's going to make sure everyone else gets *out.*

The excess of life begins to burn at her fingers and toes until her entire body sears with its heat. When she finally feels she can't take any more, her eyes shoot open, looking over the ocean's mirrored surface. In the soft shushing of the waves, Tera flicks her wrists out.

"Oriri omnes obex."

All at once, the energy charge drains. Its absence leaves her feeling suddenly cold as she stands, waiting.

Nothing happens.

She watches the waves steadily pat against sand and broken shell pieces, dragging them out to sea before pushing them back at Tera's feet.

"I don't understand," she says breathily. "Maybe it doesn't work if the barrier is water."

She realizes her hands are still outstretched and she pulls them back in, one of them navigating up to its comfort place woven within her copper curls, sniffing out the half-peeled scab.

A ripple breaks along the flat surface of the water beyond the gentle waves. She freezes, her hand sinking back down to her side. The water reverberates again. She takes a step back out of the cold tides. It lets out a steady rumble.

In the distance, out by the ripples, Tera makes out a small dark spot. Then another, and another. The horizon fills with heads, then shoulders, and eventually entire bodies as an army of corpses marches toward her.

Her grin grows wider with each added body. She snaps to attention when she realizes the corpses still need a purpose.

"Attack the tower. Get everyone out of the tower by any means necessary," she commands. "And, uh, try not to kill people," she adds.

The waterlogged bodies of over a hundred fauns storm out of the sea, marching past her. Her head swivels around as if trying to take count of each body. She wonders just how many more would've become part of her army if only she could reanimate the dead too decayed to rise.

Just as the last few corpses brush past her, she turns to face them all in their siege. She locks her eyes on the tower, seeking out every bit of warmth in the cold, breezy coastal air. Her fingertips begin to tingle, and she allows the fire spell to erupt in her hands.

The flame illuminates her face in an angry amber glow, its reflection flickering in her eyes. She pulls her hands together in front of her chest, one hand in front of the other, just like Aston taught her. In one swift motion, she sweeps both hands out in front of her, setting fire to the entire army of corpses.

"Let's see them stop you now," she tells them, joining their march from a few paces behind.

On the walk toward the tower, Tera steps through the dead seagrass. It crunches and disintegrates beneath her feet. She stops, looking to either side to see the entire span of seagrass crisp and lifeless.

"You never would've let me do this," Tera says to Don. "But I'm handling what the Council never would've touched, and you know it."

Up ahead, there's a guttural scream. Tera races forward, dodging and darting through the horde of burning corpses.

"I told you not to kill anyone!" she calls out to them, just before her eyes lock onto one of the front door guards, completely engulfed in flames. The other spots Tera, throwing her a wicked glare before snapping his fingers and disappearing.

The burning guard's screams eventually fizzle out until the sounds of crackling fire replace it. The smell of smoke, copper, and rotten steak fills the air, assaulting Tera's nose and mouth. Her stomach thumps high in her chest and bile bubbles deep in her throat. With a dry swallow, she forces it down, her head spinning and taking in the mess around her.

Dead fauns beat their hands on the sides of the tower, its wet and ancient wood reluctant to catch fire. As they gather around the structure, draxxi begin swooping down from the sky, enchanted to defend the tower from intruders. One by one, they soar to the ground, snapping at the corpses and leaving a sloppy mess in their wake. In the middle of the chaos, the fire finally seems to catch, beginning to consume the side of the old tower.

Tera watches the flames for a moment before her gaze drifts to the side just in time for one of the fauns to get snatched up by a larger draxxi. The scaled creature pulls the corpse into the air and snaps it in half. As its remains litter the ground, the front door of the tower pulls Tera's attention.

She springs to the side, obscured by several members of her makeshift army as marrow elves spill from the tower like ants from a trampled hill.

The marrow elves file out, each startled by the surprise army outside their front door. Several keep running toward the village and don't look back. Others cast water spells, extinguishing the fires of the corpses. Before they can focus their efforts on the fire devouring their stolen home, Tera shouts to her army, "Stop them!"

The remaining corpses turn on their heels, locking onto their new purpose. One of the marrow elves lobs a fireball at one of the corpses, knocking it onto its back and completely incinerating it.

Another marrow elf splits the ground before him, tripping up some of the corpses and one of the other marrow elves. He tumbles into the crack with a scream, the center of the world swallowing him whole.

The crease in the ground stretches just in front of Tera's feet, rumbling the ground. She stumbles, her arms flailing before her. Just as she loses her balance and tips forward, a hand grips her back and yanks her into the air.

"That would've been a stupid way to die!" Kiran shouts down at her.

She looks up to see Aston holding onto her from Elo's back. The young draxxi's leathery wings pound above her, struggling with all the weight of his passengers.

The flames and bodies below shrink as Tera and friends ascend further into the sky and away from the scene. When she looks down at her legs dangling in the open air, she lets out an involuntary whimper.

"I've got you," Aston calls from above. "Don't worry."

"I told him if he drops you, I'm telling Mom," Zeyla sneers.

"You got her?" Tera asks, shouting over the wind. She looks down at the lifeless sea grass far below her feet.

Out of nowhere, there's a whack. The wind whipping past her seems to stop and the ground suddenly grows closer and closer.

"Non cato!" she screams. Her fall slows to a gentle sink and she eases herself toward the wet sand of the shore.

"Aston?" she calls, the beach seeming to spiral around her. "Kiran? Zeyla?"

When her feet touch the ground, she spins to look for her siblings and friend. She spots a lump of black scales first, but a horrible wail just beyond the crispy sea grass pulls her attention. Tera takes off running, the plants crunching beneath her feet as she does. She stops when she spots the others.

Zeyla holds out her arm, inspecting a long, sand-covered scrape. On the same arm, one of her fingers stands bent at an unnatural angle. She moves almost mechanically, her eyes focused and her face calm, sweeping her healthy hand over her injured arm. As her hand moves over the wound, the pieces of sand drop off as her flesh stitches itself together and leaves behind unblemished skin. Finally, her finger eases back into place with a crunch. She looks up at Tera, her normally caramel skin looking gray.

Tera hurries over, yelling, "Are y—"

Zeyla swats her away as she stands. "Healing sickness. It'll clear. Move out of my way."

The same scream echoes through the heavy air, and Zeyla knocks past Tera as she makes a beeline for the source. Tera hurries in step behind her, nearly bumping into her sister as she stops abruptly.

Zeyla drops down next to Aston in the sand, holding her hands out over him and mumbling something with her eyes closed. All Tera can do is stare at her brother's disfigured body. Limbs splayed and bent like a child's discarded doll, he lays completely still.

Throughout her entire life, Tera has never seen her brother shed a tear before now.

His face twisted in pain, Aston lets out another harrowing cry. Acid rises in Tera's throat, burning her chest.

As Zeyla's hand travels over his right leg—bent forward at the knee—a sharp *snap* echoes out, and Tera turns just in time to empty her stomach in the sand at her feet.

She stays turned with her back to her brother, spitting up phlegm and stomach acid.

There's another scream, but it isn't from Aston. Tera recognizes it, standing upright and listening close.

"Someone, help!" the voice yells.

"Kiran!" Tera calls out, spitting one last time to clear her mouth before taking off toward his voice.

"Tera!" Kiran yells.

She follows the sound back out toward the shoreline where she landed, rushing through the dead seagrass once more. As she grows closer, she spots his silvery hair leaning down behind the large black lump in the sand.

"Are you okay?" she calls over to him as she slows to a trot, nearing the mound. It takes a moment to register. "Is that—"

"Help him!" Kiran screams, looking up over Elo's body, his eyes bloodshot and face streaked with tears.

Frozen in place, Tera stares at the young draxxi, limp and unbreathing.

"Tera!" Kiran snaps, baring his teeth as he pleads, his entire face wet.

"Uh—okay. Yes. Absolutely." She nods over and over, walking toward his body, each step gentle enough it couldn't have cracked ice on a lake.

With a deep breath, she recalls the same ritual she attempted on Aeridonis. Elo isn't a pile of ash, she reassures herself, so this should work.

Delicately, she places her hands on Elo's side, his scales smooth and cool against her skin. She closes her eyes and breathes, visualizing Elo waking and coming to life before her over and over again. She tries to pull life energy from around her, feeling none before muttering, "Suscito."

The atmosphere is still, the silence only broken by the soft crashing waves and Kiran's thick sniffles. Elo's body still lays breathless before her.

"Try it again," he demands.

Tera bites back her quivering lip, blinking away a hot tear collecting in her eye. Her eyes shoot over to the dead sea grass, desperately searching for even a single live blade of grass. Without finding any, she nods, placing her hands back on Elo.

As she repeats the ritual, Kiran mutters, "He was trying to save us."

She doesn't know how to respond, so she just focuses on the spell. Just as she casts it again, Zeyla and Aston come running over—Aston's limbs back in place.

"Oh my gods." Zeyla gasps, hands over her mouth as she looks on at the scene.

"Can you fix him?" Kiran turns to Zeyla, still on his knees beside the draxxi.

"Is he…" She looks over at Tera, who gives her a nod.

Zeyla sighs and returns Kiran's question with a hung head and subtle shake.

"Why isn't it working?" he asks Tera.

"There's no plant life left to pull from," she admits, gesturing with her head to the sea grass. "I used it all to bring back the fauns to attack the tower."

"This is *your* fault?" Kiran asks, spit flinging from his mouth. He rises to his feet and starts toward her.

Aston steps in front of him, hand to Kiran's chest to stop him. "She was trying to save us all," he says.

"She could've found another way!" Kiran screams.

"There's no way she could've known this would happen," Aston says.

Tera watches the hatred filling her best friend's face.

"I'm sorry," Tera says, her voice cracking.

Kiran just glares back at her, his face darkening.

"I didn't think about it when I used up the seagrass. I was just focused on getting you guys out, I—" Tera swallows her words, desperately searching for the right thing to say.

Meanwhile, Zeyla walks around the body on the beach, looking it up and down until she spots it. On the side of

Elo's head, she notices a shimmering silver marking. She drops to one knee, leaning in toward the symbol. Delicately, she traces her finger along the mark—a curved and curled line above an angular one. When she pulls her fingertip back, it's ice cold. She taps it against her thumb to bring warmth back into it and she looks over to her big sister.

"Tera?" she calls. "Can you come look at this?"

It takes a second for Tera's stare to break as she snaps back, hurrying toward Zeyla. Her sister points down at the symbol on Elo's face and Tera squints as she tries to remember where she's seen this symbol before. When it hits her, her lungs turn to lead.

"What?" Aston asks, noticing the change in her eyes. He walks around to where the two girls are kneeling, noticing the symbol himself. "What is it?"

Tera sucks the inside of her cheek, trying to steady her voice before speaking. "The Everdeath spell."

CHAPTER TWENTY-FOUR

ASHES

"It can't be irreversible," Kiran says, shaking his head faster and faster after Tera's explanation of the Everdeath spell.

"I'm so sorry," she says, her voice shattering on the last syllable. She lets out a short sob before collecting herself. "I couldn't have brought him back even if there were plants for me to pull from. It's not possible. I'm so so sorry."

"But who did this?" Kiran asks, his hands gently petting Elo's side. "I didn't think marrow elves were deathrisers."

"They aren't… usually." Tera sighs. "But neither are arboreal elves and look at me. I don't know who did this."

"I hate to cut the grieving short, guys," Aston interrupts, "but we've got to get out of here."

Tera and Kiran stand, following Aston's gaze to the tower. A thick cloud looms overhead, rain fizzling out any remaining fires.

"Whoever cast that spell is still out there," Tera says, watching the rain fall. "How do we get out of here though?"

"What do you mean?" Aston asks, turning to her with a furrowed brow. "You said you've got a summoning stone, right?"

Tera groans. "Long story. That's not gonna work."

"Is Trevitt okay?" Kiran asks.

"I really don't want to talk about Trevitt. We don't have time right now anyways," Tera urges. "We need another plan."

"Can we take one of the draxxi?" Zeyla asks, pointing at the scaled beasts circling the tower.

"They're enchanted," Kiran says. "Can't break the enchantment. Only the animalinguist who cast it can break it."

"Shouldn't we do that anyways?" Aston asks. "Find the caster, I mean. There's no other way to get the draxxi out of here."

"That'd be great, if we could even find her," Kiran replies.

"Is it a pretty blonde girl? Tiny, super long hair?" Zeyla asks.

"Yeah?" Tera narrows her eyes at her. "How'd you know?"

"When they moved me, they put me in her room. We talked a little and she mentioned her path," she says. "Her name is Seratellie."

"Do you know where she went?" Tera asks, stopping herself when she realizes she's been creeping closer and closer to her sister.

Zeyla shakes her head. "Not really. All I know is our door burst open and everyone in the stairwell was running downstairs and yelling. I started to run downstairs too and that's when Aston and Kiran grabbed me."

"She's got to be around somewhere then, right?" Kiran asks, wiping away at the last of the tears on his face.

Zeyla shrugs. "I guess?"

"I have an idea," Tera says, her eyes alight and a soft smile easing onto her face. "Follow me."

She ignores their questions, taking off through the dead grass and back toward the tower. The others shout behind her, but she pushes on.

Around the base of the tower, Tera's undead army has clearly diminished in number, but a small group of corpses still claws pathetically at the side of the old tower. She assumes the marrow elves must have given up on the army once they no longer posed a true threat.

"Come here," she instructs the remaining corpses. They oblige, immediately putting their hands down and shuffling over to her. She describes Seratellie to them in as much detail as she and Zeyla can recall. "I need you to find her and bring her to me."

Without so much as a nod, the corpses all turn and stumble off in different directions. When Tera looks back at her brother, he's staring back at her with raised eyebrows and pursed lips.

"Alright," he says with a sniff, "that was pretty badass."

Tera tries to force back her smile, attempting to replace it with a cool and collected composure. She pauses and then throws out a "thanks."

Just then, there's a snap right beside her. She whips her head around, looking for the source. Instead, she spots the front door guard who cast the illusion spell when she first tried to use faun corpses at the tower. Just as the four are about to run for the shore again, Garridan walks in-between them with smooth confidence.

"Where'd they go?" the guard asks in a gruff voice, his eyes scanning right over Tera and her group.

"What're you talking about, Cress?"

"You know bloody well what I'm talking about!" He spits at Garridan's feet, to which Garridan snarls his lip.

"I don't, actually."

"Why're you hiding them?" the guard asks.

Tera's jaw sinks lower and lower as she pieces it together. She looks over at Kiran, Aston, and Zeyla, but none of them seem to understand.

"What're you talking about? Seeing things again, are you?" Garridan chuckles, pointed nose held high. "Guess that's why they call you Crazy Cress, hm?"

Cress's face flushes bright red and a thick vein pulses across his temple.

"You're hiding them," Cress accuses again.

"Hmm, guess you'd know if you didn't flunk out of illusion classes back in the day."

"You don't know what you're talking about."

"A few flashy illusion spells doesn't make you an illusion master. But, you must know that."

"I'll kill you right here and now." Cress holds one hand at his head, one at his heart, palms facing outward.

Tera covers her mouth with a closed fist, eyes bulging. She looks over at Kiran and mouths, "deathriser," pointing frantically to Cress.

It takes a moment, but the new information finally clicks and Kiran's confused expression twists into rage. Before Tera realizes what's happening, he takes off toward Cress.

She watches in horror as he raises his fist in the air, and charges at the large guard.

Garridan's jaw slacks to the side and he lets out a huffy sigh.

"You won't kill him," Garridan says, projecting his voice loud and steady.

Cress catches Kiran by the throat just as he's about to land his punch. Kiran lets out a wet gasp and Cress lifts his feet off the compacted sand.

"Try me," Cress challenges.

"Well, not with the spell, at least," Garridan says. "I guess you could kill him the old-fashioned way. I suppose I overlooked that."

Tera stands in panic, still hidden by Garridan's illusion spell. She scans the tower grounds for an idea, her eyes locking on a flash of blonde from the front door.

One of the faun corpses strides over, shoving Seratellie forward, gripping her wrists tight behind her back.

The girl whines, kicking her feet and thrashing her head from side to side.

"Let go of me!" she shrieks.

Tera's eyes flick between the faun corpse with Seratellie and Kiran getting choked out by the huge deathriser. In the middle of her frozen panic, her brother casts a fire spell at Cress, clipping Kiran's ear. His silvery hair catches on fire and the deathriser drops him on the ground, using his now-free hands to swat at the flames on his own clothes.

Garridan's illusion spell over them breaks. Zeyla runs forward, grabbing Kiran from under his arms and dragging him away from Cress. Aston casts a basic water spell to drench out the fire in Kiran's hair.

"Agh!" Kiran yelps in surprise, water dribbling down his eyebrow and tumbling onto his cheek.

Tera turns her attention to Seratellie, now that the immediate threat to Kiran is out of the way.

"Can you break the enchantment?" she asks the girl.

"What?" She struggles against the faun corpse.

Tera turns to look at the corpse. "Let her go, and stay put."

It obeys, lowering its hands and waiting for its next command.

"The draxxi." Tera points up at the circling black creatures. "Can you break the enchantment?"

"Who are you?" Seratellie asks, her tiny nose scrunching at Tera.

"Friends of the draxxi. Doesn't matter. They don't belong with the marrow elves and you know it. I saw you in the valley and I know you didn't want to enchant them in the first place."

"Is it really worth it?" Garridan asks Cress.

Tera looks over and sees the guard holding his outward hands on his head and heart again, his eyes narrowed on Kiran.

"Think about it," Garridan says. "Two Everdeaths in such a short time? I wouldn't. Remember what happened the last time."

"Fedrae will kill me if I don't handle this," Cress says in a growl.

"Which is worse?" Garridan asks, his voice smooth and low.

Cress pauses, watching Kiran before lowering his hands, groaning and rubbing his chest.

Just as he does, one of the draxxi swoops down from the sky, landing beside Garridan and Cress. It rears its head back, flashing its dazzling needle teeth. Before it can snap at them, Garridan places a hand on Cress's shoulder and the two disappear. The draxxi's snarl fades as it looks side to side for the pair. When it gives up, it comes bounding over to Tera's group.

Tera stumbles backward, conjuring a fire spell in her hand.

"It's okay!" Kiran calls to her. "It's safe! She'd like to say thank you."

Tera looks between sopping-wet Kiran and the massive draxxi. Up in the sky, the draxxi begin their descent and land in the sand around the tower.

Kiran bursts out in laughter, standing and watching the sky. Zeyla and Aston join him, their mouths hanging open as they watch the meteor shower of scaled beasts coming down from higher in the heavens than they could've seen into.

A muffled sound pulls Tera's attention in the middle of the spectacle, but the group doesn't seem to notice. She looks around and past some of the grounded draxxi, spotting a blur of blonde from between the creatures.

Her chest tight, Tera takes off after it. When she passes a couple of her corpses, she commands, "Stop them!"

As the path before her clears enough to see ahead, she spots Cress dragging Seratellie into the front doors of the tower, one of his huge hands covering the entire bottom half of her face. Her icy eyes bulge open, locking on Tera with a begging stare just as Cress pulls her into the tower.

Fire spell in hand, Tera sprints toward the tower entrance, bursting through the open front door. As she does, Cress grins at her just before pulling Seratellie into the red portal with him. It swallows them up and blinks out of existence.

She stops, standing in the empty room. Her head spins around, desperately searching for a way to save the girl.

"Garridan!" she finally calls out, but he doesn't appear.

With a flustered huff, she turns on her heel and bolts back out of the tower. At this point, all the draxxi have landed and Kiran is walking up to each one with a loving smile, no doubt exchanging some kind of words with them.

"Kir," she calls out as she approaches him. "The death-riser guard guy took Seratellie through a portal in the tower. They're gone, the portal's gone."

Aston and Zeyla walk over halfway through her story, and she starts over, filling them in.

"Where was the portal to?" Kiran's smile fades.

Tera shrugs. "No clue."

"There's nothing we can really do for her if we don't know where it went," Zeyla says.

Tera shoots her a disgusted look and Zeyla puts her hands up in a dramatic display of defense.

"What?" Zeyla scoffs. "Tell me I'm wrong."

"You're—" Tera stops and groans.

"I didn't say it doesn't suck," Zeyla says, "but we can't help her. What we *can* do is leave this depressing place. I don't want to spend another minute here." She shivers, her lip curled.

"Before the rest of the marrow elves realize we're still here," Aston adds.

Tera looks around. "I don't really think they're going to try anything when we're surrounded by draxxi and their animalinguist disappeared to who-knows-where."

"Doesn't mean I want to wait around and find out," Zeyla says.

"You know I never side with your sister," Kiran says, "but she might have a point."

"How are we supposed to leave though?" Tera asks. "No summoning stones, no portal—"

"Uhh…." Kiran theatrically motions with both arms to the large draxxi beside him.

"I just kind of figured you'd ask them to go back to the valley so they could be done with all this mess. I mean, I know the marrow elves know where the valley is now, but I'm assuming Aeridonis can tell Tera some fancy new way to hide them," Aston says, looking the creature up and down with a raised brow. "Is she really willing to give us a ride?"

There's a pause, and the siblings all watch as a huge glowing grin spreads across Kiran's dark face.

"She is. And the rest of the draxxi are going to follow," Kiran says before gently stroking the draxxi's side.

Tera exchanges a look with her brother, and when she looks back, Kiran is already helping Zeyla onto the draxxi's lowered back.

"Come on!" Kiran calls to her. "What are you waiting for? Up ya go!"

He reaches out for Tera, and she steps over to him. She pulls herself on with help from Kiran boosting her foot up through cupped hands.

"Woah," she says breathily.

Zeyla chuckles from in front of her. "Bit bigger than the baby one, huh?"

As Aston steps over to the draxxi, Tera hears a soft flapping from behind her. She turns just in time for Steve to land clumsily on her shoulder, whacking her face with a feathery wing.

"Hey, bud," she greets him, blowing and flicking her tongue out to get rid of a piece of stray feather from her lip.

He caws, wiggling his little foot at her. A small scroll shakes around his ankle, bound by a piece of black ribbon.

Aston pulls himself up on the back of the draxxi, situating himself behind Tera while she unties the note.

I think we've solved it. See me first

thing before class.

Prof. Dringely

Tera rereads the note, as if it's written in a foreign language. As her mind wraps around the message, her heart races faster and faster.

Kiran hops up behind Aston and calls out for everyone to hang on.

Tera shoves the note in her pocket and Steve lets out a disgruntled squawk, wobbling on her shoulder before taking off. She watches her bird fly away for a moment before the motion of the draxxi jolts her forward.

She wraps her arms around Zeyla in front of her, and she can feel Aston hang onto her.

"Zeyla!" Kiran calls forward. "Hold on!"

She groans, and Tera can practically feel her roll her eyes. She reaches her arms around the draxxi's scaley neck mere seconds before it lifts into the sky with a powerful push of its leathery wings.

Behind their draxxi, the others start ascending. The small coastal village shrinks smaller and smaller beneath and behind them until it disappears entirely.

"Is she taking us to the valley?" Tera hears Aston yell to Kiran over the wind ripping past them.

"No. Pipwerry," he answers. "In case anyone's forgotten, I've still got a tirabet hatchling at school I'd like to check on. If Professor Aeckmage is still there, anyways. I figured you three could just take the portal home from there."

"Works for me," Aston replies.

"I'm just ready to be home," Zeyla says, hardly audible over the beating of the draxxi's wings. "I feel like I stink like old people."

"Old people?" Tera asks.

"Yeah, like mildew and musty ocean water or something. I just want a hot shower, some aidaberry tea and one of Mom's scones, and maybe a good book. Or preferably, a bad one. A trashy romance I don't have to think too hard about."

Tera scoffs, smiling to herself. All she can think about is professor Dringely finally separating her and Aeridonis. Her mind wanders to daydreams of her visiting him for tea and to show him her improved test grades. She imagines it'd be like visiting her grandfather, only less talk about the good ole days on the Pipwerry joviball team as their star athlete.

Eventually, the draxxi draws near Pipwerry. The floating islands grow near in the thick clouds around them until the scaled beast begins its descent, approaching the Hub.

Gracefully, it lands with hardly more than a soft thunk on the grassy floor before the fountain.

Kiran lets out a sigh of relief, sliding down the side of the draxxi and landing on his feet. He turns and reaches out to help Aston down, but Tera's brother is already slipping down the black scales before Kiran can get to him.

He holds out a hand to Tera so she can ease herself down, then he hurries over to Zeyla and does the same. Once they're all off the draxxi, Kiran steps over to pet her head, presumably communicating with her again.

Tera watches the two for a moment before striding over to Aston, who's giving another draxxi a gentle pat on the neck.

"Would be a cool way to get to school, wouldn't it?" she asks, her eyes looking over the creature.

He scoffs, nodding with his eyebrows raised. "Yeah, I suppose it would be."

The two are quiet for a moment before Aston clears his throat and breaks the silence.

"Do you think they'll leave you alone?" he asks.

Tera lets out a little nose huff, shaking her head. "Not with him still in my head at least."

"I didn't figure."

"Might not be a problem much longer though," she says, pulling the crumpled note from her pocket and holding it out to Aston.

She watches his eyes scan over it a couple times before he looks up at her.

"She can separate you?" he asks.

Tera nods, a smile bursting through.

"That's awesome, Tera." He hands the note back. "That's got to be a relief."

She lets out a dramatic exhale. "Yeah. I'm just ready to be done with all this. It's exciting, but I'm kind of fed up."

"Can we go home now?" Zeyla calls, crossing her arms. She shifts her weight between her feet and tilts her head at the other two, her eyes narrowed.

"I have a half a mind to just sleep here tonight so I'm ready to talk to Dringely first thing," Tera says with an airy chuckle.

That ready to get rid of me, huh?

Tera jumps at the sound in her head.

"You okay?" Aston asks.

"You're back," Tera says, her voice soft.

I never left.

"Could you see all that?" she asks.

I could.

"Don, I'm s—"

Save it. I'm honestly surprised you didn't use that potion on me sooner. He chuckles warmly.

"I really needed you back there. I shouldn't have taken it."

Aston and Zeyla both watch Tera with furrowed brows.

Seems you did alright all on your own.

They're silent for a moment, and Zeyla and Aston wait for Tera to do or say something.

I'm proud of you, Esotera.

Tera feels her eyes sting, and she quickly turns away from her siblings. She clears her throat weakly before letting out a cracked, "Thanks."

After a second, she adds, "I couldn't have done it without your help. I've learned more with you squatting in my headspace than I have in all my years of school otherwise."

So that's what I am to you, huh? A squatter? He laughs again. *A homeless, bodyless brain-squatter. I suppose that's fair.*

"Hey," Zeyla calls, snapping her fingers in front of Tera's face. "You can finish this at home. Let's *go.*"

Just then, the draxxi begin lifting off into the sky again, filling the air with heavy *thrump-thrumps* of their wings.

Where are they going?

"They headed back to the valley now?" Tera calls to Kiran.

He shakes his head, his expression flat.

"Where are they going?" Tera asks.

"Home."

They can't leave. Make him stop them!

"Kir! Tell them to come back! They have to stay in the valley, re—"

"No."

Tera looks at him, taken aback. "But the curse," she manages through confused stutters.

"I know. And I'm sure Aeridonis and the Council can figure out another solution. He's been hiding something from you." Kiran's eyes bore into Tera's, his features wearing a rage she's never seen before.

All Tera can do is gape back at him, trying to block out the sounds of Aeridonis's angry ranting in her head.

"He wasn't keeping the draxxi safe in the valley. He was using them. The Council took them from their families and trapped them in that tiny valley for years and years. They wanted to *leave.*"

I didn't like it either, but it was either that or the lives of everyone in Evalyra. I didn't have much of a choice.

"But what about everyone in the kingdom?" Tera asks, her chest tight as the last of the draxxi disappears into the dark night's horizon. The atmosphere falls quiet again.

"I already told you. They'll figure something out. It's not fair to the draxxi. They've protected the kingdom long enough, and for what? They were fed just enough to survive, they were trapped in a valley far too small for their species, and they were separated from their families. I did the right thing."

"But what if they can't?" Tera asks.

"What?"

"What if this was the only way to protect everyone?"

A panicked look flashes across Kiran's face, but he quickly stamps it out, replacing it with one of disgust.

"I'm done talking about this. I've got another animal that needs my help." He turns toward the Hub, trotting toward the door and disappearing, leaving Tera with her brother and sister at the fountain.

"Now what?" Zeyla asks, her eyes wide as she stares at her sister with crossed arms.

"Now we go home. Tomorrow, Dringely will remove Aeridonis from my head. He can go back to the Council and work on fixing this all, and we can go back to normal."

Aston nods coolly, looking between his sisters. "Sounds good to me."

With a deep breath and a sigh, Tera turns toward the Hub and makes her way inside. Zeyla and Aston follow right behind without another word. Every footstep on cold stone seems to echo through the empty building. They round a corner, walking into the portal room.

The portal master's door mocks Tera from across the room. She feels her face and hands grow hot as she stares at it, half-expecting Trevitt to come waltzing out at any point.

"Tera!" Zeyla calls, stopping herself before stepping through the Darkwood portal, setting her foot back down in the room. "What's your problem?"

Confused, Tera follows her sister's stare down to the fire spell in her own hands. "Oops. Sorry," she says, releasing the spell and shaking her hands out.

Zeyla just stares back at her with a snarled lip and raised brows before finally stepping through the deep green portal.

Aston looks over at her in silence for a moment too before following their little sister.

Tera walks up to the portal, stopping right before it and glancing back over at the portal master's door. With a deep frown, she flips it off and steps through the portal.

"I don't understand." On the Darkwood side of the portal, Tera hears her sister's voice waiver. "What happened?"

Tera looks before them at the crackling embers where Nyana the dryad once stood. Just past her, the towering trees and homes of Darkwood smolder. Thick black smoke billows out as the sides of houses drop to the earth and shatter like mirrors.

The silence of the forest chokes her nearly as much as the smoke.

"Mom?" Zeyla screams, running for the crumbling staircase up ahead. "Dad?"

Tera and Aston hurry after her. Zeyla takes a few quick steps up the scorched wooden stairs with her older siblings just behind her. Another step and the stair begins to crumble in slow motion beneath her weight. Tera shoots her arms out, wrapping them around her sister and yanking her back just before the stair gives way.

"Come on!" Aston yells at his sisters, reaching for their hands and leading them back down and away from the tree.

The entire staircase rains down in ash and chunks of charred wood. Zeyla puts her hands to her face with a wet sniffle and a muffled whimper. "They got away in time, right?" she asks no one in particular.

"They were at work when we left," Aston answers with forced coolness. "I'm sure they're somewhere safe."

The three look on as the side of their home lets out a pained groan, caving in. The embers glitter and glow in a vibrant red-orange until the structure of the house collapses, littering the blackened forest floor with burnt ruin.

Tera looks over at her brother, meeting his wide eyes. "I don't think they're going to leave me alone."

END OF BOOK ONE

About the Author

Jen Guberman isn't a New York Times bestselling author, and she has no critical acclaim, but her mom thinks her books are pretty good. She graduated from Gardner-Webb University with her bachelor's in communications & new media. She spends her free time playing video games, creating jewelry, and watering her excessive house plant collection. Jen lives with her husband and their cat, Camden, in Charlotte, North Carolina.

 @JenGubermanAuthor

 /JenGubermanAuthor

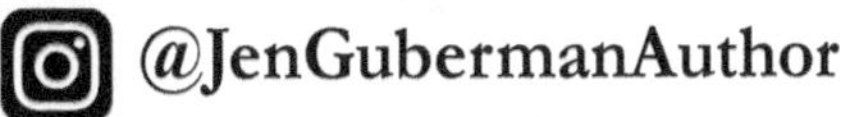 @JenGubermanAuthor

www.UberGuberman.com

IT WASN'T UNTIL TALLIS
TRIED REM FOR THE FIRST
TIME THAT HE REALIZED
HE WASN'T HAPPY.

"I haven't read a book in only three days in years, but I couldn't put this down." —LAURA L. ZIMMERMAN, Author of the Banshee Song Series

"The author made me cry before giving me the ending I was hoping for."—Amazon Review

"Absolutely timeless."—Amazon Review

"Best book I've read in a long time."—Amazon Review